True Talks

True Talks

A Trinidad Tale

Keith Chater

Published by Tablo

Copyright © Keith Chater 2023.

Published in 2023 by Tablo Publishing.

All rights reserved.

This book or any portion thereof may not be reproduced or used in any manner whatsoever without the express written permission of the author except for the use of brief quotations in a book review.

Publisher and wholesale enquiries: orders@tablo.io

20 21 22 23 LSC 10 9 8 7 6 5 4 3 2 1

True Talks

A Trinidad Tale

by
Keith Chater

This is a work of fiction. Names, characters and places are either the product of the author's imagination or are used fictitously. No reference to any real person is intended or should be inferred. Any resemblance to actual persons, living or dead, businesses, companies, events or locales is entirely coincidental. Alas, Sookbirsingh Hill is not to be found on any map of Trinidad.

'God setteth the solitary in families.'
Psalm 68: 6

"I was quiet, but I was not blind."
Jane Austen

4

For Sonia

6

Author's Note

Of course, I'm older now — quite a bit older, if I am honest — but my memory, that uncertain companion of the elderly, hasn't begun to play its tricks quite yet, although I have to admit that when I came across the manuscript beneath some old files and tax returns at the back of a closet, I had to pause for a minute to remind myself just what it was. 'True Talks' was written some fifteen or so years ago and it was fifteen more before that, that the events I was writing about took place. My initial thought, after I flicked through the first chapters, pausing, here and there, to read and remember, was to put it aside again, to ease it back among memories of things that used to be, but the truth is that what I had written was a love story and love, true love, doesn't change with the passage of time.

And what a love story it was! The inimitable and irrepressible island of Trinidad, wrapped up in the tale of a family so extraordinary on its own that it is difficult to know how to separate one's affection for the one from one's fondness for the other. At the centre of it all, of course, was Sasha, my wife, a Trinidadian to her red-painted toenails: complex, innocent, and kind, as entirely different as ever she could be from the staid, rational, Anglo-Saxon man who managed to marry her.

It is several years since we have visited that little country at the far end of the Caribbean. Sadly, the last two occasions were for other funerals, not as fraught as the one that dominates this story perhaps, but melancholy nevertheless. I have been told that the old house on Sookbirsingh Hill empty. Nicolas, our son, saw it a few years ago when visiting the island on business. He drove up the long, winding road to arrive at its gate but he did not go in, choosing rather to remember how the house had been in its glory days, in the summers of his youth.

Cruelly, too, many of my cast of characters have been scythed by the passage of time, but I hope that they will come alive when you read about them. Heaven knows, most of them were larger than life and I hope that the writing will allow you see them that way. Trinidadians — 'Trinis' — are about the most alive people you could ever want to meet. I am happy to have lived among them, to have been buffeted by their often outrageous energy, and to have called, what always seemed an awe-inspiring number of them, family.

When Sasha first read the manuscript, she issued a warning. You will hurt people if you publish this, she said: it is too close to what really happened. I disagreed with her then, and I disagree with her now. If anyone is able to laugh at himself, it is the citizen of Trinidad and Tobago. Within Sasha's family itself — and no family I ever met had a healthier sense of its self-worth — the appreciation of irony, of wit, and of the ridiculous was second to none. There were exceptions, of course — you will find them in the reading — but, generally, I think my characters can be left to look after themselves. And no family, no book, no island, can be populated only by the sanctified, after all.

Sasha's other hesitancy about the manuscript — actually it has often been more of a full throated protestation — concerns the words, the expressions and the localized grammar I have sometimes inserted into the mouths of my characters. My point, however, is that Trinidadians, including my many in-laws, were and are, in fact, bilingual. They steer, sometimes within the same sentence, between the King's English and the local patois with admirable aplomb. It is a true, true thing that when a Trini relaxes, so does his syntax. There is nothing wrong with that, either: language evolves.

My own hesitation about the manuscript, particularly in these days of political correctness, is that I might be somehow be taken to task for cultural appropriation. I am, after all, a white man and I bring that baggage, and all that it implies, to my story. When I lived and worked there, however, my entire universe was populated by

Trinidadians. I knew no one else, not even the occasional ex-patriot. Who else, therefore, could populate my book? Also, of course, I am married to a whole tribe of Indians. Any book I write about the island will not so much pilfer someone else's cultureas weave that culture into the fabric of my own experiences. And what experiences they were!

So, let's proceed. To the island I fell in love with. To the house in which it all happened. And, most of all, to Sasha and to that prodigious number of persons who I called my in-laws!

Ian Menzies
January 2023

Note: For the brave and the inquisitive — not to mention those who might become confused — an explanation of the family's sometimes bewildering genealogy is to be found at the end of the book. You will also find there a glossary of Trinidadian words, phrases and expressions: vernacular to be enjoyed.

Trinidad Tales

A Night Flight
The Provocations Of Piarco
Driving South
The House On The Hill
A Surfeit Of Sookbirsinghs
And A Bounty Of Badris
Introducing Sasha
A Short Note on C P & J
Ainsley & The Nurse
Obits, Pallbearers & The Order Of Service
The Delights Of Driving in San Fernando
Rookmin & Mathura
Mr. Jones & His Emporium
Miss Marjorie, Patsy & The Wake
Sleeping With Soames
Nessa: Commesse As Usual
Family Viewing
Sookdeo Pays His Respects
Primping, Patsy & Paulie
The Rings Are The Thing
Six Good Men & True
Nessa Explodes
The Service, A Lost Gideon & The Deluge
Interment Tales
The Cemetery Named Paradise
A Superfluity Of Flowers
Alcolada

Interlude At Mayaro
Chaos Continued
Lincoln: The Poisoner
Port Of Spain At Last
June & Ram Entertain
Murder, Trinidad Style
Meeting Irene
Sweet Pan
A Great Reckoning In A Little Room
Mr. Khan Reads The Will
Entre'acte
A Codicil Can Make A Difference
Nessa Meets Her Ex
The Septuagenarian Siren
Quiet Thoughts & Misappropriated Mangoes
The Executor Executes
Raising Our Glasses
The End Of The Story

Genealogical Notes
Some Trinidad Words & Expressions

A Night Flight

The bustle in the cabin grew. Passengers, comatose from a night flight and the alcoholic anticipation of heat and home, began to stir. Stretching legs under the seats in front of them, they leaned over their neighbours to peer out of the windows. Swollen feet inched their way back into uncomfortable shoes. Babies, sleep interrupted and feeling the effects of cabin pressure, began to bawl discomfort. Men scratched themselves awake, knuckling the night out of their eyes. Women turned round in their seats to look at the line for the lavatory, calculating numbers, minutes and necessity.

In everyone, a mental, a cultural, an almost theological shift from Canada to the Caribbean was underway.

Indians packed away curry and daal containers; women adjusting twenty-two carat gold bracelets for optimum glitter, men hoisting the knots in their ties and sucking up their gut. Nonchalant black men put on shades and palm-smoothed the slept-in velour of tracksuits never used for exercise. Their companions prodded cautiously at hair extensions and searched for chips on curved, blood-red fingernails.

Indian or black, they were coming home.

Some were returning from vacation with the spoils of shopping. Electronic appliances were in cardboard boxes or huge, patched suitcases somewhere in the belly of the plane. A cornucopia of cabin baggage was above their heads. Others, having thrown in their landed immigrant lot with the large, cold country we had just left, were merely visiting, but, Trini to their essence, they were still going 'home'. Dressed to the nines, their suitcases contained baubles to impress the natives.

Scattered among this stretching press, grains of wheat thrown on fertile brown soil, sat the occasional tourist, white to the bone. These souls, having chosen to go somewhere a little off the beaten track, had spent the last six hours at thirty-five thousand feet with two hundred people of very different apparel, attitude, accent and, well, hue. They sat mute, surely wondering what the agitation was about and what they had gotten themselves into.

In a glide pattern above the Caroni River, the plane slowly descended over the suburbs of the capital, the mangrove swamp, the rice fields, and onto the runway. A sweet, safe bump. The beat of a tenor pan began to pulse through the cabin. An exultation of jubilation.

'Home, man! We home! Oooh Gawd!'

Old Indian ladies adjusted their dentures and their orhnis, placed hands together and bobbed their heads to others across the aisle.

'Achhaa!'

Shouts surged into applause.

The voice of a flight-attendant came over the speaker announcing our imminent arrival.

'May I,' she purred, 'ask all passengers to please remain seated until the plane comes to a complete halt and the seat belt and No Smoking signs have been turned off.'

Even those who had not previously done so, now stood.

Raising the smooth cadence of her voice a tone, the flight attendant next advised her charges not to open the luggage bins above their heads until they were ready to deplane and to be careful when doing so because… Overhead bins began to click open and gruff yelps were heard as ill-loaded luggage tumbled down on the heads of the innocent and the unwary. The occasional 'fock' syncopated into the buzz of conversation.

Trinis were coming home!

The four of us took no notice of the commotion. Exhausted by the journey, we sat slumped together like ventriloquists' dummies discarded after a party. Conviviality was not our strong suit in any case. The first had hardly spoken to the second in more than five years. The first did speak to the third, but she spoke rather more often of her behind her back than to her face. The second spoke to the third frequently, but with all the exquisite inequality of the auntie–niece relationship. The fourth, me, hypocrite that I am, I spoke to them all.

It was not that we had not addressed one another when we met up at the airport for we all knew to mind our manners, but we had dispensed with such pleasantries long before boarding.

'My dear, how are you? It's been a long time.'

'Praise God, reasonably well, given the circumstances.'

'How yuh do, Auntie? What a rush! Ah jus trew ah few thing in ah case.'

'You were quite right not to dress up for a night flight.'

'I'm sure they'll arrange for you to go to a hairdresser when we arrive.'

'Oh my, what a pity your husband isn't coming. Perhaps later?'

'The dear man! But he lived a good long life. Thank the Lord!'

On the plane, such scintillating dialogue was kept to a minimum.

And yet we were all members of a family: two by blood, that divine nectar of consanguinity that chisels a permanent place on the membership rolls, and two by marriage.

In-laws!

No blood at all, not a dribble. Our place is less certain. We sit in the anterooms of decision, we toil in the vineyards of acceptance. I call all of the in-laws the 'outlaws'. Sasha laughs, but she doesn't quite deny it. Somewhere in the secret recesses of that glorious, generous heart — in which I know my place is quite secure – she regrets that I lack the blood.

***

On my left sat Agatha Badri, 'Gatha' to those who loved her, 'Ag' to the rest of us. My father-in-law's brother's wife. Ag was sixty, with skin that had never seen make-up. Her grey hair hung in a loose bun that sat exhausted on the nape of her neck, held there by a hundred pins that she shed like dandruff over the many flowered dresses she favoured. She was wearing her trademark cardigan with the raised cable pattern that resembled a noose. She had knitted it herself, eons ago. Suspended round her neck, on a black leather cord, a huge cross swung to and fro, battering what stood in for her breasts. I was never sure whether it was osteoporosis or the weight of Christ Crucified that had given her a slight curvature of the spine.

A Canadian, Ag came to the island years ago as a visiting deaconess representing her church. While going about washing clean the souls of the natives, pointing them towards a proper, pristine, Protestant salvation, she, in short order, mopped up an older husband and, well into her forties, produced first one child — many thought of it as a virgin birth — and then another, before returning to her homeland, dragging both them and their father behind her. Back in Canada, she maintained all the dowdy accoutrements of her calling, but she also opened an import-export business and became living proof that Christianity and commerce could co-exist. She was here, I felt sure, to ensure that her darling boys were remembered when the largesse was distributed. And if any of Badri's pants, shirts or merinos would fit Rohan's rather more bulky frame, all to the good. Rohan, Roh as the rest of the family called him, was her, possibly chartered, accountant spouse.

To my right on the aisle, seventy-seven years of age, hair still blacker than the soul of a psychopath, hugging herself in anticipation of all that was to come, sat Badri's sister-in-law, Fleur. Though he and she scarcely had a kind word to say about the other, truth to tell she would not have missed his passing for the world. And to be fair, in this family, attendance at the interment or immolation of a close relative was mandatory. The alacrity with which she had booked her flight showed not only the importance of the event and her commitment to familial tradition but also to the societal imperative. Even so, when Fleur came south for a funeral, the family held its collective breath that things would pass off smoothly, lo, down to the forty days. On one occasion, before my time, a deceased had, in a moment of prior delirium, bequeathed a cow to be shared jointly between Fleur and her cousin, Clarice. Solomon himself could not have divided the animal without rancour. It took teams of weary solicitors to broker a deal and decide who would receive which cut, chop and pound of suet.

Ag and Fleur had not spoken since the death of my mother-in-law, Ann, when Ag had suggested that Fleur's décolletage might be considered inappropriate to the event and handed her a handkerchief to stuff down her front. Fleur's umbrage had been a sight to behold. Her comment, that Ag herself resembled a bag lady, inaccurate as it was from the point of view of cleanliness (Ag used soap like Chanel used scent), was not far off the mark as a description of her appearance.

'Be modest in the sight of the Lord!' replied Ag.

Came the response, 'And well-dressed in his house!'

Fleur had flounced past and Ag's lips had moved in a little prayer for the other's immortal soul. The blight between the two became permanent. It had been the nodded sniffs and 'cut-eye' glances that made me determine to sit between them when we met at the ticket counter before boarding the plane,

Across the aisle, wedged tightly into the less than generous space allowed the economy passenger, sat Bianca, my friend in this mêlée. Anca, as she is known, had been four and a half pounds at birth but now tipped the scales at something approaching two hundred and fifty. For a long time, Ag anonymously sent Anca diet information, and she had also been known to refuse to sit next to her at public functions. A stance against the sin of gluttony. Alas, Bianca is also short. To complete a blighted birth trinity, she has the complexion of burnt chocolate.

You may be fat. You may be squat. But, coolie girl, you should not be dark.

In the Caribbean, shade defines you. Her mother once advised Anca never to sit in the sun in case she became darker and then confused the issue by adding that she must never sit in the shade, else she would not be visible. Multiple doses of such motherly concern have caused Anca to ricochet through life in search of a comfortable niche, keeping away from most of her family and their verbal muggings. Fleur was Anca's aunt. Living in the same city, she was also unavoidable. For Anca, the trip was to honour an uncle who once broke off an intimate conversation with Johnny Walker to squeeze her ample arm and whisper in her ear, 'Don't mind that, darlin'. The Bible says, 'Black but comely."' Next morning, he didn't remember a word he had said, but Anca never forgot.

Which leaves me. I, Ian, was Badri's son-in-law, one of two. English by birth, Canadian by inclination and affection, I, many years ago, became the first non-Indian member of the tribe. Fortunately for the mental equilibrium of my in-laws, I am not black, Muslim, mentally deficient or Roman Catholic, although white and educated have not always been counted as a significant improvement. Undernourished and underprivileged was how my sister-in-law described me at first sight. Rich might have helped. Slightly. Badri and I had maintained a formal relationship over the years. Like two declawed toms, we arched our backs and occasionally spat at each other, sharing only our affection for his daughter and my spouse, Sasha.

Sasha had been at her father's bedside for the past several weeks. He had suffered from emphysema complicated, at the end, by galloping dementia. She would have been there when he gurgled his last, but he had sneaked out in the middle of the night when both Sasha and Nurse were napping in the Berbice chairs outside his door. He fell on his head down the gallery steps and was found among the crotons when cook came to work next morning. Her shrieks were followed by the phone calls that brought the four of us to this cylinder in the sky.

The backward thrust of the engines was like a sharp clout to the head and it lurched us into awareness. Sleeping little, we had sighed our way through the night. Each one of us, I am sure, could have described the design on the bulkhead wallpaper more easily than the state of mind of our travelling companions. I had spent the night mulling over the possibility of what was to occur. Possibility is the wrong word, I think; even then we knew the probability, the likelihood, of the events of the next few days. Not the details, of course, but their shape. Flying four hundred miles an hour towards almost certain disaster with no way out other than a parachute has a way of concentrating the mind. Waking now, we swallowed great gulps of the stale cabin air to ready ourselves for the events to come and I'm sure that each of us remembered times past and other crises. We straightened our shoulders, the better to endure.

We, too, were coming home. We might be able to cope with the dead: but, oh, we would have to be careful of the living.

***

I decided to let everyone stutter along the clogged aisle, totter down the steps, cross the tarmac and enter the terminal ahead of me. There was no need to hurry and it was a moment to savour. With the last straggling passengers, I walked to the door of the plane and took a single step out onto the ramp. The wonderful welcoming heat folded itself around us like dough around so many raisins. It snuggled under armpits, sneaked behind knees and wedged itself into the farthest recesses of our nasal passages. Upper lips became instantly damp; even eyelashes clumped with moisture. I breathed in the oven of the early morning and a chilly Canadian May was microwaved from the marrow of my bones. Strolling towards the old airport building, I looked over my shoulder at the mountains, outlined dark green and purple in the dawn. The hot breeze stuck the shirt to my back, and my socks were suddenly damp.

Heat is at the heart of everything that Trinidad is. The weather is somberly foretold in every newscast.

'The high today was 32 degrees Celsius. Tomorrow, the high will be,' An upward inflection here, a slight beat for suspense. '32 degrees. On Friday, and for the Emancipation Day holiday weekend, there is a chance that the high will reach,' Pause. '33 degrees.' Pandemonium.

If you warm to the heat, you thrive like the lush vegetation: less than five miles away from the airport there is jungle. If you do not like it, you will take three showers a day until your body becomes acclimatized. The country itself has never learned to cope with it. Trinidad fires sporadically on two or three cylinders, mopping its collective brow. The pace of life can render a temperate northerner fractious until he learns to ease off, slow down and go along. Once adapted, however, fascination for this land of shimmering sunlight takes over.

The southernmost of the islands of the Caribbean, Trinidad is the most industrialized and the least touristy. There are few beaches good enough for swimming but several are just right for shallow boats to bring in cocaine from nearby Venezuela. The country has been ruled by the Spanish, the French and the British but now belongs to anyone willing to take advantage. Trinidad is independent with all the irony the word can muster. Foreign oil interests dominate finance, a colonial mindset still determines the political, judicial and educational forms, and the mass of the people keep the eye of their aspirations beadily directed towards North America. The chains of slavery and indenture have been replaced by want for material things.

Ethnically, there are probably more East Indians than people of African descent but an accurate census would be impossible to conduct and no one cares much anyway. Except, of course, the politicians who, every five years, bawl race at election time. The mosques of Islam live quietly next to Hindu temples. Shouter Baptists have staked out a place next to Scottish Presbyterians on the Christian landscape, and there is every denomination and sect in between. To accommodate them all, there are more religious public holidays in Trinidad than anywhere else on the planet. This is fine with the average Trini since he has never been convinced of the virtues of work, hard or otherwise, except as it will provide funds for a carnival costume, grog and a woman to 'wine with'.

But the place is alive! It is a scratch your belly, put your head back and roar place. A place that loves to talk, where semi-literate tabloids, read and discussed by everybody, debate politics and retail scandal. A place where wit is prized and the word 'picong' was invented to celebrate the quality of banter that goes on between men of good will.

'How he could get she?' exclaimed a man to his friend as Sasha and I stood waiting outside the Strand Cinema one evening.

'Fuh true!' replied the friend, shaking his head sadly, 'I cyar even get he!'

And the four of us laughed as they passed by.

This is the place that invented calypso and the steel band, that has the greatest carnival in the world bar none, whatever any bunch of Brazilians or, God help them, Jamaicans may think. It is the home of Solo sweet drink, off-shore oil, that damn Naipaul, Willie's ice cream, and, in the words of a now deceased Prime Minister, 'If you don' like it, get the hell outta here!' Love it — and you must — but don't be blind for a moment to its faults. If you are, you may be mocked, pick-pocketed, robbed or macheted, but you will probably admire the élan of your assailant as the deed unfurls.

Funeral or no, it was good to be back.

The Provocations Of Piarco

Entering the slightly fetid air of the terminal building at Piarco gave me a jolt of Trinidadian reality. Immigration has three categories: Returning Residents, Caricom Nationals and Visitors. Returning Residents whizzed through a choice of five open wickets, while naturally slower small islanders moseyed up at a reasonable rate to the Caricom kiosk. The longest line by far, since half of Trinidad has gone abroad and changed its citizenship, was in front of the single Visitor's kiosk.

Visitors wait.

A solitary Indian Immigration Officer eased himself onto a raised chair. His white, short-sleeved shirt dazzled, pomaded jet hair providing a blinding contrast. He stretched. An elongated, arms-above-the-head, hands-twisted-together, biceps-bulging, this-is-my-territory stretch. One hundred and fifty people groaned. Past Trinidadians, they knew the form.

'Oh, gawm. I had 'im las time.'

'He does be nasty, fuh soh!'

'I dead out an we go be waiting all day wi' dat fella.'

'Look nuh, man. Dey en got nobody else on duty in dis place?'

'Hush yuh mout, chile, he might hear yuh.'

'Yuh mad or what? He cyar hear dis far. Is half a bleddy mile.'

And the crowd did that quintessential thing that Trinidadians do to indicate wry disgust, subdued fury or half-amused helplessness. It sucked its teeth.

'Steups.'

The sound winged its way up to the front of the line where two white folk were pawing at the ground in their need to catch a connecting flight to Tobago.

'Ehye! You two dere. You firs? Come!' commanded Immigration, waving them forward. 'I ent have all day!'

Alas, we knew that he did.

For the next fifty minutes, the line hiccupped towards its goal. Babies screamed for food and tore with pudgy fingers at their mothers' blouses to get at the bounty. Grown men tried hard not to weep. At one point, a female Immigration Officer sashayed up to the kiosk and the crowd recoiled in fear that she might replace our man. The two of them cozied up, elbow to elbow to lime, to chat. It was five minutes before she took herself off and the crowd relaxed again.

Somehow in the meander of things, Ag, Fleur, Anca and I came abreast of one another and it was thus, mute but together, that we arrived at the Do Not Cross This Line sign, painted on the floor. The Officer stamped the passport of the woman ahead of us with a flourish, extended his chin up and out to clear his throat and, without looking, called out, 'Nex. Come.'

The four of us shuttled forward. It was a mistake. Four very dissimilar faces stared at him through the glass partition.

'So whey is dis den?' he asked.

He flicked the back of his fingers.

To the women, 'All yuh, get back. Wait all yuh turn.'

Gender has its privileges.

'Actually,' said I, unable to resist, 'We're all related.'

He thought about it. 'How yuh related to he, tantie?' he asked, pointing his chin first at Fleur and then at me.

Swollen up. 'He is my niece's husband.'

'An the lil bubbalups black one?'

'Her niece self,' replied Anca, on her own behalf.

Chin towards Ag, he puzzled, brow furrowed, 'An so you he lady.'

A cruel blow. Ag has a good twenty years on me.

'Well, no, not exactly. This lady is my father-in-law's sister-in-law.'
'Steups.'
A pause to rethink.
'What all yuh here for den? A fete?'
I doubted whether Ag had ever been to a fete in her life. She leaned forward to speak but Fleur was ahead of her.
'I am here,' she announced, the lead in a Shakespearian tragedy, 'to bury my brother.'
This was inaccurate but it elevated the dramatic quotient considerably.
'Umm, What your name is?'
It was a reasonable request and one sympathized with his need to move on.
'Sookbirsingh.' Fleur.
'Badri.' Ag.
'Ramdass.' Anca.
'Menzies.' Me.
His eyebrows shot up, two black birds startled into flight.
'But we are all related,' I hastened to reassure him.
His bang flopped down over one eye, the other eye glared at me.
I hurried on.
'My father-in-law died yesterday morning. I'm sure the death notice will be in the 'Guardian' today. You may have heard of him. Dr. Morton Badri? We are coming for his funeral. We are his family.' And, vaguely, to awaken him to the possibilities, 'Others are coming, too.' He peered down the line. 'No, not today. Tomorrow night's flight. We're a big family. Some of us play cricket.'
This last, though true, had nothing to do with anything. Authority sometimes rattles me.
The man digested all of this.
'Who kill 'im?'
'No-one killed him. He was quite old, he had been sick for some time and he died. I'm sorry.' I was not sure what I was sorry about, but continued, as though it explained all, 'We're being met.'

'Where yuh stayin?'

'Three of us are staying at Sookbirsingh Hill.'

'And I'm staying in St. Ann's,' piped up Anca. The officer peered into her shadow. 'My Ma live dere. She dis lady sister. But I goin Sout dis morning.'

Not wanting to get into this again, he asked, 'How long yuh stayin? When dey have dih funeral?'

Ag interrupted the flow.

'We don't know when the funeral is, Officer.' Chidingly, as to a small child. 'But dear Brother in Christ, we'll all have missed it, if you don't hurry up and let us through.'

All four of us turned to stare at her.

The Officer sucked up every particle of air inside his booth.

'Who you tink you talkin' to, Madam? You cyar talk to me like dat! Watch yuh bleddy mout! I ah officer of dih Republic of Trinidad an Tobago! And, to besides, I,' he looked her straight in the eye, 'I is a Hindu.'

We were protected from his spittle by the glass partition. Windex would be required.

'Please forgive the lady, Sir,' I spoke hastily, a grovelling penitent. 'Mrs. Badri has been devastated by the news and,' inspiration struck, 'she has a medical condition.' I rummaged through a very limited repertoire of what that might have been and turned to glare at her.

Fleur leaned forward to confide in the officer.

'Officer, this woman is not quite right in the head. Yuh know how it is.' Many Trinis have family in the madhouse. 'We'll all be gone in less than two weeks.'

She sighed, a dying fall.

With a fiddling of papers and the percussion of official instruments, the Immigration Officer orchestrated the stamping of our passports. 'I givin' all yuh ten days. Nex!' he bawled.

We were through.

'Wha dih arse you speak to 'im like dat for?' asked Anca, jello in a hurricane. 'Yuh mad, or what?'

'We must all try to educate the less fortunate. The poor man had no manners,' replied Ag, surprised as always at opposition. She looked pointedly at me. 'Roh would have known what to say. '

'Yes? Then Roh must be as much of a crass jackass as you are,' responded Fleur, on my behalf. 'How many times have you come to Trinidad, woman? Do you never learn a damn thing about how to go on. How the France you expect to get through Customs, I do not know. Ah ent able! You is a chupid, chupid woman. '

When stressed, Trini will out, even among the most cultivated.

Ag walked away from the encounter humming, but the reality was that we still had to collect our luggage.

***

The conveyor system was made of polished steel. The theory of the thing was superior, the maintenance magnificent, and, in twenty years, I had never seen it work. Luggage would arrive willy-nilly. Some was tossed, some squeezed, through the cavity in the wall into which the conveyor belt disappeared. Some would be lobbed from on high and bounce down the ramp. Some, properly pulverized, would appear without rhyme or reason at the far end of the hall, huddled together like lost sheep. Other pieces were never seen again.

We stood waiting next to the silent conveyor. Nothing happened. We waited some more. Nothing happened again.

'Steups!'

Then, amazement! A large green suitcase appeared in mid-air, high up, where the conveyer belt came out of the wall. It hung suspended for a moment and then swan-dived down the belt, landing on the grubby tiled floor. A lowing moan was uttered by the crowd.

'I tink dat one mine.'
'Oh gawd, don' let me new set ah china come outta dere. '
'Everyting go be all zug up!'
Suitcases began to erupt from the wall. The crowd took cover.
'Dese people crazy, yuh know. Dey doh know no betta.'
'All yuh wait til I get me hans on dem fellas!'
'Lawd, look at mih crosses. There mih TV. It come out dih box. An I axe dem tuh be careful.'

With a jerk, the conveyor belt began to move.

At first: bedlam.

Then, the silence of true awe descended.

Luggage began to appear from afar off and advance towards us like so many travelling tombstones. A small riot of people began to dive in among them, shielding their heads to get at their belongings. Anca rolled forward and grabbed a red suitcase. Ag yanked at hers: its wheels had been snapped off, a gash visible in its side. Fleur's and mine were found cringing together protected by a red surfboard that had half-escaped its packing and lay beached, an enormous tongue hanging out of a gaping cardboard mouth.

Darwinism in practice, we left the less fortunate to fend for themselves and moved off to Customs.

A traveller who has nothing to declare or who is craftily declaring nothing, goes through the Green Line. He stares straight ahead, hands his Immigration Card to the Customs Officer and proceeds out into the world, head held high, relief palpable as he goes. In theory. There is also a Red Line at which the honest traveller admits to an over-indulgence in worldly goods, pays the necessary tax or forfeits the item if it is on the prohibited list. The Red Line is rarely used. I have never used it myself. Like the Visitors' Line at Immigration, it is usually manned by a single soul, generally a trainee, who looks longingly at the noisy commotion across the way.

In front of us, a Creole family, father, mother, grandmother and three children, manoeuvred a rickety luggage cart along the outline of chipped green paint. Mother played navigator since father could not see over the seven suitcases and three cubed cartons piled onto the wagon. Each carton was labelled 'Fragile' in red and bound with clothesline. Each wobbled as the cart galumphed forward.

I recognized the man. His name was Sampson. He had been the janitor in the school at which I had taught years ago. A badjohn of impressive invention, I remembered.

'Good morning, Mr. Sampson. Haven't seen you in a while. How are you? Been abroad?' I said, not to state the obvious.

'Well, bless my soul, Man! Ah ent see you self for long. Me an deh missis been visitin she bruder in Brampton. Ah go up every six mont tuh keep up meh papers, oui. An Horace,' he pointed at the more hefty of the boys, 'He hafta see ah doctor fuh he asthma. Dih ole lady, she does pick up she pension, yuh know how! How yuh stop?'

I told him about Badri as we moved forward.

'When all yuh havin dih wake an ting?' he asked, adding that we might expect to see him there.

I nodded at the amount of luggage, 'You bought a lot of stuff,' said I. 'I hope they're not too strict.'

He shrugged, 'An ent afraid ah dem!' he replied, looking at the official ahead of him.

'Well, take courage,' I suggested, as he moved off.

'Fuh true,' he winked. 'Monkey know which tree to climb!'

All eighty-five pounds of Grandma followed him. She dragged a giant suitcase and held on tightly to a very small girl. The child cuddled an enormous blonde doll. Her brother nursed a pulsing black boombox with one hand and held a basketball in the other. The older brother toted two large, red, white and blue shopping bags from which protruded three two-litre bottles of coke, three jumbo jars of instant coffee, a Black and Decker drill with bit inserted, and one twenty-four pack of three-ply toilet tissue. All three youngsters carried knapsacks. Mother carried duty-free liquor bags with bottles that clanged together as she sidled along, guiding the trolley forward. Enough whiskey to demand a twelve-step program.

'Is licks like peas if ah drop dis,' she huffed, as she passed by. Under both arms, pressed to her sides like flotation devices, were several cartons of cigarettes.

They stopped in front of the Customs man.

'Where yuh card?' he asked.

'Hole up,' replied Sampson. 'Lemme get it out mih pocket.'

He pulled out a grimy, folded-over paper ripped at one corner and handed it over.

'Nuttin to declare?'

'Nah, man. Just a few small tings dih kids did buy fuh deyselves. Yuh know how!'

He flexed his significant muscles and, lowering his shades down his nose, looked the officer straight in the eye.

'Ah rite, boy. Go tru.'

Sampson braced himself, turned to give me a grin and pushed the cart forward to freedom.

'An what yuh have in dat hand baggage, madam?' the officer asked suspiciously, turning to Ag.

'Just some personal things, Brother. And my Bible, of course. No gifts. We're here for a funeral.'

Since her gestures indicated that the four of us were once more together, he took a step backwards the better to assess the very modest luggage we carried.

He pointed to Anca's case.

'Open dat one. Who it belong to?'

As Anca unlocked the case, we all leaned forward to peer inside. Neatly laid out blouses and dresses were surrounded by a number of smaller items, each wrapped in its own plastic bag. The man cracked his knuckles and began to rummage like a magician who had lost his rabbit. Seeing a piece of white cloth sticking up in one corner, he yanked at it, shaking it out as he pulled. All five of us stared at a pair of Anca's outsize underpants. Flinging them aside, he dove in again. A chemise appeared. He held it up to the light and looked at it, puzzled.

'Is a vest,' Anca clarified.

Given her weight and shape, the explanation was necessary. The Customs Officer was not convinced however, and turned the garment around and upside down before scrunching it and dropping it back. He continued to finger his way through the suitcase like a maestro in concert until he brought forth a scotch-taped, plastic-wrapped container. He shook it and we could hear liquid sloshing about.

'Is that the embalming fluid?' I asked, unable to resist.

'Is shampoo,' explained Anca, giving me a severe look.

The Custom's Officer unscrewed the top and sniffed.

'You use no-name shampoo?' said Fleur, caught between horror and disbelief. Ag moved away.

'It meh shampoo. I ent want to bring a full-up one. It does be too big, so I did put it in a container.'

'So it's not the formaldehyde then,' I added helpfully, for the officer.

He squinted at me and upended the container the better to smell it. A drop landed on the end of his nose. When he spoke, it began to make a bubble.

'I cyan smell nuttin! Yuh cyan be bringing tings into dis country dat ent got no label.'

Charmed, we watched the bubble grow. Just as he became aware of it, it burst. Tiny droplets brecked his face. Anca stifled a giggle behind her fingers. Ag reached over and took the pair of Anca's underpants from the top of the suitcase.

'Here. Wipe your face, my child' she instructed.'

And so we came through customs.

The sun shone and it was morning, the first day.

Driving South

The Benz was there to meet us.

In all my married life, both when we lived in Trinidad or when we were visiting, I had never been allowed to drive it. I have never been in an accident, had never been stopped for speeding — not that anyone ever was — and have never even scraped a car against a pole (an activity Sasha specialized in), but as Benz replaced Benz in the Badri garage, I stood on the sidelines or sat in the back seat, seething that I have never been permitted to turn the key in the ignition or even rest my hands on the steering wheel. It had been several years since I determined to be bigger than the issue and that I should slough off adolescent envy.

But I wasn't and I hadn't.

Is there a man with soul so dead he doesn't love a Benz?

Sonnilal, the driver, greeted 'Miss Fleur' finger to forehead, nodded at me and, with a bashful elbow nudge, grinned shyly at Anca. He had been in love with her since they played together behind the stables as little children — he a raggedy yard boy from the village, she the next generation of Sookbirsingh. Even after puberty hit Anca, and it hit her hard, Sonnilal never seemed to notice when everyone smirked at her burgeoning size. She would have had him too, had he been a little less innocent and more able to cope with the torrent of opposition that surely would fallen on his head. She protected him by drawing away. Now, she reached up and patted his arm affectionately.

'How your Pa, Sonny?'

'He dere, Miss Anc, he dere.'

'Hurry up and put the suitcases in the trunk, Sonnilal, dear boy, and be careful with mine. There's no need for us to stand out here in the hot sun when we can be inside a nice cool Benz.' Ag squirmed with anticipation. She had always liked her creature comforts.

'Right,' he replied, 'Where Mista Roh?'

'Mr. Roh,' A dip of the head and a sigh, 'was unable to get away, alas. He's very busy. Lord in heaven, boy, hurry!'

Sonnilal had brought Roh home from too many sprees to be intimidated by Ag. And he was a Hindu.

'Aah!' he replied.

I helped him load the car and we drove off.

Sonnilal and I chatted about the traffic and the recent rains that had brought the dry season to an end. He took the narrow two-lane Old Southern Main Road to get out onto the highway. We picked our way through Indian villages that were already awake. Women were setting out produce on roadside stalls. Their menfolk, cutlass in hand, trudged towards the cane fields. Uniformed little boys in short pants were skipping off to school with older sisters whose dark flirting eyes would break hearts very soon. Coconut palms waved in the small breeze and the sun puffed out its chest for the day to come.

As he drove, Sonnilal glanced in the rearview mirror to catch a look at Anca.

Fleur leaned forward in her seat.

'How everybody at the house, Sonnilal?' she asked, the slight adjustment to her grammar a tacit acknowledgement to being home.

'Dey ent move Mr. Morton yet, Miss Fleur. Dey couldn't get ah hold ah he Auntie, so Mr. Soames, he say dey should keep dih body home las' night self.' Sonnilal replied. 'Ah tink dey go bring up dih hearse for he dis morning.'

We absorbed this.

'Heaven preserve us! You mean to say,' said Ag, her thin voice rising as she spoke, 'that the body stayed in the house all yesterday and all last night? In this heat? That's dreadful!'

'Is all right, Miss Agatha. He pack up in ah ice box. People in the village does do so, plenty time.'

A silent splutter in the back seat.

'Heathen!' She whispered the word directly to God.

Fleur sighed.

'It's nice that he'll be there to meet us,' she said.

Accelerating onto the main highway, the car sped south, past Chaguanas and Couva towards San Fernando, the town that God forgot. A few miles before it, we turned seaward at the cut-off for Sookbirsingh Hill, midway between Claxton Bay and Gasparillo. Slowing down to negotiate the rutted road, we were enclosed on both sides by tall sugar cane ready for burning. We passed by Johnnie's Rum Shop which guarded the entrance to Monrovian Estate Village. Three men raised their glasses at us. It was eight-fifteen in the morning.

When I first came to the Hill, over thirty years ago, the houses in the village were low to the ground, some still with ochre mud walls and carat roofs. Only occasionally was there one that stood on stilts, an ever-present hammock slung below, next to rows of washing that flapped in the hot breeze. Red hibiscus in pitch oil cans guarded doors and sheaves of faded Hindu flags, high on bamboo canes, defined the occupants.

The oil boom of the eighties and the drug trade of the nineties has replaced most of this. Two storey houses now adorn the road; houses that bristle with self-approbation, some Italianate or Spanish in design, some conjured up from the roiling imagination of their owners while they were being built. We passed the village shop, barred for its own protection. We waved at the guard outside the transport company compound, and turned, eyes left, to look at the Sookbirsingh quarry that for two generations had stained the road red-brown like henna on a bride's hands. At a standpipe by the side of the road, an old man, in the middle of his morning wash, followed the car with his eyes as we passed. Sonnilal gave him a 'right'.

The car followed the curving road up the hill and a little way down the other side. There stood the big house, sheltered from the high winds that raked their way through the central hills of Trinidad during the rainy season. Braking for oncoming traffic, we paused, ready to swing wide into the open gates of the compound. In that short moment, I thought again about the old house in front of us, and the family that had lived there so long.

The House On The Hill

It was a large, wooden, estate house, the oldest such house in the neighbourhood, and for a long time its creamy white walls, jalousied shutters and shallow, red, corrugated iron roof dominated both the village and its people. Wide steps went up to the front doors. Two gigantic baskets, a profusion of green plants, swung ponderously in the breeze on either side. A wide gallery surrounded the entire building, like the promenade deck on a ship. Its balustrade hid the cushioned divans that offer a comfortable intermission during a stroll. Each member of the family had their own favourite place to sit, to relax in the deep shade. In these more dangerous days, burglar-proofing had been added to the windows, but, somehow, the effect, the symmetry of it all, has not been lost.

A large living room and a formal dining room seating sixteen made up the spine of the house. Bedrooms, three on the right and four on the left, flanked the long centre space. The wooden floor, the original long gone to termites, creaked when anyone walked on it. At the back on the right, the kitchen faced the bathroom across to the left, the two separated by another eating area large enough to seat ten for breakfast with ease.

The double back door opened to the gallery again. To the left was the laundry. Beyond the gallery and, up a few steps, a smaller, more modern, utilitarian building had been added. It did its best to fit in, bedroom, sitting room and kitchen, but seemed apologetic and embarrassed, eclipsed by the main house. This was the extension my father-in-law had been permitted to build after the death of his wife and to which he would retreat when the clan Sookbirsingh became too much for his frazzled nerves. 'Badri's Quarters' someone had christened it, and the name stuck. He hadn't lived there much during his last months. At the end, he had preferred to be nursed in the comfort of the main house.

Even in these days of burglar bars and reinforced steel doors, the big house was inviting. Breezes played coquettishly with the floor length net-curtains of the front windows. They skipped along the gallery and waved down the long centre of the building to attract the attention of those drinking tea at the far end where the bustle of the kitchen overflowed into the jostle of the back steps.

It was a house I loved.

People flowed from room to room, just as the breeze did. Built long before air-conditioning, the craftsmen who constructed it had figured out their own cooling system. Around the top of the high walls in every room, a vent, a transom, decorated with a fretwork of delicately carved wood, encouraged the air to circulate. With the breeze came conversation, for the Sookbirsinghs were a family of talkers. If I asked Sasha a question in the back bedroom, I was quite likely to be answered by her uncle Soames relaxing on the front gallery. God knows that using the bathroom, with seven in-laws sitting at the breakfast table on the other side of the wall, was an acquired skill.

Down the steps at the back, a pathway led to the gardens, to the stables behind them, and to a small grove of fruit trees, mango, orange and paw-paw, off to the right. Sitting there at the back of the house, leg hooked over one of the rattan chairs, I would look out at the outline of the palm trees at dusk, count the breadfruit on the gnarled old tree before they dropped, thump, on the hard ground, and breathe in the warmth, the laziness, the contentment of the tropics.

Facing the gallery at the side and back of the house, however, and not so subtlety altering this picture-perfect of a tropical paradise, was a large dusty barber-greened parking area with its own gas pumps. It was empty these days except for, tucked away in a far corner, an ancient tireless Cadillac, eaten alive by vines, a remnant of the glory days when Old Man Sookbirsingh owned the biggest taxi business on the island.

A Surfeit Of Sookbirsinghs

I never met Old Man Sookbirsingh. He was before my time. He built an empire in South Trinidad. His father, Bhowanipersaud, had been one of the first Indians to arrive and he had seen the promise of the place. He took the parcel of land the Crown doled out to him at the end of his indenture, worked it, and, over time, bought more pieces from other less ambitious labourers who came after. Realizing that the estate workers craved the goods to be found in far away San Fernando, he bought a donkey and loaded it up with ribbons and fabric, rubber-soled shoes and replicas of Hindu Gods, and walked through sweltering days to the barracks of the sugar estates. In time, the overburdened donkey became a weighed down, wheezing automobile. This became two. The cars were exchanged for lorries with sides that let down to display the goods in all their glory and abundance. He did not sell the cars: with a coat of paint and seats back in place, they became the first vehicles for hire on the narrow roads of South Trinidad. Before Bhowanipersaud died, he passed his vision on to his two sons and left one taxi to each of them. Sasha's grandfather borrowed money to buy his brother's taxi from him, and kept him on as a driver.

And they went to work. From San Fernando to Rio Claro they journeyed, stopping to pick up fares for both short and long hauls. He would make axle-mangling detours to Fyzabad or Barrackpore if the price was right and every public holiday saw his two cabs, twelve before long, booked to drive the sweating field workers and their families to the fresh air and sea baths of Mayaro. Then he branched out. He obtained the Monrovian Estate quarry in part payment of a debt, went into cocoa, bought an over-loader and dabbled in race horses. Along the way, he became a Christian and married a roll-up-your-sleeves get-to-work woman from Brasso, who came to be known by all as Ma.

Ma was a wizened old woman when I met her. Never leaving her room, she would sit in the shade, just out of sight of the window, a lace handkerchief always on her lap. She would raise her parchment cheek to be kissed. Like Sasha herself, she was a toucher, always reaching out, fingers fluttering to a slight caress on shoulder, brow or hand. I never knew what she thought of me, but she loved her granddaughter dearly. She made me nervous; her bright, shrewd eyes knew every corner of her room, and they watched me carefully as long as I remained in it.

Ma and the Old Man had bought a small estate, tucked just over the brow of a hill, safe from the westward-blowing winds. They built a house. The hill came to be called Sookbirsingh Hill by the local people and the road that passed in front of the house, Sookbirsingh Hill Road. The Old Man's brother, an easygoing fellow who loved best to stretch out in his hammock after work, married Ma's sister, Shanti, and built a little house down the road, almost to the sea.

Everything bore fruit. Ma and Shanti made babies. Ma made ten: Irene, Susan, James, Winifred, Jolyon, Hester, Ann, Fleur, Soames and June. Ann married Morton Badri, eventually becoming my mother-in-law. Irene, the first born and, as everyone agreed, the light in the old man's eye, bore a 'dougla', a half black, child out of wedlock for a stonemason who worked up at the quarry. She was sent away. Years later, she was still not considered a fit topic of conversation for respectable people or for the ears of outlaws. I was long married before I knew anything of her saga, so firmly had she been excised from the family.

It had been years before too that, searching one lazy Sunday afternoon for a book to read, I came across a yellowing volume, long untouched after his death, on the Old Man's book shelf. The book was Galsworthy's 'A Man of Property' and, in it, I found a wondrous genealogy with all those good Forsythe names, names now transposed to this southern-most tip of the Lesser Antilles. Ah, ambition! Yet they were fitting enough names for the children of this material man, though he may perhaps have lacked the ironic turn of mind to see the full extent of the joke. Why an Indian entrepreneur would call his son Soames, given his place in the plot, is unanswerable, but Trinidadians do seem to dip their pens into the ink of the bizarre when inscribing the names of their offspring on birth documents and baptismal certificates.

Not for them Peter and John or Betty and Sheila. Whole troops of little brown Winstons and Roosevelts attended school in the years after World War II, though hardly a Trini fought the good fight during these hostilities. Grosses of Oxydols and Persils have graced the bassinets as well as the laundry baskets of beaming Trini moms. I have had my bed made up by a Princess, and a Queen has fried my morning eggs sunny side up. I once taught a child doomed by the name Romeo Trumpet and regularly paid my respects to an ancient cousin of the Badris named Babsie, who insisted on kissing me each time we met. The whole family maintains a warm relationship with identical octogenarian twins, Girlie and Boyie. An affinity for alliteration likely resulted in the siblings Lola, Lucille, Lavinia, Lloyd and Lucan, the children of Fleur's first cousin once removed, not to neglect for a moment those siblings who are her yet more mellifluously named second cousins, Boris, Cloris, Doris, Morris, Loris, Norris and, alas, Horace.

At the time of Badri's death, Jolyon, Fleur, Soames and June were still alive. No one really knew whether Irene was alive or dead, although it was rumoured that she lived in Port of Spain, by the La Bas. Jolyon had an affection for all things female: his sisters, his wives, and any passing craft that might hove into view from Coffee Street down south to Charlotte Street in the capital. He loved his five daughters but he saw them rarely since they all lived abroad. Jolyon himself was a sedentary man. He had settled into an apartment above a store in Arima in early old age, the better to carry out his duties as a steward of the Turf Club, and, finally having learned his lesson, to keep the family just a little bit at bay. He was quite content to let his younger brother live in the big house as long as the big house maintained him as to the manor born, and since his stipend arrived regularly on the twenty-seventh day of every month, there was an easy affection between the two brothers.

Fleur was the brainy one, the one with flair. After the scandal over Irene, the Old Man came to dote on her. On race days, she would twirl round in a new dress, long white gloves to the elbow, showing off, and he, lounging in his hammock on the gallery, would laugh and take out his wallet,

'So yuh goin to races, chile. How much yuh want dis time?' And benevolently, 'Steups.'

She had him round her little finger and she knew it. She once told me the story of how it almost broke his heart when she wanted to live away from home in the dormitory at La Pique, the Canadian Mission's girls' high school in San Fernando.

'Why yuh cyar travel like dih rest of dem?' he would ask, 'Ah could send a taxi, no problem.'

'But Pa,' Fleur weaseled, 'if I could stay in dormitory, I could work harder and not waste time up an down that bumpy road, and you want me to do well, not so? And,' the clincher, 'if I don't work hard, hard, that Dulcie Ramlochan go beat mih up an she go come first in the school an...'

The Ramlochan family had buses.

Fleur took the trick and graduated at the top of her class with a scholarship that flew her away to university in Canada and, ultimately, to the proverbial 'very good job' at Bell. She never married but liked being able to divide her time between the functions and luncheons of Trinidad and life among the large professional Trini contingent in Toronto, where she could keep up with more serious subjects such as opera, literature, the stock market and the vagaries of 'couture'. Fleur loved her frocks.

June was Anca's mother and the baby of the family. She could wheedle as well as Fleur but her twirl was somehow more childish. Over-indulged in her youth — as were they all — there came a point when she wanted her own private source of largesse. Not the brightest banana in the bunch, she chose Ram Ramdass, one of the many suitors who drove up to the Old Man's front porch to inquire about the size of his daughter's dowry. Ram could talk good and he had flash. The family thought he had cash, but it was not long after the Wedding of the Year at the Naparima Bowl that Ram turned up to ask the old man for a life raft to keep his shoe emporium afloat.

'Ah cyar understan it, sah,' he whined. 'Nobody buyin meh new boot. Is a nice, nice lady boot. High heel an high top. Pretend suede. All deh fashion in New York, ah tell yeh. An deh bes' sole ah could fine.'

Just try wobbling down the Coffee on stiletto heels, calves all closed up in the broiling heat of July, thirty-two degrees in the shade, the sidewalk shimmering in the glaze of the sun.

'The onliest ting ah need to axe yuh for is a small, small ting tuh tide me over until it take orf.'

Not willing to confuse a spade with a trowel, the Old Man clarified the circumlocution.

'All yuh mean a loan,' he barked.

But June added her ten cents and the Old Man coughed up dollars.

***

Rescued from bankruptcy twice more by June's inheritance after the Old Man passed away, nothing went well for Ram until the mid-eighties when everything turned miraculously around. Coming down from up-market where he couldn't give them away, he introduced shoes for the masses, introducing them anywhere he could place them. "Ram's Shoes" appeared across the land. They walked their way into supermarkets, into parlours and into every kind of shop that could find a shelf for them. Then he opened a fleet of his own shops, shop after shop, everywhere from Westmoorings to Point Fortin. His shoes began to sell. As Jolyon said, every house on the Eastern Main Road from Barataria all the way to Sangre Grande must have had a pair of Ram's shoes under the bed and several more in the wardrobe. Everyone from the baby to Granddad had a pair.

Of course, he made he made some mistakes along the way. His nationwide 'Buy One Get One Free' sale went disastrously awry when no one realized that he was making a joke. Ram should never have attempted a witticism. He wasn't the type. The whole country turned out en masse at nine o'clock in the morning on the first day of the sale expecting to get two pairs of shoes. Ram had intended that they get two shoes allright: a right one and a left one. The police had to be called in to quell the rioters. Shoes — sandals, watchicongs, Oxfords, steel-toed workboots, ladies pumps — were hurled through plate glass windows and littered the highways and byways of the land. Calypsos were written that day, and it was fortunate that the populous did, eventually, see Ram's joke, although he always said he wasn't the man after that that he had been before.

Of course, the quality of his shoes was not of the best — the family refused to wear them — but, as he also often said, making them kept the youth of the Philippines from juvenile delinquency. His greatest success was in ladies' shoes. It was Ram who realized that the ladies of the land were less interested in wearability and comfort than flash and fashion. It didn't matter if their shoes gave up after three outings as long as they looked good at the first fete or function. So Ram gave them what they craved. He gave 'em shoes of every colour and style, for every size foot and for every budget. Then came his piece de resistance: one day he had been sitting in the car waiting for June to appear.

'Woman,' he bawled, 'what dih arse yuh doin now? We go be so late goin, they all be back before we reach.'

'Ah cyar find a purse tuh match these blasted shoes. Gi meh a break!'

'Ah'll give yuh a...'

At that precise moment, the penny — thousands of pennies — dropped. Purses, handbags, luggage to match the shoes! Why hadn't he thought of it before? Ram had driven out of the yard and was half way to the factory when June finally came out the door, but, from that day on, Ram became an enriched man. He soon acquired the yacht that he kept moored in the harbour at Chaguaramas and there were rumours of fishing boats at Cedros. He built a mansion of grey brick with what looked suspiciously like gun turrets up behind Queen's Hall in Port of Spain. His son, Royston, jetted off to Miami to take flying lessons but, having crashed two Cessnas in a row, came home chastened. He took up the study of Trinidad's coastal waters instead. The shoe business had never held much attraction for his other son, Clarence, who raised rare birds of the wild high up in the cool foothills of the mountains near Maracas Bay on the North Coast.

All in all, no one was greatly shocked when, one bright morning, the headline in the Guardian read "Ramdass Mansion Raided" and, in only slightly smaller print underneath, "Shoe King's Yacht In Drug Search", but no charges were laid. Nothing was found. June jumped up and down in embarrassment but she was soothed by the purchase of an enormous diamond necklace just like that movie star's at the Oscars. Ram steupsed mightily, but, bold-faced, returned to races the following Saturday like always. And, it was said, a police constable at headquarters, a cousin on Ram on his mother's side, put a nice piece of new galvanize on his roof in Diego Martin.

***

Today only Soames resides in the house on the Hill. A life-long bachelor, he took after his uncle more than his father. He has lived well and easily all his life. In youth, he had been denied nothing and, in maturity, he denies himself nothing. Although Soames lacked the infinite charm of Jolyon, he is both considerate and generous. He likes his creature comforts and, like all his tribe, he has a very good sense of self. If he has spent a great deal of the worth that the Old Man bequeathed him, well, he has neither chick nor child to leave it to, and everyone knows that Black Label goes down so much more smoothly than Red. Soames lives surrounded by servants, though in these egalitarian days they are to be called 'helpers'. He has a cook, a cleaner, a washer, a laundrywoman, a gardener, a stablehand though he no longer owns a single horse, a woman who comes to put the kettle on for tea every afternoon, and a driver who takes him up to Johnnie's each morning to pick up the newspapers. He is a Trini after all.

The importance of family is ingrained in Soames. He honours his sisters and he basks in the bonhomie of his brother. He does everything that the family expects of him. He even sends a man to clean all of the relatives' graves in Paradise Cemetery every year the evening before All Saints' and lays flowers on them to remember the deceased. Every last one of them. Among the living, the least worthy is to be welcomed if a drop of Sookbirsingh blood ekes its way through their narrowing arteries. Ram continued to visit the house during the very days that the country rolled its collective eyes at the bobol, the chicanery, that had permitted him to walk free. The prickly Badri was allowed to build and live at the Hill after Ann died, although the two men were far apart in achievement, pleasure and even politics.

Sookbirsingh Hill was a home and a haven for them all. Fleur flew down, June stomped in and Jolyon swung by after trips to Union Park, not to forget all the other relatives, or the old school and racing chums who might drop in for Sunday tea. On Christmas Eve, the house would be filled with any family member that Soames managed to persuade to sleep over. Mattresses would be hauled off beds, cushions from chairs, and divans were dragged in from the gallery to accommodate the overflow. Forty-nine people visited the house my first Christmas Day there. I remember the headache. Sasha and I gave presents to every one of them.

Soames, you see, also has cousins.

There is only one Sookbirsingh family in Trinidad but it threatens to run off the page when the newspaper has to publish a wedding announcement or an obituary.

As he lay dying, Old Man Sookbirsingh had scrambled to make sure that his brother was remembered in his Will. Unfortunately, the solicitor was waylaid at the rum shop by the junction and did not get there in time to witness his signature. Ma was left to carry out her husband's wishes. The two sisters lived well together and, like her, Shanti had gone out and multiplied.

And that had not been the end of it: when they married, Ma and Shanti arrived with Brasso siblings and near and dear cousins blessed with both a healthy libido and the fecundity to support it. I once began a family tree for Ann that came to include more than two hundred and twenty of her relations before I gave up, exhausted. And those were only on her mother's side.

In the next few days as many of them that were still living and able, would drag themselves over the Hill to pay their respects.

And, so far, I have not mentioned a word about the Badris.

***

Sonnilal eased the car through the open gates and drove slowly along the side of the house towards the back gallery. A tent had been erected on the asphalt. About thirty feet square, it sheltered white chairs arranged in rows facing a small table. The front row was occupied by a group of men, women and children who were solemnly drinking tea. On the far side of the table, two silver-haired men, very alike in looks, sat together their knees almost touching.

Both wore shorts and slippers and their unbuttoned shirts revealed white merinos and prosperous tummies.

The doors of the Benz clicked open, warmth flew in, and the four of us climbed out of the cocoon of its comfort. Fleur stood at the side of the car looking over to the house. She sighed the sigh of someone who has come home. The two men approached, and she smiled wryly,

'Hello, Soames. Morning, Jo. How yuh do, boy?' She embraced each in turn and patted Soames on the back.

The two men kissed her and Soames turned to bestow a brief peck on Ag's cheek.

'Where Roh?' he asked.

'He's very busy, Brother Soames,' she replied, 'His schedule is full all week. We really didn't expect Morton to pass so quickly.' She shook her head, pins flew out, and the cross bounced about a bit. 'Was no-one on duty when he died? Where was Sasha? Didn't you have a nurse? Praise God, Roh was devastated to hear the news.'

The matter explained to her satisfaction, she stretched, long, skinny arms flexing underneath her cardigan. 'Heavens,' she continued, 'you can have no idea how tired I am. I didn't get a minute's sleep all night. There's no space in those planes. And the food was dreadful as usual. Somebody should do something.'

God, perhaps?

'Get something to eat and then you can rest, darlin,' said Jolyon, when she reached out with her other cheek to acknowledge him. His lips didn't quite touch her face. 'You'll feel better.'

'Rest! I don't know when there'll be time to rest! There'll be people and noise here all day long and there's a lot to do. And we must all pray!' She sniffed. 'I hear the body is still here.'

An accusation.

'That's right. Is true. As soon as Morton died' — only those closest to Badri called him by his name —'ah sent one of the boys to Freeport to find Didi and tell she, but she gone up tuh town tuh see one uh dih girls. We had to wait until she come back in dih afternoon, an by that time it was too late to move him. So I get Dooks tuh bring up one ah them ole ice box from dih funeral home. They comin back tuh take him later on in dih morning.'

It was a long speech for Soames and he rubbed his face as he spoke, considering the probity of his decision.

'Didi get here about ten las' night,' continued Jolyon. 'Yuh never hear such bawling in yuh life when she catch sight ah he. Ah thought she was going tuh jump in dih box too.'

He turned to hug Anca as he spoke, 'Hello, girl, how yuh do? Yuh looking well good!'

'Doh make skylark, Uncle Jo, ah tired too bad,' she replied with a grin. All the girls liked Jolyon. 'Where Ma?'

'In Badri quarters lyin down,' he replied. To me he said, 'Sasha in the house. She worn out. Been up all night, and it wasn't easy before. I'd let her sleep if I were you.'

Soames reached over to shake my hand, 'How's it going, boy?' he asked.

Jolyon raised one eyebrow and, with a glance at the three women, smiled. 'Rough night?'

I shrugged my shoulders, 'It could have been worse. The plane might have crashed.'

He patted me on the shoulder.

'Come and get some breakfast,' said Soames, urging us towards the house.

'In a few minutes,' replied Fleur, 'We must say our Good Mornings to everyone first. Who is here?'

'Mainly Badris. Come and see.'

And A Bounty Of Badris

There is an endearing punctiliousness among middle class Trinidadians. They know how to behave, and they have taught their children well. Boys stand when women come into a room and men shake hands when they meet. People kiss to greet one another. Good Morning and Good Night are important things to say. The old saw 'manners maketh man' has a place here even if its implicit formality seems at odds with the harum scarum offhandedness of the society in general. We were tired, but we would never have thought of going directly into the house without paying our respects to those who had made such a point of paying theirs. Ag led the way since she was a Badri by name, if not by nature. Fleur went next, with Anca and I following along.

These were my father-in-law's family, sons and daughters of Didi, his aunt, and their sons and daughters too. Being Didi's children, none of them was actually named 'Badri', but they were Badris nevertheless. They were country folk: each one had looked up to their Uncle Morton, their educated cousin, with something between awe and bemusement. And while they had known the Sookbirsinghs for years — the Badris were expected at every celebration, invited to many of the fetes and seen at all of the funerals — the old house could still intimidate them a little. They felt more at ease in the yard.

No-one rose when we approached them. They were tired, too. We bent forward to exchange small talk, to offer and receive condolences. The usual words were mumbled and wan smiles were exchanged as Ag went down the line of chairs. If the big Sookbirsingh house always gave Didi's family pause, Ag could bring them to a full stop. She stood out after all, but also they had never known what to make of her. To make matters worse, her God confused them. Many of the Badris were Hindu and while they knew that in Ag's religion there was only one God, she gave Him such a variety of names: Yahweh, Lord, Jehovah, Emmanuel. Plus she had varying appellations for them themselves; not only Brother or Sister (in Christ of course), but also Darling, and Friend and Lamb. On one occasion she had called one of Didi's sons 'Lover' and Didi had almost fallen off her chair. Most of all, Ag's manner was unfortunate. She acted as though these country cousins were innocents alone fit for conversion, children to be led by the hand to salvation.

Almost at the end of the line, Ag came to the oldest person there, a round cherubic gentlemen sitting in his Sunday best, trilby hat balanced on the top of his head, his brown face more used to the beaming smile of openness than to the more closed countenance of sorrow.

'Where Roh?' asked Uncle Bim.

Ag sighed and smiled. 'Brother Bim, my Child.' Bim was a couple of years older than she. 'He couldn't come. He's very busy right now, you know. Work.'

'He en' comin? '

Bim couldn't quite take it in. His brow wrinkled.

As to an infant: 'Well, you know, he has a large practice and even after tax time his clients depend on him. You know how it is. '

Bim clearly did not. He turned to his wife who was seated next to him.

'Roh not comin,' he said. Perhaps she could explain.

Ag laughed a little nervously. 'I'm here to represent him.' She raised her arms skyward and smiled. 'And the good Lord is holding my hand!'

Bim and his wife looked up at her blankly.

'He own bruder self, not comin!' Bim repeated to himself. Perhaps he didn't realize that he said it aloud.

The tears began with Fleur. They were genuine tears and Fleur knew it. Her adherence to the social niceties and her belief in noblesse oblige was mingled with real affection for the family. She gently ran soothing fingers over the forehead of one, rubbed the neck of another and kissed everyone in turn, all the while murmuring the calming chat of condolence. She had the right words and she knew how to adapt them to her audience. Trinis are good with language. They use it as a weapon but they also give it as a gift. They bind up wounds with words.

She spoke to Bim in the vernacular.

'Bim, Boy, long time ah ent see yuh! How yuh do?' He tried to raise his bulk off the chair but she eased him back down, 'Relax, nah boy, yuh tired.'

'Morton gone,' he said and a single tear rolled down his fat cheek. He pushed it back up.

Fleur nodded, 'But he in a betta place now.' She turned to Bim's wife. 'Pearlie, how yuh do, girl? How the grans?' Pearlie had seven grandchildren.

'Dey dere. Dey dere.' Pearlie loved these children dearly and underneath the mournful tone was the small certainty that life went on.

'Ah hear that Victor will be takin Common Entrance nex year,' said Fleur, who made it her business to know such things.

'Is true, girl!' replied Pearlie, more animated, reaching out to lay her fingers on Fleur's arm. 'Yuh have no idea how hard dem children have tuh work. Poor little mites. Victor, he takin private lessons an all. After school. Five days ah week.'

Fleur commiserated, 'Oh my! But he'll do well. He's a smart little fellow. Perhaps he'll be bright like his Uncle Morton!'

'Yuh tink?' said Pearlie hopefully, before sinking back, reminded of the deceased. Fleur passed on to the end of the line.

It was my turn.

I had known Bim and Pearlie for years, since I first arrived in the island. I have dandled their grandchildren on my knees. I even babysat the last one, Percy, one time when his Ma was in San Fernando General Hospital. It seemed only fitting to give him a quick poke in the belly as I worked my way down the line. The third family dinner I ever attended in Trinidad, (the second was here at the Sookbirsingh house, the first at Badri's in Port of Spain) had been in Didi's house in Brother's Road long before she moved to the metropolis that is Freeport. The clan had been invited to look at Sasha's intended: I was trotted out like a carcass swinging from a meat hook. When we arrived, seventeen people were standing on Didi's veranda. Eyes examined me from hoof to forelock and, on the whole, they did not seem impressed. When I reached the steps, they stepped apart to let me into the house, as though I might have a sexually transmitted disease hidden beneath my English accent. They bowed and I scraped.

A vast — and as it turned out, an entirely typical — meal was served that day. It began with a gigantic salad: half of a scooped out, eight inch, avocado pear, filled with its own mashed innards floating in mayonnaise. Each. Several meat dishes followed with great dollops of rice and a convention of local vegetables, the names of which I did not yet know. The meal concluded with a one-pound slab of Cadbury's milk chocolate. Also each. It was the only time that I have ever invited out to dinner and had to bring three quarters of the dessert home in my back pocket.

★★★

The passing of my father-in-law was a significant day for the Badri family. It threw the times out of kilter. For as long as any of them could remember, they had been the Indians and he the only chief. He was not a warm man and I suspect that, as I did, they regarded him more with respect than affection, but it was real respect. On his side, he had achieved much in his life but he had never thought to leave them behind. They brought their problems to him, asked for his advice and they listened to his answers, but he also listened to them. They knew when to plant and what people were thinking in the countryside. He honoured Didi as his father's sister and, down to her great grandchildren, he upheld his role as head of the family, observing all the obligations that went with it, even if he could never have told you the names of the younger ones.

Bim stared up at me, his hat tipping to the back of his head.

'It all done, boy. He gorn! What we go do now he gorn? He such a bright fella. Ah ent know what go happen now. What will Ma do now? It go kill she.'

The poised, worldly-wise white man rummaged through the deep pockets of his advanced education to supply some suitable comforting phrase. I leaned forward with a brave smile, kissed him smack on top of his glistening forehead, shook his hand, and murmured, 'Bim. My felicitations!'

Fleur, Ag and I went up the back stairs into the house. Fleur held onto the banister like a climber in need of oxygen. The back dining-room seemed suspended in time. Light played on an abandoned breakfast table. Flies had begun to attack the scattered crumbs and the debris of scrambled eggs and ham on the uncleared plates. Grapefruit halves, astringent morning tartness spooned clean, lay at their side. Unexamined tea leaves decorated the bottom of cups. Those who had eaten had wandered away replete, but I was sure they were still weary from the emotions of the night.

In the kitchen, a swirl of activity seemed to contradict the finality of recent events. Women from the village were hard at work helping to prepare food: a little for the family's lunch, a lot for another evening's wake. One woman sliced bread. Two others constructed sandwiches. Honoria, the old black cook — she had been with the family for many years and had known Mister Soames when he was in short pants — was cutting cake into mouth-sized bites. And Trinis have big mouths. Her grandson was counting bottles of sweet drink, getting ready to pile them into oil drums, on ice, under the house to cool. The present cook, Clara, was scowling into the depths of the large coffee urn. Coffee is the life-blood of a wake. The urn would stand at the bottom of the back steps, and she would supervise its replenishment all evening long. Mourning is thirsty work.

Clara was running inventories aloud to herself.

'When dat good for nuttin Desmond does be finish here, Mister Soames have tuh send he tuh dih parlour tuh buy more ice. An tuh dih bakery fuh moh bread. An then dong tuh HiLo tuh pick up some ah dem Styrofoam cup an plastic plate. What I go make for dih family supper? Hmmm, oui, ah nice chicken curry. Ah got bhaji in the fridge, and Honor can mek roti good good.' She tripped over Honoria's grandson and chided him. 'Boy, move your big self!' before continuing her soliloquy. 'An Oh Lord, ah almos' forget! Ah betta mek certain ah have dem low calorie sugar business for Miss Agatha or she'll go basodie for true. An some red apple. Why dat woman want apple when it have plenty julie mango hanging from dih tree, ah ent know!
'

I shook Honaria's hand and gave Clara a tight hug. She despises the bland food I like and cannot understand either my prohibition of garlic or my preference for potatoes over rice, but we laugh at the same things and share a similar sense of the ridiculous. Besides, she once saw me naked by accident and while her peals of laughter did little for my self-esteem, they were contagious and we have been allies ever since.

I looked further into the deep shade of the house. The long mahogany dining-table was gone, replaced by a plain, coarse-looking wood box. Almost the same shape but larger than a coffin, it was painted grey. At the far end of its flat lid, a glass rectangle, rather less than a foot in width and six inches in 'height', winked when the sunlight billowed into the room as the occasional puff of air lifted the front curtains. The box was an old-fashioned icebox used in the country to preserve the dead until burial but, in this case, borrowed from the undertakers to keep Badri antiperspirant-fresh until his oldest living relative had paid her proper respects. It stood on low trestles, three feet from the floor. A bucket sat underneath it. As I watched, a drop of ice water fell into the bucket through a hole drilled into the bottom. Plink. The sound shattered the stillness of the room. I supposed that inside the box, my father-in-law, a red snapper on a fishmonger's slab, lay fighting the demons of decomposition: ice crammed between his legs from thigh to toe, ladled underneath his armpits and shoved behind his neck. Badri, finally, the ultimate in cool.

***

Badri's father, Rajeev, had been dead long before I came to Trinidad. Sasha hardly remembered him. I knew him only as a large photograph on the wall of Didi's drawing room. Over the years, the portrait had begun to fade for the sun's searchlight struck it daily, but although the edges had misted, the eyes at its centre had not. I never liked to sit directly in front of the photograph. It made me uncomfortable. I felt interrogated and I preferred to seat myself off to one side, beyond the keen intelligence of those eyes. At the same time, the photograph fascinated me. Sasha was present in the way he held his head. Our son, Nicolas, was suggested in the curve of the upper lip and, just occasionally, in the overall saturnine effect. Would I ever look at a future grandson and see the old gentleman — in the shape of a nose perhaps, the sharp point of a determined chin?

I knew that Rajeev had been a learned man, one who had sought knowledge from books as he wended his way through a prickly world. Once, as an infant, Soames had been taken to visit him and told him straight off, 'I don't like you. You look like ah man who does like too much ah books.' And, indeed, books were everywhere in the Badri household. A huge, well-thumbed dictionary was Sasha's grandfather's prized possession. She has it now and if you put your nose close you can still catch the smell of singed paper from his reading too close to a flickering candle. It also holds the slight aroma of the masala that impregnated the houses of his generation.

The story goes that it was his search for knowledge that brought Rajeev to Trinidad in the first place. The young son of a Brahmin from Uttar Pradesh, he had just arrived in Calcutta to study medicine when he met three sailors from a British Merchantman who invited him aboard to see the innards of an actual ocean-going ship. Once on board, they hit him on the noggin, locked him in the hold and the next things he saw, after several weeks of seasickness and head-banging remorse, were the docks of Port of Spain and an overseer's boot.

That, as I say, is the story.

It is amazing to me how few Indians admit to having arrived in Trinidad as indentured labourers brought out by the colonial government to serve their time and better themselves. The vast majority seem to have arrived by some kind of osmosis or had just happened to be passing through, vacationing one imagines, when they decided to tie themselves to the land and toil in the burning sun for seven long years.

What is true, however, is that Rajeev knew how to read and write, and in the evenings of his indenture he wrote letters back home for his fellow labourers — perhaps they were telling their relatives how much they had enjoyed the trip. The writing gained him a reputation of being a wise, intelligent man. At the end of his indenture, the young brahmin became a pundit. His roadside mandir, however, stood just a little down the road from where Canadian missionaries had built a church to convert the heathen coolies who worshipped gods that had strange elephant heads and sometimes even a surfeit of wriggling arms. I picture Rajeev, standing outside the little church with its coloured glass windows, listening to the lusty hymns and a minister breathing fire and brimstone over his small flock. He was intrigued, but, long before he put a foot inside the church, he got hold of a Bible and taught himself to read it. Then, he waylaid the minister on his walk home to the manse for an explanation of some of the more incomprehensible miracles and to debate the foggier conundrums of Judeo-Christian theology.

The minister, no fool he, saw the benefit of bringing a card-carrying pundit into his flock and inundated Badri with tracts and testaments. Rajeev cracked. To the consternation of the Southland, the pundit became a catechist, walking away from the little mandir up to the front door of what was to become the biggest Presbyterian church in San Fernando, Susumachar.

And he went in.

Again, that's the story, anyway.

He brought his aunt, Didi, from India to look after his house and she did so until, one day, he saw a demure young girl sitting in a pew in front of him. Her downcast eyes and large bosom caused him to lose his place in his text. She flustered him in ways that confused his newly protestant soul. The telling of his story always becomes a little hazy here. They married, had two sons and a daughter and she died.

From the time he was five years old, Morton, the elder of his sons, never put down a book while the younger, Rohan, though just as bright, had to be severely coerced into picking one up. In due course, Morton went off to university in the cold white North, one of the very first Indians to be educated there. Before he left, Rajeev, the newly minted Christian in him bowing to an atavistic Brahmin sense memory, made his son get down on his knees in front of his mother's gravestone in Paradise Cemetery and promise that he would never marry a white woman. The incident must have defined the man my father-in-law became. It certainly helped define what I came to think of him. Perhaps it also explained the slight sadness that always seemed to weigh on him despite his intellectuality and his academic brilliance.

In due course, Morton Badri graduated summa cum laude and, good son that he was, virgo intacto.

Rohan, force fed, went to England to study to be an accountant, so enjoying himself in the process that he took ten years to do it. He came back, painted the southland scarlet and met Ag. Plainly, he never knew what hit him. We saw them occasionally in Canada. Roh's sense of fun, and, I was pretty sure, his pleasures and his vices, still bubbled just under the surface, blossoming whenever his spouse left the room.

Rejeev's daughter, Rebecca, married and died in childbirth, leaving behind her a son.

Morton began his career as a schoolmaster. He taught English and Latin at Naparima College and became the vice-principal at Queen's Royal College in Port of Spain before catching the eye of a colonial administration that conjured with the idea of bringing an Indian into government. It was an innovation of immense proportions. Badri became a civil servant and soon a Permanent Secretary. Everyone knew my father-in-law and if I was an embarrassment to him, so pale and so present, the dawning looks that said, 'Oh mih God, you is dih son-in-law' could make me entirely uncomfortable with my peripheral status on the edge of his universe. I could feel for him though: in those days good Indian families preferred to keep their skeletons under lock and key.

Badri served on committees and was asked to chair them. He moderated the Synod of the Presbyterian Church and was the Coordinator of the Museum Committee of Trinidad and Tobago. The new University of the West Indies bestowed an honorary doctorate. He convened the government's Electoral Ethics Commission, not the most active of positions even then.

Despite all this, he still found time to go to Old Man Sookbirsingh and ask for the hand of the quiet, calmly gracious Ann whom he clearly adored. Since Ann's hand was all he asked for, the old man consented.

From the first, Sookbirsinghs were in awe of Morton's pedagogy. His manner didn't help. He stood up straight and he looked straight ahead. He could laugh but he rarely saw much to laugh at, although a good scotch did help. He preferred thoughtful intellectual discourse but the pickings were slim at the Sookbirsingh dining table, and his best conversations were with himself, examining the picayune phraseology of official reports and the minutiae of draft constitutions. Principled and punctilious, he remained all his life more admired than loved, and was comfortable that this was so.

Ann and Morton had two children, a pair of twins, Vanessa and Alexandra. I always meant to ask him how they came up with those names! Vanessa – always Nessa to the family — stayed home and married, only after a divorce leaving the island for the USA. Sasha — or Sash, as I sometimes call her — went abroad to complete her education. Morton drew the line at another ceremony in the cemetery, although I am sure part of him would have liked one. He knew that the far warmer Ann would have had his head. In retrospect, however, nothing short of human sacrifice would have served. In the fullness of time, it came to pass that Alexandra married white and Vanessa went the extra mile and re-married an Asian of the Chinese persuasion.

***

Another plink and my reverie was broken.

The rectangle of glass on the top of the icebox glinted in the sun. It was designed as a window for the living to look in on the dearly departed. No-one expected the deceased to open his eyes and look out, but rumours abounded of occasions when this had, in fact, happened, terrifying all concerned, not least, perhaps, the incarcerated occupant. I took a deep breath. I moved forward, mesmerized by the little window and what seemed to be the end of a nose within the box. Like the periscope of a submarine, two nostrils emerged as I approached, the angle of my vision increasing step by step. If either nostril had caused the glass to mist just one slight wisp, I would have ended my days in a padded room. But Badri was a stickler to the end. Sombre and grave, though not quite yet in one, he remained inert.

At the far end of the box, knees apart, slippered feet splayed wide, Didi sat on a straight-back chair. She was dressed in white, her face in the shade of her orhni. Very old now and almost blind, her bony hands repetitively twisted the starch out of the large kerchief with which she periodically mopped her brow. She was moaning, her lamentation low and heartfelt.

Fleur walked to the other side of the coffin and looked down through the glass window of the icebox.

'Well, good morning, Morton,' she said. 'I suppose we should speak for the last.'

Did she, perhaps, pause a moment for his reply?

'You were always a difficult man but you took good care of Annie. Lucky for you, you found her. We didn't often agree, you and I, but that's over now, for all you were wrong more often than you were right! '

She paused, mulling over in her mind what she wanted to say next.

'Morton Badri, I hope you got what you wanted out of life, but sometimes I think you didn't. Sometimes I think you wanted more but didn't quite know what it was.' She shrugged. 'Well, there's no point in us getting into that now. '

She moved round the top of the icebox and Didi struggled up to meet her. They embraced, the old woman burying her head on Fleur's breast. Didi began to sob, a silent racking sob that grew to shake the floor beneath her. It made the loaded trestles vibrate. Fleur, water standing in her eyes, stared straight ahead, comforting her.

'There, Didi, he's gone to a better place. No more pain, no more pain.'

'Oh God, Fleur. Look at mih crosses! What ah go do without he? It all finish now. What ah go do? '

Fleur was silent. How could she answer?

'Take courage,' she said, gently. 'Think of the happy times. '

'There! There! Didi,' added Ag, reaching out to pat the old lady on the shoulder. The singsong of joy was in her voice. 'Praise our good and great Lord for his life! But no one lives forever. He had a good long life. And now he's sitting with the angels at Jehovah's knee!'

Didi was Hindu down to the bindi on her tired forehead. Her brother had never attempted to convert her.

Hearing this voice, however, she jerked her head in its direction. She began to moan again, the merest smile playing at the corner of her mouth. She pushed herself round and away from Fleur, the moan growing. Ag opened her arms to receive her but Didi seemed to be peering beyond her.

'Aaahhh! Rohan! Where mih boy?' wailed the old lady. 'Where Rooooohan!'

Didi stumbled forward, her leather slipper slip-slapping on the wooden floor. Avoiding Ag, she reached her arms out to take her beloved Morton's only brother into them. Rohan: the new head of the family, its heir, the proper Badri to lead them out of this wilderness of desolation. No one came forward. For one split second, Didi stopped to breathe and the silence made each of us flinch.

Then: 'Oh Gaaawwwd, Where mih boy? Where Roh?'

A new crescendo of keening.

'Now Didi, everything is fine,' answered Ag, in a calming tone. 'Roh sends you his love. He'll probably phone to-night and you'll be able to speak to him. Or tomorrow night. The boys said to say hello to you and to tell you to take it easy. You remember my boys? Daniel and Mal?'

Short for Malachi. The other two points in her trinity.

'They came to visit you the last time we were here. Remember, Sister Woman? You came from Freeport to see us! Remember you had a bad leg and could hardly walk and wanted to see them all? And Rohan?'

It was a mistake to mention his name. She knew it immediately and would have hurried on but it was too late. Didi took a huge breath, an audible intake of lamentation.

'Ooooohh, mih God. Where he is? Where Roh?'

Ag looked pleadingly at Fleur who shrugged her shoulders and turned away, herself in tears.

And still Ag tried. 'Well, you know how busy an accountant is, Didi. A Chartered Accountant! He can't just drop everything every time something...'

This was not right.

'Some of his clients are very, very rich and they really need...'

Not a successful train of thought.

She changed tracks and attempted to raise her voice over the sounds of the old lady's sorrow.

'And he didn't like to leave the boys behind because they'll be having exams before you know it. The term is nearly over and,' rushing on, 'you know how expensive it is to fly down here but ...' desperately. 'I'm here! And dear sweet Jesus! And the Lord will be with you, too! The Lord will provide!'

These last words were lifted up into an absolute silence.

'He ent comin? Roh ent' comin!' Didi spoke the words to herself, wonderingly.

She peered over at Fleur. Fleur could not look her in the eye, but she shook her head in confirmation and mouthed the single word, 'No.'

Didi sank down on one of the chairs that stood against the wall and looked towards me. I had not realized she knew I was there. She reached out a boney right hand and gripped my left hand with it, trying to smile through her sadness.

'Mista Ee-an-uh. Betaa. You here!' She peered up into my face and squeezed hard. For some reason — respect, my different background perhaps – I had always been 'Mista Ee-an-uh' to Didi, but she had never called me 'Betaa', son, before. 'Rohan, he ent comin!'

She was telling me.

'No, Didi,' I said. 'He's not. Sasha is here. You've seen her. And Nessa will be coming down tomorrow night when she gets organized. The same flight we came on. It was all so rushed. And James. He'll be coming, too. They'll be here. '

Didi was weeping as I moved towards her. She buried her face in my waist, the buckle of my belt hard against her cheek. Fleur came to us and knelt down, resting her head against Didi's.

'Well, we can't all be here, can we now?' said Ag, standing apart. 'I know Roh would have been here if he could, but it just wasn't possible. '

It must have sounded hollow even to her ears.

Didi stood up. She kept my hand tight in hers and moved a single step towards Ag, her slipper again a gunshot against the wooden floor. Ag jerked as though hit.

'Ah man who cyar come tuh see he brother when he dyin! A man who not dere tuh wipe he brother head with Bay Rum when he dyin! Who ent dere to put he brother in dih grong! Him ent a man! Dat ent a man! Roh ent a man! '

Her voice was strong.

'Dis, dis is how he treat he?! Ah shame, ah shame for yuh. Ah shame for Roh! He a bad, bad man. He not a Badri at all!'

Some of what Didi said was lost on Ag, but she understood the gist.

She turned aside.

'Lord, Lord. Merciful Jesus!' she sighed, 'There's just no pleasing these people.'

She appealed to Fleur.

'"These people" are my people.' Fleur spoke scornfully, and walked away.

'She's an old lady and her nephew, just passed away, for God's sake,' I spoke harshly, 'He was the head of the family.'

Didi turned her back on Ag. She reached up to smooth my forehead with her sodden handkerchief.

'Betaa,' she said, nodding. 'Betaa, Lord bless yuh. You is dih head ah mih family now.'

It was far from true of course, but what a journey I had travelled through the years to hear those words.

Introducing Sasha

I met Alexandra Badri at a reception for overseas students just four days after I arrived in Canada and less than a week after she did. I had never met anyone like her in my life. This is not the place to tell the story of our life together however, except as it impacts on the events about which I am writing, though it is a tale worth the telling. The first member of the family I met was June, who visited Canada almost four years later. The three of us had coffee at an hotel near the university. The number and brightness of the lady's rings dazzled me, seven of them spread across both hands like diamond-encrusted knuckle-dusters.

She got right down to it.

'You'll be going home to England after graduation.'

'No, I may go to graduate school in the fall. '

'Sasha's going to teach in Trinidad. '

'Yes, I know,' I replied, 'She will come up for Christmas.'

'Sasha? What! An miss Christmas at the Hill!'

'Auntie, it's not all settled yet.' This was a retreat from an agreement. 'Why, we won't actually graduate until next month!' Sasha laughed nervously.

'Well, everybody waitin tuh see you home for Christmas dis year, girl. An yuh betta be dere! What yuh fader go say?'

'Actually, I may join her in Trinidad before long.' I slipped in the knife. 'I'm going to apply for a job. '

'A job! A job? Dey ent have jobs to give to expats these days, yuh know. So don't hole yuh breath.'

I was sure she would have loved to squeeze every last breath out of my body.

I met Morton Badri next. I had written him to ask for the hand of his daughter in marriage — a quaint custom, I thought, but Sasha insisted. His response came back as a series of questions. He would have to reflect on my answers before he could make a final pronouncement. What were my prospects? Did my mother work? What was the occupation of my paternal grandfather? My religion? Presuming a satisfactory religion, my denomination? Did I have any outstanding physical peculiarities? He inquired about the incidence of mental ill health among both my maternal and paternal antecedents. At the time, I didn't realize it, but this was a bit of a slippery slope for him. Both Badris and Sookbirsinghs had extant oddities in their closets.

All in all, the questions made up a long list and the good doctor sent a carbon copy to Sasha.

'Didn't he realize,' she asked, bemused, 'that you would show me the letter?'

'Perhaps he thought I might hide it,' I replied. 'I can appreciate him wanting to know about his daughter's intended, but did he never hear of the word subtle?'

'Poor Daddy. He's only looking after my best interests. I guess he doesn't trust me to find out for myself if you're 'bazodee'!' she smiled, 'That's 'nuts' to you.'

'God,' I said, 'I wonder what he'll be like when I meet him in person.'

The actual meeting took place an hour after our graduation ceremony. He had arrived in town the evening before on the way to a conference at The Hague. I did not enjoy the ceremony as much as I should have, partly because it allowed him to see me before I could set eyes on him, but mainly because of how I was dressed.

At that point in my career, I didn't own a suit, and, wanting to impress my future father-in-law, I decided to have one made for the occasion. I also hoped to be married in it at a later date. Unfortunately, the tailor didn't finish the job on time. I attended my first graduation in a suit borrowed from my roommate. David was four inches shorter than I and four inches more around the circumference. I wore the trousers, with suspenders, as low as they could go, wrapped myself in my academic gown and felt the liberating breezes of academia flowing all around me. Later, when Badri and I shook hands, my elbows stayed firmly hinged at my hips. Despite my wholly robotic appearance, he forbore to repeat his earlier mental health inquiries.

 The next time I saw Dr. Badri was a year later when I arrived in Trinidad to take up a teaching position he had found for me. I still do not know how Sasha managed to persuade him. He and she met me at Piarco. It was my first time in the tropics and it was my first time in a Mercedes-Benz.

 From the first moment I slid onto the leather seat of that Benz, I coveted it. I salivated, I oozed with envy of it. I have never been knowledgeable about cars (at that point, I couldn't even drive one), but as I ran my fingers over the soft tan leather, sucked in the cool of the air-conditioning, and listened to the refined purr of a finely tuned engine, I was caught. Trinidad seemed fine, but this, I thought, is it! I lowered the arm-rest and leaned nonchalantly against it, caressing the panel of the door with the back of my slightly shaking hand, approaching something like orgasm in the comfort of that classic sixties car.

 Ever since that day, I have always been able to pick out the hum of a Benz, whether in traffic, on the highway, or in a parking garage. Other cars don't interest me in the least, but, in that first moment, I became the Yo Yo Ma of Benzes, driven to seeking them out in my dreams. Not that anyone in the family would let me drive theirs, even after I was licensed to do so.

 Badri's inclusion as the driver of the welcoming party put a huge blight on it, as he possibly intended, and the sight of what I took to be dozens of large snakes crossing the dark road on the way out of the airport played on all my ignorance of the island. After a whispered, panicked, consultation with Sasha, these snakes turned out to be sugar canes that had fallen off the wagons on their way to the factory.

More than even the snakes, however, I had never seen so many dark people in my life. Everyone was either black, coffee or, at their very lightest, mocha. And I mean everyone. Sash had been one of a tiny minority in the Toronto of those days, and when I saw her in the airport, she herself seemed far browner than memory served. I, myself, appeared as an albino anomaly.

All of the drive into Port of Spain, Sasha chatted away from the front seat while her father drove, staring ahead into the dark. That night shaped my relationship with him. He was polite; I was polite. I asked a question; he answered it. Or vice versa. He had only the best interests of his daughter at heart but I was an embarrassment. No one in the family, Badri or Sookbirsingh, had married a non-Indian before, not even a non-Hindu.

Steups.

It was strange that Sasha was to lead the way in marrying 'out of her race', as they called it. She was totally devoted to her family, loved her aunts and uncles, and whether a cousin was once, twice or even thrice removed, — and several of them might well, I thought, have been removed with benefit permanently — she had affection for them all. Although the apex of her devotion was always her father, she was not the least like him. Outgoing and full of laughter, she possessed compassion in abundance and forgave all men their faults: her father's with alacrity, mine sometimes with an effort. She had the walk of a queen and the hips of a harlot. She still has. The one thing that Badri and I shared was our love of his daughter. She evoked a sophomoric jealousy between us, but also, I think, an eventual grudging respect.

Both Sasha and I were teachers in Trinidad: me at a boys' school deep in the country and she at a top girls' school. Life revolved around the family. Sookbirsingh Hill became a regular Saturday afternoon jaunt. Sometimes, we would stay overnight at Soames' invitation and occasionally I would go out to spree with the boys, but invariably we were back in town for Sunday dinner with Sasha's parents. Our car, a mere Morris Minor, could have found its own way there.

***

It was in Trinidad that I learned to drive.

Shortly after we were married, Sasha arrived home with an elderly Indian gentleman who fingered the brim of his hat with one hand and held a black umbrella like a truncheon in the other. Mr. Baboolal was the proprietor of the 'L' — for 'learner', I can only presume — 'Driving School'. As far as I ever knew, he was the 'L Driving School'.

I understood Mr. Baboolal even less than I understood the boys at school.

'Mash dih clush! Mash dih damn clush!' he would bawl at me, the hat on his lap protecting his private parts, as he whacked my knee four to the bar with the umbrella. 'Wha dih arse yuh doin, bass? Yuh makin joke, or what?!'

Sasha would interpret my phonetic repetition of his exhortations while she soothed my bruised arm with Limacol later in the evening.

'I think he means,' she would venture, judiciously, 'that you should depress the clutch before you change gears. He doesn't seem to think you know what you're doing.'

'Well, he's right about that anyway.'

'You should have more patience with him,' she advised me. 'He's such a sweet old man.'

'Sweet! Ouch! He's not my definition of sweet. And I'm paying him good money, and not to be beaten to a pulp either.'

'Well, you can't fire him. I think he may be some kind of pumpkin-vine family.'

A groan. 'Badri or Sookbirsingh?'

'One of Grandma Sookbirsingh's cousins from Brasso. Or a cousin's cousin, perhaps. I'm not exactly sure.'

I gave up.

After taking extra lessons from a colleague at school, I eventually passed the test, but I never did find out if Mr. Baboolal and Sasha were related, though once I thought I caught a glimpse of him across a crowded room at a wedding. The umbrella seemed familiar.

Our own wedding took place in Port of Spain and was a quiet affair, so great was the shame of the event. Only Sasha's relatives attended, although I imported David to act as my Best Man. He wore his own trousers. The only other white person there was the minister, a sunny Scot, who had been long enough in the island to have been permanently dyed ruby-red from the sun. Apart from 'I do' and 'I will', I had little to say to him, and, at the reception, he was kept segregated at the far end of the room and plied with the demon rum. He seemed to have more than the passing acquaintance with it that one might have expected from a Presbyterian missionary.

For Sasha, the day began with her father threatening not to walk her down the aisle: it finished when we were ladled into a taxi and June called out, 'Oh Gawd! She leavin she fader house an she ent know where she goin!' Sasha burst into tears.

I put my head between my knees and tried to breathe.

We remained in Trinidad for four years before returning to Canada, but we went back regularly for holidays, weddings, Carnival and, more often as we have aged, for funerals. Sasha returned for her aunts' birthdays and to see her father presented with awards as well. Three times in the past year, she had made the midnight trip home to help out as he went through a swift and bewildering decline. For years, their idea of conversation at the breakfast table had been to trade stanzas from the nineteenth century romantic poets or from Caesar's Gallic Wars, the other one providing context and subsequent lines, but, in his last days, Sasha could only listen while some loose loop in her father's brain led him, verbatim, through speeches and public addresses delivered long ago. In the deep, sad nights of those last times, he became the son and she the loving mother that she is to all who need her care.

***

As Didi held on tight sobbing into my chest, one of the bedroom doors clicked open and Sasha stood in the doorway. She looked tired, her smile was wan and tears ran freely down her face. She came no further into the room and I began to disentangle myself from Didi to go to her. Fleur removed the old lady from me and I took Sasha into my arms. We turned back into the bedroom and closed the door. The mosquito netting had been pushed to one side and we sat together on the edge of the bed. My sadness was all for her. She seemed feverish and it was long minutes, the sun of the morning rubbing itself against the pink of her housecoat, before she was able to talk. Then words poured out in a litany of reminiscence. She told me of the long days and nights, wanted me to know the details of his illness, to understand how he had been. She spoke of his delirium and the sharp shock of reality that would occasionally return when he would comfort her and they would laugh together about things long ago when the world had been fine and it had revolved properly on its axis.

She told me how once, when his eyes were bright, she had asked him what he thought of her rock marriage now, after all these years, and how he had lowered his gaze, squeezed her hand gently, and shrugged, 'All of that was in it, child! I had to tell you how I felt.'

And the subject was closed between them.

We sat together and the room became still. Sasha was quiet. I put my hand on the rise of her breast and smoothed her cheek.

'You did everything you could. He had been ill for months and it was his time. He was no longer the man he had been. He knew you loved him, you had taken care of him, and you'll always have these last memories of him. Just think how lucky you are to have had them. Everything is going to be fine.'

'Don't be too sure,' she sighed, with a rueful half-smile, 'Nurse is somewhere around! She may have gone down to Dookie's in San Fernando.'

Sasha sat up.

'Come, you must be hungry. Let me get you some breakfast and then you should try to rest.'

A Short Note On C P & J

Half an hour later we were waiting for the men from the undertakers to take my father-in-law to the funeral home in San Fernando. Dookie, Cipriani and Jones, as every Trinidadian knows, is the largest such emporium in the land. The name, however, is awkward. It is, for instance, too much of a mouthful to use to scare a small child. 'Look at mih crosses! Chile, if yuh don' behave yuhself, I go call Dookie, Cipriani and Jones tuh carry yuh orf in ah box!' lacks a certain resonance, even if bawled with all the cacophonous vehemence a genuinely infuriated Trini can muster. The acronym, Dee Cee & Jay is invariably used instead.

In fact, while most Trinidadians know who Dookie and Jones are, the firm in all likelihood having been used to bury several generations of relatives and loved ones, not many have even the slightest idea about Cipriani. This was because Hiram Cipriani barely survived the foundation of the limited liability company that bears his name. Three short days after its incorporation, Hiram was ensconced in the back of a north-bound hearse on the highway having his usual midday libation when his elbow caught the door handle. The door flew open, Hiram flew out and the hearse being closely followed, and at a considerable speed, by a large truck — not one of the Sookbirsingh's, but full of sand and gravel nevertheless — his haemoglobin flew everywhere. Not many interment establishments can make the claim that their third corpse was a full partner. Hiram had left his all his shares in the business to the other two partners in a Will signed and witnessed just before he set out that morning.

The hearse was due at eleven o'clock. It seemed disrespectful to go about any other business, so we waited for its arrival seated at the breakfast table. Subdued conversation about Badri mingled with Soames bringing Fleur up to date on the local political gossip. I passed on messages to Sasha from friends. Ag sat slightly apart drinking tea until June appeared. The two of them began a conversation about the escalating price of imported chocolates. Ag made notes. No one seemed to pay much attention to the icebox or to Didi sitting on guard at its side. Time stopped and the accelerating heat of the morning oozed over our tired bodies.

'So, Anc, what's the boyfriend situation like in Toronto?' asked Jolyon, with a grin. 'It's about time dis family had a wedding. A good looking girl like you must be have to beat dem off with a stick.'

'Right, Uncle Jo,' replied Anca, 'it just a matter of deciding which one ah want an den ah'll send yuh a plane ticket tuh come to dih weddin.'

'Ah wish!' June turned from Ag to comment on her daughter's single state. 'She'll never fine ah man if she doh lose some weight. Who go marry she?'

'Wha yuh mean?' replied Jolyon, rising to his niece's defence. 'Plenty men would be happy to have she. Ramdass'll give yuh a sweet dowry, girl.'

'Well, yuh know, Uncle Jo,' Anca batted her eyelashes at him. 'What I really waitin fuh is fuh yuh to axe me!'

'Girl, ah couldn't keep up with yuh these days at all. '

They both laughed.

'Ah doh know what so funny! Is serious business we talking about here,' her mother pouted, 'She ent getting any younger.'

'But she still sweet,' said Jolyon, and he pinched Anca's plump, brown cheek. 'How about makin a match for she with Ainsley? '

Ainsley & The Nurse

Ainsley Surujnarine Gokhool was Badri's sister's child. Rebecca Badri had been a joyous woman but she died having him. Some felt he had not been worth the sacrifice. While the doctors tried to save the mother, a shrieking Ainsley had been left on a gurney near the door of the delivery room. A nurse, coming in in a hurry, had knocked against the gurney and the baby, in swaddling cloths, had rolled off, luckily caught, like a football in flight, by an orderly as he fell.

'Ah got im!' bawled the orderly just as the doctor sighed, 'We lost her.'

Ainsley's father took one look at his new son and left the hospital. It was three days before he came back. During that time, Ainsley never ceased crying. He had an unprepossessing face even then and nurses who would normally gather in the nursery to smile at the newborns avoided him. His father took him to the country where he hired a wet nurse to do the necessary and still Ainsley never stopped crying. Paediatricians and pundits were consulted to solve the riddle of the wailing infant but no one could shut him up. Then, one day, Gokhool took him to an obeah woman in the next village.

The story is part of Badri family lore.

The old Negro lady carried the child out the back door of her house and laid him naked in the dirt on a banana leaf and said to Gokhool, 'Dis chile does be one unlucky chile. Ah never see anyting like dis chile. Ah see a black cloud follow he all dih days ah he life. He a po-me-one fuh true. An he go cause big big trouble for he family. Where dih mudder?'

'She dead,' answered Gokhool.

'She right,' replied the woman, and shuddered.

She put a white worm on Ainsley's chest. Gokhool watched as his son and the worm wriggled together in the sunlight.

'What ah go do?' he asked.

'Take he tuh ah orphanage.'

'Steups, woman, ah cyar do dat! What people go tink? '

The woman shook her head and rubbed goat fat and mango juice all over Ainsley's sticklike arms and legs. Still he cried. Then, with a quick gasp and an incantation, she squished the worm dead on the baby's chest with the back of her hand.

Merciful silence fell.

Unfortunately, he began again the following morning and has hardly ever stopped since. Ainsley will cry at a harsh word, a hangnail, the sight of an injured puppy, the nation's unbalanced budget, a faded flower or a lost cricket match. He had gushed great tears when he heard that Sasha and I had a son, and he wept waterworks when Clara's youngest passed the Common Entrance exam. Undifferentiated lachrymosity is his long suit.

Unable to cope with such distress, his father began to parcel him out to different relatives until it was time for him to go to school. Then he was sent to board with Didi in Freeport. Didi couldn't do much with him. He didn't study, his manners left much to be desired and he continued to bawl at the drop of a hat. His greatest pleasure was in going out to the main highway with a little notebook in which he would write the license plate numbers of all the Sookbirsingh taxis that passed by and the exact hour at which he saw them. Over time, Ainsley expanded his research to include other companies, and then all the taxis in the island.

He came to manhood with an encyclopaedic knowledge of the hired-car industry in Trinidad, avid to share the minutiae of his information on makes and models, their age and maintenance, gas mileage and passenger comfortability whenever it might be needed — and also when it was not. He whimpered his way into a job at the Sookbirsingh company headquarters in Port of Spain until the drivers threatened to mutiny. He was then banned from the premises and eventually from the cabs themselves, but to this day he remains a connoisseur of taxi physiognomy.

After a period of prolonged unemployment during which his main occupation was to rock himself, sobbing with self-doubt, in the hammock of any relative willing to put up with him, a stray thought wafted into his head. He would become a barber. Sent off to Canada to study the trade properly, he could not get used to the cold and hated the icicles that hung like stalactites from his unhappy eyes. He packed his bags and returned home. He was allowed, once, to cut Jolyon's hair: good-natured even in adversity, Jolyon referred to it ever afterwards as the Massacre of the Mane. I have seen a photograph in which Joylon, a large scotch in his hand, appeared to be sporting a modified Mohawk. In a move of self-preservation, Badri and Soames set Ainsley up in a little shop over the hill in Claxton Bay where the damage to the local population would be out of sight. But Ainsley adored his family and he would turn up for Sunday lunch at Sookbirsingh Hill and for afternoon tea anywhere. He liked, he said, to spree with the boys. 'The boys', all a generation older than he, had other ideas. Ainsley had one virtue: it was the easiest thing in the world to buy him a Christmas present. A handkerchief is an extra arm to Ainsley, a vital appendage, an expected accessory. His dresser drawers must be full of them.

Anca roared with laughter. 'Put meh on a bed with Ainsley an ah'll flatten him in one.'

June sniffed.

'Every chalk have he cheese, but ah tink ah'd rather have she die an old maid than marry Ainsley.'

'Yuh safe anyway, Anc,' said Soames, 'Ainsley does only go out with dih help.'

'How yuh mean?' asked Anca.

'Is so!' agreed Jolyon, 'Clara did see Ainsley and Nurse dong by dih parlour at dih junction eatin crab-back!'

'What yuh say? Gimme breeze! Nurse?!'

'Is true! An dat was a few months ago. It goin from long.'

Joylon laughed. 'An yuh know what he say when ah tell he ah see him with she? He say, "You see me? You see me?!" An he swell up. "You ent see me wit she. Not me!"'

Everyone laughed.

'Don't worry. He told me last week that it was all over,' said Sasha. 'She was too bossy, he said. He hadn't told her yet, but he was looking for an opportunity.'

'So there yuh go, Anc. Yuh still have a chance!' suggested Joylon.

'Not wit Nessa about to arrive in dih picture,' laughed Soames.

'All yuh remember how Ainsley used tuh like Nessa when dey small?' asked June.

'He used to follow her all about. She couldn't get rid of him,' agreed Sasha.

'Ainsley still likes she too bad,' said Soames. 'Look at he looking at she when he tink nobody know.'

'Hah!' I said. 'Better not tell Nurse. She can't stand Nessa. And she'd break Ainsley in two.'

June stopped the laughter with a serious question.

'When yuh goin tuh tell Nurse she could finish dih work, Sasha?' she asked. 'Now yuh Daddy gone, there's no need for her.'

Sasha frowned. 'I can't just tell her to go. I thought I would wait a few days until the funeral is over and, meanwhile, she can help sort out Daddy's medicines and some of his things. Help out generally, you know. '

'If yuh take my advice, yuh'll get rid ah she as soon as all yuh can.'

It was not like Soames to be so firm. The occasions when he offered so definite an opinion were few and far between.

'Between she and Ainsley, they go drive everyone mad.'

'Why, what's going on now?' I asked.

It was difficult to imagine that Nurse, almost as scrawny as Ainsley, could have had such an effect on such an easy-going man. On the other hand, I had heard the stories about her. For me, her main claim to fame lay in the fact that she had once reduced my wife to the use of four letter words. One four letter word, anyway. I had thought I had been the only one to do that.

***

Nurse first came to the attention of the family when Bim hired her to look after his mother while she was recovering from a bypass operation ten years previously. Didi could not abide the woman but she knew her job. When Ann became ill — cancer took her in a few short months — Nurse was rehired to make her comfortable and to stay with her during the night. She had been bossy then, but she was, I was always told, efficient, willing and, if not exactly gentle with the patient, well, she made sure Ann received her medication, ate a little something and was neat and clean. Nessa, however, held to the opinion that her mother declined as quickly as she did to avoid being under Nurse's care.

When we were first introduced, I found it difficult to believe what I had heard. Nurse – her name was Lillian, but I never heard anyone call her that — was a small, dark, Indian woman with permed hair. She had a penchant for pink, except for the white ankle socks she invariably wore, whatever else she had on her feet. Although Hindu, she wore three delicate gold chains, each bearing a cross, around her neck. She looked like a teenager, but we calculated that she must have been pushing forty, hard. There was initial gossip about whether she was, somehow, related to the Sookbirsinghs. Fleur, consulted as the expert in such matters, had a theory that she was the outside child of a second cousin once removed from near La Brea.

After Ann's death, Nurse somehow managed to stay on in the old servant's quarters at the back of Badri's house and, when he moved to the Hill, she came with him. She took a room in the village. Badri was a bit of a hypochondriac, and, according to both of his daughters, Nurse set about making herself indispensable. A little cough, a spoonful of elixir. A pulled muscle, how about a rub? Then, when Badri began to build his own quarters, a further use was found for her: whatever else, Nurse was competent.

She was dispatched to the builders in Port of Spain, sent to buy a toilet and appliances in Miami and, nearer home, put to oversee the day workers. It was in this last that she perfected the habit of command. She began to accompany Badri to meetings, to purchase tickets for plane trips and to balance the only book that Morton had little interest in, his cheque book. Since both Sasha and Nessa lived abroad, they could only be grateful for the attention their father received, but Nurse's control accelerated when Badri's health began to decline.

His annual physical examination turned up a growth in his belly. Nurse decided that an operation was indicated and, before telling his children anything about it, arranged the day and the hour. They were not amused. Nessa was having surgery of her own at the time, but Sasha booked a flight and, landing to Trinidad on the morning of the operation, arrived at the hospital just as her father was to go under the knife. She and June remained in the waiting room throughout. Nurse was nowhere in sight.

When the procedure was over, June went home and Sasha sat in a chair next to her father's bed. Worn from the night flight and from worry, she fell asleep. She was startled awake when Nurse took her by the elbow and pulled her to her feet, poking a finger into her chest.

'Girl,' poke, 'if yuh cyar stay awake,' poke, 'an' watch yuh fader fuh when he wake up,' poke, 'den yuh no help atall!' Double poke. 'Move out an ah'll sit here an mek sure,' poke, 'nuttin does go,' poke, 'wrong.' Poke.

The nervous tension of the long flight through the night and worry for her father overflowed. Sasha snapped. She grabbed Nurse's pointed finger and twisted it backwards.

'Don't you fucking talk to me like that, Nurse! Don't you ever point your finger at me, and don't you ever dare touch me again or

I'll break every,' ah, the blessed glories of repetition! 'fucking bone in your scrawny little body. You hear me?' she hissed at her. 'You've done a lot for Daddy, but don't ever forget that I,' she arched the digit, 'am his daughter and he,' arching further, 'is my father.'

Still holding on to the finger, she led a yelping Nurse to the door and pushed her through it.

Nurse's version of this was retailed throughout the family to anyone who would care to listen. How Sasha had used 'the F word', twice, and had almost broken a finger which, to prove her point, Nurse wore in a bandage. In truth, the family had never heard anything like it: Sasha swearing?! Nurse gained some momentary sympathy from the telling, but overdid the asking for it. Sash was truly appalled at what she had said, and privately blamed me for the general lowering of her standards, but, in some secret place, I suspect she exulted. Jolyon gave her some comfort and perspective when he laughed and said,

'In two twos everyone go forget about it, and, in any case, remember dat dih higher monkey climb dih more he show he ass. An is Nurse we talking about!'

Sash laughed ruefully. 'I can't believe I said it! But I meant what I said! Perhaps she'll learn something from what happened.'

'Yuh makin joke,' replied Jolyon. 'Dat woman learn when cock get teat!'

Eventually, Didi intervened and told them both to behave and to remember that what they should be concerned about was Badri. The two of them shook hands. Nurse used her other hand. In the long run, however, the incident strengthened Nurse's position: Sasha felt so guilty that she let Nurse get away with a lot of things she shouldn't have. The incident also underlined, for both Sasha and Nessa, just how much they relied on Nurse's being there. Neither could easily pick herself up to fly to her father's side at the drop of Nurse's cap.

In those last months, Nurse was in charge. She moved into Badri's quarters, slept on a cot in his living room, paid his bills and hired assistants — they never remained very long — to help look after him. She fussed.

'Ah goin tuh dih junction tuh see if ah could get a nice piece a king fish fuh dih boss dinner.'

'Ah don like he colour dis morning. Ah goin tuh call Dr. Ramdeen tuh tell he tuh come tuh dih house today self.'

'All yuh, don make so much ah blasted noise! Daddy restin.'

Thus did Badri become 'Daddy' to Nurse, though never when his daughters or Didi or Soames could hear.

'Where are they now?' asked Fleur, 'I'm surprised they're not here.'

'They went to pick out the casket.'

'Oh dear God, save us, Sasha! What does Nurse know about such things! Nor Ainsley either. I hope you told her to make sure it's tasteful.'

'And not too expensive,' added Ag, 'Really, you should have waited and I would have been happy to go. The Lord loves a helping hand!'

'Heaven knows what she'll choose,' agreed Sasha, 'but I couldn't listen to her any longer. She was going on and on about all that had to be done. It was easier to let her go.'

Soames shrugged. 'It was either she go to Dookie's an supervise down dere, or she stay an tell everyone what tuh do up here. Ah thought Didi was goin to give she a hot slap las nite when she said not tuh let Honaria's children in tuh see Morton.'

'Why shouldn't they see him?' asked Fleur, indignantly. 'They've known him since they were in short pants.'

'Nurse said only close family were to be allowed in tuh see him. And them, one at a time,' explained Soames. 'Don't worry. Ah tole her tuh watch she mouth and stop it.'

'She is ah ass.' A statement from Jolyon.

'Jo! Mind your mouth!' said Fleur, but no one contradicted him. Anca giggled. Ag pretended not to hear.

Sasha took Didi a cup of tea. Soames began his usual thorough reading of the morning newspaper while Jolyon, Anca and I moved out to sit on the back gallery. Fleur needed to unpack. The group under the tent had disappeared, gone home or to friends for a rest. They would return for the wake. The yard was still, except for a pot hound that meandered lazily around, sniffing the chairs. Sonnilal sat off by himself, in the shade of the Benz. Every so often he would look over in the direction of the house.

'That dih boy fuh you,' said Jolyon to Anca quietly, making sure that June could not hear. 'Ah doh care who say what!'

'Doh make pappyshow, Uncle! What he want with meh?' giggled Anca, 'ah fat, black, lil, coolie girl. Yuh crazy or what! Anyway is too late now.'

'Rubbish,' I said, 'He toutoulebay! If you lifted a finger he'd come running and you know it.'

'Yes, an Ma and Pa would kill him and den dey'd kill me self! Anyway, ah cyar see Sonny shovelling two feet ah snow up dere in Canada,' replied Anca, with a regretful laugh.

Sasha joined us and we looked out at the day in companionable silence.

***

A horn blasted out on the road and a large black Mazda, old but immaculate, roared to a stop next to the Benz. Nurse was at the wheel. A little man, a pencil thin moustache residing above full red lips, like a rubber mat on top of a mattress, sat beside her. He was weeping. So short that he looked like an infant behind the dashboard, the man opened the door and slid down from the seat. A cushion fell to the ground. Nurse climbed out of the other door, slammed it shut and yelled over at Sonnilal.

'Boy,' she said, 'Wha yuh sittin dere fuh? All yuh don know dere is tings to do arong ere? Is a man dead up dere! We ent pay yuh tuh do nuttin. Get up an move all ah dem blasted chairs. How yuh tink dih hearse go be able to come in here an pick up Mr. Morton, just so?'

Coming towards the back steps, she shouted up to Jolyon, 'Where Mista Soames? The hearse go be here in five minutes. Ah just come ahead a bit tuh get all yuh ready. Morning, Mista Ee-an-uh.' She nodded to me. 'Yuh betta help. Miss Sasha, ah'll tell yuh what ah decide about dih casket when dey gone.'

She was clearly furious about something.

'Okay, and nice to see you, too, Nurse,' I replied.

Ainsley (for it was he) tottered towards the house and came up the steps. He was sobbing quietly, tears streaming down his cheeks, mucus seeping out of his nostrils.

'Ah tell she!' he whispered to Sasha. 'Ah thought she go kill meh.'

Sasha rolled her eyes at me.

'Why did you tell her today, Ainsley? Honestly, why didn't you wait?' Sasha was both sympathetic and annoyed.

Ainsley stumbled sideways, pushed over by the weight of her words.

'She say how she want tuh move in wit meh, Sasha! Ah frighten! An what Nessa go say?'

Nessa would have given him a good thump.

Sasha sighed aloud. 'Go and lie down. You're worn out. Go inside and rest,' she said.

Her suggestion, however, resulted in a fresh paroxysm of tears. He leaned his head against the doorpost. 'An Uncle dead, to besides!'

'What on earth is the matter with him?' I whispered to Sasha.

'You know how soft he is,' she replied. 'He always cries. You know that. But since Daddy died, he can't seem to stop.'

'But if he broke up with Nurse, they should be tears of joy,' I suggested.

Jolyon leaned over and said to Sasha, 'He fall!'

'Uncle Jo, for God's sake, hush!' hissed Sasha back at him, wanting to laugh nevertheless.

Aloud to Ainsley she said, 'Ainsley, I'm so sorry. You really should go and lie down.'

To Nurse, who was coming up the stairs having dealt with the help, Sasha said, 'We were just sitting here talking. We didn't realize what time it was. You're right. Everything will have to be moved. '

Everyone stood.

'Let's get the chairs out first.'

Before the task was complete, however, the men from Dee Cee and Jay arrived, led by Mr. Lancelot Dookie himself. An enormous half-Indian, half-black man who habitually walked with a Bible under his arm and a cell phone in his hand, he shook hands with everyone and squeezed Fleur tight to his chest. Old now and stooped, it was an honour to the family that he had made the effort to oversee the operation.

'Well, bless my souls!' he said. 'Is a sad, sad day. Ah go miss Morton too bad meself. He meh partner from long.'

We already knew, without a word ever being said, that there would be no charge for the funeral. Dookie and Badri had been in First Standard together and, against all reason, they had remained friends. There was also the never spoken fact that Dookie had loved Ann all his life long. He had adored her.

We stood quietly as the men carried the icebox out. I put my arm around Sasha's waist while she wept. Soames peered down at the bare wood floor and Fleur turned away. Nurse hovered. Didi lifted up her head and began to splinter the air once more with her cries, while Ainsley flopped down like a rag doll onto one of the chairs and wailed.

Obits, Pallbearers & The Order Of Service

An hour later, Soames brought his copy of the morning paper, folded open to the death notices, and dropped it on the table in front of Fleur.

'Look trouble here today,' he declared. 'Yuh see this?'

'Oh, is it the announcement?' she asked eagerly, putting on her reading glasses, 'Let me have a look.'

Soames stood over her as she read.

'My God, who put this in?' Fleur tapped the paper with a manicured fingernail. 'I can't believe my eyes!'

'Nurse did tell Sasha she will do it fuh she yesterday,' replied Jolyon. 'What happen?'

We read over Fleur's shoulder.

Sasha was in the shower and could hear every word. She turned off the water.

'What did she do now?' she called out, ominously.

'Oh, Sasha. Ah cyar believe ah see it wit' mih own two eye,' exclaimed Anca.

'Gih me breeze,' said June. 'Ah never see more.' She laughed nervously.

Jesus, I thought, Nurse better watch her fingers.

Fleur began to read.

'"Badri, Morton Sunil. After a"' she paused and lowered her voice, hoping, perhaps, that Sasha would not catch the words, '"tedious illness."'

Everyone looked up at the transom to listen for a reaction. None came.

Fleur cleared her throat.

"'Of Port of Spain and Sookbirsingh Hill Road, Monday 14-04-94. Brother of Rebecca (deceased) and Rohan (his parts" — she stressed the unusual ess — "in Canada)."'

She took a breath and stammered.

"'Relic of the late Ann."'

'Oh, mih fader lifted!' said Anca, as she peered on tip toe at the paper.

Fleur continued reading, albeit with a slight stutter, emphasizing each syllable as though she could not quite believe her eyes.

"'Father of Vanessa and James Wong Howe and Alexandra and Ian Menzies and grandfather of Nicolas. Uncle of Ainsley."'

'Ainsley?' Sasha's voice echoed ominously off the bathroom tiles. 'Only Ainsley?' she asked.

'My boys! O Sweet Lord, my boys! No-one ever remembers my boys!' announced Ag, the martyr. 'And they loved their uncle so. Just wait till Roh hears about it!'

'Shall I go on?' asked Fleur with little cough, and, not waiting for a reply, she began again, "'Cohort of..."' She stopped. 'I can't read the rest.'

June continued for her. "'...Lillian Savitri Ragoo..."' Who's Lillian Savitri Ragoo?'

I think that, even as she asked, she knew the answer.

Then, very faintly, 'What's a cohort?'

'Christ!' I said, aloud.

'Dih woman got more guts than ah calabash, Sasha,' said Jolyon, starting to laugh. 'Yuh know how yuh Daddy always like tuh tell she she his cohort. He like dem Latin word too bad!'

'She have bad mind!' said June, shaking her head. 'She kiss mih arse stupid!'

'Everybody is going to mix cohort with 'co-inhabit'!' said Fleur, quietly.

'Or co-whore!' whispered Anca, looking down at her lap.

'Or consort!' announced Ag, quite loudly, towards the transom.

We heard the water being turned back on. At the same moment, Nurse appeared at the back door like an apparition.

'Where Miss Sasha?' she asked, brusquely. 'Ah want we tuh finish dih Order of Service tuh take tuh Dookie's.'

Sasha swept into the room dripping wet, wrapped in her housecoat. Her arms were tightly folded as though to hold herself together.

'I'll take care of that, Nurse,' she said, and snatched the draft from her hand. 'There is no need for you to bother yourself. Thank you very much! And for your information, you were not my father's cohort, however 'tedious' that may seem to you!'

Nurse saw the newspaper. She shrugged.

'Ah was only tryin to say how close, close Daddy an I was.'

'Daddy!' Sasha exploded. 'He was not your Daddy!'

'Dih woman need a good cut arse!' muttered Soames.

The eighty-five pound caregiver was not to be denied.

'He did say how ah was like ah daughter to he. An he call me dat in he Will, to besides.'

'What dih France!! Which Will you see, woman?' asked Soames.

'He make ah new Will las August when ah took he tuh town tuh see he dentist. We went by Paulie Goberdan after dat.'

Incipient chaos!

Paulie Goberdan was a friend of Ainsley. He was a solicitor, though it had taken him a dubious number of years to pass his exams. On the one occasion the family had used his services, they had not only lost the case, they also had to pay costs for all the parties involved. The presiding judge, one of the ethical few, a religious man and a family friend, took Soames aside afterwards, to ask what else he expected, hiring such a jackass in the first place, adding that, 'the blasted Virgin Mary sheself would ah lose she place in the inn if she arrive wit Goberdan.'

'Goberdan wasn't Daddy's lawyer,' said Sasha, her voice on a steely even keel. I knew that voice.

Nurse was defiant.

'Is true. But dih Doc wanted to change he Will dat day, an, since Assraf Khan does be in San Fernando, he say tuh go to Paulie since he nearby.'

'Do you have a copy of the Will?' asked Soames.

'No, Mista Soames. Mista Paulie does have it lock up.' Did I imagine, that she said these words slyly? They certainly seemed bathed in molasses.

'Morton was out of his mind last August. He wouldn't ah know what he did sign,' exclaimed June. 'Ah remember dat day. All yuh brought him by us an Ram an dih yard boy had tuh carry he up dih stairs. He ent know where he was.'

'Oh no, Auntie. Dat does be was ah different day. Dis day he was fine,' said Nurse, sweetly.

'What nancy story yuh telling! Ah ent remember him goin to no dentist two times,' said Soames.

'Oh yes, Mista Soames. Yuh remember him went when he toot fell off he denture an he nearly choke, and then again tuh collect the repair denture deh nex week self.'

Soames boiled down. 'Umm,' he said. 'Is true talks. But who tell yuh tuh take Morton all about deh countryside tuh see solicitor?'

'Was dih Doc self tell meh,' stated Nurse, with an alarming degree of complacency.

'So what was in the Will, Nurse?' asked Fleur, all innocence.

'Ah ent know, Auntie,' Nurse relied, equally so. 'Dey lef meh in dih courtyard an went in tuh Paulie office.'

'What Ainsley know about this?' asked Joylon.

'Ainsley?' she asked, genuinely surprised. 'Him? He get on so bad when he hear dih Doc have tuh go tuh dih dentist that ah tell he tuh stay home.'

It was a known fact that Ainsley fainted at the sight of blood.

'And I don't suppose that Paulie told either of you about it afterwards?' I asked. 'Except, of course, to say that Badri called you his daughter in it!'

Soames spoke. 'Watch meh good, woman! If any nasty commesse does come out of dis business, I, Soames Sookbirsingh, go do for you!'

Nurse lifted her thin shoulders and shrugged, 'How yuh mean, Mista Soames! Paulie couldn't ah tell meh what in dih Will 'cause dat is corn — fee – den – tee – all.'

Stretching the word out, she wagged her finger at each one of us in turn until, I think, she remembered Sasha was in the room and quickly hid it.

'If all yuh don want my help on dih service, ah goin tuh lie dong.'

'Ah ent trust that Nurse one bit,' announced Anca, when the door closed. 'An as for dat papesy Paulie Goberdan, he ah ass.'

'Well, yuh know dey say' "Where molasses is, fly must be!"' said June, nodding her head sagely.

'I bet she made sure my boys are not in the Will,' moaned Ag. 'That's what it's all about. You saw she made sure they weren't in the death notice. Roh will have something to say about this! Wait till I tell him! Oh, brothers and sisters in Christ! He may come down.'

I wasn't sure whether she meant Roh.

'Well, at least we'll find out if there's anything at all that can lure him to his brother's funeral,' snapped Fleur.

She turned to Sasha.

'Don't fret, my dear. If Nurse got him to put something in a Will that shouldn't be there, it'll be easy to show that your father didn't know what he was signing.' The expert was in her element. 'Badri was in and out of his mind for the last year. Everyone knew it. Even Paulie Goberdan and Nurse wouldn't try anything.'

'Perhaps we should check with Ainsley to see if he knows anything,' suggested Soames.

'Soames,' I chided, 'would you tell a secret like that to Ainsley? You'd have to be crazy. We would have heard about it months ago.

Whatever happened, neither Paulie nor Nurse would be foolish enough to tell Ainsley. '

Fleur agreed. 'We'll just have to wait until after the funeral when the Will is read. In the meantime, Soames can phone old Khan and tell him what we have heard and see what he thinks. Badri was one of his oldest clients, after all.'

'Is true, girl,' agreed June, patting Sasha's hand, 'An remember, God doh sleep.'

***

I went to lie down while the women sat on the side gallery working on the Order of Service. I had hardly punched the sweating pillow into shape before they erupted into gales of laughter and I got back up to see what was going on. They were looking over the draft that Sasha had taken from Nurse. Even Ag was smiling.

'Lord Save us! She has herself down to do a meditation.' Pins flew as she shook her head.

'And no hymns!' said Sasha. 'Just the soloist singing 'My Way.' Frank Sinatra's 'My Way!''

'What's wrong with 'My Way'?' asked June, a bit miffed. 'Is a sweet, sweet song. Dey does sing it often at funerals.'

'Not at my Daddy's funeral, they don't,' answered Sasha, with force. 'Can you imagine Daddy even listening to 'My Way'? Anyhow, Nessa would have a fit.'

Nessa having a fit is not a pretty sight.

'Who is going to read the lesson?' I asked.

They began to laugh again. 'That's another thing,' said June. 'She want Bim's son Stanley. An Stanley have tie tongue. How dih boy go be embarrass!'

'The congregation go be rollin in dih aisles,' said Anca.

Eventually, readers, texts and the hymns 'Into Your Hands' and 'What A Friend We have In Jesus' were decided upon. I briefly argued for 'O Love That Wilt Not Let Me Go' until Sasha pointed out that, since I hadn't been all that fond of the man in the first place, it might be better if I kept quiet.

I did until they came to the subject of pallbearers.

'We need six,' declared Sasha.

'Whole six?' wondered June.

'I agree,' said Fleur. 'Four is sparse. As though you can't afford more. Eight, too show-off-ey.'

'Yuh don pay fuh pallbearers, tantie,' said Anca, kindly.

'I know that, Bianca. Do you think me a fool? It's just that it looks more caring with six, but eight is a crowd.'

'Well,' I said, 'if I know Nurse, she's picked out one big heavy coffin, so you'd be better find six good strong men and true.'

They went to work picking the candidates. It was a big slate: there were cousins in abundance on both the Badri and Sookbirsingh side of the family. James Wong Howe and I were chosen immediately. James had the advantage of weighing in at about three hundred pounds soaking wet, but he would have enough trouble squeezing down the narrow aisle at Susumachar by himself, without being attached to a coffin handle. Sasha did not wish to offend her sister by leaving him out, however.

'If Roh were coming, he'd...' said Ag, before catching Fleur's eye and thinking better of it.

The conversation continued.

'What about Bim?'

'Too old.'

'Soames and Jo, a bit too old too, yuh tink?'

'True talks. We all getting old.'

'Yuh ent go axe Ram? Whappen tuh Ram?'

'Of course, Uncle Ram, Auntie June. I was just going to say his name.'

A third then.

'Achhaa.'
'If Stanley cyar read, he could still carry!'
'Is so.'
The fourth.
'Dookie self might like tuh beh axed.'
'Ah eh able, Anc. He in charge. He ent have time tuh tote casket!'
'I would like someone from the village.'
'That's a good idea. Vijay?'
'No, Auntie! Not he!'
'Why not! We've known the family for years. Vijay's grandfather used to drive for the Old Man.'
'No, Auntie, ah cyar say, but is not a good idea.'
'If yuh cyar give a reason, chile, hush yer mout!'
'But Ma, yuh know as well as I. Remember. At he daughter weddin?'
'Oh Lord, Yes. Horrors! She right. He,' she hesitated, but it was the only word to use, 'he fart when he walk she dong dih aisle!'
A pause.
'Hmmm. What about Charran? Yuh need a Sookbirsingh cousin.'
'Is so, an he have more money than God.'
'Awright.'
The fifth.
'Now, one more.'
'We should have one of Dr. Morgan's boys. Daddy did the eulogy at his funeral.'
'Do you think a black man carrying Morton's coffin...?'
'What's that got to do with it, Ag, for God's sake? But he's out of the island.'
'What about Kendrick Gooroodayal?'
'He was close to Daddy, is true, but he might come in ah dress.'
'Ah eh able!'
'What about Ainsley?'
'Ah prefer Kendrick in he dress.'
'But Ainsley really should be one of them.'

'Steups.'
'What if he cry?'
'If he cry!? He bong tuh cry!'
'He'll cry anyway, if you don't ask him.'
'Hallelujah!' said Ag.
Ainsley was the sixth.
Eight would have been better.

And so they made their decisions.
'What o'clock yuh go have dih funeral?' asked Anca, who suffered from the heat.
'One in the afternoon,' replied Sasha, standing up to go back into the house. 'I know it's the heat of the day but the Happy Workers have the church booked for a function in the morning and Sonabai Ramkhalawansingh's funeral was already booked at three.'
'Sonabai!! Dead??' said Fleur, startled. They had been in dormitory together. 'No-one told me. How did it happen? She was in Canada last summer. I had her to dinner.'
'Is all hush hush, Fleur!' June explained. 'No-one supposed tuh know.'
This meant that everyone knew but were pretending they didn't.
'Dey say she did kill sheself. She was havin an affair with she granddaughter boyfriend. An when dih girl fine out, Sonabai an dih boy drive out to Point Lisas an burn up dey self in dey car.'
'But Ma,' said Anca, 'She must ah be eighty year old.'
'Not at all!' Said Fleur. 'Not a day more than seventy-three! Well, she was always good for herself.' She considered the logistics of the matter. 'I won't be able to see her before, but I imagine they'll put her in the family plot at Paradise Cemetery so I'll be able to walk over and visit when we get finished with Badri. I imagine a lot of people will be going to both funerals.'
'Oh yes,' said June, 'Some people will bring along ah basket fuh ah picnic.'

'But it go be awful hot fuh Uncle at one o'clock in dih midday sun!' said Anca, sadly.

'The Lord will provide,' said Ag, bracingly.

'Well,' I whispered to Anca, making sure that Sash was out of hearing, 'It may be even hotter when he gets where he's going.'

Anca steupsed.

***

After lunch, Sash and I went across to Badri's quarters to lie down. She was worn out from the events of the last few days and I was still feeling the weariness of a night flight. We lay together on the bed and the hotness lapped at us. Sasha told me again about the last few days and her sadness at her father's passing. She reminisced, although I had heard most of the stories before. It was her time to remember and tears washed her eyes as she smiled just beyond my shoulder, looking with affection at her memories. After a while, Sasha, who cold sweats in the heat, got up to take a shower and I fell asleep, happy to be with my wife and back in the warm cocoon of a place I love. Bittersweet.

When I awoke, Sasha was asleep beside me, hair damp, her neck still perspiring. I put on a shirt and a pair of short pants and went quietly out into the middle of the afternoon. The door to the main house was pulled in and everything was still, so I walked into the garden to look at the fruit trees and the old overgrown stables. The yard-dog decided to accompany me and lazily wagged her tail as she walked in my wake. I looked for reassurance that all the things I expected to see were properly where they should be. I own nothing here but have a tremendous feeling of empathy for it. The old Pride-of-India tree was more battered than before, but it was still there. Bunches of ripening coconuts clung together high among the palms. Oranges --- I have never get used to the fact that oranges are green here --- hung down from three trees near the back wall. I peered through the locked gates that led to the abandoned stables and thought about looking for the key to go in, but I might have disturbed someone. In any case, I am afraid of snakes.

The dog flopped at my feet and I turned to look back at the house. Only then did I notice Anca and Sonnilal sitting under the branches of the breadfruit tree. They didn't notice me and I pretended not to see them.

Then, suddenly, as it does, the afternoon turned from merely hot to sultry. The sun disappeared behind curling grey clouds. The breeze became a wind, stirring up the dust in the yard and swirling through the upper branches of the fruit trees. The dog hoisted herself up and trotted off to seek shelter. I smelled the rain before it came but the heavy drops were only seconds behind. They hit me on my shoulders, wetting my shirt before I could even begin to run back to the protection of the overhanging roof and the safety of the house. I could hear people inside begin to catch at the boisterous curtains and close the windows. I stood at the top of the steps drenched and turned to look at the downpour. It beat a tattoo on the corrugated iron. It bounced off the dry ground, bringing the brown earth up with it and it carved out little rivulets where everything had been flat before. Anca appeared, fleeing towards to the house, clothes sodden. She raised her hands into the air to welcome the cooling wetness and I heard her gurgle with pleasure. Then she twirled around and I knew it was not only the rain that delighted her.

Ten minutes later, the sun came out again.

Since everyone was awake, we decided on an early tea and, on the spur of the moment, Sasha asked if I was too tired to drive her to Dookie's. She wanted to see for herself how everything was at the funeral home. Nurse was out. She had put herself in charge of finding anthurium lilies for the church: they were Badri's favourite flower and she knew, she said, a place where she could get top quality cheap. Ainsley was off cutting hair somewhere. Since no one ever let me drive the Benz, we climbed into the old Nissan that had belonged to Ann and set out for the town of San Fernando, capital of the Southland.

The Delights Of Driving In San Fernando

San Fernando was built round the base of a hill. Unfortunately, they used the hill to build the town. The result is that the scarred remnants of a pockmarked hill, yellow and sear, great gouges gone from its landscape, dominate the view from near and far. There is enough of the hill left that the roads still wind along, going up, down and around, generally causing palpitations among the innocent.

The town itself feels as though it was cobbled together rather than designed. One way roads predominate. If you miss your turn, it can take half an hour to get from Cross Crossing to Harris Promenade, when all logic says that you should be there in ten minutes. Cross Crossing itself, the new improved version, seems to have been designed by a blind civil servant with an arthritic drafting hand. Norman Tang Street goes down at forty-five degrees to a Stop sign. Wump! Rushworth Street goes up forty-five degrees to a traffic light. The faint of heart – I list myself among them – idle the car in the hollow of the incline, pray, guess when the light will turn green and accelerate, mightily, through a main intersection. The first time I tried it, I changed my underwear afterwards. I still ride my clutch when doing it. Don't even think about Chacon Street, up or down.

Sasha, born there, takes it all in stride.

The old buildings of the town cluster along the narrow streets begging for breath. They crush together and the whole place could do with a good vacuuming. The suburbs are not much better. The best thing about them is their names, names to conjure with, from which dreams are made: Paradise Pasture, Les Efforts, Retrench, Vistabella. The drivers of Marabella are suicidal, the denizens of St. Joseph's Village so afraid of crime that one can rip one's eyes out walking along its narrow streets should any coil of barbwire fencing spring loose. Not that Trinidadians walk anywhere, of course. In those days the commercial joy of the town was its mall, Gulf City, a great, gloomy, green aerodrome of a building that encouraged the slough of despond on entry.

The citizens of San Fernando, mainly Indian, love the place. It is a mark of pride to have come from there — and one can see the point of leaving. I am a Port of Spain man myself. The best thing that ever happened to San Fernando was the building of the bypass that allows one to go directly from Sookbirsingh Hill to Princes Town – no prize itself — and on to the beach at Mayaro, keeping the town and its skeletal hill firmly off to one's right, always feeling its heat but not having to dip into its confusion.

San Fernando's other great attraction is its cemetery. We will visit that in due course.

***

As we edged along the busy two-lane road looking out for taxis picking up fares at the end of the working day, I remembered another visit when vehicular San Fernando imposed itself on my calmer reality. Sash and I were still getting used not only to being married but to being married to each other. We had been to a matinee and then for Chinese food at Mahsang's, still wrapped in the adoration of our mutual affection. I have always considered surviving the events that occurred that evening an indication of the depth of my love for my wife and of our mutual commitment to a successful union.

Newly licensed, me driving, Sasha said, 'Let's go over the hill.'

'Okay,' said I, not wishing to seem unmanly, 'but not Chacon St.'

Sasha laughed. 'My own private coward!'

'I'm serious,' I said, 'and you'll have to direct me.'

I could not, even today, tell exactly where we went. The road was narrow, unlit and, at every intersection, deep run-off channels for the rain meant that the little Morris Minor dipped and bucked as we drove along. At times, the bonnet of the car seemed to point straight up. Sasha did not help by giving her navigational directions at the last possible moment.

'Turn left here. No! No wait a minute, they've changed the road. Go straight on.'

'Go straight, right?'

'Right. But then go left, not right.'

'Okay,' I said again, just a little bit frazzled, peering into the darkness in front of me, foot, as ever, riding the clutch to make sure we would not roll backwards into oblivion. I came to a Stop sign on the top of a cliff. 'Here, right?'

'Right! Left.'

The car turned ninety degrees and was attacked by the pitch black of the night.

'Where now?' I bleated.

'Straight on. Just go straight until you turn. You'll see.'

Then she said words to conjure with.

'Don't worry, the hill isn't as high coming back down as it is going up.'

By the time we reached Pointe-a-Pierre Road, my hands were two claws on the steering wheel and there was a geyser of sweat between my shoulder blades. I was still looking for the logic of her words, playing them over and over in my newly-wedded mind, when the left rear tyre blew. Could it get any worse: on the by-ways of San Fernando hill, at night, with a clearly obfuscated spouse and a flat tyre? We rolled to a stop. I had never changed a tyre in my life. Locating the spare would be an accomplishment.

'Can you change it?' asked Sasha. Accusation, not to mention doubt, sang in her voice.

'Of course,' I replied, 'No problem.'

'You sure?'

'Well, I think so.'

And I did.

Eventually.

Squatting there, loosening the lug nuts, nearly gave me a hernia. It is not good for a man to cry, even in frustration, in front of his bride. The occasional car drove by paying no attention to us.

Sash hovered. She is good at it.

'Hurry up. You don't want to be out here by the side of the road at this time of night.'

'No.' Yank. 'I certainly,' Tug, 'don't.'

'Well, go a little quicker then.'

I jacked up the car, changed the tyre and jacked it down again. It took some time, I will admit. When, eventually, I picked up the old tyre to lug it to the trunk, the damn thing weighed more than I did.

'Don't get your shirt dirty and watch your pants,' warned Sasha.

My shirt was drenched.

'Yes, dear.' Through clenched teeth.

We climbed back into the car.

I started the engine, turned on the lights, let out the clutch and we drove off. After no more than five yards, Sasha grabbed me tightly by the arm and shrieked.

'You forgot to put the wheel back down on the ground. We're going on three wheels!'

In a reflex action, I lifted my hands off the steering wheel and took my foot off the clutch. The little car bucked and frolicked down the road a few yards before coming to a standstill. The headlights gazed mournfully out into the night ahead of us.

I took a deep breath.

'What?' I said.

'Can't you feel it?' replied my bride, the university graduate. 'When you took the jack away, the wheel didn't come down onto the ground. The car will fall over!'

My future passed in front of my eyes. I opened my mouth to speak but, for long seconds, nothing came out. I took a deep breath and turned to Sasha, prying her hands off my arm.

'That, my dear, is impossible.' I smiled, charm personified. 'The car wouldn't go if the wheels, all four of them, were not on the ground even if we have just come over a hill that is higher when you are going up than it is when you are coming back down.'

It seemed a good time to clear that up, too.

'Get out and check.' Sasha pushed me out of the door. 'You'll see for yourself.'

'Sash,' the reasonable man replied, 'You saw me change the tyre. You were breathing down my neck when I did it.'

'But when you took the jack off you must have left the car up.'

'How the France,' we were on the verge of our first quarrel here, 'would I manage that?'

'You didn't know what you were doing.'

This hurt. I had paid particular attention to avoid giving such an impression.

'You get out and check,' I suggested, but I added, because a marriage should be worked on, 'Let's both get out and check.'

We stared at the tyre together. I ran my fingers round its circumference, caressing where it met the asphalt. I took my bride's hand and gently led it to touch the rubber.

'See? Dear,' I said, gently, Annie Sullivan and Helen Keller, together again.

Sasha kicked the tyre. Hard.

'It fixed itself.'

'What?'

'The car came back down on the tyre. It seems fixed.'

'How did it do that, Sash? Tell me.'

'You're the man. You should know how.' And she pushed me playfully.

I lost my balance and sat down in the gutter.

We drove off in silence. Sasha listened for the sound of all four tyres on the asphalt and I contemplated my fate. Only when we got to the open countryside, and after a heated discussion in which both of us believed we had right on our side and also I offered a detailed explanation and a considerable degree of sarcasm, did she begin to laugh.

'And don't tell anyone!' she ordered.

This was the first time — it was to be far from the last — that I was to receive this command over the years.

Rookmin & Mathura

We turned down Edward Street and picked our way along the debris of the town, past the cavernous hospital towards Harris Promenade and the intersecting streets that make up the downtown San Fernando in which Sasha spent her early childhood before moving to Port of Spain. Rookmin, Ma Sookbirsingh's youngest sister, lived on Irving Street and all kinds of cousins used to populate the streets crossing it. Many have moved out to the more affluent suburbs, but Rookmin had stayed behind in a dilapidated gingerbread house, surrounded by the history of her family. She was an old lady now. After her husband, a sugar estate overseer, died from an infection when he stood on a rusty nail, leaving her with a whole wash of children, eight of them, Rookmin moved into the Irving Street house and raised her family there. She made sure that each one of them received a fine education and found a wife or a husband, fine or otherwise. In earlier days, her temper had been legendary but she had mellowed with age and its infirmities, and now liked to sit on her porch watching the world go by. No one in the family dared to go to San Fernando without dropping in or they would bear her wrath.

'Oho, so yuh does talk tuh me now! Ah is an ol lady an all yuh does be too grand tuh come see meh. Meh sister must be turning ovah in she grave to tink yuh shame tuh visit Tantie Rookmin. Is a sad ting! Ah remember when ah held yuh on meh knee.'

In my case, at least, this was wildly inaccurate.

The miscreant would squirm until, at length, Rookmin would sigh, shake her head and shrug.

'Yuh tink it easy? Steups. Ah so unlucky, wet paper go cut meh.'

This was her favourite saying, her mantra.

Like all of her generation, Rookmin had a great sense of family and she loved a good party. She liked to go to races and was one of the last ladies to be seen wearing a hat and white gloves there. She believed in noblesse oblige and the correctness of things. When she left the sugar estate, she brought with her two servants, Mathura and Anastasia. It didn't matter that she couldn't afford them, they came with her husband's family and they were her responsibility. Anastasia, a jolly black lady from Biche, worked alongside Rookmin in the kitchen for Rookmin's plan was to open a parlour near Naparima College and sell roti and aloo to the boys at lunchtime. Over the years, she made a great deal of money at it.

Mathura was another thing entirely. Wizened and bent at the end of a long life, Mathura was good for nothing, and Rookmin often told him just that. He had been one of the last indentured labourers to arrive from India in his youth, but on the sugar estate he had begun a life-long love affair with the elixir that sugar produces. White, dark or puncheon, it was all the same to Mathura: rum was his passion. Rookmin put him in a room under the house and, when visitors came to call, he would emerge to open car doors, give a scrawny salute and carry parcels.

'Don't gie he money! He charge up awready!' Rookmin would command, for Mathura's hand was always out. There were few visitors who didn't slip a coin or two into it. Mathura always remembered who you were and he made you feel like visiting royalty. He was extraordinarily gentle with young children — Rookmin's, their cousins, the little black children next door who came with their mother to wash and iron, our son Nicolas when he was very small — and they were all equally enchanted by Mathura, always seeking him out, knocking on the door of his tiny room to ask him to come out to play. Perhaps it was the fumes he breathed over them.

'Ah go send yuh back tuh where yuh come from,' Rookmin would threaten.

'Ah eh able! Look at meh crosses,' she would complain.

Mathura would cackle and retreat, only to be found sitting with the dogs at the back door later in the evening eating his rice and daal as well as the little extras that Anastasia would provide, to which Rookmin would turn a blind eye.

'Is so he stop! What ah go do with he?' she would ask lifting her eyes to heaven. 'What is to is must is, it can't are. Steups. Ah so unlucky, wet paper go cut meh.'

***

And then one morning the door to Mathura's room remained closed. He didn't come out for breakfast. Anastasia put down his enamel plate and his water bottle as usual, swatting at the flies and kicking the dogs when they came too close. After some time had passed, she stood at the top of the back steps and bawled.

'Mathura! The missis, she say tuh come eat yuh food. Now! Doh make skylark.' Silence. 'Yuh go ketch yuh royal arse, if yuh don't come. Boy, yuh is a chuppid, chuppid coolie man!'

Rookmin stood beside her and they listened.

'Yuh all right? Or what? Please yuh mind!'

It was Rookmin herself who eventually went down the stairs, ducking her head to walk under the house to the door of the little room.

'Mathura, boy. Yuh all right?' she called out, gently.

He was lying on his pallet, curled up, cuddling a bottle that stood upright against his chest. He had inserted one finger in its mouth to make sure that it did not fall or spill, but he had finished his last drink. Rookmin looked around the little space and sat on the ground beside him. She sighed.

'He cold like dog nose,' she said to Anastasia, shaking her head.

His watchicongs, his slippers, were arranged neatly at the door and his dark brimmed hat was hung on a nail. There was nothing else. She kept his spare shirt and pants upstairs to make sure he wouldn't sell them. He had done that more than once.

'Well,' she said, quietly to herself, 'Shroud eh have pocket.'

What Mathura didn't have in life, he had in death, however. Rookmin went upstairs, got on the telephone and called the whole family.

'Mathura dead,' she told them, 'We havin wake tonight and dih funeral tomorrow self.'

She laid him out in the front parlour and she put his obituary in the newspaper. She sent her eldest son to buy a suit. It created an uproar.

'She bazodee!' said the neighbours.

'Ma, Mathura never wear suit in he life,' pointed out her children.

'Rook, yuh head eh make tuh wear hat alone,' said June. 'Think! Yuh have children tuh educate. What yuh spending yuh money so for?'

Rookmin sighed. 'Watch meh good. Mathura my responsibility. Ah look after he in life an ah go look after he in death. So hush yuh mout. Jus be sure all yuh at dih funeral.'

A large crowd gathered on the banks of the Caroni River. Mathura was, as far as anyone knew, a Hindu. People came by private car and taxi from all over. Rookmin had put the family name in the newspaper and many thought he must be one of her children. Some people thought that she had wasted their time: a few laughed at her behind her back but she didn't mind. She minded more when they tried to take the new jacket off him so that it wouldn't be burned.

Afterwards, the whole family went back to Irving Street and we drank a toast. Rookmin didn't allow anyone, not Soames, not even Badri, to drink whiskey that day. Only rum was served. The ladies were allowed to add coke to taste. The next day she sent her boys under the house with orders to demolish the little room. They took the door off its hinges, lifted out the pallet and took away the ancient piece of linoleum that had been on the cement floor. They pried the little ledge off the wall and then they broke down the walls, piling the lumber in a corner near the hedge.

Mathura was no more.

Mr. Jones & His Emporium

After sipping a rum and coke and reminiscing about Badri for a while with the old lady, we continued on to Dee Cee and Jay. The establishment is on a narrow side street, quite a distance from the main road, across the way from a primary school. We interrupted a game of cricket being played by ten-year-olds in uniform when we drove into the parking lot. Five immaculate hearses were lined up in a row. From their shine, they had been washed and polished recently. Four were black, the fifth a powder blue. Sasha examined them as we walked by.

'Why would anyone want a hearse that colour? Blue!' she asked. A frown passed over her face. 'If Nurse has ordered that, that, thing for Daddy, I'll kill her.'

'Not even Nurse would do that!' I replied, hopefully, as we passed into the building. Mr. Jones, a cadaverous black man with immense hands, from one of which trailed a white handkerchief, came forward to greet us. He drooped theatrically.

'Miss Sasha! What a sad occasion fuh such a unexpected pleasure!'

I knew for a fact that Sasha had phoned ahead to say we were coming.

'May I take dis opportunity tuh express my personal condolences to you at dis most difficult time.'

His lower lip quivered and he reached out to lay a huge paw on Sasha's shoulder. He placed the other over his heart.

'But we mus' all rest with the Lord so that He will abide with us. Who are we tuh know dih times and dih seasons?'

He sighed. The handkerchief dangled.

'But Miss Sasha, we're not ready for a visitation as yet. Your Daddy is still with the cosmetologist. We'll have him perfect fuh yuh to view in dih morning. But now is cat in bag... '

He left the thought hanging, tragically raising the back of his fist against his forehead. I caught him peeping out from behind the handkerchief to check the effect.

'We understand,' I answered. 'That's fine. The family will be here tomorrow to see him, but Sasha wanted to go over the arrangements and to see the casket.'

Mr. Jones flashed a megawatt grin that disappeared as soon as it came.

'Come, let us go into dih chapel an we can talk in the blessed peace of that place.'

He turned on his heel and led the way into the Divine Chapel of Tranquility — or so it said over the door. The gentle twang of a Country and Western version of 'Just a Closer Walk With Thee' oozed out of speakers and we sat down in the front pew. Mr. Jones pulled up a chair in front of us.

He and Sasha talked about the arrangements. The close family would pay their respects tomorrow evening. Then, on the morning of the funeral, the body would be brought back to Sookbirsingh Hill so they could say their final farewells at home. From there, they would ride back to San Fernando in procession to Susumachar Church. After the service, we would continue on to Paradise Cemetery for the interment. Mr. Jones himself would co-ordinate all of the arrangements.

He took the notes that Sasha had prepared about the Order of Service and reviewed them professionally. They discussed the finer points of whether it was to be 'A Service of Thanksgiving' or 'An Act of Divine Worship'. The former won. Sash disappointed Mr. Jones by insisting that the Order of Service would indicate that Badri had been born and had died rather than that he had had a sunrise and a sunset, but he took the news reasonably well. He was more determined that the coffin be briefly open in the church so that latecomers would be able to, as he put it, 'to see the dead for the last' and Sasha hesitantly agreed.

This did not, however, make him magnanimous in their discussion about wreaths. Sash had decided that both she and Nessa would each put a rose on top of the casket. No wreath should lie there. Mr. Jones was alarmed. He laid his hand on my bare knee.

'Yuh ent want a nice show ah flower, then?' The remnants of elocution fled. 'First tuh begin, people go say yuh cyar afford tuh have a good show ah flower.'

He squirmed in his seat and his mouth tightened in disdain.

'I meself, ah ent like too much ah show, but yuh know how dey does be!'

He gulped great gobs of air.

We knew, and he knew that we knew, his sister owned the largest (and Dee Cee and Jay endorsed) flower shop in San Fernando, with branches in Port of Spain, Arima, Tunapuna, California, Pointe Fortin and Penal.

'But ah always say dat is dih sweet smell ah flowers dat get we tru putting dih dead in dih grong for dih las.' He nodded sagely.

When Sasha pointed out that her objection was not to flowers per se, but only to flowers on top of the coffin, and that she had already ordered several wreaths from Miss Floribunda Jones, he was manifestly relieved.

He trilled, 'Matter fix. We want everyting tuh be dih best fuh Doctor Morton Badri.'

He looked to the right and the left as he said this as though expecting opposition.

'Ah was just say tuh Miss Bessie – she our bes' cosmetology technologist — dat ah hope she go make he like a livin ting. Dey can do so much dese days, darlin.' Enthusiasm for his craft, or for my knee, continued to have a profound effect on both his grammar and his pronunciation. 'Yuh'll tink he go wake up an talk.'

I laughed a little nervously.

'Well, let's hope he doesn't.'

Both Sasha and Mr. Jones looked at me and I felt that elucidation was in order.

'I mean, if he woke up in the coffin, people would be fainting in the church!'

They were beginning to stare.

'And we'd have a hard time getting the lid on.'

Mr. Jones withdrew his hand as though I might be contagious.

'Could we see the casket, please?' I asked, clearing my throat.

Mr. Jones walked us through to the display area. Caskets for a pandemic packed the room. We moved sideways among them. In the middle, on a raised dais so that the other caskets seemed like suppliants before it, stood an enormous mahogany model, its huge maw of a lid wide open. Mr. Jones undulated towards it, hands above his head as though getting ready to dive in.

'Tell me that's not it,' I whispered to Sasha out the side of my mouth, although I already knew better.

'Is dih top ah dih line! Dih Fontainebleau Sarcophagus.' Each syllable was enunciated triumphantly. Fon-tain-blue Sar-cough-ay-guss.

The casket could have slept two with ease. It appeared to be about seven feet long and along each side was a rail held in place by giant copper handles that hinged onto the casket itself. Three on each side. The curve of the lid resembled nothing so much as the ceiling of Union Station in Toronto and seemed almost as large. The whole thing was lined inside with a deep puckered and frilled satin-like material that appeared to be pink, although we were assured that this was because of the lighting in the showroom. It was true that Badri's mind had often muddled at the end but it appeared that he was to reside in a padded cell for all eternity.

Mr. Jones was delighted with the casket. Sasha, unusually, was speechless.

'Isn't it a little big?' I ventured. Badri was five eight. 'I mean won't he move about a bit inside?'

'No, no, no!' replied Mr. Jones, 'Yuh see, once he in, he settle dong on dih foam.' And he pressed his foot-long hand deep into the satin, bringing it up again to show us the depression that remained. 'He go be well comfortable, fuh true. Like he sleepin in he own bed.'

Sasha continued to stare at the imprint of Mr. Jones's hand.

'Is this the casket Miss Ragoo chose?' she asked.

'Is the same one self she did pick, oui,' he confirmed. 'She see it and in two twos she say, "Dat is dih casket fuh dih doc." An Dookie say, "Fuh dat!" Dih lady does have good good taste. Yuh know Lance want tuh sen yuh fader off in style. He won't tek a penny fuh dih funeral.'

This was the sticking point.

'You don't think there's a few too many frills for a man?' asked Sasha, hopefully.

'Yuh makin joke! Dey don have different caskets fuh men an fuh women! An frills does be the fashion dese days.'

Mr. Jones would be the man to know.

'Will it be able to go down the aisle in the church?' Sasha asked, doubtfully.

'No probs! Just tek it slow an easy.'

'They'll have to take it slow and easy. We're going to need two more pallbearers to carry it.' And I added the words: 'At least.'

'Well, there's June's boys,' Sasha replied, thinking about it.

Mr Jones clapped his hands. 'Oh yes, dat Royston, he such a sweet fella. A real saga boy! An so much ah muscle!'

I swear he rolled his eyes.

It was then that I made a huge mistake. I knew in my heart it would take eight men to push the thing, let alone lift it, but it was chauvinism sautéed in stupidity that spoke.

'No,' said I, 'the six of us should be able to manage it.'

'You're sure? Once they print the Order of Service it will be too late to change your mind,' Sasha reminded me.

'No, we'll be fine. Six good men and true!' I sounded like an idiot and regretted the words even as they came out of my mouth.

'One of them is Ainsley,' she reminded me. Sasha has a vein of common sense that will counteract my airiness every time.

'But another is James,' I said, trying to contribute.

'Oooh, he does be a big one!' declared Mr. Jones, with a shudder.

'We'll be fine!' I said and sighed.

Famous last words.

Mr. Jones led us out to the car park, guiding me in the right direction with a hand in the small of my back.

'Which is the hearse that Daddy will use?' asked Sasha, a nub of apprehension in her voice.

'Dat one on the lef. Ah axe dih nurse lady if she ent want dih one blue like dih Queen Muder blue, but she say no.' He shrugged, tragically. 'An now it book for Sonabai Ramkhalawansingh self! Jus tink! Dat nasty woman goin tuh she las reward in dat nice conveyance. Look at meh crosses!'

I would have to compliment Nurse on her forbearance.

Miss Marjorie, Patsy & The Wake

The wake was already in progress by the time we returned to the house. Cars were parked along the side of the road and we had to leave the Nissan and walk. The evening was humid and still. I felt as though I could push the warmth ahead of me like a cushion of heated velvet. Stars were beginning to punch their way into the country dark. The on-and-off twinkle of fireflies, jouncing just feet above the ground, lit our way. As we came closer, we could hear the murmur of conversation mixed in with the clicking of the crickets and the croaking of frogs in the ditches on both sides the road.

A cigarette glowed in the shadows where someone stood out of sight, hired by Soames to protect the living while we mourned the dead.

'Good night, Miss Sasha,' he said. 'Ah sorry for yuh trouble.'

I did not catch the voice.

'Thank you, Moses,' said Sasha, 'It was his time to go, I guess. I'll send a boy out with a drink for you later. You by yourself?'

'Saul up dih trace behin dih house, Miss. All yuh be fine.'

Kidnapping is a cottage industry in Trinidad and storming fetes a national pastime, so it was wise to take precautions even at a wake. Moses and Saul were men from the village and Soames might well have thought that it was better to pay them to guard us than to leave them free to consider the alternative.

We turned into the gates of the compound.

In the darkness, a voice began to sing 'What a Friend We Have in Jesus'. It began in too high a key and the solo became strident with vibrato as the verse rose towards its crescendo, 'O what needless pain we bear,' but we felt the emotion, the simple truth of the unschooled singer, and the worn old words. 'Can we find a friend so faithful,' seemed fresh again as we listened. I heard Sasha, beside me, take a sharp grab for air and then she sighed. I took her hand in mine, lifted it to my lips and kissed it. We stood in the dark — 'And we'll find new courage there,' — until the hymn was over. It was followed by a beat of silence before the night sounds, and the murmur of the people, began again. Sasha turned her face into the crook of my neck and began to sob. Her body sagging slowly down, and we dropped to our knees on the asphalt of the driveway. I stroked her hair and, in tune with her sadness, wept beside her.

'You awright, Miss Sasha?' Hesitant, the voice in the shadows asked. 'Mista, yuh want meh tuh carry she inside?'

'No,' I replied, 'Thank you. Just give us a while and she'll be okay.'

As we moved forward towards the house, we saw that the tent was packed with people and dozens more melted into the darkness around it. The whole village was there in its Sunday best. I recognized family members who I only met at events like this and nodded at others with whom, in other circumstances, I would have joked and laughed. A couple of men who I had taught with years ago had driven down from north and several old teacher friends of Sasha from Port of Spain were seated quietly together. You could see the city folks' surprise at the number of people present: this was a country wake and it reached back to a less sophisticated time of obligation and civility.

Our friend Lincoln was there, Port of Spain personified. He had been at the house before and I knew that he had visited Sasha and her father more than once in the last few weeks. He waved from the other side of the tent. Even sitting down, he towered over the people around him, a tall, slim, black man in a bulky tam, his straggly moustache and goatee framing a wide, white smile. He stood up and came towards us, the bow of a ship gently parting the people on both sides of him. In the largely Indian crowd, he stood out. He knew it too, and, being Lincoln, he exulted in it. Coming alongside, he encircled Sasha's shoulders with his arm, hugging hard. His long fingers took my hand in his and he pulled me towards him. We bobbed in his embrace. He sighed.

'Girl, it had tuh happen, but dat doh make it easier for yuh. Ah sooo sorry!' he breathed the words, gentle and long.

He kissed Sasha on the top of the head.

'Go!' he said. 'People waitin tuh speak tuh yuh. We'll talk later.'

He winked at me over the top of her head. 'An you, you tek care of your lady.'

We made our way slowly through the tent. Sasha stopped to acknowledge the condolences of people she knew or who knew her, before we came to where Ag and Fleur sat, next to a lady minister dressed entirely in black except for the inch and a half of white clerical collar that seemed like a gash at her neck. Her face was covered with buttons, a permanent pox of prior adolescence. Fleur stood up when she saw how Sasha looked. Ag frowned. The Reverend Motilal put out her hand for it to be shaken.

'How are you, my dear?' she asked, eyebrows arched.

***

Patsy Motilal's charge was the Jaipur Presbyterian Church down by the sea at the junction. She had preached at the wake last evening and would likely do so again tomorrow night, but it was a surprise that she was here now. Sasha had told me that Patsy had hoped the funeral would be from her church but this was unrealistic, if only because of Badri's long association with Susumachar. Beyond that, there was Patsy herself to consider. She was an acquired taste, and Sasha, who was generally full of the milk of human kindness, tended to curdle when they met. I, for one, could never shake the thought that Patsy had joined the ministry to fund an education, rather than from any commitment to God or the good of her fellow man. She was a woman full of condescension towards those who could not give her a leg up on her career; quite likely, I suspected, to step over them when it was necessary. Soames insisted that her congregation was afraid of her, but Soames was not necessarily a good judge since he never got out of bed in time to attend a morning service. A better indication was the way her Elders and the Clerk of the Session always walked three feet behind her echoing her opinions. Fortunately, they did not echo her voice.

Patsy had first set foot in North America when she went to Miami as the travelling companion of a lady who was to undergo an operation there. Unfortunately for all concerned, the lady died and Patsy had to return home somewhat more precipitously than she had hoped. In the five weeks she was there, however, she acquired what was to become her prized possession, something that she never lost and which she worked hard to perpetuate as the years went by. Her accent. Her American accent. It was hard to place where this accent originated, midway between the Ozarks and the Mississippi perhaps, but, years later, it still startled whenever she opened her mouth.

A sermon by the Reverend Motilal was an event to be avoided at any cost. Even Ag would have agreed. The solemn strangeness of her voice was matched by the paucity of the ideas she used it to express. And these she expanded upon at an excruciating length. She had the ability to deaden one's posterior more effectively than the most powerful anaesthetic. The voice is part of it, too. At first, it is mesmerizing, alto tartness dipped in Oprah honey, Jed Clampett out of Scarlet O'Hara, but, occasionally, she will become excited, and a cadence of the rankest Trinidadianese will pop out. No one is more surprised than Patsy when this happens, such dirt on her nice new shoes, and she will ramp up the volume and her articulation, to continue.

'Ahs ah wus sayin'.'

No, Sasha had rendered unto Patsy all that the situation required, and, in any case, she had wanted to ask Miss Marjorie to speak tonight. From the expression on her face, Patsy had turned up to protect her territory. To makko and scoff.

Long ago, Miss Marjorie's mother, Mistress Octavia, ran the parlour a little way up the road on the Hill. Sasha bought snow-cones and sweet drinks there as a child during August and Christmas holidays. Octavia had also run her own church. In the last years of her life, however, she sat in the shade of an ancient frangipani tree and bawled 'Hallelujah' at the passing cars. Marjorie took over both the parlour and the church. Sasha had known Marjorie from childhood. Marjorie had worn her hand-me-downs, but while Sasha played with all the village children, Marjorie played with no one. She counted the coins for her mother in the shop, read her books on the front step, shifting sideways to let customers pass, but she rarely spoke and more rarely still did she speak to other children.

When I first met her, she was a grown woman. New to Trinidad, I was sent to the parlour by Clara to buy an item that she had forgotten to put on the grocery list. To this day, I am not sure if Clara wasn't playing a joke.

'Good morning,' I said, hesitantly, standing in the doorway of the wooden parlour.

Marjorie was behind the counter. She didn't look up. She was reading, her angular face fixed in a frown of concentration. The book was the Bible.

'Good morning,' she replied, turning a page. 'What I could do for you?'

'Um,' I asked, 'do you sell sugar here?' It seemed like a reasonable question. The shop sold very little. There were about five or so packets of cigarettes on a shelf and three Caribs stood side by side next to half a dozen sweet drinks. A few fly cakes were on display in a glass container, but I could not see much else.

Marjorie looked up, the frown slowly clearing from her face until it seemed as though the sun had come out in the dark parlour.

'Chile,' she announced, although we were about the same age, 'where yuh tink yuh is? Do weh have sugar! Look all arong yuh in dis land!' She stood up and spread out long thin arms to illustrate where I might look. 'Dis Trinidad! Yuh never see come see or what?'

She began to laugh. Such was the joy in her laughter that I began to laugh with her. She looked me up and down. I was wearing shorts as usual and her eyes swept upward from my knees to the neck of my open shirt. Around my neck was a crucifix worn more for fashion than as a statement of faith.

Her laughter stopped. Deep, searching, brown eyes looked keen and bright. They were the eyes of a puritan.

'So yuh does be a Christian den, broder?'

A serious answer was required: one that might affect not only how the woman would view me but, in some strange way, how I might come to view myself in the future.

'I try,' I replied.

The eyes softened.

She nodded.

'All ah we mus try, friend. Dat is all we can do, as man. An den the Lord Jesus be happy fuh all ah we.'

She nodded again, the smile returning.

'An we have plenty sugar, chile. Ah telling yuh, dis Trinidad!'

★★★

That was how Miss Marjorie and I became friendly: not friends exactly, but two people who wished each other well and followed each other's progress through the years.

Whenever I came to the Hill, I would visit the parlour for sweet drinks or to buy ten cents worth of dinner mints and to chat. Miss Marjorie always seemed to know we were visiting and after the birth of Nicolas, Sasha and I received a card sent from the 'Emmanuel

Church of Christ, Our God', her church, in the mail. I used to think that Sash was a little jealous of Marjorie; certainly Marjorie was one of the few people who was more my friend than hers in Trinidad. And yet, I still hesitate to use the word 'friend'. Miss Marjorie kept the Good Book close, but she kept people a little apart. I never went to her church, knew very little about her theology and we never socialized. We saw each other only at her parlour or, occasionally, when I might happen upon her walking by the side of the road, I would give her a ride to the junction. She had no relationship at all with Sasha.

It was Soames who asked Sasha if Miss Marjorie might speak at the wake. Her church, of which she was now the Minister, board of governors and caretaker, was a white concrete block of a building, forty foot square, about two hundred yards down the road. We could hear singing and clapping hands there most evenings of the week. Many of the local black people were members and we would see them walking by, ladies in white, men in black suit and hat, on their way there. Each one carried a Bible. They would call out, 'Good night,' as they passed by. Sitting on the front gallery, I would hide my rum and coke behind the leg of the chair until I heard the service start. Sometimes Soames would shout to one of the children to come to the gate to take a blue note to be put in the collection. He knew the church from attending funerals and, very occasionally, Honaria could shame him into attending a prayer meeting by commenting on the parlous state of his immortal soul. He would be treated like visiting royalty.

These days, Miss Marjorie was a very dark, thin, middle-aged woman almost six feet tall. I had not seen her in the tent until she stood up, languorously unfolding herself out of her seat. She nodded to me. She was dressed completely in white, a long loose skirt six inches below her knee, her blouse sleeves rolled up to the elbow. She wore an open waistcoat and on her head, no hair left visible, a tight bandana. The planes of her face, gauntly perspiring in the evening heat, shone like the facets of a diamond and in the darkness those blacker eyes glowed as they looked around at the crowd.

In no hurry, she waited until we were silent.

'Sistas and broders in Chrise,' she began, 'dih Lawd giveth an dih Lawd taketh away. Mista Badri, he gone, but dis ent no sad day, bruder. Dis ent a day fuh cryin, sista. No! Dis is dih day, he, a poor sinnah, a man in he pain, a man restless in he mind, dis is dih day he see dih Lawd.'

'The Lord be praised!' chirped Ag, from the front of the crowd.

From the folds of her skirt Miss Marjorie brought out a Bible, so old and battered that its corners rolled back in half circles. She held it up.

'How ah know? Yuh axe mih how ah know? Ah know from dih Good Book.'

This was her beginning.

As her words gathered momentum, so did her voice. It was a voice of conviction and confidence. Sometimes, she almost shouted and a rasp began to rub against the back of her throat.

'An yuh axe how ah know dis man does be save? An how ah know him be raise up from dih dead? Because ah read dih Word. Dih Word ah dih Lawd. Hallelujah!' The crowd stirred. 'Lemme show yuh, chillen.'

She licked a boney thumb and used it to page through the book. Finding the reference she was looking for, she slapped her palm down onto the page. Bam!

'Firs Corinthians. Chapta Fifteen. Lemme read dih Word, sistas and broders.'

Holding the Bible in her left hand, she lifted her right hand up, palm outwards in front of her.

'"Lo! Ah tell yuh a mystery. We shall not all sleep, but" — listen tuh what ah telling yuh, sistas and broders in Chrise, listen tuh dih words — "we shall all be changed." Hallelujah!' Again a stir. '"We shall all be change."'

She read as though she was seeing the words for the first time, the wonder of new knowledge in her voice, '"In a moment, in dih twinkling of ah eye, at dih las trumpet!" Oh yes, Lawd!'

The crowd, even some of the old Hindu ladies, clapped their hands and called out 'Hallelujah.' Only the near members of the Reverend Motilal's flock seemed unmoved. I looked over at Patsy. She was fingering the neck of her clerical collar and sucking on her lower lip.

Miss Marjorie looked upwards and pointed her finger into the night sky.

'"Fuh dih trumpet will soun, an dih dead will be raise." Amen an Amen.'

She sounded out the next word syllable by syllable.

'"In-de-struct-able!"' She paused for a long moment, '"an we shall be change." Hallelujah!'

This was the beginning of her sermon. She carried her audience with her, bowled along by the power of her towering conviction, to its end.

When she was finished, she prayed briefly, the Bible clutched against her chest, long arms crossed at the wrists, fingers fanning out to her emaciated shoulders. Then she asked 'Sista Agata' to say the Lord's Prayer, and bowed her head until it was finished. Finally, she moved to where Sasha was sitting, knelt down on one knee, took hold of both of her hands, and began to sing.

It was the voice we had heard earlier.

'"Will yuh anchor hole in dih storms ah life? When dih clouds un fole dere wings ah strife..."'

The crowd took up the words of the old hymn.

'"We have an anchor..."'

Sasha and Miss Marjorie sang together, the one looking into the eyes of the other, each firmly grasping the other's hands. At the end of the last verse, in the quiet when the singing ceased, Miss Marjorie stood and gently smoothed the back of her hand over Sasha's brow.

Then, she nodded to me and turned to walk away through the tent, out into the night.

Sleeping With Soames

We were tired but the night was far from over. There were people to be met. I shook hands with Ram and embraced his sons, old partners in crime — although that was not necessarily the best expression to use around the Ramdasses. I caught up on family gossip with a variety of cousins and swapped stories about my father-in-law with his cronies. Ag sat next to me for a while and I listened to her complain that it was well after the time everyone should have left so we could all get to bed.

Anca, hearing this as she passed by, laughed.

'How yuh mean!' she said. 'Nobody ent goin home yet. Dih night young. Yuh want meh tuh turn up dih broom an see if they does leave? Dey say dat help. Anyhow, nobody in dis house sleep much till Uncle bury!' And she added, sotto voce, moving away from us, 'Ah wonder if Roh sleepin.'

Before long, however, my whole body was straining for rest, and seeing Fleur go slowly up the back steps, holding on to the banister, made me want to follow her. But Sasha needed my support. Then there was the matter of where I was to sleep. On the drive from San Fernando, Sasha had broken the news that, because of the numbers involved, the women would bed down with the women and the men with the men. I had been delegated to sleep with Soames since he and Jolyon together would have made for cramped quarters and Soames flatly refused to sleep with Ainsley. Sasha had been conciliatory when she broached the subject but there had been a giggle in her voice.

It would not be the first time that Soames and I had shared a bed.

Sasha and I had been married six short months when we arrived at Sookbirsingh Hill for my first Christmas Eve there. The house was crowded and Sasha took me aside to whisper that they would be putting mattresses down in the living room to accommodate some of the younger people. Then, almost as an afterthought, it is a way that she has, she slipped into the conversation the fact that I would be sleeping with her uncle. I quite liked Soames, but half the time I could not understand what he was saying — when Nicolas was six he solemnly announced that Uncle Soames should come with sub-titles — and I certainly had never envisioned bedding down with him. Her enigmatic, 'Have fun,' left me perplexed.

I went off to bed while Soames was still out spreeing with the boys. I fell asleep on my side of the bed and, in my own semi-alcoholic haze, did not hear him come in, find his pyjamas and join me under the mosquito net. The sleep of the innocent. The sun woke me early on Christmas morning and I lay there, stretched out on my back watching the rays of light as they played with the breeze through the netting. Then, marginally more awake, I remembered where I was. I glanced over at Soames and saw that he was lying towards me on his right side. His face was half buried in the pillow, his mouth almost closed and his left eye open. He was looking at me.

'It looks like it's going to be a nice day,' I said, clearing my throat.

It seemed only polite to say something: after all I was a guest in his house, not to mention his bed.

He did not answer.

'I still have some presents to wrap,' I said. 'I should get up.'

Soames had never wrapped a present in his life — his sisters did it for him — but I expected some pleasantry by way of reply, even this early in the morning. None was forthcoming. I glanced over to make sure I had not imagined that he was awake, and saw that he was still looking at me. Except that, when I looked again, perhaps he wasn't. He was certainly staring from a three quarter open eye, but now I felt a dribble of doubt. Perhaps he wasn't actually looking at all.

A small part of me began to congeal.

I eased myself over onto my left side and we lay face to face, two feet apart. Dust motes played in the sunbeams that lit up his face. He looked fresh enough. I lay there gaping. He stared back.

'Hi there,' I whispered, very little nonchalance available, all savoir-faire departed, essaying a slight wave of my hand in front of his face. 'You up yet?'

No response.

I jerked my head off the pillow to see better with both eyes, and examined him. He seemed okay, though perhaps a little paler than usual.

'Soames,' I asked, a little sternly. 'Are you awake?'

And, with more than a hint of desperation, I added, 'Say you're awake.'

Nothing.

I began to flush. All over. Should I call out to Sasha for assistance or get out of bed to go find her? O God, if he were dead, let them not blame me! A small panic was coming to maturity in my breast. Quite quickly, in fact. Is there etiquette on the correct way to lie in bed with a corpse? Perhaps it is an Indian thing, I thought. I eased away, pushing my bottom into the netting, preparing to turn around to pull the net loose, plant my feet on the floor and flee. As I did so, slowly elbowing myself up from the mattress and reaching out to free the net, Soames snorted. It was a cross between a snore and a honk, so I will call it a snort. It had an epochal effect on me. I leapt into the air and careened into the net becoming entangled, ripping it apart as I tried to escape. Suspended from the ceiling by a hook and a thin tape, the net was flung from side to side like a small sail in a high wind. The tape snapped and the whole thing began to fall. I collapsed backwards on top of Soames, and shot back into the air as he uttered an almighty roar, flinging both arms sideways to escape my body and the shroud that was slowly descending on him. We both screamed.

A dozen of my new relatives — including Badri – appeared at the bedroom door. Sasha seemed to think it was all extremely funny.

'Didn't I tell you?' she explained later, still holding onto her side with laughter, 'Uncle Soames always sleeps with one eye open. He cannot help it. It just won't close. Everyone knows!'

'Well, I didn't know!' I answered, grinding my teeth.

'Well, my love, you do now!' She roared with delight.

And so to bed.

Nessa: Commesse As Usual

Next morning, Sasha and I drove to the airport to pick up Nessa and James. Ag declined our invitation to come along. No doubt she would have her fill of her niece-in-law in due course. The plane was late as usual, so we waited on a bench outside the terminal. After a while, Sasha wandered off to get a better view of the purple hills of the Northern Range. She came back with the news that the plane had broken down in Barbados and it could be several hours before it would arrive. The story was that a door had fallen off and they were going to have to fly another one in to replace it: nothing untoward for the national carrier. We debated what to do and had a good laugh at how Nessa would behave and how James and the crew would need to cope with her.

Rush hour traffic into Port of Spain was underway and as we had no wish to sit in gasoline fumes for an hour or more, we decided to have breakfast in one of the villages nearby. Sasha relaxed away from the bustle of the house, and in the sunny morning we might have been on vacation as we moved from stall to stall looking at the abundance of fruit and the wares on display. We bought a paw paw which the woman cut lengthwise for us, scooping out the little brown seeds so that we could bite at the yellow-orange flesh and savour its sweet, sickish taste. It is my favourite fruit. Sasha laughed when the juice ran off my chin onto my shirt and called me a pig. I said the same about her when, head thrown back, she slopped the milk from a coconut down her dress.

We sat at the side of the road, sticky from our endeavours, and watched the world go by.

Across the road, a new house had been built, all pillars and a winding staircase leading up to a large patio surrounded by the protection of omnipresent burglar bars. A newly painted wall hid the downstairs portion of what was really a mansion from inquisitive — or worse — passersby. An electronic gate was also part of the paraphernalia of keeping them at bay. More to my taste were the words someone had neatly painted on the pristine cream of the new wall. Black letters a foot high requested passersby to 'Please do not urinate on this wall. Thank you.', in capital letters. I nudged Sasha to look and we scoffed at the owner's hope that the message, so politely stated, might be obeyed.

Signs in Trinidad have always been a source of amusement to me. Probably my favourite was a hand-painted one, quite dainty really, in red about two feet long, that asked "Low self-esteem?" A telephone number followed. I have never yet met a Trinidadian with an esteem problem, and I have often regretted not taking the telephone number, just to see if anyone had ever called. The most annoying sign I ever saw was hardly unique, but I will always remember the first time I saw a version off it. The words "Fock Off Vernon" were scrawled on the outside wall of a public convenience at Curepe Junction. I was new to the island then and had a burning need to improve the spelling. Sasha dissuaded me, pointing out that it was far too public a place for a white man to be seen doing anything at all to the wall, even from a very laudable devotion to pedagogy.

To my surprise, I saw Anca and Sonnilal strolling towards us on the other side of the road. Their arms were linked as they walked. Sonnilal swung a large shopping bag in his free hand.

'Look at that,' I said to Sasha, pointing them out, 'you never know what you'll see if you take the time to look.' When they came closer, I called out, 'Hey, Miss Ramdass, is that man bothering you?'

Anca and Sonnilal stopped and turned toward us in surprise.

'Oh meh God,' said Anca, 'What you two doin here?' She was laughing.

'I think that is the question that we should be asking you!' I replied. 'Sonnilal, you lost?'

He had the grace to look sheepish, but draped a proprietary arm over Anca's shoulder nevertheless.

'Ah takin Anc tuh tong tuh fetch some ting fuh she muder.'

'An since when is town in this direction?' asked Sasha. 'I thought it was over there.'

They both grinned.

'Never mind that, what the two of all yuh sittin there at dih side of dih road like two po-me-one?' asked Anca. 'Yuh marry so long, an yuh behaving like teenager!'

'We behaving like two teenagers?! How about you!?'

Sonnilal leaned over and kissed Anca on the cheek as if to say, 'So there'.

'Papa yo!' declared Sasha, 'He think he nice!'

We all laughed, but Anca called out, 'Watch me good! Mine yuh don't tell Pa or ah'll give allyuh a good tump. Is trouble if Pa hear anyting before ah ready to tell he.'

'Be careful, Bianca. You know how Uncle Ram can be,' warned Sasha.

Anca shrugged. 'Cut eye doh kill. An he cyar make meh cut cloth at Salvatori.'

'True, but take care. If there is anything we can do, let us know, okay?' And more lightly, 'And if you can't find town, Sonnilal, you better buy a map.'

'Yuh right bout dat,' laughed Anca. 'Son cyar find gazette paper in ah latrine!'

She pushed him playfully.

'How yuh mean!' he said, grinning. 'Yuh tink ah kiss meh arse chupid, or what!'

They waved and went on their way.

We talked about them for a while. Mismatched, physically, financially and in almost every other respect, they nevertheless seemed perfectly suited to each other. We wished them well but could see no easy solution for their dilemma.

'You know what they say,' said Sasha, shrugging. '"Every chalk have he cheese."'

I thought about it, shaking my head. 'I really hope so.'

By the time Nessa and James finally emerged from Customs, it was almost noon. She was in a wheelchair, pushed by a porter: the refrigerator-shaped James walked behind carrying the luggage. When Nessa saw us, she bounded out of the wheelchair, coming towards us at a trot.

'They're insane!' She waved her arms around to encompass the airline, the airport and the entire country. 'Imagine! They leave us sitting in the plane with no air conditioning for an hour and then tell us that a door fell off! Madness! They wouldn't let us off. We just sat there boiling until I got up and walked out. James, watch the bags.' Coming up to Sasha, she offered her cheek to be kissed. 'You're looking tired,' and then to me, 'Where's the car? Help James with the bags. He has a hernia.' Turning back to her sister, 'What's going on at the house? Has anyone come to blows yet? How's Ainsley?'

'Why were you in a wheelchair?' asked Sasha, bemused.

'I always travel in a wheelchair. Better service that way. Where's the car? James don't fiddle with that bag. And don't lose it. My medicine is in it.' And to the world in general, 'Why are we standing here?'

***

Vanessa Badri is not a difficult woman as long as she is allowed to express her opinions. You don't have to agree with them but, by God, you have to listen to them. She has an opinion on everything under the sun and, like water from a tap that will not turn off, they pour out of a mind hot and clear. She had been a married woman when she first met the enormous James Wong Howe and, within a month, she left her spouse for him. It was an act that stunned Indian society in Trinidad. Not only was James Chinese, but the man she left had been the catch of the season. Krishna was a 'star boy', a dazzlingly handsome, young doctor from a good Hindu family. He was also, as she later explained to Sasha, the most boring person she had ever met, completely self-centred, and, it turned out, unfaithful as well.

What she saw in James, no one knew. He spoke little, was a computer nerd by trade and had the weight and looks of a somewhat decrepit sumo wrestler. They have no children, didn't want any they said, couldn't stand the thought. In fact, Nessa was not able to have them, but she adores her nephew and demands to know everything that is going on in his life. Long ago, she substituted her health for the child she could never have and she worried about it incessantly, coddling herself outrageously, though always with an element of humour in her tales of woe. She is devoted to her physical state but is convinced that it is parlous in the extreme. She is, in fact, as healthy as a horse.

Nessa loves fashion but she does not indulge in it, preferring to swathe herself in large flowered muumuus that dust the ground whereon she walks. She also enjoys gossip: which Trinidadian doesn't? She enjoys spreading it, too, like thick raspberry jam on warm toast, and she has also, on occasion, been known to invent it. She and James live in Thunder Bay – the reason they were so late in arriving — where she hates the climate, the vegetation and the people, but puts up with it because she clearly adores her husband — the 'Chinaman' as she calls him in her own inimitable way.

Once in the car, she wanted to know everything about everything and approved or disapproved as we went.

'I should tell you that it sounds as though Nurse got Daddy to change his Will,' Sasha told her.

'What! Change his Will? How? What's Daddy's Will got to do with the Nurse? The little harpie! James, move over, you're hogging the whole seat.' She pushed his bulk aside and leaned her elbows on the back of the front seat. 'Have you seen the Will? I don't suppose they'll read it until after the funeral. There should be a copy at the house. No? No matter. Ian, close the windows and turn on the air-conditioning for heaven's sake. So much humidity is bad for my sinuses and I'm beginning to sweat like a bull.'

She took a breath.

'How is Auntie June and that crook she's married to? Anca came down with you didn't she, Ian? As fat as ever? She's going to keel over one of these good days, see if she doesn't. An what about my boy Ainsley? Still in love with me?'

We told her about Nurse and Ainsley's parting of the ways with her.

'She's a sly one and no mistake! Don't worry. I'll flirt with him a little bit and he'll forget all about her.'

'When you flirt,' I suggested, 'don't go too close or you may get wet.'

'Still?'

'You don't really expect him to change do you?'

We laughed.

We told her about the funeral arrangements. She disagreed with almost everything but shrugged it off once she had told us we were wrong, stupid or inefficient. And why.

Sash told her about the sleeping arrangements.

'Well, I'm sleeping with the Chinaman in the back room. It's the only mattress in the whole place that is hard enough for my back. The rest of them are like sleeping in a swamp. And that bed won't collapse with him on it. Ian, don't pass that truck. He'll only pass you back going down the hill. James, will you sit still! You're giving me a backache right now with your moving around. God, this car is cold. Open the windows a little bit, the cold's not good for my asthma.'

We arrived at the house during lunch. Nessa strode into the kitchen and opened the fridge looking for water. Only when she had quenched her thirst did she greet the people seated around the table.

'Hello, Uncle Soames. Jo. Auntie June. Ainsley, what on earth are you crying for now?'

She bent over and gave him a big kiss on the cheek, winking at me while she did it. I swear he simpered.

'Didi, you're looking well. How you do? Bim boy.' And to Fleur, 'Good to see you, Auntie.'

She took the top off a tureen and peered inside.

'Calalloo! James serve me some calalloo and rice. What are you all standing up for? Not so much as that. Remember my stomach. Ainsley, you look like you're about finished. Go and bring the bags from the car. We're in the back bedroom.'

Its current occupants could move.

'Watch the hand luggage, it has my medicine in it. Where's Auntie Ag? Don't tell me she's getting her hair done! That'll be the day! I should go though. I hope someone made an appointment. Sasha, don't forget to wash yours.'

Clara, who knew all the family gossip, put her head around the kitchen door.

'Miss Nessa,' she said, 'it have more rice in dih pot. An melongene. Yuh want?'

June replied for her. 'Bring it in, Clara. Better belly bus than good food waste!'

'Eat yuh food, beti, girl,' said Didi who was beaming at her grandniece, hands clasped in front of her. 'Yuh looking nice, darlin.' She paused. 'Yuh hear Roh cyar come?' She sniffed. 'He busy.' She spat the word.

'Don't worry, Auntie, we'll get along quite well without Uncle Roh or anyone else who doesn't have time to come.'

I was sure that Nessa would have several dozen well chosen words to say about her uncle's absence, but they would be said in private to Sasha.

'What are you all standing up for,' said Nessa. 'Sit! Eat your food.' So everyone sat down and we ate.

No one would ever imagine that the Badri sisters were twins. It would be difficult, in fact, to find two sisters more unalike — in looks, in temperament, or in manners. Nessa has manners, but doesn't mind them. Sasha minds them to excess. Nessa is fair and resembles the Sookbirsinghs; Sash is darker and has the eyes and mouth of a Badri. Both like to talk but Nessa listens best to what she herself has to say, while, for years, Sasha listened too much to what others had to say. Once when Badri was in his cups, he took Nessa by the hand and declared, 'Look at this one. She is a chip off the old block.' Then he gave Sasha a hug and said, 'And this one, she is her mother's child.'

In one way, they are united, however. They are devoted to the family. Family provides both of them with the best sense of who they are. They believe in blood, its benefits and the obligations it engenders. James and I know our place — we have discussed it quietly together — and we know that we lack the blood. Sasha and Nessa — or, as Nessa insists, being the older by half an hour, Nessa and Sasha — are dipped in its communal memory and linked together by the ties that it binds.

You see it when they meet, in how they greet each other, in how they gather each other up in the bad times and are happy for each other in the good. They do not always get along, from politics to religion, from music to fashion they disagree, but scoff at one and the other will scratch. Compliment one and the other is likely to purr. Nessa loves a confrontation, Sasha prefers peace. But the triumph of the one is the delight of the other, and turmoil for one of them is indignation and apprehension for the other.

***

'So tell me, Auntie June,' said Nessa. 'What's happening with Anca?' We had told her about our encounter. 'Any boyfriends?'

'How I go know? What she do in Canada ah ent know! She go die a ole maid.'

'Is there no one down here?'

'Steups. Ah tell she tuh come home an Ram go find a nice likkle boy from dih country fuh she, but she ent mind me.'

'Umm,' said Nessa. 'No boy from the village?'

I kicked her under the table.

'And you, Ainsley!' He had just returned from carrying in the luggage, 'What are you doing with yourself these days?'

Ainsley burst into tears. Great wracking sobs snorted forth. He wiped his nose on his shirt-sleeve. Ainsley adored Nessa. You could see it in the way he became shy around her and made even less sense than usual when he had to speak to her. As a child, he had learned that her verbal thrusts were almost as bad as the physical blows she bestowed upon him when he refused to join in a game or didn't understand her jokes, but he worshipped her nevertheless. Even now, he would ogle her from behind his hand, moonbeam her from under the brim of his hat.

'Uncle dead,' he said. 'Yuh Daddy dead,' and he shook his head, sadly.

'Yes, Ainsley, but the world goes on,' Nessa replied, the words addressed partly to herself.

Then she turned to Nurse who was standing in the doorway, sucking on a chicken leg.

'Well, Nursie! What's this I hear about a Will?'

'Ah ent know nothin about yuh fader Will. Ah ent even seen it.' Nurse addressed the room, 'All yuh have bad mind. Ah dih one take care ah dih boss when he daughters away in Canada an ah don expect a penny more than mih wage fuh all ah do. But what I get from dem anyway? Ah ent get a 'thank you' fuh meh trouble.' Her eyes narrowed. 'Just cause ah mek a mistake in he obituary. Steups.'

'Nurse, we know that you did a lot for Daddy,' said Sasha, with what I am sure was forced patience, 'and we're very grateful that you were here to help take care of him. Don't think that we aren't. But you have to realize that he was our father.'

'And not yours' hung in the air.

Nessa looked at Nurse, but she didn't say a word. No doubt she would have something to add later in private. I am sure everyone in the room was as astonished as I was at her forbearance.

'Pass me the roti, please, Auntie June,' she said.

'Eat, girl. It well morish. Yuh want Clara to hot it up?'

'Yuh want tuh fire one wi dat, Nessa? A scotch?' asked Soames.

'No uncle, but if you have any coconut water, it would be great. I'm parched in this heat.'

'Clara, it have coconut water fuh Miss Nessa?'

'Ask me dat! Yuh tink ah ent have water fuh she? Steups.' Clara sighed. 'How many of all yuh want coconut water?' Mock vexed. Nessa was a favourite of hers. 'Ah ent got time fuh dis!'

She slammed the fridge door and we heard her filling the glasses.

'Mista Krishna came tuh dih wake las night,' said Nurse, looking sideways at Nessa, 'an he bring Latchmi.'

Nurse knew all the family scandal. Latchmi was Krishna's second wife. Nessa and she had gone to school together.

'Ah tink she pregnant again.' To June, 'How many dat, Miss June?'

'It's four, as if you don't already know,' said Nessa, answering for June. 'What's he doing in Trinidad?'

'His Ma has cancer. She ent well at all,' said Soames, who in his youth had dated the lady in question and gone to school with her future husband. 'Prakash well worried. Yuh should go an see her, Nessa.'

Nessa laughed. 'I don't think she'd want to see me, Uncle! And I certainly don't want to see that saga boy son of hers, although someone told me he gets better looking with every passing year. I hear he has a woman on the side in Mississauga. I've got a mind to tell Latchmi to check it out.'

'Mind your business, Nessa,' warned Fleur. 'That family has enough to cope with just now without you spreading tales.'

'Perhaps yuh'll see Krishna an she at dih funeral,' suggested Ainsley, snidely.

Was he still jealous of Krishna?

While they were speaking, Ag came up the steps. She had been out spreading the word of the Lord and bulk-buying local canned vegetables for shipping to Canada. She nodded at James and kissed the air near Nessa, who told her that she was looking hot.

'I am hot! Sometimes I think that the Lord made this place a little like Hell so that we poor sinners can know what it is we have to avoid. It was so hot in San Fernando that I thought my head was going to explode.'

Several of us conjured with this thought.

'I saw one of your cousins, Soames. She came right up to me. I can't remember her name but she was so happy to see me. I think she said her mother lives in Couva or Cunupia or somewhere.'

She looked at the table, platters still half full of food.

'Is there anything left to eat? I'm starving. You'd think they'd serve snacks.'

June called out to Clara in the kitchen, 'Bring some more rice, for Miss Agata, Clara. An hot up a piece a chicken fuh she. Dis well cold! Hah!'

Soames, bristling from Ag's comment about San Fernando, said, 'I goin tuh lie dong. Ee-an-uh snorin all night an ah ent sleep a wink. What time we going tuh Dookie's dis evening?'

'Five o'clock, Uncle,' said Sasha. 'We don't have to stay long and I'd like to get back for the wake by seven.' A pause. 'Ainsley, I hope you're coming.'

'Ah comin, oui, but ah want tuh be back early. Paulie comin dong fuh dih wake tonight.'

'Well, we wouldn't want to be late for Paulie, would we now!' Nessa stood. 'I'm going for a walk. If I lie down now I'll have indigestion and it's not good for my circulation to lie down straight after a big meal. James, see if you can find an umbrella. I'll get sunstroke with so much sun in the heat of the day. Sasha come with me and we'll talk.'

Family Viewing

Everyone except Ag dressed to go to the funeral home. Three cars followed one another in solemn procession. We gathered in the Dee Cee and Jay's parking lot and, by virtue of her age, Didi led the way into the chapel. She insisted that I give her my arm to lean on but Soames gently took her from me and said, 'Ee-an-uh with Sasha, Didi.' Ag hardly noticed. She was upset that no one had told her that she should have worn black and she had kept on about it in the car until Fleur had had enough,

'Well, we can always pass by Gulf City and sit in the car while you run in and buy something suitable that you should have had the sense to wear in the first place.' Sarcasm is one of Fleur's strongest suits.

Mr. Jones was there to greet us. He looked Ag up and down and said, to no one in particular, 'Well, perhaps she luggage get lost.' And then, in all innocence to her face, 'Is Mr Rohan parking the car?' And continued, 'Come along. He's in the chapel.'

He didn't mean Roh.

The room was more subdued than yesterday. Soft candlelight played on a casket that had been positioned at the base of an only slightly less than life-size cross. The cross was an iridescent neon which give new meaning to the expression 'in the pink', although on the darker brown faces of the assembled mourners it had a pucey-purple effect, as though they were all desperately trying to hold their breath.

Everyone, Didi most of all, was subdued, taken aback by the chapel's ambiance — a guitar version of Amazing Grace twanged over the amplifiers — and by the size of the casket in which Badri lay. He was dressed in a dark pin-stripe suit, and wore a white shirt with a blue tie. His hands were linked together and his fingernails reflected in the light. June moved forward, putting her hand over his as though to cover the artifice. Didi stood at the head of the casket peering in with some difficulty because of its height. Nessa and Sasha were at the side, an arm around each other's waist. Badri really did look to be in the absolute bloom of health, as though he might vault over the side of the casket at any moment and suggest a game of tennis.

Ainsley's knees buckled when he saw his uncle and he slumped down on a straight chair next to the casket. Water flowed from between his clenched eyelids, like the overflow from a leaky weir. Fleur reached into her purse and took out a man's handkerchief. She shook it loose and handed it to June. Then she opened a bottle of cologne and poured some into the handkerchief as June held it. Unsatisfied, she shook out more and took back the handkerchief. I caught the aroma of Badri's cologne and looked down. Had he moved? We knew the scent. Fleur moved in front of Nessa and folded the handkerchief into the breast pocket of Badri's suit, patting it into place.

'There you are!' she said, breaking the silence.

'He looks good,' said Nessa. 'He lost weight since I saw him.'

'They did a really good job on the face.'

'I like dih way dey comb he hair.'

'Do you think he should be wearing his glasses?' asked Sasha, 'Would they make him look funny?'

'I don't want him in glasses,' declared Nessa, 'what does he need them for anyway?'

'But he always wore glasses.'

'Not when he sleepin tho',' suggested June.

Nurse said, 'He bein bury wearing dem gold ring?' It was an accusation. Two rings were visible on Badri's hands: his wedding ring on his left and a heavy gold and onyx ring, a diamond set in its square face, on his right.

'Why not?' replied Nessa. 'His wedding ring was from Mummy and I never saw him without the other one.'

'I think he got it in Brussels,' agreed Sasha. 'He always said the diamond was first class.'

'It would look nice in ah ring fuh one ah you girls,' said June.

'Well, it's staying where it is!' said Nessa.

Sasha nodded. 'I don't want it.' She shrugged.

'Don't be touchous, but is a lot ah money tuh bury!'

'Ma!' warned Anca. 'It not your ring.'

'Is a waste,' declared Nurse, and, repeating an earlier comment, she added, 'an what would he need dem fuh now?'

'Well, Nurse, if we took them off they'd go to Roh and I'm sure that Roh wouldn't want them and that he'd much rather they remain where they are right now,' said Sasha, firmly.

Ag cleared her throat but she did not speak.

'Is good gold! Twenty-two carat,' said Nurse to Ag.

'Auntie?' asked Nessa. Daring her.

Ag tried to laugh, 'I'm sure I don't know what to say. Roh always admired those rings and it would be a nice remembrance for him, don't you think?'

'Well, Ag,' said Nessa, turning to face her aunt, 'if you want them you're going to have to take them off his fingers yourself because I don't think anyone here is going to help you.'

'What a pity Roh couldn't spare the time to be here to do the job himself,' said Fleur, pushing fire.

Ag stood rigid, her arms crossed in front of her to ward off these verbal blows.

'It does seem such a waste,' said June.

Anca elbowed her mother to be silent.

'Ah could do it fuh yuh,' said Nurse, 'if yuh like.'

'No, no, Nurse!' With a supreme effort, Ag feigned nonchalance. 'If his daughters don't want their uncle to have them, then they'll have to stay where they are.'

We stood staring down at the rings, thinking about what had been said.

It was at that moment I knew for sure there was going to be trouble, that we would not get through the next few days without something happening that might have a far reaching effect on the family. I had not been certain before, but now I began to listen not only to the words we spoke, but also to how and to whom we said them, how we treated each other in the everyday tasks we had to carry out. I glanced at Sasha and she frowned back at me. She felt it, too. Her father's passing might be more than a death in the family. It might also change the family as we knew it.

Sookdeo Pays His Respects

Everyone comes to pay their respects to the dead.

We had hardly reached home when a car pulled into the yard. It was too early for the wake. Anca went to see who it was. She returned, grinning.

'It Senator Bedase.' She looked around coyly, her eye settling on Sasha, 'An Sookdeo.'

A murmur of amusement shimmered in the air. Smiles of devilment lit up several faces, and gleeful glances slid back and forth from Sasha to me around the room.

'He come!' announced Nessa to Sasha, mock solemn.

'Behave yourself,' replied her sister. 'Or I'll box your ears! All of you, behave yourselves!'

Her order might have been serious, but from the look of them all, she could have had no expectation that they would obey. Soames and Fleur went out to greet the guests, and everyone hushed, to hear what was said. Only Didi had no appearance of anticipation, no expectation of amusement on her face. She looked over in my direction with a slight frown of concern. Sasha did not look at me at all. She sat up straight, demurely playing with the stem of her glass.

'Yuh boy come!' Jolyon whispered in her ear.

Two persons entered with Fleur. A dark, solidly built, middle-aged woman, rouged, every hair in place, and a well-covered middle-aged man, also dark, but with thinning hair and glasses that had slid to the end of a beaky nose on a very shiny face. He was carrying, rocking it like a babe in arms, one of the largest watermelons God ever produced.

Nessa stifled a guffaw.

'It's Laura and Sookdeo,' said Fleur, unnecessarily.

She had the grace to keep a straight face.

Soames stood behind them, beaming into the room. Sookdeo, nodding at everyone, lurched over to Sasha as she half rose from the couch. He bent forward to kiss her, passing the watermelon awkwardly into her arms. Its weight pressed her back onto her seat and, for a moment, it appeared that he would tip over on top of her. I watched, nonchalance personified. June was looking at me sideways, trying to hide a smile behind a hand that went through the motions of tidying the front of her hair. Jolyon did not even bother to hide his grin.

Sookdeo was Sasha's old boyfriend. Long ago, as teenagers, it had been assumed that they would marry. Sookdeo was one of the few young men who Badri allowed to come anywhere near either of his daughters. He was from a good family, and Ann and the boy's mother had had a plan since the two children were at Grant School together. About the only person who disapproved of their plan was Sookdeo's older sister Laura, now the senator. A bossy, bumptious woman with a bosom the size of her ego, she had outraged the Sookbirsinghs when Rookmin reported hearing her say that 'dih girl look like ah horse.' It was hardly comforting for the family that Laura had mixed the girls up and had made the comment about Nessa. Sookdeo took absolutely no notice of what his sister had to say.

From age sixteen to the time she left for university, Sasha and 'Sook', as she called him, were an item. He paid court in Port of Spain, in San Fernando and points between. By all accounts, and she will admit it, she accepted his attention with all the innocence of the late nineteen fifties, and returned it. As far as I am aware, her father never felt constrained to demand the details of his mental health or of his future plans. He was not particularly happy that Sook's company had been the one to import his beloved Benz, but he was willing to put his future son-in-law's lack of advanced education aside if he had to. Just this once.

Then she met me. For quite a while, as I have figured out over the years, she did not know what to do. She held hands with me and wrote long letters to him. She renewed her acquaintance with him during summer vacations, told him about her friend at the university, and came back in September. Gradually, the scales tipped in my favour. Whatever his attraction, and I still do not know what that might have been, I made her laugh. At the end of her third year — she told me this long afterwards — she went home and broke it off. She gave him back a necklace and a bracelet and he returned all the letters she had written him. Joylon was so annoyed when he saw the huge pile of aging envelopes that he insisted Sasha burn them. In retrospect, it is surprising that the family received me so warmly into her affections: certainly they never given me an inkling of just how much they had preferred her former beau.

I remained in the dark about Sookdeo. Even Jolyon kept the family secret from me. In the end, it was the senator herself who let it slip at races one Saturday afternoon when Sasha and I had already been married for some seven or eight years. This woman I hardly knew turned to me during tea and said, 'So you dih fella who tief meh brother girl. Yuh break he heart!' I had no answer to give and, indeed, am not sure that she wanted one. In fact, I had no idea what she was talking about, though from the appalled looks of the people with us in the stands, they certainly had. Sasha was in the paddock with her uncle at the time and June waylaid her on her return, getting to her before I could. It was evening before I prodded her for an ever-widening explanation. Badri was furious when he heard what had happened, and refused to have the Senator in his house afterwards, but I knew that he had been embarrassed for Sasha rather than for me.

Sash and I made a joke of the whole thing. I had never seen Sookdeo (he never went to races), and it was years more before I did meet him, but whenever any strange man would appear — halt, maimed, ancient, a beggar on the street, the comic in a Bollywood movie – I would lean over and whisper a question in her ear, 'Sook?'

We finally met at a wedding. We were about to leave when I saw Badri speaking to a pleasant enough looking fellow about my own age. I went up to them and Badri, in a most unusually enervated voice, said, 'Have you met Sookdeo?'

'No,' said I, with surprising aplomb, 'I haven't. How do you do?'

'Ah! Well!' he replied, 'nice to meet you.'

'Nice to meet you, too,' I lobbed back my riposte, adding airily, 'At last.'

We shook hands as I inquired of my father-in-law, 'About ready to go, are we?'

Sookdeo never married and Sasha has been teased ever since because of it. Part of her still feels guilty and I know that her affection for him remains. She will never hear a word against him, would have played matchmaker if she could, but the families have drifted apart over the years. Although we expected to see them at the funeral, it was a surprise that the two of them had turned up this evening. Or perhaps it wasn't. From the way Sookdeo looked at Sasha, one could never doubt that he still loved her. If the size of the watermelon was any indication, he was still in the heat of passion.

Brother and sister shook hands round the room and sat down. Sookdeo was a quiet man, comfortable in himself, content to leave conversation to his sister. She had gone into politics to hear herself talk. Her love was horses. Rumour had it that Jolyon and she once went to Miami for a weekend at the track and that they had had a quick fling after the serious business of racing was over for the day, but although he was quite willing to be ribbed about it, he always had a ready reply.

'Yuh cyar bring dat woman tuh bridle, an ah prefer a craft with a smaller saddle dan she.'

Everyone was in need of a pick-me-up, and they joined us for a drink. We chatted about Badri.

'I really didn't think it would have happened so quickly,' Sasha sighed. 'I mean, we knew it wouldn't be long, but I thought he would just slowly fade away. I never thought he would have the energy to pull himself out of bed and fall like he did.'

'Ah know exactly what yuh mean, chile,' interjected the senator. 'Ah remember ah had a horse once, Monopoly's Rant. He have a bad diarrhoea, but he getting betta an dih trainer say next day we could take he out tuh pasture, but den, dat night, he kick he stable door dong and he break he leg. An we have tuh shoot he!'

I opened my mouth to reply, but the warning in Sasha's eye made me close it again. We watched each other across the room, each taming the line of our mouths into a wavering approximation of seriousness.

In bed later, I said, 'Watermelon a little heavy, was it?'

'You are a bad man,' she replied.

'Not at all! But was she saying we should have shot your Dad? He didn't have diarrhoea, did he?'

Sasha gave me a sharp cuff on the back of the head and sighed.

'Sook would have given me a Benz!'

Another event occurred that evening which was to make us laugh both then and later, and which also showed us that however much man — or, in this case, woman — may attempt dignity, the gods can still choose to play their tricks. After the wake, as the family sat in the living room, too tired to pull ourselves upright and go to bed, Sasha declared that she had a headache. I brought her a glass of water and two aspirin. While the desultory conversation continued to slowly wind down, Sasha sleepily took off her stud earrings, a gold and diamond pair that her father had given her many years earlier, and laid them on the arm of the chair next to the water. I saw her drink the water from the glass.

Jolyon stretched and said, 'Well, I goin tuh mih bed.'

'Give me your glass,' I said to Sasha, 'I'll take it to the kitchen.'

Sasha picked up the glass and looked down at the arm of the chair.

'Oh, my God,' she said. 'I swallowed an earring. I thought the aspirin felt sharp!'

One earring and an aspirin sat next to the coaster that had held the glass. We stood staring at her.

'What am I going to do?'

She put her hand over her mouth, eyes wide awake now, and began to laugh.

Primping, Patsy & Paulie

A funeral in Trinidad is not only a religious affair and the opportunity to mourn the passing of the deceased, it is also very much a gathering of the living, a social event for people of goodwill. Not a fete, certainly, but perhaps there is something of the country market about it, more subdued and respectful no doubt, but with a feeling that the bustle of business will carry on regardless, a realization that, after the deceased is honoured, life will go on. It took me, the staid Protestant from a Northern clime, a long time, accustomed as I was to a small gathering in a chilled chapel, to become used to the tropic buoyancy of the occasion. Woven into its fabric, for they are Trinidadians after all, is that exchange of conviviality shared by people who have not seen one another for a while, sometimes a long while, and who have things other than mere dour regret and sombre sympathy to muse upon.

Then, there are the womenfolk. Women bring to the occasion a fine feeling for the observance of cutting-edge feminine apparel, the discussion of which is recognized as an integral part of accepted post-interment conversation, for while the fashions worn are likely to be somewhat more muted than usual, given the limited colour palette that is acceptable in such circumstances, Trinidadians are quite capable of wearing those dark glasses of bereavement that also permit a sideways glance at the length of a hemline or the latest Jimmy Choo.

Fleur and Nessa had been up early and were gone to the hairdresser. June appeared at the breakfast table with her hair still locked around the cardboard innards of toilet rolls, the whole swathed in the paper itself. No Southern stylist for her. She moaned about a headache and having had to sit up most of the night to keep everything in place. Much womanly whispering had gone on, late into the night, about what to wear, and how much to sacrifice to comfort or comportment in the broiling afternoon heat. We men knew better than to get involved, well recognizing the looks of determination that had settled on the female faces that appeared at the breakfast table. Honaria was grumpy about having to come in to press the ladies' dresses, for as she told everyone in earshot, she had her own outfit to sort out. Only Ag had the temerity to stand over her to see the job was done right. The others knew that Honaria would have been mortified to ruin a pleat or to stamp even the least expensive frock.

Everyone was wearing black, which fortunately comes in many shades, except Didi who wore white. Then Anca came out of the bathroom, unpressed, in purple, a large rather soft plum, with a black-feathered hat. She pirouetted before the group, causing her mother to gag slightly at the sight of so much voile in one place.

'She looks like a giant eggplant,' muttered Ag to me out of the side of her mouth, not without a certain satisfaction. There was, I had to admit, a degree of truth in what she said.

'Why dih hell we wear stocking in dis country, ah ent know! Dey make meh well hot!' Anca exclaimed.

I had reason to agree with this statement. Sasha had shaken me awake earlier, careful not to disturb Soames, frantic about stockings. Hers were full of ladders. I was dispatched to the supermarket at the junction in search of one-size-fits-all pantyhose. My objections were to no avail. I explained that ladies' stockings were not the kind of item that any self-respecting Trinidadian male would place on a checkout counter, but was given short shrift.

'You're not a Trini,' she said.

'How about a male?'

'Yes, but a Canadian male. You're emancipated.'

'You mean Trinidadian males are not emancipated? I didn't know. I thought there was 1833 and all that.'

'Just get up and go and buy them after you eat your breakfast. And shut up!'

'Doesn't sound very emancipated to me!'

She reached through the net and slapped me on the backside.

Harassment!

'Up! Now!'

I had never understood why a perfectly good leg had to be covered by exactly the same shade of brown, and was about to agree with Anca, when Ainsley appeared in the doorway. He was wearing a new suit, a crisp clean white shirt, shoes so well polished that any passing lizard would have been able to see its face in them, and a tomato-red silk tie.

'Dih tie a bit bright, boy,' commented Jolyon. 'Yuh ent have nuttin a bit darker than dat?'

'Is new,' Ainsley mewed.

'Ainsley, take off that tie!' ordered Nessa, 'You're not going to a fete, for God's sake. Or a whorehouse.'

The faucets opened.

'Boy!' said Didi, 'take off dat tie before ah give yuh a cut arse meself! Is yuh uncle dead! Yuh ent have no shame? An stop yuh snivelling!'

Soames came into the room as Ainsley retreated. He was resplendent. He too had been to the hairdresser — not Ainsley, a barber at the junction — for a shave and a trim. Every silky, silver hair was in place, swept straight back from his forehead. The white point of a pocket-handkerchief stood at attention in his suit coat, and the gold of his belt buckle caught the morning sunlight.

Everyone was settling in for a subdued second cup of coffee when the hearse came into the yard, swinging round to back towards the empty tent.

Against all expectation, it was on time.

***

Only a few people had been invited to the house for this private family viewing. Most of the Badri clan was absent and I was struck by the fact that my father-in-law was to be buried, as he had lived, surrounded by a surfeit of Sookbirsinghs. Everyone filed out onto the back gallery as Dookie himself came round to open the back door of the hearse and supervise the unloading of the deceased. Sonnilal had removed the tent chairs and set up trestles for the coffin to rest on. He helped Dookie's men hoist it in place. When a sharp crack rang out as the leg of one trestle struggled to carry the weight of the mahogany, Sonny gave it a sharp kick, warning it to do its duty.

'Oh Gawd, don't drop him,' yelled out June. 'Ah yuh go kill him!'

When Dookie began to unscrew the top of the casket for the viewing, the family came down the stairs single file, Didi leading the way. As we moved forward to stand around the coffin, consciously or unconsciously we arranged ourselves in twos: Didi and Stanley, Charran and his wife, Sasha and myself, Nessa and James, June and Ram, their two boys, Anca and Jolyon, Fleur and Soames. Ainsley stood next to Ag. Nurse stood apart.

The sound of a car engine made everyone turn round. Patsy Motilal drove into the yard.

'What is she doing here?' asked Fleur.

'What he doin' here?' asked Soames. Sitting in next to her in the passenger seat was Paulie Goberdan. 'Ainsley, you know anything about this?'

'Paulie does be Patsy cousin, so dey comin tuh dih funeral tuhgether.'

'But what they doin here, boy?' asked Soames again. 'No-one invite dem.'

'Patsy tell meh she might drop in tuh say a prayer.'

'Over my dead body,' declared Nessa.

Jolyon, trying to keep it light, said, 'Nessa, we don't want trouble. She here already.'

Sasha was rattled by Patsy's arrival. She had learned yesterday that the regular Susumachar minister had been taken ill and would not be able to perform the service. She and June had sat together on the back gallery going through a list of names to find a suitable substitute. 'Suitable' shortly gave way to 'available', but, by common consent, Patsy was not to be asked. Perhaps she was here to offer her services.

'Never!' said Sasha aloud to herself. She had found a retired minister I had never heard of, the very name of whom had caused June to frown.

'Do you think we should?' she said when Sasha suggested they telephone him. 'He'll charge you the earth to come out at such short notice. I wonder who will be doing Sonabai?'

'Better to pay too much than have to listen to Patsy. Daddy would be furious if it was Patsy. And I won't ask Auntie Ag. Daddy would die all over again if I did.' Sasha laughed. 'Anyway, if he's 'doing' Sonabai, as you call it, Auntie June, perhaps he'll give us a bulk rate!'

We huddled together like dumb insolence as Patsy and Paulie approached. Jolyon, straining to remain affable, went forward to greet them. The tension of the moment was sidestepped, however, when Honaria and her family came into the yard followed by Clara and her daughter, Duchess. Sonnilal's sister, Vashti, was with them and Anca peeled away from the family to greet her.

Everyone came towards us together.

'Ah ah ah ssss orry fu fu fuh yuh loss,' said Paulie, as he approached Ag, holding out his hand.

The Goberdans had been family friends from way back. An 'Old Man' Goberdan and Old Man Sookbirsingh had arrived in Trinidad on the same boat, but the Goberdan bloodline had thinned over the years. Paulie was a pale, round-faced, round-bodied man with flat feet and a big bottom. He was myopic and he stammered.

'Whu whu where Ru Ru Ru Roh?'

It was Ainsley who answered.

'He busy, Paulie. Yuh know how hard it does be fuh a good accountant tuh get away wid appointments schedule, an client wid back taxes tuh pay?'

Evidently he had been speaking to Ag.

The new arrivals paid their respects at the side of the casket and everyone commented how well Badri appeared to be inside it. Honaria wiped her eyes with a huge white handkerchief that she pulled with a flourish, like a magician, from between her breasts. She ran a black hand along the frills of the casket's upholstery to neaten them and gave a grandson a hefty clout when he coughed on the corpse.

'Mine yuh manners, chile. Close yuh mout when yuh cough on Mista Morton,' she instructed.

Dookie, complimented on Badri's appearance, came forward to explain some of the finer points of the mortician's trade. The others moved away from the casket to stand at the bottom of the steps leading to the house. Anca and Sonnilal's sister went inside and came out with small glasses of orange juice. For a while, everyone stood sipping and talking quietly. Then Clara and Duchess brought trays to collect the glasses.

We gathered round the casket.

The morning seemed more humid than usual. Ten minutes earlier, the day had been sunny, light breeze frolicking with the dust of the yard, but now a storm was coming. Heavy drops of rain began to pound against the roof of the tent and everyone moved forward, almost badgering the casket, to keep out of their way. The wind picked up and hurled the rain at us through the sides of the open tent.

'Into dih house!' called out Soames and, amid little shrieks of laughter, he began to herd people up the stairs.

Sasha and I remained where we were, she sheltering her father's face from the downpour. Ainsley, hiccupping with grief, stood holding his head between his hands as though the end of the world was imminent. Nurse and Ag also stayed, watching as Dookie and one of his assistants began to lower the lid of the casket. June was there too.

She helped Ag tuck in the frills. I turned Sasha away and then we, too, ran into the house.

Twenty minutes later the sun was shining again. Someone must have told Patsy that her services were not required. She stood sullen, frowning as Sasha said a prayer before placing her father's Bible at his side in the casket. Nessa, her stiff upper lip suddenly as strong as tissue paper, put a picture of Ann on the other side. Then Dookie lowered the lid. Honaria wiped away the little rivulets of rainwater from the gleaming wood with her kerchief as Ag began to sing the hymn 'Abide with Me'. Patsy joined in. Nessa looked at them, eyes blazing, but Fleur raised her eyebrows in a warning. She gave a minimal shake of her head and pursed her lips. Then she joined in. The words were slowly taken up by everyone. Those who did not know all of the later verses hummed along with the others to its end.

While the casket was being loaded back into the hearse, we separated into the different cars that would carry us to Susumachar. Soames had brought in three extra vehicles for Honaria and Clara, their families and for neighbours who might wish to come along. He directed Nurse to join them. When the convoy was ready, we waited while he locked up the house, leaving Sonnilal's sister inside it. An empty house, even a house of mourning, can be a temptation. Vashti had volunteered to stay, to wash the breakfast things and the glasses, and prepare tea for our return. It was quite a procession that followed the shining, black hearse out of the gates and up the hill. People in the village stood outside their front gates as we drove by. The younger men and women merely watched the parade, but the old men saluted and their womenfolk adjusted their orhnis and lowered their eyes.

The Rings Are The Thing

Sasha, Nessa, Ag and I were seated in the back of Badri's Benz, the lead car behind the hearse. James sat in the front seat with Sonnilal, who was driving. For a while no one spoke: each one of us remained wrapped in our own private thoughts.

Nessa broke the silence.

'I'm going to kill that woman! Who does she think she is, butting in like that? Of all the nerve. Arriving just so. And opening her big mouth to sing! It's a wonder she didn't start to pray as well.'

'Ah heard Mista Soames tell she dat Sasha was to say dih prayer,' interrupted Sonnilal from the front.

'Actually, the hymn kind of made everything complete. I wouldn't have dared sing it!' said Sasha. 'But it was what we needed before we set out.'

'Ha! What right did she have to horn herself in where she didn't belong?' Nessa had another thought. 'And who told her to bring that Paulie? What? Ainsley needed his boyfriend to hold his hand? Of all the blasted nerve, the two of them!'

'Well, if you ask me, the whole thing was a waste and a washout. Literally a washout!' Ag was pleased with her choice of words. 'And the servants butting in so I could hardly get near the coffin.'

'Honaria has known Daddy for forty years, Ag,' said Sasha, 'and she has been so helpful these last months. I don't know what we would have done without her.'

'She had no right to push me aside. She just elbowed me to one side to look in the coffin, and those little children with her.'

'They're her grandchildren, Ag,' I steuppsed, 'She wanted them to see her pay her respects for Badri. They're just kids. They didn't mean any harm.'

'I don't see why your Daddy had to be there in the first place, Sasha. Everyone can see him at the church and to open him up in that tent in the broiling sun doesn't make sense.'

'Soames wanted him there. Soames was trying to show his respect by having him leave for the church from the house. He didn't have to do that.' Nessa was upset. 'And Sasha wanted to say a prayer. What's wrong with that?'

Nessa had argued both against bringing the body to the house and the idea of having any prayer at all, but she defended her uncle and sister against Ag as a matter of course.

'What right do you have to say anything, anyway?'

'Shhh!' said Sasha.

James turned his head in the front seat. 'Vanessa!' he warned.

Nessa's head was hot and her feet were aching from standing. Her blood pressure, her one true medical concern, would need monitoring as soon as she got home. Besides, she loved a good fight and everyone knew she had little time for her uncle's wife. She slid down the slope into Trini.

She turned to Ag.

'Yuh only here because Daddy's damn lazy brother cyar stir himself tuh pick heself up an come to he own brother funeral. His own brother! What happen, he too poor to buy ticket an come tuh meh father funeral? Sending container here and container dere! Why don't you climb in ah container along with the fabrics an fashions and yuh flour an sugar and ting and save the fare that way? Yuh don't have no shame? Everyone see that Uncle Roh ent come! Everyone asks about it. "Where Roh? Where Roh?" So don't criticize what Sasha wants, you hear mih?'

Nessa sank back in the seat and burst into tears. Sasha, caught in the middle as always, closed her eyes.

Nessa wasn't the only one to be vexed, however. Ag had heard 'Where Roh?' too often since her arrival. She had told me this in a series of furtive whispers on the front gallery the previous evening. No one asked about her, she complained, no one seemed to care that she had flown through the night to be there, to do the Lord's work, to minister to the family and look after any poor lambs that might go astray. She knew that they didn't like her. No one liked her. All they wanted was to know where her husband was. At that point, she had broken down sobbing and told me, holding tight onto my arm, that Roh was probably at the office right then having an affair with his receptionist, but she'd never tell his nieces that. Oh no! And I better not either! Jesus would save him in the end, yes, the Lord would bring him back, back into His arms and into hers as well. And then she had prayed.

I hadn't the remotest idea what to say.

Why do people tell me these things, I moaned to myself?

For almost twenty years, I had been the one who defended Ag against her critics. She did not understand the family she had married into and they certainly didn't understand her. A daisy among orchids, she radiated white-bread, provincial Ontario in a world of twelve-grain dough. How she had hooked up with Roh was a mystery. She had never been comfortable in his world. She was, I think, a little afraid of her husband, even though I always thought he was terrified of her. He did not understand either her Canadian conventionality or her basic insecurity, her loneliness even. He loved to party and she loved to pray. These days Roh went his own way while Ag, well, Ag busied herself with her church, her business enterprises and her two boys, who were more like their father than she would ever want to admit.

Ag was almost hysterical. 'How many times do I have to tell you? He's a chartered accountant.'

'So he's a blasted accountant,' yelled Nessa back at her. 'He's not a brain surgeon.'

'People make appointments to see him. He has a waiting list. People rely on him. He's not just some low grade computer repairman.'

Ag had gone too far. Nessa reached over Sasha and slapped her aunt. Sonnilal could have turned off the air-conditioning and the car would still have remained frigid. It was James who, several kilometres down the road, endeavoured to reintroduce some warmth.

'Sasha,' he said, tentatively, 'I thought you decided that your Dad was going to be buried with his rings. What made you change your mind?'

'What do you mean? I didn't change my mind.'

James and Sasha spoke as conversationally as possible, chitchat back and forth to cover the devastation.

'No, I noticed it when Nessa put your mother's picture next to him in the casket. He had no rings on either hand.'

'You're making joke!' declared Nessa, recalled to life, her accent caught between two cultures. 'James, you sure? Did you see? Are you sure you could see? I'm sure I saw his wedding ring when Dookie opened the coffin at the start. Yuh must be imagine it.'

'I'm pretty sure,' replied James, judiciously. 'Ian, did you notice that he was wearing them?'

'No, but I really wasn't looking, you know,' I said.

'Sasha, what about you?'

'I'm sure he had them on.' She frowned, trying to remember. 'At one point, the little diamond flashed in the sunlight. I'm sure. You must be mistaken, James.'

Ag glared out the side window, taking no part in the discussion.

James shrugged in the front seat, 'If you say so.'

'Don't be an ass, James. She does say so,' said Nessa, 'You're blind as well as fat!'

Typically, she tried to laugh off the very tension she had caused; a tension that still filled the car like a wagonload of nerve endings.

'No, Nessa, James right.' Sonnilal spoke with some deliberation. 'When Miss Sasha put in dih book, ah say tuh Vashti how dey ent leave he wedding ring on he finger when he an he mistress so close in life. An Vashti say, perhaps it cost too much a money tuh leave so, an ah said, no, dey ent tink ah dat.' He hesitated. 'An ah see Ainsley wit he hand restin on dih side ah dih coffin.'

His voice trailed away. He looked at the two sisters in the rear view mirror, clearing his throat.

'Oh my God!' said Nessa, each word a paragraph.

'Let's wait until we get to the church and they open the coffin again,' I suggested, the voice of reason. 'We'll be able to see then. There's no use even thinking about it before we're certain.'

'Oh my God!' repeated Nessa, 'Oh my God!'

Six Good Men & True

A large number of people were already standing in the sun waiting, when the funeral cortege pulled into the grounds of Susumachar Church. It would have been unmannerly to go into the church, and the blessed sanctuary of its shade, before the arrival of the deceased, but our procession had been held back by an accident on the bypass. While we sat in the frigid atmosphere of our automobile waiting for the police to pull two drivers and their trucks apart, the mourners at the church were threatening to spoil from the heat. The looks we received when we climbed out of the car seemed more surly than sorrowful. Rookmin's daughter Mira spoke for many when she grabbed Mr. Jones by the elbow.

'Where dih France yuh been? It makin well hot an we standin ere meltin in dih bleddy sun an all yuh takin yuh cool time to get here!'

Mr. Jones shook off her hand to organize the pallbearers. I saw Nessa speaking animatedly to Soames as I took my place at the back on the right hand side behind James. We were to carry the casket from the hearse into the church. June's husband, Ram, was on the opposite side from me. The casket came out of the hearse on runners into our waiting arms. The six of us sagged under its brutish bulk.

'Jesus!' said Ram, as we took its full weight among us, 'dis ting heavy! What it made of?'

'Hole up a thecond. Ah need tuh thee if ah cyan get a betta gwip!' declared Stanley from the front end, letting it go. The casket dipped a little and we held on tighter.

'Yuh mad or what! Don't leave go, fuh Chrise sake!' yelled Ram, his knees buckling slightly.

'Oh thit, thory.' Stanley apologized, straining. As always, Stanley wore his signature shiny black boots: one was unzipped and his trouser leg was caught in it. Its tongue flapped when he moved.

At Mr. Jones' direction, we turned the casket towards the steps of the church and staggered forward. James grunted each time he moved a leg and I could see sweat welling up on the back of his neck.

On the other side of the casket, I heard Charran, the rich cousin, gasp.

'Oh God, what dey got inside dis ting? Dey put Morton foot in cement or what? Ah cyar take dis, fuh true.'

'We're nearly dere,' said Mr. Jones, 'we only have tuh go up the steps. Soon finish.'

We stood at the bottom of seven steps. I counted them. The casket faced forward like a wounded bull.

Ram grunted. 'Ainsley! Lift dih damn ting, nah man! What yuh doin wipin yuh face?'

'Dih sweat in meh eye, Uncle.' A panting wheeze and a sob from Ainsley came over the vast gleaming brownness of the lid. 'Ah cyar see!'

As we hoisted the casket up the first step, gasping to a pause when we got there, I had the feeling that my left hand was even wetter than the rest of my body, and I looked down. My fingers were turning blue from holding hard onto the rail, but blood was oozing from where my index finger had caught on the sharp edge of a screw. My beautiful blood was trickling down the side of the mahogany. I yelped and let go. Look Ma, no hands. The coffin swayed at my end and Ram grunted.

'Fock!' he hissed desperately, between clenched teeth. 'What happen?'

The casket moved forward up the next step and I grabbed back at the rail, smearing gore hither and yon.

'Oh God!' screamed a woman standing nearby, at the bottom of the steps. 'The body bleedin! Dih coffin full ah blood!'

She staggered backwards into the arms of the man behind her.

James, in front of me, was panting. Short puffs between contractions at a Lamaze class. He turned sideways and bent forward to rub his forehead against the lid of the casket, trying to wipe the sweat from his eyes.

'Next step!' commanded Mr. Jones.

The six of us heaved: Egyptian slaves building the pyramids. The noonday sun beat down. Thirty-three in the shade. The collar of my crisp white shirt felt like a piece of dishcloth and my boxers were awash.

'Only a few more,' trilled Mr. Jones. 'Easy now!'

The casket was at a twenty degrees angle. Ram and I shuffled our feet, pawing at the ground to keep our grip. Somehow, Ainsley's hat came off his head, slid over the top of the casket and hit me in the face. I smelled bay rum as it tumbled to the ground.

'Ah cyar do dis no more, Uncle. Ah go dead!' The usual sob in his voice was buttressed by the certainty of his despair.

Ram took some time getting his reply out. He took a breath between each word and between the syllables of the longer words.

'You let go dis focking ting, Ainsley, and I go take yuh in meh boat down Cedros and drown yuh wit meh own two hand.'

'Lift!' yelled Mr. Jones, and we tottered up a step.

'An I go help yuh!' Charran's voice had morphed into a high castrati. It dripped with both sweat and sincerity.

I was aware of the crowd standing behind us at the bottom of the steps, waiting to get out of the sun. Little steupsing sounds could be heard and a wave of animosity seemed to flow upward. I looked at James' jacket in front of me. Perspiration had oozed under the armpits and down the centre of the back. Each hair on his head seemed to have a droplet of water attached to the end of it like a bead and his huge bulk was wobbling.

'I think I'm going to have a coronary!' I heard him say to himself in wonderment.

'Well, wait till we get this effing thing into the church and you can lie down on a pew and have one there,' I replied. 'We can all have one. Two if we feel like it.'

'Lift dih cathket fuh dih lath't,' squeaked Stanley from the front end and we all heaved again.

Each one of us made a different sound to support our effort: 'Hup', 'Hummmpf', 'Aaarrr',' Pprruuh', 'Ugghhh', 'Eeeeckthh'.

We shot forward at the top of the steps and the front end of the casket came to rest on the gurney that had been placed there to receive it. The back end, held by Ram and myself, was suspended in mid air. Everyone loosened their grip thinking it was secure. Inside, Badri's feet rose up and his head dipped downwards. I felt him move. To a man, we grabbed. I heard Ram bang his chin as the heavy mahogany rose towards a degree of equilibrium, and his clenched teeth glared at me across the gigantic dome. His eyes were crossed. I never felt closer to him in my life.

Mr. Jones flustered his way up the steps, waving his hands.

'Wait! Just hold it until ah get everything ready fuh all yuh.' He eased the gurney under the sarcophagus, and, at last, the six of us were able to stand off to the side, broken. The whites of James' eyes were pink and veined, and, I notice that Ainsley's Adam's Apple was bobbing up and down as he sucked in the agonized breaths of the marathon runner a hundred yards before the finishing line.

'Ah tink ah pee meh pants,' said Ram, looking down, but it was just the general wet that covered all of us.

As we stood there, each one a eunuch, Nessa bounded up the steps and instructed Mr. Jones, 'Open the coffin! Now!'

Nessa Explodes

What happened next occurred in a blur of exhaustion. Later that evening, James and I sat on the front porch and shared our memories of it.

Nessa had not been able to open the casket immediately. The pallbearers first had to push it down the aisle on the gurney to stand it in front of the chancel steps. James and the casket itself could not go abreast unless he went sideways. He trailed behind exhausted, his face the colour of the meat in a watermelon. Ainsley was forced into a balletic pas-de-deux when the unsteady gurney shifted and the hinges on the side of the casket snapped at his scrotum. Only when everything was at least in place, were the pallbearers were allowed to sit down. It was nearer to a wholesale collapse.

Mr. Jones, now accompanied by Dookie himself, set to work fiddling with some levers and opened the top half of the lid. A sharp glance went between them and, shielding the body from those nearby, they reached in, one on Badri's left, the other to his right, giving a pull upwards, followed by a tug. Dookie did some quick tidying up before nodding at Soames who had been keeping people back. Once again, however, it was Nessa who moved forward first. Her hand went to her throat and I heard a sharp intake of breath. She shook her head at Sasha.

The final viewing began.

Family was first. There was no order to who followed — friends, co-workers, colleagues, ministerial fellows, cousins and more cousins. Everyone peered down into the open casket as if to make certain Badri was really dead. Some said a few words, occasionally someone wept. Rookmin stood on her toes, leaned in and kissed him on the forehead. I sat in the front pew and watched in a daze. Sasha sat next to me, holding my hand. James sat on my other side and stared straight ahead, still sweltering like a marathon runner. The mourners, having viewed the object of their grief, moved off to the pews, fanning wildly with hymn books, the Order of Service, the sport's page of the 'Guardian' or anything else that came to hand. Fleur took out an elaborate Chinese fan and cooled herself. No doubt, the slight smile playing at the corner of her mouth was in honour of her foresight.

The line of mourners was almost finished when an old man in an orange Nehru jacket came bouncing into the sanctuary, followed by four ladies wearing saris. The pastel blues and greens, all interwoven with golden thread, floated down the aisle behind him until they came to a stop in front of the casket. In an arena of black crows, they were pink flamingos. The old man, hands together in prayerful respect, began to recite something in Hindi and the women joined in the refrain. All five bowed towards the deceased, and then they turned towards where we were seated. They bowed and namasteyed. The old man smiled at Sasha and Nessa, wagging his head from side to side in the Indian way.

'Mr. Seeram!' Sasha's face lit up. 'It is so good to see you, and we can't thank you enough for agreeing to speak today.'

Nessa rose as well and the old man was beginning to embrace the two of them when Didi, seeing him through the fog of years and the weight of her cataracts, totally misunderstood what was going on in front of her eyes.

'Roh!' she bawled, hands thrown arthritically into the air. 'You come!'

Didi stumbled forward, colliding with a bump against the old gentleman. The bump caused him to fall backward so that he collided with the open casket. The wheels of the gurney slewed round and the lid of the casket lid banged shut. Badang bang! Every member of the congregation jumped. Mr. Seeram was now seated on the floor almost under the casket with Didi draped across his lap. I wondered how a man of his size and age could cause the thing to move so easily when it had nearly killed the six of us to lift it. A murmur of consternation rippled through the church. The saried ladies fluttered around like flowers blown about in a hurricane, until presenting a rather broad backside to the congregation, Mr. Seeram managed to rise, his infectious smile still in place. 'Achaa,' he said, and, never once having lost his dignity or his composure, whispered soothing words into Didi's ear until she calmed down and, finally, understood. She took him by the hand and led him to sit next to her in the second row, waving at Bim and Pearlie for them to make room.

It was a considerably discombobulated Mr. Jones who had to reopen the casket to allow the immediate family a final look at the deceased. Nessa and Sasha approached the casket last leaning together, each with an arm around the other's waist. James and I stood at their side in support. I looked down at Badri and he seemed unperturbed by all that we had put him through, though his suit coat was just a little bit hunched around his shoulders. Sasha reached in to straighten his tie.

It was then I saw that he was not wearing his rings.

***

The final closing of the casket took place while we were still absorbing the fact that the rings were missing. I was momentarily apprehensive that Nessa might stop the proceedings to take photographs, but she merely opened her eyes very wide, and mouthed the word 'Gone' to Soames and her aunts. Lip readers might have thought she was merely commenting on the obvious — that the deceased was no longer with us, albeit in a somewhat bizarre and bug-eyed fashion — but even as we absorbed the information about the rings, our minds were diverted by Ag who — of all people — began to wail. She lacked the professionalism of Didi, but she made up for it in enthusiasm. Having no one to comfort her, she hugged herself before staggering back to her place in the pew where she collapsed in a heap on the surprised wood. Once there, she sat sobbing violently, pins spinning out as her bun slowly unravelled behind her.

'Hit her,' Nessa hissed at me, 'she's hysterical.'

'You hit her!' I replied, 'I'm not going to slap a woman in front of all these people. Not even Ag.'

'Oh, for God's sake!' said Nessa standing up and moving in front of her. Ag threw her hands round Nessa's waist and sank a runny nose into her stomach.

We could hear muffled cries.

'He's gone. Another precious angel for the Lord, but I'll miss him so much. We must pray! O Great Jehovah, take up thy servant and give him succour.'

Nessa was facing the whole congregation. She told James afterward that she was horrified to see that everyone was staring at her, waiting to see what she would do. She forced a sad smile to her face and leaned down to speak into Ag's ear.

'Behave your bloody self or I'll pinch your nipple!' she whispered.

And she did.

Ag jerked her face and hands away from Nessa's waist and managed to strangle her next sob at birth. She opened her mouth, looking around wildly for support, but nothing came out and only those closest by had heard a word.

The Service, A Lost Gideon & The Deluge

It was a fine service.

The church was packed. All of the windows were open but I felt, dressed in a dark wool suit and tie, as though I was seated in the middle of a furnace. The flowers on the chancel steps were already beginning to wilt. Some of the congregation evidently intended to pay their last respects to Sonabai Ramkhalawansingh in addition to Morton Badri. since icy-hots — thermos bottles — protruded from handbags and several people had brought sandwiches. For them, it would be a long afternoon.

The congregation sang the good old hymns lustily and with meaning. Ag read one of the lessons. Mr. Seeram gave the eulogy. He had been a school chum of Badri's who had begun life as a Hindu and later converted to Christianity. He returned to the mandir in his forties, however, at the urging of his wife and daughters. When questioned about it, he would shrug his shoulders and say there were many ways to God and sometimes the signposts were pointed in the wrong direction. My father-in-law always blossomed in his presence, a bud unfolding its petals in the sun. Seeram, as everyone called him, had a wonderful sense of humour, loved to laugh and was, in many ways, the quintessential Trini. Carrying a somewhat skewed vision of reality, a deeply-felt humanity and his fractured grammar with him to the lectern, Ivor Seeram brought Badri alive with his remembrances and, at times, we were even able to laugh.

Sasha smiled through her tears.

She smiled even more when the minister, about to conduct the prayers, asked the congregation to look about them on the pews to see if they could see his Gideon Bible. He had put it down somewhere and didn't know where it was. It had, he said, a special sentimental attachment for him.

'Sweet Jesus,' I whispered to Sasha, 'What kind of a preacher have you got here? Where did you find him? What sentimental attachment was he entertaining in Motel Six when he swiped the Bible?'

She squeezed my hand hard and told me to behave, but I felt her complicity in the absurdity of what he had said, and began to work on the joke implicit in it. God apparently did not agree. Just as the minister began to pray, the sun was pushed behind roiling grey clouds, winds swirled around outside besieging the building, and the rains came. Suddenly, the church was dark. The downpour became so heavy it drowned out what was going on inside. It felt as though we were behind a waterfall looking out. The congregation huddled together, but although the windows were open we did not get wet. The rain fell straight down and the service continued.

'Ma!' I heard a reedy voice, a row or two behind us. It was Percy, one of Pearlie's grands, aged five. 'Why it rainin?'

'Shhh, boy. Jesus make it rain.'

'Why, Ma, why he make it rain?'

'Hush, chile! Jesus want dih rain fuh dih crop.'

'But, Ma, why Jesus have rain fuh Uncle funeral?'

'Boy, watch yuh mouth! Jesus could do what he want.' A pause. 'An he looking at yuh. So behave!'

'He looking at me, Ma?'

'Oui, he looking at yuh good.'

A longer pause.

'Ma, Ma, where Jesus? Tell me nuh! Ah ent see he? Where he looking at meh?'

Slap.

The downpour continued. Sasha nudged me while I was searching for the page for the next hymn.

'The grave is going to be a mess. We'll be knee deep in mud if the rain doesn't stop soon.'

The soprano mimed her solo, the announcement that after the service the cortege would proceed to Paradise Cemetery for the interment was met with gloom, and the doxology was sung at a snail's pace, perhaps in the hope that, if it could be prolonged long enough, the benediction might be pronounced to a clear blue sky. As it was, after what was possibly the longest Amen in the history of Christianity, no one moved. There was nowhere to go. I saw the minister glance at his watch: Sonabai's cortege was due in at three, if, that is, it could get there through the torrent that would shortly overflow the drainage ditches, flood the gutters along High Street and stop traffic.

Behind us, people were whispering about what they should do. Should they follow Badri to the cemetery or wait here, or come back for Sonabai later on? Would there be time to return by three o'clock? Was it true that Sonabai's boyfriend's father was going to storm the funeral with his sons to say that she shouldn't be permitted a church funeral? If that was true, no contest, they would stay. On the other hand, if the rains stopped, they could go and watch Badri's interment, and remain there to find a good spot from which to watch Sonabai's burial. After all, the fireworks might well be at the graveside and they'd been to one service already.

Meanwhile, the rain sheeted down. A thousand percussionists beat on the tin roof. Badri lay, dry and comfortable, in solitary state. Even the mourning party paid little attention to him as we consulted one another about what to do next. The minister circulated among his flock but kept giving nervous glances at his watch.

Nessa leaned across me, hissing at Sasha, 'The Chinaman was right! Daddy wasn't wearing his rings! Did you see? He wasn't wearing his rings! What are we going to do? It couldn't have been Ainsley! He wouldn't do such a thing!' Doubt. 'Would he?'

She spun round in her seat and looked over the back of the pew to where Ainsley was sitting in the row behind. One look, however, was enough to give her pause. He was slumped forward on the pew, his face buried in a handkerchief so wet that water dripped off the four corners onto his lap. His eyes, occasionally visible between dabs, had become narrow slits in the puffiness of his face. Nessa didn't have the heart to accuse him.

She turned a gimlet eye on the person next to him.

'Nurse! You took Daddy's rings!'

'Ah ent know wha yuh talking about,' Nurse replied, taken aback. 'Ah ent take nuttin!'

'You lie! It must have been you. Who else would take them?'

'Shut yuh blasted mout! It ent me. Why ah would tek two ring when Dih Doc leave meh plenty ting in he Will?'

Nurse stopped short. She had said too much.

Nessa opened her mouth and declared over the sound of the rain, 'O ho! That's interesting. That's very interesting. And how do you know what is in my father's Will?'

Alas, in the space between her exclamation and those three short sentences, the rain ceased. The words 'in my father's Will' were heard half way to the back of the church. They echoed in the humidity. Even so, Nessa might have continued, had not James laid his hand on his wife's arm and ordered, 'Not now, Vanessa. Later.'

She sat down with a thump.

The pallbearers had lugged the casket down the church steps and were only half way to the hearse when the rains began again. The family retreated onto the porch and huddled there, looking out at the six of us holding up the casket. Rain drops bounced six inches high off the top. Its slope made us their target. We slogged forward, the deluge invading our eyes, running down our noses, cascading onto our chests, disappearing down the front of our trousers and soaking the hair of our nether regions as it went. And still I was sweating. Mr. Jones stood off to the side under a large black umbrella,

Finally at the hearse, we hoisted our burden so roughly into it that Badri's head must surely have bounced. Ram and I gave the casket a last shove and it moved forward on the rollers. Ram, looking at me in defiance through the rain, reached round, took hold of the door handle and slammed it shut. I shook his hand. The six of us ran back up the church steps to escape the rain but our loving relatives refused to give us entry. We were wet, they declared rather unnecessarily. We huddled together before slinking off to sit in our various cars, thoroughly waterlogging the upholstery and not giving a damn.

Interment Tales

For many Trinidadians, the highpoint of a funeral in Trinidad is the burial. The wake is catharsis in the immediate aftermath of death and, as such, helps family and friends cope with the new reality, but it is a time of adjustment. The mourners must organize both the coming event and also themselves, their dress, their posture, their expectations. So many families have relatives abroad that it may be several days before, as in Badri's case, everyone can arrive home to pay their last respects. The date and the hour of burial is often negotiated in overseas calls in which even time differences have to be taken into consideration.

You might, after all, have to wait several hours twiddling your thumbs until dawn breaks in Bayswater before safely phoning Auntie Minnie to tell her that Brother Cedric was cleaned up on the bypass by an over-loader that pushed him into a drainage ditch. Those unfortunate enough to reside in Red Deer, Alberta, or, like Nessa, Thunder Bay, Ontario, first have to bring themselves to civilization before they can find transportation south. In the case of an unexpected death, Aunt Minnie might also have to cope with the fact that her credit card is already maxed out and she will have to negotiate a loan to purchase a ticket. The few carriers left operating on reduced schedules in the wake of airline cutbacks and petroleum scarcities can demand exorbitant prices and they don't care that your brother or, worse, your Ma has gone to her eternal reward. They want theirs.

The good news is that at least the body is where you want it to be, in its final location if not its exact resting place. Monumental difficulties lie ahead for the family whose deceased lacked the foresight to get himself home for the big event. Or who hasn't been home for years but had made it known, put it in the Will in fact, that they wanted to be interred in the Land of the Calypso.

I have warned Fleur, who has made it quite clear that she wants to be buried next to her brothers and sisters in the family plot, that I intend to load her still warm corpse onto a wheelchair and hie us to the airport, she propped up in dark glasses between Sasha and myself, for the quickest possible flight south. It will be a task requiring both an injection of adrenalin and a talent for deception. Will she go in as a Visitor? Apart from the length of time waiting in line, no small thing itself in the heat, just how long might they allow her to stay? Will we then push her along the Green Line, nothing to declare? Whatever the challenges, it will surely be easier than having to deal with the red tape involved — not to mention the cost — in loading her properly into the bowels of the plane and hieing her home, cargo.

There is the cautionary tale of a woman who died in England. I do not recall her name but I was told that I met her once at Mayaro, years ago. All arrangements having been made by reputable morticians at each end, she was put on board a flight at Heathrow, family and friends providing a weepy farewell. Such was the expense of getting her home that she had to leave a sister and two nephews behind, clutching copies of the paperwork as the coffin disappeared. They weren't able to afford the trip. At the other end, a not inconsequential contingent — family friends, neighbours interested in the very concept, unbelieving acquaintances — waited at Piarco. And they waited. For reasons unknown, the deceased had been routed through New York and it was known that she would have a three-hour layover at Kennedy. No problem. It wasn't as though she would require conversation or even sustenance on the voyage. However, she never arrived, and by never, I mean ever.

The welcoming committee dwindled when she didn't appear, the presumption being that she had missed her flight, but for the relatives this caused a dilemma. They could hardly leave. If she came in on a later plane, she would be in no position to take a taxi home. So they stayed, becoming more mulish as the hours passed. Phone calls to England didn't help. They were all asleep there and could only blearily insist that everything had been fine at their end. What do you mean, she hasn't arrived? Shoving faxed copies of bills of lading into the faces of the airline officials didn't get anyone very far either. The baggage handlers did not appreciate being yelled at and told to look for a coffin. It was not something, they said, professionals to a man, that they might have missed. Everyone turned up again the following morning to meet the next flight — actually more turned up because the news was getting around — but the deceased still didn't show. At Heathrow, her sister insisted on waiting in the Arrivals lounge just in case she returned. Perhaps the Americans had turned her back at Immigration for not having a visa. Vast numbers of transatlantic telephone calls began to be made, among relatives, between morticians, between airlines, and, eventually, between governments.

The sister in England collapsed and was taken away for bed rest. The National Health diagnosed her as delusional and possibly paranoid. A second cousin from Tunapuna continued to stand guard at Piarco day by day and then week after week on the off chance that Auntie might arrive unexpectedly. The family wanted to sue the funeral home in Trinidad that had the contract to bury the body but the mortician said he couldn't very well bury what he had never received and washed his hands of the affair. The airline flying into Trinidad said it never received the body and shrugged its shoulders. The airline that flew it to New York said it would keep looking but pointed out that, ultimately, it was not responsible for lost — how could they put this delicately? — luggage. And wanted to know if Auntie had insurance? The initial funeral home sued the airline, successfully, for the loss of its coffin, but it deemed it unseemly to sue for the replacement cost of the deceased herself.

To this day, no-one knows what happened. Is she eternally commuting among the terminals of JFK? Was she inadvertently dispatched to Pago Pago or Azerbaijan? Is she lying, uncollected, in the some Left Luggage Department, suitcases and skis piled on top of her? Does she, perhaps, lie in the gloomy nether regions of an airplane cargo bin, forever circumnavigating the globe unnoticed, and long since decomposed?

Presuming that you do have your corpse safely at hand, after the wake comes the funeral service. This is a solemn and formal event as we have seen. Whether religious or secular, everything has to be choreographed for it to go well. This is a time when people hold themselves together: weeping is muted, processions orderly. Precedence rules. It is at the service that one has to be seen, for not everyone will proceed to the cemetery. 'Did she go to dih funeral self?' is asked second only to 'Did she send flowers?' It is at the funeral, walking down the aisle of the church, viewing the body for the last time if there is an open casket, that fashion can be shown to its greatest advantage and when the degree of one's grief — the shape of it, if you will — is most eloquently displayed. This is when one's relationship to the deceased is publicly defined. In what row of the pews will you sit? Sit too far back and you are the merest acquaintance; too far forward and you may crowd the family and appear pushy. Should you wear pure black or would battleship grey suffice? Pale lilac is not an option.

Will the family think enough of you to ensure you have a ride to the cemetery after the service or will you have to hire a taxi? Or, heaven forbid, walk? And so it goes. But there is, at the end, a containment about the service, a feeling that things should be unruffled, precise: perhaps that is why it is called an Order of Service. This document is a road map, an itinerary, a list of the players and, to the very quality of the paper on which it is printed, embossed or with curlicued font, a statement of worth and an estimate of the affection for the dearly departed.

And yet for all this, it is the burial that is uniquely Trinidadian, the venue where Trini comes into his own. Things happen in the cemetery that are talked about for years afterwards. Here limers and loiterers linger alongside the bona fide bereaved. The nosey stand shoulder to shoulder with the grief-stricken. And one can expect the unexpected. I have gone from grief to guffaw in front of open graves at a variety of cemeteries and such is the sense of humour of the average Trini that even the chief mourners have been known to split their sides between tears of loss.

Hurrying from work to attend a burial, too late for the church service, I once joined the wrong crowd and helped bury the wrong dead. It is difficult to unarm oneself from distraught people who are very glad you came and who hold onto you with vigour, even as you try to explain that you have never seen them before in your life, are very sorry for their loss, but that you must be in an incorrect section of the cemetery. They tend to not want to let you go.

Then there was the time I was offered a ride to the burial, but our half of the procession got caught in a traffic jam — remember I am talking San Fernando here — and we arrived an hour late to find the interment complete and the family climbing into its limos to depart. Since the five in our car had fortified ourselves with several nips of rum while waiting by the roadside, I am ashamed to say that our conviviality placed us somewhat apart from those who had just beheld their loved one being lowered into the ground. A particularly ribald, though entirely true, story about the deceased was greeted by a silence with more granite in it than any of the nearby headstones. Nor was the situation helped when four more cars pulled in behind us, disgorging a substantial number of grieving revellers wanting to halloo the deceased.

***

The interment of Mahadeo Joseph was probably the most memorable burial I ever attended. I should, however, clarify this statement for I attended the first burial, the one that did not take. I was not invited to the second.

Mahadeo was one of Rookmin's sons' in law. He was an enormous man, three hundred pounds, about six six. He lived in Manchester and was visiting Trinidad for the cricket. The West Indies were playing Australia in the fifth test at the Oval. Mahadeo was staying, turn by turn, with practically any relative he could find to take him in. His base of operations, however, was Rookmin's house. She gave him her own bed, it being the strongest, although not without kitchen comments to Anastasia about his general worthlessness and how inconvenient it was. It became a great deal more inconvenient when Rookmin took him a cup of tea two mornings before he was due to leave the island and found him stone cold dead.

The doctor determined Mahadeo had suffered a massive heart attack during the night. His wife, Rookmin's daughter Sarojini, consulted in bleary old England, declared that she did not want him back and that he should be interred in the family plot in Paradise Cemetery. Rookmin steupsed, bought herself a new posture-pedic, and went about the business of getting him underground. She had never liked the man and saw no need to spend a significant amount of money, so she did not go to Dee Cee and Jay but to a smaller emporium on the road to Port Fortin.

For Rookmin's sake, but also to make certain sure he was gone, the family showed up in droves at the church and we got through the service reasonably well. It was a closed casket, this being cheaper. There was considerable whispering about the fact that he was being buried so quickly and also that his wife did not show up. As far as anyone could see, and we all tried to look, Sarojini hadn't sent a single blade of foliage, not a solitary withered zinnia. By the time we got to the lip of the open grave, the heat had frazzled us. It was the last day of the test match, and we were genially wishing ourselves anywhere else. Then things began to happen.

The pallbearers, eight of them, security against Mahadeo's enormous weight, manoeuvred the casket over the open grave and began to lower it. The gravediggers, however, had miscalculated the length of the hole. It was too short. The casket hung above the open pit but could not descend into it.

The crowd ooohed.

The gravediggers were recalled and directed to dig again at the feet of the deceased while the pallbearers, cursing not at all silently, were instructed to lift the casket forward out of the way. Mahadeo's legs thus hung suspended over empty space at the whim of the pallbearers all of whom were sweating like Swedes in a sauna.

The crowd aaaahed.

When he was satisfied with their work, the funeral director told the gravediggers to stand out of the way and allow the pallbearers to lift the casket back over the grave. The pallbearers tried to do his bidding but the two at the bottom end skidded on the lumpy clay and the handles slipped out of their perspiring hands. The casket wrenched itself from the grasp of the other six pallbearers in quick time and accelerated at an angle into the grave. The crowd held its breath. I was standing in the second row behind Rookmin and her daughters, looking up the length of the coffin, and what happened next occurred so quickly that I could hardly take it in. The closed coffin hit the mud, there was a mighty thump and the viewing lid, which was supposed to have been nailed down, swung open.

Mahadeo lay safe inside: there, but not quite in state. His head was turned to the left. His chin, pushed down hard, snuggled against his shoulder. This, in part, answered how they had managed to load a six six man into a normal sized coffin. All this would have been enough, but to our horror, no cosmetic work had been carried out and no one had bothered to compose Mahadeo's features. The coffin was to have remained closed after all. His eyes, protuberant in life, were popped wide open in death. His face was suffused with blood, his tongue purple. It lolled — if the tongue of the dearly departed could be said to loll. He looked for all the world as though he had been throttled.

The sight caused such an intake of breath from everyone present that our collective heads looked deranged. Two people in the front row fainted. Women began to shriek. Several swooned. The rest of us stood transfixed. Those who could not see jumped into the air to get a better view.

Then – I cannot explain exactly how this happened — the bottom half of the coffin lid began to come apart. It swung off its hinges, slowly wedging itself between the casket itself and side of the grave. We could now view Mahadeo, the man in full, framed in his lidless resting place. All of him. He was dressed in a jacket and tie and appeared neat enough from the waist up. From the waist down, however, he was almost naked. Jockey shorts were just visible beneath the white tails of the shirt, his legs were bare and extremely hairy. He wore socks, a small hole in one big toe, but no shoes. Worst of all --- and here the residue of my questions was answered --- to fit him into the confined space of his final resting place, his knees had been bent and turned sideways. He seemed to be genuflecting towards the sun that was now shining merrily down on him.

One of the gravediggers was so taken aback at what he saw that he skidded on the mud at the edge of the grave and slid down into it. Downward velocity caused him to stumble forward and embrace Mahadeo on the diagonal. The gravedigger roared but Mahadeo did not seem to mind: the two of them practised what appeared to be a waltz hold for the afterlife.

Pandora's Box had been opened. Mourners fled from the scene, tripping over flowers and wreaths, dodging round gravestones, sprinting for the gates. The funeral director also fled, though more for self-preservation since Rookmin was in full flight after him. The company went out of business in the scandal that followed. The whole incident was written up in one of the tabloids, you might remember it, along with an exposé of funeral practices in general.

When we had all calmed down, there was considerable amusement at Mahadeo's fate among the family — out of Rookmin's hearing, of course. He hadn't been liked ever since, years before, he had attempted to steal a bottle of champagne at a cousin's wedding and had had to be restrained in the parking lot by the father of the bride. But it was a spectacular way to go, however you looked at it. His final interment took place early the following morning with only half a dozen people in attendance. This was one occasion when Rookmin did not want us there. Mahadeo had a different casket, and, I am told, was trousered, but his feet remained shoeless. The funeral director had run off with Mahadeo's shoes and Rookmin wasn't about to spend one red cent more than she had to on her good-for-nothing son-in-law. She had spent too much already.

The Cemetery Named Paradise

When I die I want to be buried in Paradise Cemetery. Fernando maybe beyond belief but its cemetery is a marvellous. The large, rolling expanse stands apart, out of time, surrounded the city. From the higher ground, where the Badri family plot located, I could look down and across, the whole vista laid out in front of me. The huge, umbrella-branched, samaan trees are fewer these days but they add an enchantment and a serenity to this landscape of crammed gravestones and mausoleums.

The narrow roadways that criss-cross the cemetery were quickly being clogged with vehicles from our procession. We had followed the hearse inside but we had to walk the last twenty yards. The hearse was too long and too wide to turn onto the unpaved side road that runs near the cemetery wall next to the spot where Badri would be buried. He was to lie in his mother's grave, the necessary number of years having passed to allow them to open it and place him there. We could see gravediggers putting the finishing touches to Sonabai's grave, off to my right in the distance,

Once again, the pallbearers assembled at the rear of the hearse. We were beaten now and our suits had begun to steam in the afternoon sun. Ram and Charran took out shades and put them on to protect their eyes from its reflection on the shining marble tombstones all around us. Ainsley looked like a poster child for malnutrition. His overworked handkerchief had given up the ghost and was pushed half way up his jacket sleeve. He stood squeezing his eyes with the backs of his hands. I cupped my own hands over my eyes and squinted at the white canvas awning that had been erected adjacent to the open grave. The canvas magnified the light, seeming to shimmer in the breeze. Could this, I wondered as we stumbled forward, be what is meant by going towards the light? We tottered through the awning, turned, and the open grave lay dead ahead of us.

Only then did Sasha's comment about what the rain might have done to the ground really register. Great mounds of clay had been dug out and piled to the left of the hole, but the rain had turned everything to ooze. The sides of the grave were slick and silky. Wading pools of wet mud were surrounded by mountains of sludge. I heard Ram, not the most religious man I know, say, 'Jesus!' and Stanley, hardly more so, muttered, 'For Chrith'th thake!' Had we been paid, we would have gone on strike. At Mr. Jones' order, Stanley and Charran stepped forward off the gravel pathway. They sank into the mire before them. I heard Charran moan in a strangulated voice, 'Meh foot, Oh Gawm, ah cyar see meh foot!'

'Hurry now, in case it starts to rain again,' urged Mr. Jones and, although there was not a sign of cirrus in the sky, we shunted ahead.

Immediately, Charran called out again. 'Wait, ah los meh blasted shoe. It come off when ah lif meh leg!'

'Don' mind that,' ordered Mr. Jones from the pristine dryness of the pathway. 'Go!'

When I put my own good foot forward into the mud and tried to lift it, I had to curl my toes to keep the shoe on. Each step was accompanied by a suctioning sound: a bunch of plumbers trying to unclog a row of toilets. Skidding about, we finally manoeuvred the casket to rest on two oak cross-beams that would be removed when it was time to lower it into the grave. Our legs vibrated from the weight of our load and from trying not to slalom off the precipices of ooze.

In front of me, James released his hold and his feet slid out from under him. Both legs disappeared into the grave and his enormous belly crashed against the side of the casket. Only might and main prohibited the laugh that wanted to erupt from within my twisted soul. Only James' girth saved him from a full, foot-first descent into the abyss. His forehead cracked against the side of the casket. He peered upwards, a look of bewildered terror on his face. The rest of us heaved ourselves away, leaping from our burden, desperate to seek the asylum of the gravel we could see so close by. The crowd, totally fascinated, edged closer even as we struggled, but it was left to the gravediggers to rescue James, though not before he had sprawled full length in the mud and one shoe had fallen, lost for all time, into the grave.

And the sun shone brightly down.

The immediate family sat under the awning on two rows of chairs. They would let neither James nor Ram join them and Sasha shooed me away with a giggle, wrinkling her nose. We stood off to one side. Other people pushed together behind the awning, trying to absorb its shade by osmosis. More adventurous mourners climbed on the railings of nearby graves and, some few gifted persons balanced on top of tombstones to obtain a better view. There must have been well over two hundred people. The minister appeared, looked about and wrapped his gown round him, holding it above his knees in an attempt to keep it clean.

The Reverend Chesney Gupta was not someone I had known before, even by reputation. And his, apparently, was not good. He had taken an early retirement rather than let Synod audit his private bank accounts. At his last charge, the sterling silver communion plate had gone missing along with the Christmas candelabra. Nothing could be proved, however, and even those who doubted his honesty admired his religiosity. These days, he made a small living filling in for sick or vacationing ministers and otherwise performing marriage ceremonies or conducting funeral services. We had been warned that once he got going he was difficult to stop and also that he could be rather absent-minded at times.

He moved to the front of the awning to say the final prayers and Badri's benediction. From where James and I were standing we could see him in profile. He closed his eyes, threw back his head and raised up his arms, balancing himself on the balls of his feet. His Gideon Bible was nowhere in sight.

'Oh Lord,' he began. He had been educated in England and the accent was Oxbridge, more Anglican than Presbyterian. The vowels were syrupy, long and mellifluous. 'We worship and magnify Your wonderful name.'

'Amen and Amen.' Ag endorsed the sentiment.

'We come before You today bowed down with an enormous sadness, feeling low, feeling confused, feeling angry in our grief. We know that there is a time and a season under heaven for all things but we wonder why, why You have chosen to take the one we loved so deeply and so well from us at this particular time.'

Sasha began to weep.

'Why do we have to say 'Goodbye' to one so adored, one who meant so much to us, Lord? Why do some go forward into Your eternal harbour of rest while we, who loved them so, find ourselves still beached on this earthly shore?'

'Oh Sweet Jesus, why?' echoed Ag.

Nessa began to sniff, a handkerchief to her eye.

'Yet we realize that it is not for us to know the details of Your plan for any of us, and, while we are sad, we know that we can find comfort in our faith, in our remembering and in Your presence in this place today.'

The Reverend was rocking gently, backward and forward. His eyes remained firmly closed. He was smiling with God.

'And so we bring to You our sincere and heartfelt prayers of thanksgiving and intercession for your dear, devoted servant this afternoon. We give thanks for her life and we offer our prayers of intercession for her immortal soul as she prepares to meet with You for that great reckoning in Your Kingdom beyond.'

Hold on a minute! Her life? Her immortal soul? She!?

'Lord, we have so very much to be thankful for. Your servant had a long life, was surrounded by a large and happy family and, from everything I have heard about her, she was, in so many ways, a fulfilled woman.'

I'll say.

The mourners were staring at the minister in awe.

Even Ag was silenced.

Sasha stopped crying in mid-weep and Nessa lowered her handkerchief.

'We know, however, from the unfortunate way in which she met her end that she was deeply unhappy and in need of Your help, Your succour, Lord.'

Nessa began to flap her handkerchief at Gupta, waving it just out of reach of his backside. His eyes remained closed, a slight frown of concentration on his still uplifted face.

'And we pray for forgiveness on her behalf, knowing always of Your loving kindness.'

Nessa was swatting desperately now, but she hadn't been able to touch him. She cleared her throat. The rest of us stood like statuary.

'For we remember, Lord, that You loved a sinner and we pray that our sister will be forgiven seventy times seven.'

Oh shit!

Nessa looked hopelessly around for assistance. The Reverend took a stentorian breath and a measure of sternness entered his voice.

'We ask for Your eternal forgiveness on her behalf, that she should have felt the necessity of taking her own life and, in doing so, taking with her that of ... the young man... to whom she was... so... unfortunately... bound....'

Was it doubt that had entered his oration?

Like an unwound clock, the Reverend Gupta slowly ceased ticking. He licked his lips. He frowned. His eyes remained steadfastly closed. The assembly held its breath. Was he hoping against hope that if he opened his eyes he would find that everything would turn out all right? Slowly, he did open his eyes. He blinked. He scanned the crowd, but the people he saw in front of him were as likely to have been at Badri's burial as at Sonabai's.

'Oh God!' he said. It sounded more like a cry and a prayer for himself than for the deceased, whomsoever that might prove to be.

I have never seen a crowd of Trinis so quiet. We were trying to absorb what we had heard, many, I think, wanting to imprint the occasion on their mind's eye for future telling. Someone might even base a calypso on this! The Reverend opened his mouth, still not daring to turn round to look at the family behind him. The very principles of time were suspended in the heat of the afternoon. Then, slowly, and only from the knees up, he swung round. His feet remained pointed towards the open grave. When he saw the handkerchief in Nessa's outstretched hand, he slowly closed his eyes again and shook his head.

Like everyone there, he remained dumb. Not even Nessa had a word to utter. Then, in a voice I, fortunately, have never had directed towards me, Sasha who broke the silence.

'Leave!' she hissed, pointing in the direction of the gates of the cemetery. 'Get. Out. Now!'

The Reverend Gupta slunk away, leaving the floor, so to speak, to a dogged and determined Patsy, who, dripping with self-satisfaction, moved forward and suggested that it might be an appropriate moment for a hymn while the casket was being lowered into the ground.

★★★

Muddied as I was, I went to stand next to Sasha. Didi and the older women were wailing in unison and Patsy's voice, leading the singing, somehow complemented them. Nessa stepped forward and threw a rose into the grave, but Sasha remained still. Her arms were wrapped tightly round herself, keeping herself together. Our fingers were linked but, otherwise, we did not touch. Pearlie was weeping quietly and Soames stared, out of focus, at the ground between his feet. Fleur sat erect, assessing what was going on in front of her, the corners of her mouth drawn down in concentration. Ag, who was now covered in loose, streaming grey hair like an Old English sheepdog, dabbed the corner of her eye with a handkerchief, clutching her cross convulsively. For a man who had never encouraged them, there were tears everywhere.

The gravediggers began to attack the mountain of mud and to shovel it onto the top of the casket. The thunder of clay falling on its roof made me flinch, snapping my eyes shut reflexively over and over again. The crowd sang lustily to drown out the harsh loneliness of the sound as enormous spadefuls followed, the muscular arms of the diggers straining to complete their task. Tiny driblets of liquid mud, the blood of the dead, flew off the ends of their spades, splattering the dresses and the suits of the bystanders, and yet everyone remained where they were. They would complain, and bitterly, of ruined garments later, but this was the moment to show proper respect and to honour Badri for the last time. Also, they wanted to see what might happen next.

I feel sure that no one could have predicted it, however.

Ainsley had been standing off to one side, his suit steaming in the sun, trousers lacquered with mud. He pushed his way through the people lining the gravel road and took two stumbling steps forward to the edge of the grave. Then he just stood there, interrupting the rhythm and arc of the gravedigger's swinging shovel. In considerable danger of decapitation, he began to bawl.

'Nyeeeeeee, Nyeeeeeee. Nyeeeeee.'

Ainsley peered at the grave while the crowd peered at him. Patsy, catching his movement forward out of the corner of her eye, stopped mid-note. Didi, herself no slouch in the bawling department, was clearly taken aback, and ceased momentarily with a strangling breath, before resuming half an octave higher.

'Nyeeeeeee, Nyeeeeeee. Nyeeeeee.'

'For crying out loud,' hissed Nessa. 'Stop him, for God's sake!'

Sasha whispered, 'Ian, get hold of him. Bring him back!'

'Bring him back, what the hell for?'

'We can't leave him there.'

'He can come back when he's good and ready, can't he?' I had a thought. 'He's doing it on purpose.'

'Rubbish! Why would he do it on purpose? He can't help it. It's Ainsley.'

'For heaven's sake, stop the man. Where's James?' asked Nessa, looking around? James was unavailable. He had retired behind the Benz, stripped down to his underwear and was lying inside on its back seat in a dazed heap.

'Nyeeeeeee, Nyeeeeeee. Nyeeeeee.'

I let go of Sasha's hand and, muttering at the injustice of life and the exigencies of petticoat government, stepped forward gingerly into the mud. The gravediggers had filled in the grave and were banging with the backs of their spades at the mound they had made above it. I slogged forward as best I could until I was able to place a hand on Ainsley's shoulder. I turned him around and he fell against my chest. His hat came off — again — falling behind him. As it fell, a shovel pounded it into the mud. Ainsley leaned against me and his buried cry pulsed through me. I took him by his skinny arms and lifted him away from me. We remained connected by a string of mucus that swung like a trapeze from the end of his nose to my lapel.

Very slowly, I closed my eyes: this too would pass.

'There, there,' I muttered inanely, not knowing what else to say and not wanting to say anything at all. 'It will be all right.'

From behind us, I heard Nessa, martyrdom in her every syllable, command, 'Bring him here! Ainsley, come here!'

I turned him round and led him back to the walkway. Nessa held out her arms and he fell into them. Then, very slowly, he oozed down the length of her torso and lay in a puddle at her feet. Out of the corner of my eye, I saw Nurse cross her arms and smile.

A Superfluity Of Flowers

Another imperative in a Trinidadian funeral is flowers, and it took time transferring the wreaths and bouquets from the hearse and the other vehicles used to carry them to the grave. They were placed profligately all about, the myriad colours responding to the sun. Soon they began to hide the clay and place a carpet of civility over the mire that surrounded it. Mr. Jones and an assistant removed the cards that accompanied each tribute, placing them safely in their pockets.

The cards are to be handed to the family who will pick through them afterwards so that each can be properly acknowledged. The family also notes the names of all persons who have not sent flowers. If, after inquiry, it is discovered that they had not been out of the country or in hospital or in gaol, the relationship is weighed and its worth re-evaluated. There is no worse blunder surrounding the burial of the dead than to not send flowers. It is a thing remembered, lo, unto the next generation.

So many bouquets and wreaths had been received that they were piled willy-nilly on top of one another, and it would be quite a task to sort out who had sent what. The svelte line of Mr. Jones' suit-coat bulged with the cards he had collected, accentuating his hips.

When everything had been put properly in its place, the gaiety of the blooms and their very profusion began to subtly alter the mood of the occasion. Hymn singing continued but it began to give way to conversation. At first, this concerned itself with the blooms themselves, then with the service and the deceased, but soon it became more general to include the weather, the humidity after the rain, The Reverend Gupta (alas), and the crucial decision of whether or not to wait for Sonabai's bier to arrive. Did anyone have a radio?

Had anybody heard the score? People began to circulate. Now, finally, the women could comment, most often in a few pithy words spoken behind artfully placed linen handkerchiefs, about the outfits.

People who no longer talk to one another, cannot abide the sight of one another because of an argument, a change in social station or a law suit, will come face to face at a funeral and propriety demands that they exchange a few words. Family rifts, deep gullies of enmity, have been mended when the combatants have fallen into each other's arms at the side of a newly filled grave containing the remains of a mutual friend, even if both sides had publicly sworn that they would never again have anything to do with the other. It is a spectator sport to watch what is going on: the eddy forward, the initial retreat, the awkward, circumspect rapprochement, the final weepy reconciliation.

Even more interesting is the scorpion-like dance that occurs among the bereaved where some secret division has occurred in a family. There might be some slight hope that open gossip about it has not been retailed across the deep South, that the whole world is not in the know. This is generally a faint hope: gossip is mother's milk to the energetic Trini and 'commesse,' scandal, is absorbed airborne through their pores like moisturizer on the driest of skin.

'Look nuh boy, Lallie walk right past Mannie! She ent sof at all!'

'No, no wait. It look like they go speak! Move a likkle an see if yuh cyar hear what she say.'

'Girl, see how he give she a cut eye!'

And Lallie hisses at Mannie between gritted teeth, 'Kiss me!'

If Mannie responds, whispering violently, 'Woman, is so yuh stop? Well, it tek two hands tuh clap. Watch meh good. Ah ent go kiss yuh if you is deh las Auntie ah have left on the face ah dih blasted earth,' well, the chances of reconciliation are few and very far between. Lallie is likely to flounce away accompanied by the nudges of all those who are not so surreptitiously watching. If, on the other hand, she raises her voice, or worse her hand, and answers Mannie back loudly, there is the danger, the delight, of a public brawl and the last, merest chimera of family unity will collapse in front of everyone.

Horrors!

I have seen performances on these occasions that deserve the highest accolade: Aunties at war who have swapped smiles and energetic conversation, giving more signs of mutual adoration than the Magi; cousins who have slapped each other on the back and laughed uproariously when they would have dearly liked to insert a sharp instrument between the third and fourth vertebrae; nephews who have worked vigorously to ruin the reputation of nieces who now admire how well they look, declare that it has been too long, and are so glad to see them appearing so well.

Of course, these are other people's families.

On this day, all was sweetness and light, although clouds had had begun to hide the sun again and a breeze was moving along the byways of the cemetery, rustling between the graves. The crowd had begun to thin out. Some people looked at the sky and debated whether to wait for Sonabai to arrive. Others decided to go home. Soames said he would head out and dropped the keys to the Benz into my surprised hand. It wasn't the right moment and I handed them to Sonnilal without thinking. We stayed a while under the awning, chatting with friends, and then said goodbye to them as they left to go about their lives again.

Eventually it was quiet. Sasha and I and Nessa and James, he dishevelled but again dressed, sat facing the flowers that almost reached our feet on the pathway. We did not speak and when no one else remained, the four of us walked quietly away.

That night young men scaled the walls of Paradise Cemetery and carried away the flowers, ripped apart the wreaths and plundered the bouquets. They sold their spoils down the Coffee next day.

Alcolada

I awoke about thee o'clock in the morning. The net on Sasha's side of the bed had been pulled loose and the door to the room was ajar. I lay a while listening for her return and to the noises of the night, watching the reflection of the moon on the long wardrobe mirror. After a few minutes, when she didn't come back, I got out of the bed and walked into the living room, but she was not there and there was no light in the bathroom. I felt my way to the rear of the house and saw that the inner back door had been opened, though the burglar bars of the outer door were still pulled in. I stepped lightly on the old wooden floor so that I would not disturb the sleeping house. Sasha was seated on a divan in the back gallery, her back against the wall. The outline of her breast showed against the thin cotton of her nightdress. She was looking at the night sky.

'Are you all right?' I asked. 'You shouldn't be out here by yourself.'

'I'm fine,' she replied, reaching out her hand, 'Come.'

We sat side by side. We couldn't see the moon but its light illuminated the yard in front of us with an almost tender paleness. The tent was gone. Trees across from us cast inky shadows and those high enough were outlined against the night sky. There was no wind. Even the branches of the palm trees seemed to hold their breath.

'Look at the stars,' said Sasha, pointing upwards. 'I miss seeing stars in Toronto, the city blocks them out. But here there are too many to count.'

It was true. So many stars had punctured the dark sky that heaven itself seemed to peep through.

'Are you all right?' I repeated.

'I'm fine,' she answered, patting my knee and we sat quietly together in the tranquil dark.

'Where do you think he is now?' she asked.

I thought about my answer.

'He believed in an afterlife,' I replied. 'I think he'll be there, wherever it is. He used to talk about reincarnation, didn't he? Not exactly a staunch Presbyterian belief!'

'I think he is somewhere around us,' said Sasha, thoughtfully. 'I think that his energy is still here and we'll be able to feel it. '

She sat silent a while.

'Don't laugh, but when I went for breakfast yesterday morning, I felt that he was in the room, right there with me. I could smell the sweet smell of the Alcolada that Nurse used to dab on him every morning. You won't believe me, but I could smell it. He was sitting right there, next to me at the table. We sat, just the two of us. Together. And then Clara came in with the tomato chokka and the smell was gone.'

For a long moment I said nothing. Her wistful recollection, her hope, hung in the night air.

I smiled.

'Well, the garlic in the chokka must have driven him away.'

Sash squeezed my hand and smiled to herself in the darkness.

Interlude At Mayaro

The next morning we broke one of the cardinal rules of proper behaviour following a funeral. Sasha did not feel at all comfortable about it and Fleur was a little scandalized that we should even think of such a thing, but our time in Trinidad was limited and we decided that, if we went early enough, we could be back before teatime, when visitors were most likely to arrive to offer their condolences, and no-one would be any the wiser. We would go to the beach.

The sun was shining, and it wasn't, as James pointed out, as though we were having a party or anything. Nessa was all for the idea since it would give us an opportunity, away from the older members of the family, to talk, something we couldn't safely do in the open breezy house. I had been finding pieces of clay and dirt all night in the most peculiar places and itched for a sea bath to clean myself off. In anticipation of going with us, Anca had stayed overnight after her parents returned to Port of Spain, and, at the last minute, Ag announced that she would come along, just for the ride. Oh, Happy Day! Then, Jolyon said he could carry his radio to listen to the match and that it might be fun to go.

Mira, Rookmin's daughter, had heard us talking about the trip the night before so we had invited she and Partap, her husband, to come along. Sonnilal made a detour into San Fernando to pick them up. I made a stop in the village to collect Percy, Pearlie's grandson, who had awakened from a sound sleep the previous evening at the mention of the beach and demanded to be included. There were three cars in all. Clara packed a lunch for us from the mountain of food left over from the wakes and we set out at nine o'clock. Not bad considering Trinidadians have no sense of time and are always late: we had intended to leave by seven-thirty.

We drove along the bypass before turning eastward towards Rio Claro. It takes about two hours to get to the beach at Mayaro. For the first forty-five minutes, the two-lane road wends its busy way following the ridge of the hills, a steep slope, sometimes a drop, on both the right and the left. Houses on stilts are able look passers-by in the face. The potholes were deep and wholesale subsidence sometimes narrowed the two lanes to one undulating track of asphalt. There is no place to widen the highway even if the Ministry of Transport wanted to do so. It can be a knuckle-whitening experience to drive this stretch of road and the taxi drivers who pelt along it are the icing on the cake.

Arrival at Princes Town is always a relief but, invariably, I manage to forget that this bustling centre of commerce makes San Fernando appear leisurely, congestion free and calm. I suspect that there is a municipal ordinance in Princes Town stating that nothing is allowed to be more than eleven inches away from the next nearest object. This applies to merchandise on display in all its shapes and sizes, to buildings, to vehicles passing through and to the local inhabitants. The town is as clogged as a backed-up drain. I navigated the Nissan along the narrow main street, taking care to avoid the elbows of sidewalk strollers that might enter the open window and hit me in the eye.

Sasha, out of her mind, insisted that we stop to buy doubles from a roadside vendor. I obeyed, of course, so she climbed out and the traffic began to back up. It also began to honk. The car behind me attempted to pass by turning into the oncoming traffic. Someone would have to give way. Unfortunately, both vehicles were taxis. The drivers sat on their horns and glared at each other. I stared straight ahead.

Sasha hopped back in the car, declaring, 'See that didn't take long, did it!' She was oblivious to the uproar all around us.

We were able to go faster on the second leg of the journey. I had hoped to stop near the little mud volcanoes in the Devil's Woodyard near Hindustan Road, but Ag said she was tired of sitting and, in any case, she couldn't imagine why I would want to see any more mud after yesterday. It was a palpable hit, so we kept on going. It is a glorious drive and the approach to Mayaro village through the palm trees is worth every bit of the effort to get there.

Sasha had me stop again to buy fruit in the market and we all climbed out to stretch our legs before going on to the beach house, a few miles further down the Guayaguayare Road. I was looking for starch mangoes when we heard a woman begin to scream. Not the wailing, keening kind of scream I had been getting used to in the last few days, but a raw, jagged hysterical scream of terror. It was followed by a crash. Sasha dropped a pommerac in surprise and it rolled under the vendor's stall out of reach.

'What in the world is that?' she asked, turning around.

'Oh, precious Lord, someone's been hurt!' declared Ag.

'It sound like a fella been shot,' declared Percy, with relish, moving off in the direction of the noise. 'Leh we fine out what happnin.'

'You stay here,' I commanded, but he was already gone.

'Ah think ah know dat scream, yuh know,' said Jolyon thoughtfully.

The noise had come from the other end of the small covered market and we could see a crowd gathered around something on the ground. As we looked, Percy emerged from the crush of people and darted towards us. He was grinning.

'Is Auntie Mira!' he called out.

'Oh my dear Sweet Jesus! Is she hurt? said Ag

'No. She see ah cyat!' He answered gleefully. 'She see ah cyat and she gone off!'

It was quieter now but we could hear someone taking deep, jagged breaths and whimpering loudly. Nessa emerged from the crowd coming towards us. She raised her hands and looked towards heaven.

'Look at my crosses!' she said, 'We stopped and were walking along looking at the vegetables when Mira begins to scream like a mad woman. I nearly had a heart attack, I tell you.'

Anca pushed her way out of the crowd, a large melon grin on her face.

'Then she fell on the floor and her eyes rolled up into her head,' continued Nessa. 'Oh my God, what a thing! I never saw anything like it.'

'Is was dih cyat!' said Anca. 'Dey bringing she now.'

'A cyat! A tiny little kitten curled up on the stall, fast asleep among the bhaji!'

'Is she all right?' asked Ag.

'Ah tink so,' replied Anca, 'Partap give she a good hot slap an she seem tuh calm down a bit. He vex too bad.'

The crowd opened to let Partap and Sonnilal through. Between them was Mira, her hands hugging her shoulders and her head resting on her husband's chest.

'Oh, mih God, mih God, mih God!' she panted, when she saw us. 'A cyat!'

'Foolish woman,' said Partap. 'Yuh see a cyat an carry on like this.' And to us, 'Every time she see cyat is dih same ting. What ah go do?'

He had another thought.

'Even a bird! Yuh should see she when she see bird. A little tiny bird self land on dih bleach in dih yard an she gone off. Screamin she bliddy head off.' He shook his head. 'What ah go do?'

Mira and Partap had been happily married for twenty years and he knew perfectly well that there was nothing he could do. With the possible exception of Percy, we all did. Mira, the soul of generosity and the kindest of women, had a fixation about cats and small birds. Large ugly corbeaux didn't bother her. It was, in a sense, a family thing. Sarojini hyperventilated when the word 'snake' wriggled its way into polite conversation and Soames himself could not bear to feel sterling silver cutlery touch his teeth. All his life, he had shamed his sisters by dining off stainless steel. At any rate, we were in an appropriate place to be reminded of such things. The beach house we were visiting had belonged to Tantie Neeta, the mad aunt. Neeta had been another of Ma Sookbirsingh's sisters but she was long dead and I had never met her. She had married well: her husband, Dr. Kissoondath Beharry, had owned half of south Trinidad, if the stories were true. They had been riotously happy until the birth of their child, Shakuntala, who — everyone knew the story — leapt out of the birth canal with an eyetooth already grown in her head. Neeta took one quick look and was never the same again. What might have been diagnosed as post partum depression these days was plain crazy back then. She was kept locked up in a bedroom of their house on Gransaul Street until the neighbours said that the noise was scaring their kids. Sasha remembered her from when she was a child.

Dr. Beharry took Neeta to Mayaro where the sea breezes seemed to bring her calm. He put her in a beach house with a full time nurse. She languished there for years, cackling into the wind that swept down the sands, frightening the village fisherman bringing in their nets. She became the family warning.

'If yuh don behave, ah'll send yuh by yuh Tantie down Mayaro!'

Any family oddity, even among the Badris where there was no blood connection, was blamed on 'dih ole lady down by dih beach.'

'Watch out, girl, or yuh'll en up like yuh Tantie Neeta wit a screw loose!'

The house was empty now, available to anyone in the family who wanted to spend a weekend. We stayed there whenever we came to Trinidad, with giggles and ghost stories to fortify us, along with a good tot of rum, against the spooks in the night. It was said, although I never saw her photograph, that Neeta and Mira resembled. Mira never liked to hear this, and didn't particularly like to go into the house either, but she loved the beach and wasn't about to be kept away from it by anything, not even a cat.

***

We sat around two old picnic tables in the shade of the palm trees looking out at the sea. The Mayaro breeze is strong and sandy. There was much to talk about but the place itself provided a counterpoint for our thoughts. Miles of the lightest brown sand ran in both directions, the tide was high and breakers hungrily pounded the shoreline. Oil derricks were just visible on the horizon. It has always filled me with awe to think that the first thing beyond them, except for the occasional ship, is Africa. I liked to search where the sand joined the palms trees looking for lost treasures that had been thrown up, I imagined, by the tide and which now lay hidden on the edge of the new world.

Further down towards the water, I knew that I would find the beautiful, angry remains of jellyfish, opalescent purple murano glass bodies still shimmering in the sun, tendrils trailing, hidden viciousness for bare feet. And the sea itself, crashing against the sand, not the gentle aquamarine of a picture postcard, but dark, determined and dangerous. No wonder Sasha's generation cannot swim. Surrounded on all sides by water, they have spent their lives bathing in the froth of the tide, being wise and unadventurous in no more than eighteen inches of water. And they are correct, for, on most holiday weekends, the long coastline from Manzanilla to Mayaro will claim at least one unwary victim caught in the undertow and carried away by its currents. Both the Sookbirsinghs and the Badris have stories to tell about that.

After a long while, the sand, hurled at us by the constant breeze from the sea, became too much and we turned our backs on the ocean. The women took out the food and we men organized ice and drinks. I sat in my chair, spread my legs out in front of me, leaning back, looking upwards through the waving fronds of the palms into the sun that stood above us in the middle of the day. This was the life! Later on, I would lie out, a small, pale, bleached mammal, and broil for a while, basting myself with oils until an angry pinkness set in. Only then would I drape a towel from neck to toe, leaving my eager head as a sacrifice to the gods of tanning. Sasha and the other natives circle the shade becoming effortlessly darker by the minute, the objects of my absolute envy.

***

As I might have expected, it was Nessa who shattered the reverie of the afternoon.

'Well, did anyone actually see Nurse take the rings?'

'Nessa, we can't say she took them, if no one saw her,' cautioned Sasha.

'Who else would have taken them? Not Ainsley. Not Dookie or Mr. Jones. It only makes sense that it was she.'

'But look nuh, why would Nurse want tuh tief dem?' asked Jolyon. 'What she want with yuh fader wedding ring? Or deh other one. She cyar wear them, dey too big. An someone go see she, too besides!'

'Perhaps she want dem just fuh so,' suggested Anca, with a shrug.

'If you had taken them off in the first place,' sniffed Ag, 'this wouldn't have happened. The diamond ring should have gone to Roh.'

'Who could have taken them apart from Nurse?' I asked, trying to deflect the storm clouds. 'Ainsley certainly didn't. He couldn't have stopped his bawling long enough to get them off your Dad's fingers.'

'Ag was bending over the casket at the very end!' announced Nessa to the sea breeze.

And they were off. Dislike conquered discretion.

'You are a lost child! Sinful and evil. Mark my words. Hell will await you if you don't mend your ways.' Nessa did not react. 'Wait until I tell your Uncle!'

'And you are only here to see what you can get! And you think Uncle doesn't know?' Nessa could contain herself no longer.

'I won't sit here and be spoken to like that,' said Ag, standing up and flouncing off towards the beach house.

'Well,' I said, 'that didn't help, did it?'

We sat in silence, running the conversation over in our heads.

'But wait ah minute,' said Mira, hesitantly, 'what all yuh sayin? Ah tink ah see Auntie June takin off Badri ring. She ent tell yuh?'

'Ma? Wha Ma want with two men ring?' asked Anca.

'You're sure it was Auntie June?'

'Ah sure, oui. It was sheself.'

'Why didn't you tell someone if you saw something?' flared Nessa?

'Who ah go tell? Ah thought all yuh know!'

'Anca, you know anything about this?' asked Nessa, turning in her seat to face her cousin, the turn an accusation.

'Me? No. An why Ma want Uncle ring? It ent make sense.'

June had more rings than a telephone.

'Well, she's greedy enough!'

Anca had her own troubles with her mother but she didn't appreciate her cousin's comment, which, incidentally, was far from true. June was generous to a fault, even if her gifts often had more weight in their cost than in their taste.

'You ent have ah right tuh say that! What she do you? Ag right, yuh a crass idiot in truth!'

'Mira sees your Ma taking my father's rings off his dead body and I'm a crass idiot?! Well, I like that. It's not as though she was falling down hysterical from seeing some cat, you know. She saw what she saw.'

'What yuh mean?' exclaimed Mira, on the verge of tears. 'Ah cyar help it when ah see ah cyat. Yuh tink ah like to have a fit, just so? Yuh tink it easy fuh meh? Partap, why yuh let she say such tings tuh meh, boy!'

'Nessa,' said Mira's stalwart spouse, 'it just bad mind tuh say dat!'

'Why yuh speak bad of Anc's Ma? She yuh Tantie!' demanded Sonnilal, entering the battle.

'And if you weren't so afraid of her, she'd be your mother-in-law.' Nessa threw the words back at him.

'Dat our business, woman!' declared Anca, standing up and shaking her finger at her cousin.

'Apologize, Nessa. You really can't say such things to people,' sighed Sasha, the vain protector of the peace.

'I just want to know what happened to Daddy's rings!' said Nessa and she burst into tears.

Jolyon, James, Sonnilal, Partap and I, mere males all, looked from one to the other. Jolyon lifted his shoulders and James his eyebrows. I cleared my throat but Sasha squeezed my hand hard to keep me quiet.

'Mira,' she said, 'when did you see this? Are you sure that Auntie June took the rings?'

'Ah see she wit meh own two eye. She slip dem in dih pocket ah she dress. Too besides, why ah go lie?'

Anca groaned.

'Yuh absolutely sure, Mir?' she asked.

'Ah see what ah see, girl. Ah sorry.'

Ag, who had trickled back towards us, flew into the circle of chairs shouting at Nessa, 'You see! You accuse me and it is your aunt, your own aunt, a criminal just like her husband and her sons. Lord, protect me from these sinners!'

Anca, still standing, twisted round, and shoved Ag hard against the chest with both hands.

'Doh you speak of mih Ma an Pa like dat! You is ah nasty woman!' she yelled.

Ag fell backwards and landed on the hard sand with a shriek.

Percy, long silent listening to the latest bacchanal in the family, his ears flapping in the Mayaro breeze, began to cry. We had forgotten he was there.

'Come, Percy, my lad,' I said, hoisting myself out of my chair, 'let's go for a walk and let the adults sort it out.'

On the trip back to the Hill, Sasha gave Nessa a well-sliced piece of her mind.

Chaos Continued

We were home in time for tea and for the evening visitors who would keep on coming for a week or more to pay their respects, invariably staying too long on the long, soft couch in the living room. That evening the family sat on hard back chairs and listened politely to the conversation of condolence but I, for one, kept thinking about what Mira had said. It didn't make sense, except that, in a certain way, it did. June would not want the rings for herself, but she wouldn't want them to be buried, even if she had to hide them away so that no one would see them. Her affection for her nieces was real. June was a flighty, self-absorbed woman, but she wouldn't have done anything to hurt them. I didn't envy her when Nessa tackled her about it. As for Nessa herself, she had shouted herself out and by tomorrow would be wondering why people were vexed when all she had done was say what she had to say. She had insisted many times in the past that she never bore a grudge — and it was true — but she never seemed to learn that others might.

The living room was full that evening. Guests came and went, playing out the ritual of commiseration, offering the solid support of friendship. The primary guest was an elderly gentleman of African descent, Alvin McHalsey-Cormeau, a retired high court judge, who had sat with Badri on various committees over the years. There is no one as proper, as punctilious even, as an educated black Trinidadian of a certain generation. Dressed in a light tan tropical silk suit and tie, he managed to look as though he had never been hot in his life. Everything about him was ordered, including the expressions on his face. His wife, seated next to him on the couch, was a symphony in starch. Her garments creaked when she sat down. Both she and the judge had a ponderous, weighty manner of speaking and the accent, forced from the bridge of the nose through pinched nostrils, was pure Noel Coward. They seemed to have come from a different world, but, in their own way, they were warm and their friendship with Badri, if on the surface absurd, had been one of long standing.

We were listening to a long story from Mrs. Cormeau about their granddaughter who had a good job at the Bank of Montreal and a beautiful house in North York, when Sasha excused herself and disappeared from the room. She returned minutes later as our communal eyes were beginning to glaze over during an even longer tale of the success of another granddaughter, this one in Washington, the capital, of course, not the state, currently responsible for cataloguing the law books of a long deceased Justice of the.... And on and on and on.

Sasha stood behind me, reached over, unclasped her hand and dropped a small metal object into mine. I had no idea what she had given me until I looked down and saw an earring sitting in my palm. I was so surprised to see it there, as dull and tormented as it looked, that I lifted my open hand and it jumped up into the air, before bouncing onto the carpet. Everyone looked at the earring's progress until it came to a final resting place at the feet of the speaker. Her septuagenarian spouse peered down, and, following the line of his immaculately pleated trouser leg, leaned over to pick it up.

'A nice piece, Alexandra, my dear, but I think that you will find it will be vastly improved with a little polish. It seems to have been deprived of light. Was it lost?' he asked, examining the object through horn-rimmed, half-moon glasses.

Nurse had spent the evening sitting, ankles crossed, on a hard-backed chair next to the couch. She spoke for the first time.

'How yuh guess dat, Judge?' she marvelled. 'Is true, she lose it.' Then she uttered words Sasha would never forgive, 'It just now come out she battam!'

***

The evening ended in chaos. As soon as the last guest left, the whole family had turned on Nurse and, a fox at bay, she had retreated into her room until Soames, more enraged than I had ever seen him, rousted her out again. I'm sure he was on the verge of telling her to pack her bags when, suddenly, he clutched at his chest and sank back onto the couch gasping for air. Fleur immediately became hysterical and had to be pried off him. In her desire to help, she was in danger of suffocating the man. Jolyon, whose own heart was not good — he had had two triple bypasses — became chalk white, no mean feat for a man of his complexion, and abruptly sat down next to his brother. Ainsley, as was to be expected, wept. We were beside ourselves. The quarrel was forgotten and Nurse was needed in the rush.

During the next several minutes, I thought that we would be giving Dookie repeat business, but, gradually, order and better breathing were restored. Ainsley was dispatched to fetch the doctor — anything to get him out of the house, Sasha said — and we all had another cup of tea.

Everyone was calming down when Nessa took it into her head to say,

'Well, you'll have a quiet day tomorrow. We've' — meaning the four of us — 'been invited for lunch at Auntie June and we'll carry Anca home. We weren't going to go but it seems,' no pause here to consider June's three siblings, 'that it was Auntie June who took Daddy's rings off his hand in the casket, and I want to know why.'

Fleur jerked upright as if she had been shot.

And it began again.

It took quite a while to repeat what Mira had told us. Jolyon continued to say that he did not believe it. Fleur kept repeating,

'Nonsense! I never heard such nonsense in my life!' over and over. Soames, still a trifle unsteady, said little, but shook his hand at Nessa as though warding off an evil spirit. The doctor was taken aback when he arrived. The first thing he did was to ask for a cup of tea. He poked and prodded all the members of the older generation, took their blood pressure and felt their pulses. Fleur recovered sufficiently to say that she had not seen him at the funeral: it was an accusation, and the poor man admitted that he had not been able to make it.

'A patient at the Health Centre keel off just as ah was settin out, Auntie,' he said.

I looked at him hard but I did not recognize him although there was a general Sookbirsinghishness about his features. Something about the flatness of the back of his head, perhaps.

We went to bed with nothing resolved and it took me a long while to fall asleep. I was looking forward to the visit tomorrow since it would be my only outing to Port of Spain. I had arranged to stay overnight with Lincoln and visit a pan yard in St. James while the others returned home: my only time off the family leash for good behaviour on the trip.

I lay there thinking about the life in Trinidad that Sasha and I had had, years ago, when we were newly married and carefree, with a whole existence beyond family and the ties that bind. We used to dance and go the movies. Sasha always liked to take people along with us, and afterwards, at Johnson's Snackette or standing at a stall somewhere around the Savannah, there was great camaraderie and laughter. Lincoln was one of our best friends: we had known him at university and, later, he had taught at the same school as I did. He was the only black teacher and I the only white one, so we had come together for mutual support against the tribe of circling Indians who were in charge.

Lincoln: The Poisoner

I never knew where Lincoln Curley found the money to go to university. In any case, he never seemed to have any and was always on the borrow. He was, however, always meticulous about paying you back. Sasha hadn't known him in Trinidad. He spoke vaguely of growing up in Belmont. He and she had belonged to two different worlds even if those worlds were just a few miles apart. At university, he was always protective of her. He thought her too innocent by far to face the ways of North America, and the English boyfriend not likely to be of much help either. As it turned out, North America needed to be protected from Lincoln Curley. A case in point was the incident of the pepper.

Lincoln lived in a rooming house but ate his supper in any one of many cheap restaurants near the campus. One evening, he was seated at the counter of a diner when two young female students from his pysch class sat down next to him. Now, one thing Lincoln liked better than one young woman sitting beside him was two young women and he began to chat them up. They were well into a friendly conversation when the cook brought him his meatloaf and mashed.

Lincoln would tell happened next with a flourish.

'Ah look at dis nasty food. It looking real miserable, man. Ah brown plank ah meat an ah whitey pile ah lumpy potato. Not even a grain ah rice self. So ah reach in meh pocket an ah tek out meh peppa. Ah import dis peppa all dih way from Montreal, an, boy, is was hot. Ah well shake up dih bokkle an den ah shake it on meh food, good good, yuh know how.'

'"What dat?" one ah dey girl axe.'

(Editorial license permits me to say that the young lady, born and bred in the Ontario of the early sixties, would never have said 'What dat?' in her life, but this was Lincoln's story.)

To which he replied, 'Dat is peppa. Ambrosia tuh give all yuh Canadian food some spice! Tuh wet meh taste buds an smooth dih food as it go down meh palate tuh feed meh starving belly. Dat is meh muder milk. Dat is elixir from dih gods. Perfume tuh mend mih mind an flex mih body!'

'"Lemme just try a likkle on meh chicken", one ah dem girl say, an ah tell her, is not fuh she. She ent have dih stomach fuh it. Dih in-tes-tin-al for-ti-tude fuh peppa. It too strong. But she ent like dat and she say she'll just put ah bit on dih side ah she plate. An dih other one, ah blonde, man, a true true blonde, she say, "Go let she try it. An me also to besides"'

Lincoln gave an elaborate shrug.

'What ah go do? She put she hand on meh knee and ah ready tuh open mih heart tuh she, gi' she anyting she want! Papa yo! Well, yuh know, soon dey suckin in air and drinkin up water and dey eyes crying, an poppin out dey head from dih heat. An ah sayin, "What ah tell allyuh?" An dey saying, "No, no, is well good," an beggin fuh water. So anyway, ah finish meh food an ask dey girl if dey want tuh come by me fuh coffee, but dey say dey not feelin so good, so anoder time. An ah gone.'

Lincoln paused before continuing, relishing the telling of his story.

'Man, is dih middle of dih night an ah sleepin when ah hear a bangin at dih door. Ba dam bam. When ah open it, is two police standin dere and, behind one ah dem, dih likkle blonde girl, cryin. "Dat dih fella," she say, a she point at meh. "Is he try tuh poison we!" Dey march in tuh meh room, an me standin dere in meh merino. "He does have it in a bokkle in he coat!"'

At this point when telling the story, Lincoln would shake his head sadly and suck in a long, succulent breath. The wide gap between his front two teeth made him a highly adept and enviable steupser.

'Fuh dat! It tek meh two hour tuh tell dih police is mih peppa before dey does believe meh. An ah tired an ah have ah eight o'clock lecture nex morning. Ah tellin allyuh, dih moral uh dis story is — Lincoln say don give out yuh treasures tuh no papsie white girl just cause she bat she eye at all yuh. It ent worth it, man!'

Lincoln had many such stories to tell. Many were against himself. Trinis know how to laugh at themselves. He once told me the story of how, when he had just returned from Canada and was full of himself and his accomplishments, he went to a fete and asked a young woman to dance. While they were dancing, he told her all about himself, what he had done, how well he had done it, and what he was going to do in the future, generally making, as he admitted with a sad shake of his head, an ass of himself. Eventually, the young lady interrupted him and asked, 'What is your name again?'

'Lincoln,' he said, proudly. 'I is Lincoln,' surprised that she didn't know who he was.

'Who? Lincoln?' she asked again, 'Abraham Lincoln?' and walked away.

Port of Spain At Last

Driving along the Beetham Highway into Port of Spain the next morning, I was reminded of the first time I arrived there a lifetime ago. On that occasion, it was late at night and Sasha and Badri took me to a boarding house in Woodbrook and left me there. She was to pick me up after work the next day so that we could go to their house for dinner. I woke in the morning and looked out the window into the blinding light of my first day in the tropics.

After breakfast and a chat with my pleasant, light-skinned landlady, a half Portuguese woman, I ventured out. I had grown up in a provincial English town and the first time I saw a black person I was a teenager. Then I went to Toronto and there were precious few of them there either in those days. But I walked out of that house that first morning into a bustling world that teemed with them. They were walking the sidewalks, driving the cars and riding the bicycles. I never felt so pale in my life as on that first day. The sun itself was another shock. It was hot. It had no mercy as it beat down on me as I staggered along unacclimatized, not yet appreciative of its virtues. Where was I? What had I come to? I completed my walk rather more precipitously than I had intended and returned to sit on the landlady's veranda, contemplating the vista from the safe privacy of the shade.

I sat there until it struck me that sitting was not the answer, although, at that point, I was not sure what the question was, and I stood up to go out again. The people were no fairer and the sun was even stronger, but this time the walk proved more pleasant. The shock was wearing off. I found time to notice the architecture, the traffic, unknown plants in the front gardens of houses. I saw how deep the gutters were in the streets and that the grates were built to receive large amounts of water, not at all the sedate trickle of a more temperate clime. I only realized that the traffic went along the left side of the street when I was nearly killed crossing the road.

I gazed at the tall palm trees. I could not have recognized the difference between a coconut and an imperial palm that first morning, nor, in some cases I must admit, between an Indian and an African, but I found the very act of walking exhilarating, each step an exploration, a discovery. I had no local money, but I went into a grocery and saw different vegetables, read strange brand names on the canned goods, and caught the unusual smell of the establishment. Leaving the store, I saw an almost naked person approaching me and I crossed to the other side of the road. I passed a television station and came upon a huge, green, open space. A racecourse grandstand stood in the middle of it, a distance away. It seemed to be an enormous field. I was on the edge of the Savannah.

That day, I walked by other places that I would come to know well, to be entirely familiar with, then looking at them with the newest of eyes. I stopped by the gates of a school. The playground was crammed with small, dark, uniformed children and I wondered if the school at which I was about to teach would be like this one. I came upon a cemetery, alight in the searing sun, right by the main road, chock-a-block with gravestones, and tried to peer over the wall to obtain a better view of a burial in progress. Even then, a funeral!

I had become aware of how burningly warm I was in my long sleeved shirt and dress pants so I turned onto a major road and, not quite sure whether I was going in the correct direction, came across the naked gentleman again, now sitting on the curb. Seeing him somehow gave me confidence. I was going the right direction and I hardly even hurried by. I arrived back in a great mood, full of questions for when Sasha would arrive after three.

From that day forward, I have loved the city of Port of Spain — ah, what an exotic, romantic name — so totally different from anything I had ever seen before, so beyond what my mind had been able to imagine. Over time, it would became better known to me, its suburbs and its core, its attractions, the best ways to get around. I came to accept both the destitution of Shanty Town and the wealth of Goodwood Park. The luxury of the upside down Hilton impressed me but Sasha always preferred the more romantic Normandie, where we would dance the night away. I would walk from Independence Square towards Park Street, shop at Stevens, Todd and Fogarty's, stare in the windows of Y. De Lima's. Venturing further, I learnt where to find a pirate cab, a taxi, on Henry Street to take me home to Maraval, sharing it with Trinis hot and tired after work. I listened to Sasha sing in competition at Queen's Hall. Soames took me to races at the Savannah and Jolyon showed me the old cathedral and the tiny latticed houses of the old town. In the four years, that we lived there, it became home.

The city has changed considerably and I have been warned it is no longer always safe to walk everywhere because of 'choke and grab' and the poverty that will not go away, but I still enjoy its life and vitality, its contradictory torpid effervescence, its sweaty edginess. I am comfortable there.

I sat in the back seat of the car looking out of the window, examining the sights as we came into town. I feel certain that I had a smile hovering near my face as I put my fingers against the glass to acknowledge that I was back, whether the city was interested or not. The traffic was ferocious as always and we had to maneuver our way slowly along Wrightson Road, past the side of that first cemetery, round the Savannah to St. Ann's and on to June's.

'Whitehall has been painted,' I heard myself say pompously and laughed at myself that I could feel some kind of ownership of the Prime Minister's Office.

Sasha, who knows me to a tee, knew what I was laughing about and said, 'Dih boy tink he ah Trini!' And she laughed too.

June & Ram Entertain

When the car drew up in front of the Ramdass compound, the large ornamented iron gates were closed and Sonnilal had to speak into an intercom.

'Dis place like a jail,' said Anca, scornfully. 'Ah cyar even walk on dih grass or laser beams go set off a siren and scare meh to death. Daddy had tuh get rid ah Clive dih gardener, an he with us from long, cause he keep forgettin and dih neighbours complain about dih noise. If a mango fall in dih night, dih blasted alarms go off.'

'Well, at least you should be safe from burglars,' I suggested.

We went up the circular driveway and came to a stop in front of two massive mahogany doors, shiny with brass fittings. The doors opened and a smiling June came out in a dress made from a pink and gold sari material. Nessa had promised to behave — a promise that really meant very little — or, at least, not attack her aunt before we actually got inside the house, but Sasha and Anca were on edge and it showed.

'Come in, come in, we'll go through to dih pool,' June said. 'Fleur ent come? Where Ag?'

'Ag not feeling good an she stay home, Ma.'

Ag had been left pouting in her bedroom.

'Thank God fuh dat!' said June. 'Anca, tell Sonnilal tuh go round dih back. Cook will give he food in dih kitchen.'

Anca mimicked the words behind her mother's back, but all she said was, 'Yes, Ma. Ah gone.'

We went through an over-decorated house into the garden. Inside, heavy polished furniture with ivory inlay was the order ot the day; outside, a mini jungle, surrounding a kidney shaped pool, blocked out the sounds of the city. The multitude of plants reached out to tickle the back of your neck as you ducked by.

Ram was relaxing under a large umbrella with a drink in his hand. He didn't get up.

'What all yuh want tuh drink?' he asked. 'Clarence, tek orders.'

'It's a lovely pool, Uncle,' said Sasha.

'It bleddy expensive,' he replied, 'all dem chemical an ting, an a boy tuh tek out dih blasted leafs an all. It go bankrupt meh yet.'

'It dih only ting ah have that give meh joy an he want tuh full it up with cement!' complained June.

Since she was wearing enough jewellery to dress a shop window, we didn't take her too seriously. Nessa was clearly about to erupt if she did not say something soon, and James sat down next to her, giving her an occasional evil eye, to make sure she stayed in line — not the easiest of tasks at the best of times, and this was definitely not the best of times.

'Auntie,' she said at one point, 'Soames sent some breadfruit and mangoes. Sonnilal had it, he must have taken it to the kitchen,' she looked over at Anca, 'since he's eating there.'

June saw no bait to take.

'Ah know yuh ent come with yuh hand shaking,' she said, laughing. 'Let's go an eat.'

We sat down at an enormous round table with a lazy susan the size of a wagon wheel in the middle of it. Ram had designed it himself. I felt as though I was in a pricey Chinese restaurant, but Ramdass food is always excellent and I always looked forward to it. June could not cook to save her life but whoever she had in the kitchen was worth her weight in ghee. I would rather eat at the St. Ann's house than at any family house on the island. Every meal is a feast. This simple lunch, as June called it, included curried shrimp, goat, chicken, Chinese vegetables, white rice, roti, and, specially for me, potatoes in their jackets. Even Nessa couldn't find the time to broach the subject of the rings while tucking into a full plate, washing the food down with a generous rum punch. Ram kept telling James and me to 'fire another one' and the drinks flowed freely. He was feeling no pain himself.

Then, Nessa burst the bubble.

In a voice of burnished innocence, she said to June, 'Auntie, someone says you took off Daddy's rings off just before they closed the casket.'

The next sound to be heard was the sound of knives and forks clattering onto plates as they slid out of our panicked hands.

'Who tell yuh dat?'

'Is it true?'

'It could be that they saw wrong, Auntie,' suggested Sasha hastily, looking for a way out.

'No,' replied June, judiciously, 'it not wrong. It true. Ah tek dem awright.'

Ram choked on his drink, and spluttered, 'What for yuh did that, woman?'

'Yuh tink ah tief dem, Nessa? Is yuh bad mind. Yuh really tink ah tief yuh Daddy ring?' asked June.

Turning to Sasha, she continued, 'Chile, ah took dih ring, so dat when all yuh realize yuh shouldn't ah bury dem, ah have dem safe. Is foolishness tuh bury valuable ring like dat.'

Anca began to cry. 'Ah tell yuh, she ent tief them. She have a vault full ah she own already.'

June stood, only now realizing the full implication of what was being said. 'Well, ah never see more! Don't look at me like dat, Nessa. Cut eye doh kill, yuh know. Yuh tink ah tief yuh ring? Why I do dat? An yuh tell meh daughter dat I tief dem! Lawd, look at meh crosses!'

She began to cry.

Ram, having recovered from his shock a little, stared into an empty glass, and didn't seem to care one way or the other.

Nessa held her ground.

'What right did you have to take them? You knew we wanted to leave them on his fingers. His wedding ring from Mummy! And he always wore the other one. What business was it of yours? You aunts are all alike, minding people's business.'

Sasha rose to move between the two women.

'Auntie, really,' she said, softly. 'You shouldn't have. It wasn't what we wanted.'

June fled the room in tears, returning a moment later. She threw the two rings onto the dinner table. One of them landed on James' plate. He flinched.

'Take them,' she said, pulling herself up to her full height. 'Take them an good riddance. See if I try tuh help yuh in future. An leave meh house now.'

Anca held onto her mother's arm. 'Ma, yuh don't mean it, don't be so touchous! Everybody upset!'

'Upset! Of course, ah upset. An you no help! Yuh tink ah ent know what yuh doing, sou-souing arong wit dat coolie boy from dih village. Givin him sweet eye when yuh tink no one looking. Watch meh good. You stop seeing dat boy or yuh can leave wit dese ungrateful wretch.'

With the mention of Sonnilal, Ram woke up. 'Yuh seein dat coolie boy? How yuh mean! Ah go break every bone in he damn body,' he roared.

'You leave he alone!' Anca roared back.

Her father hauled himself out of the chair and raised his hand to slap her just as Sonnilal appeared in the doorway from the kitchen.

'Leave she alone,' he shouted. 'Hit she an ah go kill yuh!'

He pulled a knife from his back pocket and opened its blade. We were beginning to look like a bad amateur production of West Side Story. I folded my napkin neatly, next to my half-eaten food, and stood.

'I think,' I announced, as calmly as I was able, 'that perhaps we should leave before someone says something they'll regret.'

'Too late fuh dat!' June swung round to me in a rage, 'Take yuh wife an yuh damn sister-in-law, an tek meh daughter if yuh like, an leave. Ah ent want any of allyuh in meh house again!'

***

We sat on the pool terrace at the Hilton and drank. Nessa was furious yet exultant, although, at the same time, she knew she had gone too far. James looked as though he would have skinned her alive if someone had handed him the necessary implements. Anca, who had melted into Sonnilal's arms, was sobbing quietly. Sonnilal had never been to the Hilton before and was gazing around, awed by the luxury of the place, while he tried to console her. How often would he be able to bring her back here again, I wondered? Sasha kept suggesting that we go back to St. Ann's and apologize. Right now, before it was too late. I played with Badri's two rings, turning them over in the palm of my hand, wondering whether they were even remotely worth the amount of trouble they had caused.

'Nessa, did you have to? What will Uncle Soames say?' Sasha's voice was grief-stricken.

'Well, somebody had to say something! She took the rings!' replied Nessa, scornfully. 'Why shouldn't I ask her?'

'But did you have to do it like that?'

'Like what?'

'So accusingly.'

'She took the rings, Sasha. How else was I supposed to say it? Anyway, she'll get over it. Everything will be all right in the morning.'

'Not with me,' sobbed Anca, 'Ah ent goin back. Ever.'

'Just wait until Ag hears about this,' I said, wryly, 'Whose side will she be on?'

'And Auntie Fleur! It's her sister! My God, Vanessa, do you never think before you speak?' Sash was furious with her sister.

'Oh you, Miss Priss! You wanted to know. You just wanted me to do the dirty work. She stole your father's rings.'

'But she didn't mean to steal them. She was keeping them for us. She thought it was a waste.'

The argument continued until it was time to leave. Each of them, however, made sure that she didn't go too far either in recrimination or by saying something that could not easily be taken back. James and I looked at each other over our drinks, knowing the score and treading warily. We knew what would happen next, that Nessa would boil down and Sasha would play the peacemaker. I think we also realized, however, that too much had been said for there to be a quick reconciliation, particularly since Anca and Sonnilal had also become embroiled in everything. Anca would defend Sonnilal against all comers and her father would never forget a knife pointed at his throat. I have to say that I would agree with him there.

It had been arranged that I would remain overnight in Port of Spain with Lincoln, while the rest of the group went back to the Hill. The thought of what was likely to happen there made me determined to return with them, but Sasha was adamant that I stay in town. It made sense in a way. Although I would have liked to have been there to support her in the confusion and argument that was bound to occur, I had to agree that she would do better handling Fleur and the uncles without me, and, if Nessa kept on as she was, I was liable to lose my cool and give her a piece of my mind, which would not have helped anybody.

It was also a fact that, as an outlaw, lacking the blood if you wish, I tended to keep out — even was kept out — of the more acrimonious family quarrels. It was an interesting phenomenon. It wasn't that my opinion would not have been listened to, and even valued, but rather that such quarrels were, in some way, private and demeaning to how they viewed themselves. I had noticed that Badri, too, had always tended to step away when Sookbirsingh ructions began to erupt. James, I knew, would keep in the background — although, in his case, his presence might well be required to prevent Nessa from coming to blows with some of the combatants. Certainly, Sasha knew my opinion about what had happened and could represent it, should she feel it might carry weight.

There was also the matter of the Will. Sasha and I had decided that, since I would not be needed when it was read, I might as well stay away. We had discussed what she would do depending on what might be in the two documents and I was confident that, although she might like my support in case there were any surprises, she would not need it.

Lincoln had undertaken to carry me to a pan yard to hear a steel band practicing that evening and I was eager to be there. He had also piqued my interest on the phone by whispering that there was someone he wanted me to meet, but that I was not to tell Sasha as it might upset her, and not to tell anyone else either. He had been very cryptic, saying also that we should not go later than eight o'clock or we would be too late. I hadn't any idea what he was talking about, but Lincoln was like that: secretive, a little mysterious and well aware of the impression he was making.

Murder, Trinidad Style

I met Lincoln at his flat behind Queen's Royal College, dropped off by the others before their journey south. Lincoln, in punctilious form although he had never liked Nessa, invited everyone in for tea but Sonnilal wanted to beat the traffic and get away before rush hour. After they left, I sat under Lincoln's ceiling fan to cool off, Earl Grey at my elbow, and I asked him whom it was he wanted me to meet. He was clearly nervous about what to reveal, part of him enjoying the situation, while another part seemed to be worried whether he was doing the right thing. He asked me twice if I had mentioned anything to Sasha and when I asked him what I could have told her, he was reassured.

'You can tell her yourself, man, when you see her if you decide you want to, or should. But I didn't want her to know about it beforehand. I was told not to, that she shouldn't know.'

'Well,' I replied, 'you've certainly whetted my appetite.'

'Let's wet it some more! How about a rum and coke?'

We sat a while and chatted. This was a very different Lincoln from either the poverty-stricken university student or the posing teacher of his young manhood. Somewhere along the years, Lincoln had discovered who he was and relaxed into himself. He had always had a private and a public face. His private face was the face of friendship but his public one could be calculated and slightly theatrical, sometimes pretending, sometimes almost pretentious. It was like his surname which began life as a single word, Curley, only becoming double-barrelled when Paxton and the silly little hyphen was added in his salad days. In later years, more secure and mature, both mercifully disappeared. One felt that he had come to know who he was and didn't need to pretend to be something he was not anymore. Even his accent had changed.

Lincoln brought me up to date on politics, wanted to know what books I had read recently and what plays in Toronto were worth the money. He told me about the school at which we had both taught. I never thought he would have kept up with its progress, but he seemed to know chapter and verse about its accomplishments and what had been happening with several of our old colleagues.

I was reminded that 'liming' — meeting up with your friends for a drink — included a passion for ole talk, gossip, and that Trinidadian men are as devoted to it as much as their womenfolk are. Calypsos and the tabloid press tell stories, put a satiric spin on them or find a humorous slant to a serious situation, but you don't have to be a calypsonian or a journalist to know how to tell a story. Trinidadians learn that lesson with their mother's milk.

'Did you hear what happened to Selwyn Jankisoon?' he asked.

'No, I haven't spoken to Selwyn for years.'

'An you ain't going to speak to he soon, my friend.'

The accent was already beginning to fray at the edges. Liquor and the talk would loosen both his tongue and the way he spoke. In any case, you don't tell a good Trini story in the King's English. Trinidad is a republic, anyway.

'What happened?'

'He was principal at dih government school in Arima, an he take up with one ah dem Senior Cambridge student, a big, buballupse, creole girl from Grande. Dey say one day she fader an muder turn up at he school an cuff he dong and tell he tuh leave she alone, or he go find out. Den dih talk is, he get she pregnant. Well, one weekend he lyin in he bed, a car drive up and call out he name. He next door neighbour hear dih talk. Dih fella in dih car say how Selwyn school on fire an, if he come quick, he could give he a lift.'

Lincoln started to laugh.

'He come rushin out dih door in he merino and he watchicong yellin, "Come leh we go!" an den all dih neighbour hear is screamin an getting on, an Selwyn bawlin, "Oh God, don kill meh, don kill meh," before dih car drive off.'

Lincoln shook his head.

'When dih neighbour come dong tuh see what happen, he find Selwyn lyin in ah pool ah he blood. He did be have twenty-two lash wih a cutlash an dih machete did nearly decapitate him. Dey kill he fuh so!'

'But that doesn't make sense,' I said.

'As man! Dat is what I say! Black people don know 'bout cutlash. Dey does blow yuh head off with a gun or dey bash yuh brain in wih ah calabash, but cutlash is coolie people weapon.'

'So did the police arrest the father of the girl?'

'Dey arrest him, oui. Dey go straight tuh he house an pick he up. But dey ent find no weapon, an dey ain't find no blood in he car or on he clothes.'

'So they let him go?'

'Ab-so-lute-ly. It turn out dih man bruder is ah Inspector from San Juan, so dih fella ain't even charge. Dey let him go, an he at he work by lunch.'

'Wow,' I said, 'that's amazing. Not even to question the man. Typical in this wonderful land of yours, but pretty bad as well.'

'But wait, nah man. Dat not dih end ah dih story. When Selo muder hear her boy dead, she take in with a stroke an she dead next morning. She kick off! An she have tree son as well as Selo, and, when dey see dere muder dead, they off straight to dih girl fader house, push in he door and do fuh dih whole family. Dey find dem all dere. Fader, muder, dih girl, two picknee, and an ole grandmoder, to besides. All dey kill dere wit cutlash self! Half Selo family sittin in death cell on Frederick Street! Did yuh ever see more?'

'Only in Trinidad,' I said, shaking my head with laughter.

'Is true talks,' replied my host with a sigh, shaking his head.

'But who killed Selo then?' I asked.

Solemnly shaking his head, Lincoln replied, 'No one know.'

He sighed again, looking at the clock on the wall. 'But see the time. We should be going.' Lincoln was reverting, his cultivated accent taking charge again. 'But first, I want you to change your clothes. We is we, but yours are too good! You look like a foreigner!'

'Ask mih dat, nuh! I is a foreigner?!' I replied, mocking, but he went into his bedroom anyway and returned with a pair of khaki pants and a hot shirt.

'At least you're wearing sandals,' he said. 'My shoes are too big for you to walk in!'

'Never happen, boy!' I replied, 'Steups.'

Lincoln threw back his head and we laughed.

Meeting Irene

Finally fitted out to Lincoln's satisfaction, we took a taxi downtown, before setting off, on foot, along Independence Square towards the old cathedral. I hadn't seen it for years: it was no longer an area where I would feel comfortable wandering around by myself. We passed it by and moved further on into the oldest part of the city.

'Where on earth are we going?' I asked.

We stopped to buy snow-cones from a little wagon at the side of the street. People were looking at us, but Lincoln sat down on the curb and motioned me to join him. The sidewalk was dirty and, although the gutter was dry, it was cluttered with the detritus of the bustling city. I eased myself down beside him. He, dreadlocks spilling out from one side of his woollen cap, looked entirely at home, but even in decked out in his clothes, sockless and wearing sandals, I felt out of place. I felt a tension in myself that I didn't like, just as I didn't like to acknowledge that there were places I should probably not visit in the city.

'Lincoln, what's going on?' I asked. 'You're going to have to tell me sometime.'

He sighed. 'Do you remember in college where I said I came from?' he began.

'Belmont,' I replied, looking around, 'but this isn't Belmont.'

'No, it's not and I lied. I was born and raised in Laventille. But, in those days, you didn't go to Queen's Royal College and say you came from Laventille, so I said I came from Belmont.'

Laventille climbs the hills above downtown Port of Spain. I knew little about the place except that the houses were small, the poverty considerable and no one in the family went anywhere near it. Looking up the road towards it now, Laventille seemed both a reason for excitement and a cause of apprehension.

'Okay, but why are we going there?'

'My mother still lives there. She won't leave. I've asked her to live with me or she could live with my sister,' – I hadn't known he had a sister — 'but she says she was born there and she will die there. It's her home.'

'So you want me to meet her?'

'No! Yes! But she's not the reason we're going.' He paused to gather his thoughts. 'The other day I was home to see Mammy,' he smiled at his use of the word. 'I was telling her about this funeral I had to attend. Your father-in-law's funeral. My Auntie, she's not my real Auntie, she lives next door, was visiting and as we were talking I mentioned that his name was Badri.' Lincoln paused. 'Auntie said she knew him.'

He looked down at his feet and paused again before continuing.

'I said to her that she couldn't know him. Well, that put her in a state. She drinks too much and it's not good for her, but she kept on insisting that she certainly did know him. She was his sister-in-law, she said.'

I was completely lost.

'What? Who?'

'His sister-in-law. She explained the whole thing. She knew what she was talking about. I know her well enough to realize that she was telling the truth, even if she was half charged by the time we had finished.'

'But who is she? What's her name?'

'Well, she's called Irene. Auntie Irene. She said she was the oldest sister, the oldest in her family. I'd never heard her last name and I've known her all my life.' He paused. 'Sookbirsingh.' He rushed on. 'Then, when I told her that you, Dr. Badri's son-in-law, was going to stay over a night with me, she said to bring you. She knew about you. Knew you were white. I didn't know what to say!' He shrugged. 'I asked her if I should bring Sasha, too, but she said she didn't want to bother her, but to bring you.'

I was totally confused. I had heard about Irene, of course, but only a little. Sasha's knowledge of her was hazy at best. I did recall that once, when we were discussing the family, she told me that she suspected that she and Nessa had only been given an expurgated version of Irene's story. I was pretty sure, too, that Sasha didn't know whether her aunt was alive or dead. I certainly couldn't begin to imagine how a Sookbirsingh had come to live in Laventille, or what I would ever say to her when we met.

With his fingernail, Lincoln poked at the remains of his snowcone and interrupted my thoughts.

'I would never have gone to university if it hadn't been for her. Mammy can't hardly read, but Auntie Irene was always reading — the papers, Mills and Boon novels, religious tracts, anything she could get her hands on. But she also read serious things; big thick volumes with small print. When I was about eight years old, she took me by the hand down to the public library in Woodford Square and got me a library card. It was the beginning of a new world for me and I adored her.'

He shook his head and laughed ruefully.

'I didn't even realise she was an Indian until I was about twelve and she told me stories about the cane fields and how they burned the sugar to harvest it.'

He stopped, putting his head on one side looking off into the distance.

'Now she's old and sick and she drinks too much — even then she drank too much — but I know I would never have left here if it hadn't been for her. She changed my life. She helped me with my homework. Mammy couldn't — she could only cuff me down when I didn't want to do it. Auntie Irene had six children of her own and they've all done well. Over the years she had three husbands but she was never married that I know of, and now she's alone, still next to Mammy, still reading. When she isn't drinking. Even when she is.' He shook his head, wryly glancing at his watch. 'Come, if we don't get there soon, she'll be too drunk to know.'

***

And so we climbed the narrow streets of Laventille. There were fewer burglar bars there. People sat out on the front steps of their tiny barrack-like houses chatting with one another in the cooling air. A group of men turned from a heated discussion to look at us, but seeing Lincoln they waved and called out 'Goodnight'. I would have thought they were planning mayhem, but Lincoln said they were probably talking about cricket. He was amused at my nervousness and advised me to relax. Eventually, we turned onto a side road, not wide enough for a car, and came upon a small house, the single front step of which touched the dusty pavement. A narrow double door was half open and the light from a lamp peered hesitantly into the city dark.

'Mammy, you dere?' Lincoln called out. Now, it was he who was nervous. He glanced at me to see how I would react.

'Lincoln, is you?'

'Oui, Mammy,' said this most independent and sophisticated of men, 'Is me.'

An old lady, short and stout, came to the door. She beamed, and her son leaned over and kissed her on the top of her head.

'Go quick,' she said to him, after he had introduced me, 'before she too gone tuh know. Come back when yuh finish.'

Lincoln led me to the house next door. It was set back a little from the road, behind, on the hillside, made out of wood that I don't think had ever seen paint. The one window that I could see was without glass. A shutter, hinged along the top, was propped open with a stick, and pink net curtains floated in the evening breeze.

'Auntie! Auntie Irene!' Lincoln called out gently from the bottom of the steps.

A tall, very dark woman appeared in the doorway. Her head was bound with a flowered handkerchief. Her dress was old and faded, but clean and starched. It belonged to another age and it hung loosely on her. Her face, almost black from the sun, was gaunt, almost wizened, but, as she stood there in the doorway, there was perhaps a resemblance to Fleur in the way she carried herself. Sookbirsingh women walk like the royalty they know themselves to be, and Irene held her shoulders high and her head back in that same almost strutting way. Sasha has that same magisterial stance and there was something in Irene's eyes that reminded me of my wife as well.

She slopped a tumbler full of a brown liquid in her hand.

'Auntie, dis is Ee-an-uh, I was telling yuh about.'

'Come, let me see yuh, boy,' she said, holding out both hands, and also the glass, towards me. I moved forward. Setting the glass aside, she took my face in her hands and looked down at me.

I knew neither what to do nor to say.

'Ee-an-uh,' she said. Then, correcting herself: 'Ian.'

She rolled the word around her tongue. Her breath was liquor, one hundred proof. She squinted as though to fix my face in her memory. I think I must have been the first member of her family she had touched in forty years, even though I was white and there was no blood.

Then she said, 'How yuh treat meh niece, mista man? Yuh treating her well good?'

'Yes, I am,' I stammered, 'I didn't know to bring her. Lincoln said not.'

She turned into the house and I followed her inside. Lincoln stood behind, on the bottom step.

The front room was ten feet square. It held a small table, a kerosene lamp, two Demerara chairs and books. Books everywhere: on the floor, behind the chairs, on a small bookcase made of planks and concrete blocks. Everything was immaculately clean, the floor scrubbed like Irene herself, the books showing not a speck of dust. Even the glowing lamp betrayed no errant dust mote floating in the air. Irene sat down on one of the chairs. It was low to the ground and her knees were high, level almost to her face as she looked at me.

'Sit,' she commanded, 'an tell mih all about them.'

I hardly knew where to begin, but I told her why we were in Trinidad. I told her about the death, the wakes, the funeral, then about my history with the family, what the house on the Hill looked like now and how the funeral cortege had left from it. She hardly spoke a word, devouring every one of mine.

Eventually, I stopped speaking and we listened in silence to the slight sizzle of the oil lamp. It was well past eight o'clock. She nodded her head. She reached up, pouring rum from an open bottle into her glass and then more into another glass that stood beside it on the table. Half a glass of neat brown rum. It was an enormous amount and there was no coke in sight.

'Come,' she said, 'fire one with me.'

The old woman reached forward and we clinked glasses. Irene cackled. I realized that she was not sober, that she was holding herself steady with an effort, that the drink was fighting her natural dignity and grace. It might overwhelm her, but there still echoed in her something of long ago, a still alive sense of undefeated self. I could see that she had hardly any teeth in her mouth and, not wanting to embarrass her, did not want to look at her too closely, but I was fascinated by everything about her.

'Tell me about yourself.' I spoke gently, leaning forward.

She lifted her shoulders and shrugged.

'No need for that. Tell me how my brothers are? Are they well? Jo! How is my darlin boy, Jo? And Fleur? And little June? How is that husband of hers? Is he still keeping out of jail?'

The more we spoke, the more precise her speech became, patois slowly being left behind.

'How much do you know about them?'

'I read the papers. They used to be in the society pages, and then you could always see pictures of Soames and Jo in the Sports when their horses won,' she sighed. 'Now if I want to see them, I turn to the obituaries.'

'You should have come to the funeral.'

She laughed, head back, mouth wide open.

'No, it's too late for that! I have another family here.'

She peered around the room.

'Sasha would like to meet you.' I was sure of it.

She corrected me. 'Alexandra. I have a picture of her singing at Queen's Hall. Would you like to see?'

'Yes, but no one calls her that these days. It's Sasha. She's Sasha to everyone.' I laughed. 'I sometimes call her Sash.'

Irene opened a book that had been lying next to her on the floor and took out a faded piece of newsprint. In a photograph, Sasha was singing, joyous, eyes alive, on a stage. She was wearing a blue dress. The photograph had been taken at a music festival just a few months after we had been married. I had seen it before, so many years ago, in the newspaper, and I well remembered the day. I had been in the audience, proud of her success.

'I saw her that day' said Irene, pride for Sasha in her voice 'I was there when she won!'

'So was I!' I replied. 'Isn't that amazing?' I remembered I had a picture of Sasha in my wallet. 'Would you like to see a photograph of her now?'

It was a one of the three of us; Sasha, m and Nicolas. I explained who he was, told her what he was like. Time passed. She was becoming sleepy in front of me.

'Would you like to keep it?' I asked, gently.

She shook her head, but there was a wistfulness in the gesture.

'It's okay. I have another at home. Next time I come, I'll bring lots of pictures,' I pressed. 'And I'll bring Sasha with me, if you like.'

She nodded, but her eyes were closing. She brought an almost empty glass to her lips again before, without opening her eyes, placing it on the edge of the table. I put my own glass down, hardly a sip missing, beside it.

I thought she was asleep, but very quietly I heard her say, 'Tell them I love them. Tell them all, I love them still.'

I sat with her for a while longer until I heard Lincoln returning and then I stood. I picked up my glass from the table and carried it out to the doorway, pouring away the rum as quietly as I could onto the ground at the side of the steps. Lincoln looked up at me. There were tears in his eyes. I took the glass back inside and placed it quietly next to hers on the table.

'I will,' I said.

Sweet Pan

Steel band music is close to the soul of Trinidad and you have to be there to hear it. It doesn't record well, somehow missing the raw kankalang of the percussion, the real sound of wood beating on metal, and the mellow undertones that flow from the tenor pans. Listen to it live in concert or, even better, during practice under the stars in a yard. They were already playing when we arrived at the top of the narrow street in St. James and made our way between parked cars towards the sound. People were sitting on the curb outside the gates and on the bonnets of their cars. The faintly sickish smell of ganja blended with the haze of the evening. Music hung there pulsing in the air, smooth yet vivacious. Alive. Grown men and women did little private dances in the warmth, and sweet pan enveloped the night.

Lincoln marched ahead of me into the yard and shook hands with several people he knew. The multi-coloured tam sat high on the back of his head. His passion these days, he had informed me back at the flat, was music. No more film. I knew he had passed on that long ago. He was largely finished with the theatre too, though several of his plays were performed regularly throughout the Caribbean. He had turned to pan music and Rastafarianism and become a connoisseur of both. What did I want to know about the instruments, about the band, his friends asked me. Had I heard steel pan before? Lincoln explained that I used to live not far away, had been married at the little Woodbrook Presbyterian Church a few streets over, and their politeness after being introduced was replaced by camaraderie.

One of the men passed me some weed and would not take no for an answer, so I went over to a row of bleachers, where people of all types, tourists even, were listening to the rhythm of the music, and lit up. When a new set began, I leaned back, closed my eyes and smoked. Sound was everywhere. It was in my hair, its energy bounced around in my chest. It hummed. It flared. It was honey on the landscape of my mind, incense in the night. I opened my eyes to look around the yard. Young boys, as entranced as I was, dangled from the branches of a mango tree in one corner.

I could see the music ahead of me, coming towards me. It entered my mouth, my nostrils and my very pores with its velvet perfection. After days of death, I needed to be alive again. Tears jumped into my eyes. Ah Trinis, I thought, what a place you have. Don't spoil it. Keep your beautiful, decaying, corrupt, exasperating Eden and allow me to share it with you every now and then.

Lincoln slouched down besides me, spreading his long legs in front of him. He threw an arm around my shoulder and looked up into the night, smiling.

'Dis dih life!' he said, taking the last piece of the smoke from my hand. 'Dih gifts of God, for dih people of God.'

It didn't seem like blasphemy at all.

He shook his dreadlocks and laughed.

When we came back to his apartment after midnight, music still in our heads, echoing through our tired bodies, playing itself in our weary steps, there was a message from Sash on the answering machine.

'Make sure you're back here for lunch. The Will will be read at two o'clock and the solicitor has asked that you be there. So mind you manners and come. You must be in the Will! If you don't want to take a taxi, I'll ask Sonny to come and get you, but let me know. Uncle Soames told Nessa off, but there wasn't too much trouble. I think he's very tired. Auntie Fleur was upset too, but she's get over it. I phoned Auntie June, but she wouldn't take my call. I could strangle Nessa. I miss you. See you in the morning.'

A Great Reckoning In A Little Room

Assraf Khan's office is the upper floor of a house behind Harris Promenade, not far from the courthouse and just across from Paradise cemetery. We had to circle the area twice to find a parking place. Trinidadians are great litigants and the crush of vehicles demonstrated that the legal profession was thriving. We left the car in the hands of a security guard who, it turned out, had once driven a taxi for Soames and who looked like a kid at Christmas over the prospect of driving a Benz around the block searching for a space. With Sasha and me were Nessa, Didi and Soames. Each had been asked to be present.

'Ah ent know what I goin tuh the reading for. It ent make sense!' mused Soames, who was missing his time out on the front gallery with his newspapers. 'What Morton up to?'

'I wonder the same thing,' I said. I had been picking at the thought all night. 'And why not James?'

'Daddy didn't know James as well as he knew you. Nessa and James have only been married ten years. Not that long compared to us,' replied Sasha.

'Yes, but he liked James. Heaven knows, he never liked me.'

'How can you say that?'

'Because it's true, that's why. If everyone hadn't warned him to behave, he wouldn't have given you away on your wedding day.'

'That was almost thirty years ago. He had changed his mind since then. And you know it.'

'Well, I don't like it.'

'Sweet Jesus, stop whining!' interjected Nessa. 'Nurse is the one we have to worry about. She's up to something and we're about to find out what. If she was playing with Daddy's mind these last months, I'll take her to court so fast her head will spin.'

The Nissan was somewhere behind us, Ainsley driving, carrying Nurse, Honaria and Clara.

'Relax, both of you,' said Sasha. 'Daddy wouldn't do anything foolish. How many times did you see anyone push him around, even at the last? I'm more concerned that Ag wasn't invited. She's been in a foul mood ever since she heard.'

Sasha had told me that when Mr. Khan had phoned to say that Soames and I should be there, Ag took the phone and demanded to know why her name had not been mentioned. Mr. Khan apparently replied that she was not named as a beneficiary in the Will. She, spluttering into the phone, replied that she should be there to represent her husband, and, she presumed, her offspring, but Mr. Khan must have indicated – I could just hear him saying it — that this would not be necessary at this time and that he himself would represent the interests of Roh or any other individual who might, or might not, be mentioned in Badri's Will.

Ag was not discouraged.

Roh, she informed the solicitor, had instructed her to attend on his behalf. After listening to what was said on the other end of the line, she slammed the phone down, called for her Maker's assistance, burst into tears, and refused to say what Mr. Khan had said to her.

On the other hand, she had plenty to say to me privately about the fact that Honaria and Clara were to be there. It would have been difficult to say it in front of Badri's daughters and she was no longer speaking to Fleur. She did complain all the way through lunch that Clara had put far too much salt in the chicken. She also commented to James, me sitting there in plain sight, that she noted that he, another in-law, obviously wasn't in the Will either, even if I was. Some people apparently had favourites, she declared. James shrugged and said that I knew his father-in-law far better than he did and everything was fine with him.

I had never considered myself a favourite of Badri, far from it, but I was intrigued that, somehow, I was apparently mentioned in his Will even if it was as, as I suspected, 'my dear daughter's protoplasmic spouse'. In any case, I would not have missed being there for anything. I had been back at the Hill by ten o'clock in the morning, ready to go.

Nurse had been very quiet during lunch, no one was speaking to her much anyway, but for a thin woman she had a very fat and satisfied smile on her face. She declared that the chicken tasted just right. Everyone was in agreement that her employment would be terminated after the reading of the Will. Initially, there had been talk of letting her go before Badri was buried, but, it had been decided in whispered gallery conversations, that this would have been both too precipitous and too obvious. Then, when he heard about the codicil, Soames wanted her gone immediately, and it was only the combined front of Sasha, Fleur and Nessa that dissuaded him. Nessa pointed out that if Nurse was still with them, they could at least keep an eye on her.

Keeping an eye on her had already proved necessary. Everyone had heard Nurse screaming at Ainsley on the side gallery earlier in the morning. She had lambasted him with harsh words and, if they heard correctly, used more than a few physical cuffs to persuade him to make up with her. The breeze had carried their discourse to every part of the old house and everyone sat there congealed with embarrassment for them both. It might have been better had he fought back more and wept less, but it was all over when Nessa went to tell the two of them to behave themselves, or else. With Nessa, 'else' was a considerable threat, and not one to be taken lightly

Ainsley's car arrived just as we were about to climb the stairs to the solicitor's office, so everyone went up together, single file. The old wooden steps creaked and we seemed to be raising a significant amount of dust getting there. At the top, we rang the bell and were ushered into Mr. Khan's office.

The old gentleman was a contemporary of Badri, cut from the same cloth. The kind of man who felt most comfortable at a fete in a three-piece suit. He was known to be a stickler for the legal niceties and, in truth, he looked a little like a stick himself. Tall and brittle, he reached out a boney hand to each of us, indicating where we were to sit. Honaria and Clara, dressed to the nines for the occasion, were directed to the very back row, next to his secretary. I was placed in the row in front of them, as was Ainsley. Nurse sat on my other side. Sasha was directed to the front row, along with Nessa, but I was surprised that there were a number of empty chairs between us.

We were hardly seated when the door opened and Paulie Goberdan appeared. He nodded to Soames two rows behind Sasha, and not quite catching her eye, shook Sasha's hand. Nessa would not look at him, and he moved on to Mr. Khan, who elaborately directed him to a chair next to his own. It must have been placed there for just this purpose. The old solicitor, a man of few words and less frivolity, went back to reading the documents in front of him, frowning as he did so. This didn't worry me too much. He was not known as much of a smiler. He made a steeple out of his hands and silently tapped two forefingers together.

Heavy footsteps were heard coming up the stairs. They ceased briefly and then began again. The door opened and Ivor Seeram, Badri's eulogist, came in puffing. Now this was interesting! No one had calculated that he would be in the Will. With a wide smile on his glowing face, he looked around. Seeing Badri's daughters, he bounced over to kiss them warmly on both cheeks before settling himself down next to Didi in the row behind. He turned round to acknowledge Soames before beginning a whispered conversation with the old lady.

I had the feeling that I was back in church. We were seated, I imagined, in the pews of a musty old chapel, the chosen few gathered together for worship. We spoke in subdued voices, respectful of where we were and our purpose in being there. Mr. Khan's heavy brown desk, piled high with documents and the bulging binders of his profession, had the appearance of a communion table encumbered by the accoutrements of the faith. The two solicitors, acolytes both, were seated behind it, ready to serve us the bread and the blood red wine of Badri, based on the gospel he had left behind.

Even the air of the place supported its sanctity. Mr. Khan kept the louvers of his office firmly closed, protecting our doings from the pagan hurly-burly of the world outside. The only daylight that was able to eke its way inside came where the windows had buckled with age and wear and tear. Dust motes floated freely, visible when they were caught in the narrow slats of sunlight that, in two or three places, penetrated the general gloom. I bowed my head in the silence and did not quite know what to do with my hands. A psalter would have been appropriate: perhaps it would have kept them still. I said a silent prayer.

'Oh Lord, may this turn out better than I think it will.'

Was this what a life came down to: the dry distribution of a man's belongings in his lawyer's chambers, a great reckoning in a little room? Would we apostles survive the service that was about to begin? Would a doctrinal schism be the outcome of what we were about to hear? Would we cleave together and, forsaking all others, go forth united. I had my doubts. Then Nurse stirred in her chair beside me and I woke from my reverie. I followed the progress of a small, black beetle zig-zagging across the floor in front of me. As I watched, Nurse moved her small, ankle-socked foot sideways and ground it underneath the sole of her shoe.

So much, I thought, for the hopes of the innocent. Once again, I knew that there was going to be trouble.

***

Mr. Khan, looked around, clearing his throat. 'Just one more, I think,' he said, turning to Paulie for confirmation.

'Um, yu yu yes, su su sah,' replied Paulie.

One more! I wondered who could that be?

The door opened and June stood framed in the light behind it. She scanned the room, twisting her purse nervously in her hands. Everyone turned round to look at her.

'Ah,' said Mr. Khan, 'come in, Mrs. Ramdass. Do sit down. We were waiting for you.'

I felt reasonably sure that no one in the room had been waiting for June, and that they were just as surprised as I was to see her there. Sasha half rose out of her chair to greet her but June went quickly to sit next to Soames. Soames looked as though he could not have been more surprised if she had arrived stark naked. The old solicitor waited until the whispered mutterings that had spread like poison ivy across the room ceased, and cleared his throat once again.

'Well, Vanessa, Alexandra, ladies and gentlemen, shall we begin? We are here this afternoon to read the Last Will and Testament of your father, and, if I may be permitted to say it, my good friend, Morton Badri. Morton,' he smiled briefly, as though fearing it might cause his face to splinter, 'was my friend of many years standing and, as I know you are aware, I was also his solicitor for many, many years. It was, therefore, somewhat of a surprise, indeed shall I say a shock, when, umm, Mr. Paul Goberdan,' Mr. Khan peered down his nose at Paulie, 'advised me recently of a document that he had in his possession and with which he thought I should be acquainted. As you will be aware, Mr. Goberdan is himself a solicitor practising at 45 Roberts Street in Port of Spain.'

Good grief, I thought, at this rate we will be here all afternoon.

'The document, after a careful perusal is, in point of fact, an addition to the last Will and Testament of Morton Badri, properly written and witnessed September 15 last, in Mr. Goberdan's, umm, chambers.'

He pointed the end of a finger at Paulie, as though indicating something not quite fit for human consumption.

'Mr Goberdan and I are agreed that its contents constitute not a new Will but, rather, that it is, from the internal wording of the document, an, umm, addendum.'

He held up a single sheet of paper and looked at us over the top of his glasses.

'Yes, indeed. This is an, umm, addendum to the Will I have in my possession and which was signed here in my chambers some two and a half years ago.'

Mr. Khan raised his other hand indicating a folder in which we could see several sheets of paper.

'While, if I may be allowed to say so, this is not the way I would have preferred such an important procedure to be undertaken,' he peered at Sasha and Nessa as though they were somehow to blame, 'there is no doubt in my mind that Mr. Goberdan's processes were, umm, satisfactory in a legal sense and consistent with the standards of his profession.'

Mr. Khan managed to say this as though he himself was in a completely different, not to say a higher, profession. He surveyed the room.

'Are there any questions so far?'

'Yes!' announced Nessa, her voice cracking through the sanctuary of the place like a whip

Mr. Khan blinked. I felt certain he was not used to, and would not take kindly to, interruptions. On the other hand, he surely knew Nessa.

'Yes, Mr Khan,' she repeated. 'How do you know that Daddy was in his right mind last September, and that he was capable of making a new Will?'

Mr. Khan spoke to her as to a child, 'Ah, my dear. Not a new Will.' He wagged a finger in the negative. 'An, umm, codicil. That is to say, an addition to the extant and legal Will.'

He held up and shook each document in turn.

Nessa was not to be waylaid.

'But how do you know he was 'compos mentis' last September? Ever since he had a stroke, Daddy hadn't been well. Sometimes, he knew what he was doing and, sometimes, he didn't.'

Mr. Khan pulled himself up even straighter in his seat.

'That, my dear, is something upon which I am not competent to comment. Perhaps Mr., ahh, Goberdan would like to respond to your question. Mr. Goberdan?'

'Ah, umm, yu yu yess,' said Paulie, stumbling to his feet. 'Ah ah ah cu cu cu can assure yuh dat Duh Duh Duh Doctor Badri was fuh fuh fuh fine dat day. He wu wu wus very bright an he knew what he wanted. Dih whole ting oh oh only took a few mih mih mih minutes.'

Paulie had his listeners with him: they were cringing but they were with him. However, he was taking so long to say what he wanted to say that we sat curdled in our embarrassment, willing him to finish so that we could move on, doubt snookered by empathetic humanity.

He finished his thought. 'An An An nuh nuh nuh Nurse Ragoo ah ah agree.'

'Nurse Ragoo! What does she know about Morton's state of mind?' asked Soames.

If not a nurse, then who? I wondered.

'Ah cyar remember if Morton properly in he head fuh most ah las' year, never mind las' September.' Soames was adamant.

'Den why yuh let he sign cheque an ting?' responded Nurse, in her best little girl voice. 'If he head ain't right, how he could sign cheque?'

Soames' mouth opened but no sound came out of it. It was Nessa who replied.

'It was all right for him to sign a cheque because we knew what he was signing,' said Nessa.

Soames nodded.

'Dat ain make sense! It all right fuh he to sign something if allyuh want it, but not if dih Doc want it!' Nurse had a point and she stuck with it. 'Ah tell Mista Goberdan about dem check signin when he axe me about dih Doc being good in he head.'

Paulie nodded his head so vigorously that it seemed in danger of falling off.

'Ah, Ah axe Nurse if huh huh huh em em employer was in in in su su su sound mine, in in fu fu fuh…'

'Possession of his faculties,' supplied Mr. Khan, with some asperity, wiping saliva from a document lying in front of Paulie with a large pocket handkerchief.

Paulie was not to be deterred.

'Fu fu fu full po po po osess ss ssion ah ah is fa fa fah…'

Everyone in the room, Honaria and Clara, and old Khan's secretary included, was nodding encouragement as he tried to spit out the words.

'Faculties, for God's sake!' bawled Nessa.

'Culties,' finished Paulie, mopping his brow with a shredded Kleenex. He sank down into his seat.

'And, of course, Nurse Ragoo is a qualified medical professional, after all,' said the old solicitor, the soul of unctuous mellifluousness by comparison to Paulie. 'But,' he continued, 'should the family wish to challenge the content of the codicil by judicial processes through the courts, of course, you would have that right.' He smiled bleakly. 'After you have, umm, heard what it says, perhaps.'

Chastened by his logic, we nodded.

He rolled on.

'My proposal for how we shall proceed is that I will read Morton's Last Will and Testament and then attempt to answer any matters arising from its content, etc., etc.'

He actually said, 'etcetera'. Twice.

'Then I will hand over the floor, as it were,' a glimmer of humour was intended here perhaps, 'to Mr. Goberdan so that he can read the codicil himself, and, umm, respond to questions concerning, umm, it.'

Mr. Khan Reads The Will

And so we heard from Morton Badri for the last time.

The Will was in the usual dry, legalistic language of wills everywhere. Even had Badri wished it otherwise, Assraf Khan would have beaten him back onto the narrow track of lawyerly correctitude. There was enough that was legalistic and pedagogical in my father-in-law that he would not have strayed very far anyway. And yet, the cadences of Assraf Khan's reading notwithstanding, there was, I found, both in its provisions and in the way that certain phrases caught the ear, enough for us to know, without the slightest aroma of Alcolada wafting its way among the musty law tomes around us, that Badri was in the room with us.

It was a detailed document but I can remember long passages verbatim.

The first shock came when Mr. Khan read, "'I appoint Assraf Khan, my solicitor and friend, and my son-in-law, Ian Menzies, joint Executors and Trustees of this my Last Will and Testament.'"

This was so entirely unexpected that I swallowed the dinner mint I had been sucking surreptitiously under my tongue.

"'I trust that the obligation imposed on them in this manner will not be onerous, and I rely on their innate honesty and fair-mindedness in carrying out my wishes.'"

I had never been permitted to drive his Benz, but I was to administer his last wishes and carry out his bequests! I was beyond surprise. True, I would have a co-executor, but never had I thought he would have considered me for this. "Fair-minded" was not necessarily an adjective I always think to apply to myself, far less one I thought he might apply to me. Perhaps he really was out of his mind. My next thought was: you crafty old man, I'm going to have to clean up after you.

After apologizing to me for not having felt able to give me prior warning of the provision, Mr. Khan asked if I was willing to take on the responsibilities requested of me. A rat caught in a cage of Badri's devising, everyone staring at me, I nodded, numbly.

'Shall I continue?' A short pause for consent. '"I leave all of my property wheresoever situate, beyond the specific and specified items listed in the attached memorandum, to be shared equally between my two children, Vanessa Juno Wong Howe and Alexandra Demeter Menzies."'

Well, I thought, that was easy enough.

Mr. Khan turned a page of the document in front of him.

'These,' he said, 'are the items that Morton listed in the Memorandum.'

'"To Baylmatie Indrani Chatterjee,"' for a second I hadn't the slightest inkling who he meant, '"my Aunt, I leave the sum of fifty-thousand dollars on the specific condition that she, and a companion of her choosing, visit the great land from whence she came, the land of our ancestors."'

Didi began to wail. She rocked backwards and forwards on her chair and everything stopped while we tried to comfort her. She tugged at her orhni and pulled it forward so that her whole face was covered.

After an appropriate interlude, the old solicitor continued.

'"To Ainsley Surujnarine Gokhool, the son of my dear deceased sister Rebecca Gokhool, I leave the sum of twenty-thousand dollars and also my gold Rolex watch, which I know he has admired in the past. I leave it in the hope that, as he watches time tick away before him, he will not waste it in his own life, but will become more positive and active in seeking out a useful future."'

Ainsley let out a groan, covered his eyes with his sleeve and began to snivel. Like an old car in need of servicing, his shoulders began to shake as the weeping gained momentum. He drew quiet honks of breath into his lungs and his moustache vibrated.

'Tank yuh, Uncle,' he blubbered.

Dammit! Thanks, Badri for leaving me to deal with that. And not only Ainsley, I thought: half the family had had its eye on that watch. Nessa had told Sasha that she wanted it for James, and I had no doubt that Ag had it on her inventory for Roh and the boys. Badri had been inordinately proud of the watch, its accuracy and its value. Being a great believer that a watch tells the time and that a Timex can do that as well as anything else, I was not interested and certainly I had no expectations in the matter. I could, however, see that there would have to be some fancy footwork around the issue. There might be more to this executor business than meets the eye. My eye anyway. I was beginning to suspect that Badri's eye had had a twinkle in it.

'"To my friend Ivor Seeram, I leave my father's Hindi and Sanskrit manuscripts and also the telescope that belonged to him. I must state my warm affection for a friend very different in outlook and interest from myself, and my regret that we have not been closer in these last years of our lives."'

Double dammit. Here was trouble. Ag had had her eye — sometimes literally — on the old telescope ever since her arrival, quite openly stating that since both James and I wore glasses, we would not be able to use it to its full effectiveness and she would carry it home with her. Roh had much vaunted twenty-twenty vision. Perhaps Badri was even craftier than I thought: the pitfalls of the executor job were growing. Sasha turned round and smiled at Mr. Seeram sitting behind her and, in her usual way, reached out to touch his arm.

'I am honoured,' said Ivor into the silence of the room.

Mr. Khan cleared his throat again.

'"To Soames Harold Sookbirsingh, my brother-in-law and friend, I leave all the furniture and the appliances in the flat that stands in the grounds of his house, together with the cases of wine therein, with the request that one case of burgundy be used at a family dinner wherein a toast is to be offered on my behalf for everyone's good health. And, if it be their wish perhaps, a toast to me in return. It is my hope that Soames will allow my daughters and their families the use of the flat as a place in which they may stay when they visit Trinidad in the future."'

Soames nodded solemnly while the provision was being read.

There was no problem there, except, perhaps, that Roh should have been mentioned by now. The old solicitor better hurry or there would be nothing else left to leave.

Mr. Khan paused. He looked around the room and then began to read again, rather more quickly than before, I fancied.

"'To June Aimee Ramdass, the sister of my late wife, Ann, I leave Ann's twenty-two carat gold rope necklace."'

The necklace in question had been bought in Calcutta while he and Ann were attending a conference. When Ann died, all her other jewellery had been given to Sasha, Nessa, and various female, family members, a ring here, a bracelet there. He had kept the necklace back, a keepsake for himself, he said. No-one had minded. To which one of his two daughters would he have given it anyway? I doubted that either of them even remembered much about it until Mr. Khan mentioned it.

"'June is an admirer of beautiful things and I leave this necklace to her in thanks of the many happy times we have spent together since Ann's passing."'

Holy shit, I said to myself. What the hell is this?

I saw June half rising from her chair, hand fluttering uncertainly up towards her neck, mouth opening slightly as though she wanted to speak but did not quite know what to say. No one else in the room moved and she sank back down. What could it possibly mean? Badri and June had never been close as far as I knew. They had little in common. One loved the challenge of intellectual thought, the other loved clothes. One read philosophical treatises, the other flipped through the pages of fashion magazines. One bought books, the other bought, well, Bvlgari.

Once, while Ann was still alive, I overheard Badri consoling June when she had — apparently — been considering whether or not to leave Ram, but this was quite a leap. I could imagine what Nessa was going to say and I was not sure that even Sasha would be able to accept a completely innocent view of the Will's innocuous words. What the France would Fleur say? The image of me dropping the necklace into June's hot little hand was followed by another: the expressions on Badri's daughters faces, as I did the deed. The man was a demon coming back to haunt me.

I was beginning to feel clammy in the enclosed space of the room. Surely there could not be much more. And what could be in the second Will that could be worse, I wondered?

'Almost finished,' said Mr. Khan, half to himself, a plain measure of relief in his voice, I thought.

'"To my grandson, Nicolas Menzies, I leave the sum of one hundred thousand dollars to be held in trust by my Executor, Ian Menzies, and administered by him for his college education. Education is the key to success in life: learning itself the key to peace of mind."'

Well, this was something like! Learning had always been Badri's reference point, the touchstone through which his favour might be found. Nicolas, the only grandchild, was about to go to college and, even in TT dollars, this was a considerable sum.

'"To my nephews, Daniel David Badri and Malachi Moses Badri, I bequeath the sum of fifty-thousand dollars each to be used specifically for their education, and also similarly administered by the same executor."'

Ag's sons were also in their late teens, each the size of a small elephant, and, while completely amiable, not the brightest pucks on the ice, not likely to achieve entry into anything more learned than remedial summer school. Admittedly, the Will was a few years old, but I would not have thought Badri that optimistic, or that blind, even then. I must have groaned aloud. Everyone turned to look at me.

'Sorry,' I said, clearing my throat. I added, plumbing new depths of inanity, 'How about that!'

The image that leapt immediately to mind was of me explaining to their mother that, No, I will not hand over fifty thou to each of the twins, and certainly not for hockey lessons, that sport being for nine months of the year their favourite, and sometimes their only, topic of conversation. Badri must have spent his declining years thinking of ways to torment me. No wonder he went out of his mind in the end. I closed my eyes and waited for the other shoe to drop.

It was a boot.

'"To Miss Lillian Ragoo, for her kindness, devotion and solicitude to both myself and my dear wife, Ann, I leave my Mercedes Benz, remembering the many times and places she has driven with me, and her great admiration for the vehicle."'

Shit in a bucket.

Nurse had been slouching when her name was read, but she sat up when the bequest was read. She looked over at me, lifted her shoulders, fluttered her eyelashes and grinned. Slyly, I thought. Several other thoughts jumbled their way through my head at the same time. You lucky devil you! Badri, you bastard, you wouldn't even let me drive it and you leave it to bloody Nurse! God! Handing over the keys to her is something old Khan can do. I won't.

These thoughts must have been broadcast by the dust in the air for Nessa said, 'But that clause must be void, since he bought a new Benz after the Will was written.'

'Dih Dih deh Will ent su su say which Bu Bu Bu Benz. It only say Benz!'

The words exploded from Paulie and Nurse nodded, vigorously.

So also did Mr. Khan.

Soames turned in his chair to look at Nurse. He didn't speak, merely raised his eyebrows, but it was clear that Nurse's days were numbered.

'"And,"' continued Mr. Khan, with a slight, but surely heartfelt, sigh, '"I leave to Honoria Dobson and Clara Butcher five thousand dollars each, with thanks for their assistance to me in the house at Sookbirsingh Hill. I honour their loyalty and their industry."'

'"Finally,"' he began again.

Finally?! I said to myself, appalled. Where the hell is Roh? Don't tell me you put him after the help! Ag must never see the bloody Will!

'"Finally,"' he repeated, '"before the disposition of my estate to these my beneficiaries, and at the convenience of my Executors, I ask my daughters to each choose three items from among my possessions as tokens of specific remembrance for themselves and to allow each of the following persons to choose, similarly, two suitable items as they may wish: Rohan Rabindranath Badri, Agatha Wopping Badri, Ainsley Surujnarine Gokhool, James Wong Howe, Ian Menzies, Jolyon Stuart Sookbirsingh, June Aimee Ramdass, Bianca Jane Ramdass, Royston Raul Ramdass, Clarence George Ramdass, and Miss Lillian Ragoo."'

Hallelujah! Ag got in at last. And he named Roh and her first. But great, Jumping Jehoshaphat, Lord God Almighty, otherwise he had omitted his brother completely!

Mr. Khan looked over his battered audience and placed the Will on the table.

'Any questions?' he asked.

Hardly waiting for us to assemble the jumble of our thoughts into a coherent inquiry, he hastened on, 'Ah yes, here it comes! I have arranged for tea and a little light refreshment before we continue. Thirsty work, I am sure you agree, mmm?'

'What about the codicil?' asked Nessa, not to be put off.

'Tea first, I think, Vanessa,' he replied, firmly. 'Alexandra. Perhaps I could impose upon you to pour.'

Entre'acte

Everyone except Ainsley stood up, although no one was quite sure what to do next. June immediately sat down again and began a close examination of her open-toed shoes. Nurse also seated herself again and began to crack her knuckles finger by finger, tiny explosions in the hushed room. Nessa turned round, scowled at both of them, and was about to say something when Soames leaned over, put a hand on her shoulder and whispered what I am sure was a warning. The old solicitor fiddled with the different objects on his desk, setting everything at the correct geometric angle: the ink-pot precisely aligned with the leather blotting-paper holder, an antique telephone with the mahogany in-tray, and so on. Not a computer in sight, I realized, in this room of ledgers and tin document cases.

Paulie, having hoisted himself out of his chair, puffed out his cheeks in a silent whistle. He glanced sideways at Mr. Khan but the older man paid no attention to him. Paulie opened his mouth to speak to him, but, obviously thinking better of it, closed it again, running a finger under the front of his collar before shaking the knot of his tie from side to side as though it had come alive and was about to strangle him. He glanced at the back of Nessa's head, but his eyes quickly moved on to Nurse further towards the rear of the room. She was still preoccupied with her fingers, however. Ainsley sat off in his own wonderful world of water. I tried to get Paulie's attention but he would not look at me.

Sasha was bent over a small table pouring tea into cups of the most delicate china. I could see the steam rising out of the spout of the teapot. She had a look of intense concentration on her face and I knew that it was not from fear of spilling the tea. She would be thinking about how to calm Nessa, how pleased she was for Soames, how she was going to handle me when I got her alone. As if reading my mind, she glanced over at me, raised her eyebrows and gave a small smile. Then, she opened her eyes wide and, fractionally, shook her head, a private signal between us; part warning, part jest. I narrowed my eyes in return, and pulled down the sides of my mouth into a pout. I saw the smile enter her eyes before she looked away and I knew she would not look at me again. There was no need.

Mr. Khan's secretary handed me a cup of tea and offered a chocolate biscuit. I shook my head and she offered them to Ainsley. He took two. I turned round to see whether Honoria and Clara had been given tea. They looked uncomfortable standing there but not unpleased, taking it all in, round-eyed. I moved over to speak to them.

'He a nice man,' said Honaria of her benefactor, 'Is sad fuh Miss Nessa and Miss Sasha. Dey go miss he too bad.'

'He leave a nice apartment fuh dey tuh visit. An Mista Soames be glad tuh see all yuh,' added Clara, judiciously. She leaned towards me and whispered, 'But Mista Ee-an-uh, how he give dat nasty Nurse a whole Benz?'

I shrugged my shoulders. Clara knew, it was a joke in the house, that I coveted my father-in-law's Benz – Soames's as well, if it came to that — and now, she realized, the chances of my even driving it were gone forever.

I whispered back, 'Don't fret. I'm the Executor. I'll hand it over to her with no gas in the tank!'

'Mista Ee-an-uh, yuh bad mind fuh so!'

The three of us laughed quietly, and the two women looked a little more relaxed. I moved away to speak to June who jumped up with relief when I approached.

'Well,' I said, 'it's hot enough in here. Plenty of surprises, eh?' Not the most felicitous opening. 'How are you doing? Did you drive down?'

June held on to my arm as though it were a life preserver.

'Oh. Ee-an-uh,' she lamented, 'ah ent know he go give me dat necklace. What will Sasha tink?'

I wasn't sure what Sash would think, but I knew what Nessa would.

'Don't worry about it, June,' I replied, as airily as I could. 'If he wanted it to go to one of Ann's sisters, you were the one he would choose. We all know it wouldn't be Fleur! And besides, you came down to see him often.' Perhaps more often than we knew, I thought. 'You didn't think he would leave it to Didi, did you?'

'Dey already tink ah tief he ring,' she said, looking at her nieces. 'An now he leave me Ann necklace!'

June rubbed the upper part of her chest with the back of her hand as if seeming to imagine how the necklace might eventually rest against it. She gave a tiny shrug and whispered to me.

'So Nurse get he Benz! Papa yo! No one know dat!' She could have added the word 'either'. 'Sometimes he get a likkle crazy, even three years ago. Dey say he have likkle strokes an he mind go piece by piece.'

'Well,' I said, 'we'll see how crazy he got when Paulie reads the codicil.'

'Oh God,' she replied, 'Ah hope it ent have more foolishness! Nessa go kill someone before dis day done.'

We heard Nessa, Ivor and Soames suddenly erupt in laughter across the room. I nodded to June and walked over to speak to Sasha again, bending over to whisper in her ear.

'It's a good job he's been buried already. I'd love to get my hands on him. I don't want to be his executor, for heaven's sake.'

'It shows he thought a lot of you. It's an honour.'

'It's a pain. And anyway, how can I even be an executor? We don't live here and I'm leaving the day after tomorrow.'

I thought about stamping my foot for emphasis. It would have made Sasha laugh.

'We'll have to come back,' she replied. 'Mr. Khan will do most of the legal work anyway. We'll have a meeting to give out the small things in the flat tomorrow morning.'

'Well, I guess it won't include the Benz!' I sighed.

Sash laughed again. 'You didn't really expect him to leave you his Benz, did you?'

'Of course not! What would I do with it? But to leave it for Nurse! The whole of South Trinidad will be talking.' And I steupsed.

'You're just jealous,' she said, giving me a smile and an elbow against my ribcage.

'And what about your mother's necklace?'

She whispered back, almost hissing at my face, 'You should have seen Nessa. I thought she was going to say something.'

'Don't worry, she will,' I pointed out, ruefully. 'Let's just hope that we all make it out of here alive.'

Sasha frowned. 'What do you think Paulie will have to say?'

'Whatever it is, don't sit too close or you'll be soaking wet before he even gets started. Look how he's sweating. He may outdo Ainsley.'

I pondered.

'Just wait until Ag hears about the Rolex! She was saying on the plane that it should go to Roh since he was your Dad's only brother. I thought it might too, because of the blood business! But Roh isn't even in the Will, for crying out loud. What happened to all of Badri's pious talk about blood?'

Sasha frowned again. 'I was wondering about that,' she said. 'Didn't he make the Will about the same time as he and Uncle were quarrelling about that piece of land in Toco, and, you remember, he said Uncle Roh got the best of the deal? He must have thought that was enough. They made up later, but he might have forgotten about the Will. Anyway, Uncle won't mind. He'll be happy that Daddy left money for the boys.'

I groaned. 'Yes, but what about Ag? She's not to going to be happy, is she? Sweet Jesus, could you tell her for me?'

Sasha smiled. 'If I know Nessa, she'll be the one who tells her. As soon as she sees her.'

'Anyway,' I advised, 'you just keep quiet and listen. Don't get yourself upset. We'll talk about it all later. Knowing this family, we'll be talking about it for the next twenty years.'

A Codicil Can Make A Difference

Mr. Khan coughed us gently back to our seats and the room became quiet again. Everyone was looking at Paulie. When he realized we were all watching him, he gulped. Perspiration was visible on his upper lip and across his forehead. He ran his tongue against the one and wiped the other with the cuff of his shirt, waiting for the old solicitor to give him a sign to begin. Apparently, the only part of his head that was dry was his throat. As he waited, he tried to clear it with a rattling, hawking sound. His slightly thyroid eyes seemed to protrude even further.

I thought for one delightful moment that he was hyperventilating. A strangling sound emerged as he fought to speak.

'Ah ah ah cyar ru ru read. Hu hu hu here!'

Paulie thrust the document at Mr. Khan and plonked himself back down onto his chair gasping. Mr. Khan, of a different generation and made of sterner stuff, turned the paper over in his hand, satisfied himself of its provenance, turned it back over right side up and began to read.

To himself.

We sat, Golden Retrievers attending the frisbee, ready to hang on his every word, but no words came forth. He slowly raised a hand.

'I would just like to familiarize myself with the,' he paused in midsentence and peered at what he was reading even more closely, 'umm, contents of the codicil.'

As if he didn't already know! He shot Paulie a glance and, like Paulie before him, cleared his throat.

'It's, um, quite short. I will read it in full.'

For God's sake, get on with it!

'"I, Morton Sunil Badri, on this Fifteenth Day of September in the year of Our Lord Nineteen Hundred and Ninety-three, in the city of Port of Spain, being of sound mind,"' he had the grace to look around the room as he said this, '"make the following codicil to be added to my Will previously written and witnessed in the presence of Mr. Assraf Khan, solicitor, etc. etc,"' he motioned with his hand to indicate omitting words. '"All provisions of that Will remain in effect, except as they are specifically altered by the content herein."'

The old solicitor cleared his throat once more and swallowed again.

'"To my nurse, Mistress Lillian Ragoo, my mainstay and support through these last trying months, who has been like a daughter to me, I leave the sum of twenty-thousand dollars with my sincere thanks for her care and devotion to me at all times."'

Everyone sat up straight, except for Nurse herself, who was thoughtfully examining her pointed patent-leather shoes. She began to rub a scuffed left toe with the back of her right sock.

Holy God in heaven, I thought. There's going to be hell to pay!

'You thief!' shouted Nessa, as she flung herself round to face Nurse. 'You're not going to get away with it.'

Her chair toppled over as she leapt out of it. It was a scene out of a melodrama.

'Ah ent axe fuh nuttin!' announced Nurse, her high, light voice caught between indignation and delight. 'But to besides, what allyuh do fuh Daddy?' Nessa became more enraged at the use of this last word. 'You safe home dere in Canada, behind God back. What you do fuh he? Is me! Me tek him tuh dih doctor, me pay he bill, me clean up he nastiness! Why he cyar leave me a few likkle dollar? Ah earn every cent.'

She tried to move towards Nessa. I grabbed her by the shoulder to stop her.

'Yuh tink ah ent got betta ting tuh do wit meh time than take ah ole man tuh dih toilet? He ent give me a ting in life, he too blasted cheap, only tinkin about he Alexandra dis and he Vanessa dat. So he blasted well betta give it tuh me in deat. Is mine, fuh true!'

She shrugged me off but Soames moved between them, a hand against her chest.

'Ladies and Gentlemen, please. I'm not quite finished.'

Mr.Khan raised his voice above the melee and spoke as calmly as only he could in the circumstances.

'There's just a little more.'

Everyone turned round to look at him. Had the door had opened at that moment, we would have looked like a tableau in a wax museum, a minor painting by Rembrandt or one of his school.

More?!

We didn't need more. We had enough already.

Mr. Khan stood in the shade behind his desk, holding the codicil in the air above his head. Surrounded by churning particles of dust, the document caught a beam of sunlight and seemed to be illuminated there like a religious artefact. I saw Nurse frown and glance over towards Paulie, but Paulie was as transfixed by the paper as the rest of us. I was sure that, whatever was to come next, Nurse did not know about it.

'Shall we continue?' said Mr. Khan. He repeated the question. 'Shall we continue?'

He paused while we settled ourselves.

And then he said the following extraordinary words.

'"And, overturning a provision of my original Will, I leave to my son-in-law, Ian Menzies, my Mercedes Benz, as an extra token of thanks for the work that is involved in being my Executor and as a gesture of my growing esteem over the years, knowing that he will take care of it and that it will keep him coming back to Trinidad in the years to come.'"

Silence, to coin a phrase, reigned.

'Yuh damn lie!' shouted Nurse, first to find her voice.

Soames turned to face her and began to laugh. He clapped his hands on his knees, put his head back and roared. I could see the gold fillings in the back of his mouth. It was most un-Soames-like behaviour. Soames liked a good joke but this was way beyond that. It was clear that he wanted to say something but he could not get the words out. Instead, he pointed at Nurse and continued to erupt, a volcano of amusement. Tears coursed down his cheeks. Mr. Khan was clearly distressed at such behaviour in his chambers but he did not know what to do about it.

Then, Ivor began to laugh, too. It was a great explosive guffaw. I did not know Ivor well, but I knew enough to know that he usually had a twinkle in his eye. At that moment there was a wide grin on his face as well. He beamed at Soames and punched him on the arm. The two of them rocked forward and back on their chairs like hysterical schoolboys. Little specks of spittle flew from Ivor's mouth arching through the rays of sunlight that crossed the room. Soames took a long breath, held it for an instance and spluttered a veritable waterfall of wet. He wiped his mouth with the back of his hand and tried to say, 'Sorry', but could not quite get the word out.

We were transfixed by the sight of them. Both were mopping their brow, mouth and eyes, but they continued to laugh and, every time one of them tried to stop, the other would start him off again.

Nurse stood up.

'Yuh damn lie,' she yelled again.

Her words produced paroxysms. Just her standing there seemed to be the funniest thing Soames and Ivor had ever seen. I began to worry that one or both of them might have a coronary on the spot.

'How yuh ain't tell meh dat?' Nurse shouted at Paulie.

'Ah ent know he leave dih dih dih Bu Bu Benz fuh yuh be be be before!' replied Paulie.

Even before he got the words out, we knew that he wanted to take them back.

Mr. Khan turned, drew himself up to his full height and said to Paulie, 'Mr. Goberdan, you told Miss Ragoo about what was left to her in the codicil!'

It was a statement, not a question.

For reasons beyond my comprehension, this was screamingly funny to Ivor and Soames. They began to roar again. The rest of us looked askance at one another.

'I shall report this to the proper authority in due course,' Mr. Khan continued. 'They will not look kindly at your behaviour, I am sure.'

Paulie evidently could think of nothing to say. He opened and closed his mouth, looking for all the world like a fish thrown up by the tide that knows it wants to get back to the ocean but lacks the legs to do so.

Soames' hand fanned the air in front of Nurse's face.

'Yuh damn arse!' He spluttered and stuttered the words caught in a maelstrom of merriment. 'Yuh ent know twenty-tousand dollar,' for we were talking Trini dollars here, 'can buy only a likkle bitty share in Badri Benz!'

And they were off again.

But so were we. Nessa began to laugh. June joined in. Honaria and Clara tried to be circumspect but they took up the refrain. A gorgeous grin appeared on Sasha's face. It had been a long time since I had seen so much open laughter there. Mr. Khan permitted himself the inkling of a smirk. Only Didi was unable to take the whole thing in. She looked annoyed, offended by our levity on such a solemn occasion.

'You lose, Nurse! Oh God, you lose!' I cackled.

'Shut yuh mout, boy.' She flung her arm towards me, trying to wave my words away. 'Is my Benz! Uncle leave it to me!'

'But then he took it back again. He didn't realize the value of the Benz. He was out of his head after all.'

'He crazy! Ah go contest dih Will.'

'Which one?' I asked. 'Mr. Khan said he knew what he was doing when he made the first Will and Paulie just said he was in his right mind when he made the codicil. And so, Nurse,' I was laughing myself now, 'did you!'

Nessa Meets Her Ex

Sasha wanted to be back at the house in case visitors came by, so we didn't waste time standing about after Mr. Khan finished. I agreed to meet him the next morning to go over what he called 'the, umm, administrative arrangements' and then we were on our way. June left even before we did. Not much was said in the car. It was difficult to know where to begin, and Didi, who hadn't understood everything that went on, was blowing her nose in the back seat. Even Nessa didn't want to say too much in front of the old lady. If we were unusually silent, the atmosphere in the other car was far worse. Clara told me later that Nurse didn't say a word and Ainsley put his foot down on the accelerator and didn't bring it back up again until he swung into the yard and jerked to a stop. Not much scares Clara but she and Honaria held on to each other all the way home, afraid that they'd never see the five thousand Badri had left each of them.

When we pulled into the yard, I half expected to see Ag standing on the back gallery waiting to hear all the details of the Will verbatim, but parked behind the Nissan was a large black SUV.

'Why would anyone want an SUV in Trinidad?' I asked, 'The place is only forty miles long.'

'Ask Krishna. It's his father's!' replied Soames, glancing at Nessa.

Nessa moaned, 'Not now!'

'Just take it slow and easy, Nessa,' advised Sasha. 'And mind your manners.'

We found everyone drinking tea in the living room. Fleur was making polite conversation with Prakash on the couch. Ag was seated on the edge of her chair facing Latchmi, their knees almost touching as they whispered together. James, stolid and beyond chubby, faced Krishna, Nessa's ex, across the coffee table. It is difficult to describe just how handsome Krishna is. Nuns have been known to lose their place on the Rosary when he strolls by. But surface is all. Like many Indian men in Trinidad, hopelessly spoilt by their parents, he has never been allowed to grow all the way up. He is obedient but devious, clever but a bit dense, masculine but soft. He stands at the centre of his own universe and everything revolves around him, at least in his own mind. Nessa thanks her lucky stars that she escaped from the force of his gravity.

She marched into the room ahead of us.

'That's a big car, you've got there, father-in-law. Which jungle are you driving in these days, you need that monster?' She gave Prakash a hug. They had always got on well.

'It drive good good, Vanessa,' said the old man, pleased. 'An it go over pothole easy too bad.'

'Watch it doesn't roll over. How's Ma?' She and her mother-in-law had never got along and, after the divorce, unfortunate things had been said on both sides.

Prakash shook his head sadly. 'She not good at all. Too much ah pain! Dey say dih cancer spread into dih bone.'

Nessa hugged him again.

'Take courage, Pa, as Didi says,' she said gently, and moved on to greet Latchmi.

Latchmi and Nessa had been at La Pique together. Petite and passive, Latchmi had been the more lively Nessa's best friend, seemingly content to be in her orbit. It had been quite a scandal how quickly she had taken her place in Krishna's bed when Nessa left it. Nessa hadn't blamed her, however: she knew that Krishna had gone after what he hadn't been able to have before. Everyone said that only Latchmi's fecundity kept them together these days — that and the petticoat government his mother imposed on the whole family, even, I suspected, from the sick bed.

'Latch, girl, how are you?' Nessa kissed Latchmi and smiled. 'Putting on a bit of weight! Too many children will do that. One of the benefits of being barren is I keep my girlish figure.'

Nessa was nervous. Krishna could still do that to her.

'And how are you, dulaha mine?' she said, looking at Krishna but moving over to James, leaning against his meaty arm.

'I'm good,' said Krishna.

'Ha! You don't think saltfish of yourself at all! I was speaking to my husband,' she replied, patting James, and adding, as an airy aside, 'Boy, do we have news for you!'

Ag's ears perked like newly brewed coffee when she heard this, but Nessa walked up to Krishna and turned her cheek towards him to be kissed. Nessa might be nervous but she could play cat and mouse when she wanted to.

'How's Mississauga these days?' she asked. All innocent.

'Actually, we livin' in Oakville.'

Same thing, I thought, all 905.

'When did that happen?'

He shrugged. 'Mississauga becomin too ethnic.'

She laughed. 'You're a bit ethnic yourself.'

'A lotta Indian from India.'

'Ahh, but from what I hear, you still go back.'

James intervened. 'Do you still have your office there, Krishna?'

Nessa turned to Latchmi.

'Keep an eye on him, Latch,' then, as though wanting to soften the message, she added, 'He's still the best looking man I ever met. And still quite the saga boy, I hear.'

Having faced Krishna, Nessa was in her element. She turned to Fleur.

'Auntie, you should have been there! Daddy made Ian his Executor along with old Khan.'

Ag spun round towards me.

Thanks a lot, Nessa, I thought.

'And left him the Benz!'

'Hmm!' said Fleur, wonderingly. 'By the time you're finished, you may think that a very small reward. I know the work involved.'

'You may be right, Fleur,' I muttered.

'He was very generous to Didi,' said Soames.

'He left Uncle Soames everything in the flat,' added Sasha.

Soames shook his head. 'There was no need for that. And you already knew you could visit whenever you like.'

'He left Ainsley his gold watch,' said Nessa, pushing fire.

'His watch! His Rolex?' Ag spoke sharply. 'To Ainsley? That Rolex was for Roh! His brother!' She made Roh sound like the Saviour himself.

'Well, that's what he put in the Will.' I sounded indecisive, even to myself.

'What does Ainsley need with a Rolex?'

'Daddy wanted him to have it,' said Sasha. There was a warning in her voice. Ag heeded it and was about to move on. I decided to pre-empt Nessa saying any more.

'And he left the old telescope to Ivor Seeram.'

'To Seeram! To Ivor Seeram?' She could not believe it.

To soften the blow, I added, 'He left you something from the flat.'

'What?'

'You have to pick it for yourself. Tomorrow. We'll all pick tomorrow.'

Ag was not deterred.

'What about Roh? And the boys? What did he leave for the boys?'

Krishna and his family sat there plainly fascinated, but Fleur had no intention of letting us wash our dirty linen in front of them, close though the two families had been through the years.

'Prakash,' she said, 'you can't be interested in any of this.' She flashed a look of scorn at Ag. 'We can talk about it later. Something more to drink? Latchmi?'

Sasha had decided I might as well earn my Benz.

'Ian,' she suggested, in a voice laden with honey 'why don't you take Ag to Badri's quarters and tell her everything.'

Ag was out of the room before I had time to stand up.

***

The thirty minutes Ag and I spent in the flat were some of the most repetitive and the most religious I have ever endured. I would say something and Ag would invoke the deity. Then, she would repeat what I had said as though I was an imbecile and couldn't possibly have meant it. We began with the Rolex, continued via the telescope and worked our way through the other provisions. She was appalled that her spouse had been left out of the Will and tried to blame my intelligence, my comprehension skills and, eventually, my hearing before she began to accept that it might be true.

'Woe unto him on the day of Judgement! May the good Lord forgive him! He was the most miserable of men. God give me the strength to forgive him in the purity of my heart.'

I knew of no answer to such statements.

The roof really fell in when it came to the boys' education. Their inheritance added up to a reasonable amount of money, even in Trinidadian dollars, but she balked at the idea that I controlled it, and that I wouldn't, couldn't, hand it over to Roh or, better yet, directly to herself.

'What do you know about investing money?' she asked.

The correct answer was, not a Hell of a lot.

'Well, I also will have to invest for Nicolas, so I guess I'll have to learn.'

'You get money for him? As well as the Benz?'

'They are two different things,' With some asperity, I tried to explain. 'I think the Benz was for being an Executor'. And for having to deal with you, I added under my breath.

'It's not right! He must have been mad.'

She caught the idea and clung to it.

'That's it. He was out of his mind. He should have been locked up. He had no right writing a Will. We'll contest the Will.'

'Ag, if you think that Sasha and Nessa are going to court to contest their father's Will and tell the world that he had lost his marbles, it's you who is insane. In any case, Mr. Khan will be against you and so will Paulie Goberdan.' Though not Nurse, I'll bet. 'You'll only cause trouble in the family.' Clutching at favourable straws, I added, 'He didn't leave Fleur anything at all.'

She brushed Fleur aside while she worked towards a fine fit of fury.

'That woman! She doesn't deserve anything. Even the servants got more than me. Some little knick-knack, I'm allowed to take. And that awful Ainsley gets twenty-thousand. It's not fair.'

I was becoming annoyed.

'It doesn't have to be fair, Ag. It was Badri's money and he could do what he wanted to do with it. Don't be so blasted petty. You never cared for him and, God knows, he never cared for you.' Somewhere along the way, I had snapped. 'Leave it alone, for Christ's sake. Neither you not Roh ever lifted a finger to come down here when he was ill. Even I came. He cried, Ag, when Roh didn't come to see him. So shut the fuck up!'

If Ag was justifiably horrified at my language, she wasn't about to do as I demanded.

'Wait till I speak to Sasha, she'll get me my money.'

'You can tell Sasha anything you like and I can't stop you, but I'm Badri's Executor. Not she. And his wishes will be carried out.'

It sounded pompous, even to me.

'I'm going to phone Roh, right now.'

'Not from a telephone in dis house, yuh not!'

We both jumped.

Soames stood in the doorway. He looked at both of us, but he spoke to Ag.

'No more, woman. Sasha been through enough. Yuh want to argue wit someone, yuh argue with me. Leave she alone. Matter finish.'

Ag opened her mouth to speak.

'Ah jus throw Nurse out dih house, an ah'll throw a next one out if ah like. Leave Morton in peace!'

The Septuagenarian Siren

Not surprisingly, Fleur hadn't had the energy to go to Sonabai's funeral as she originally intended, but I had promised to drive her to pay a condolence visit to the family if she wanted. It seemed like a good idea to get out of the house and I offered to take her that evening if she was up to it. Of course, I had an ulterior motive: I could drive the Benz! No one could stop me! Sasha thought about coming with us but decided to stay home to pour oil on troubled waters. I told her that Trinidad didn't produce enough barrels a day for that, but she felt she had to try. Plus, she wanted to talk to Anca and see if there wasn't some way she could help smooth the waters there.

'You mean the waters between June and Anca or those between June and you?' I asked.

This was unfair, but I didn't see how she could effect the one without the other. Anca was returning to Canada with me in two days in any case. Soames was unhappy about aiding Anca, but he wasn't about to throw her out of the house. Anca had whispered to me at breakfast that she thought the solution to her problems was to become pregnant. Sonnilal would marry her, a baby would help his immigration chances, and her mother would be mortified.

'In any case, meh clock tickin,' she said.

She and Sonnilal had spent most of the afternoon together somewhere doing God knows what, and they had returned just as Krishna and his family were leaving. Anca looked tired. Sonnilal looked drained.

It was such a relief to get away from the house that we were half a mile up the road before I fully realized that I was sitting behind the wheel of the Benz and that it, at least, was humming along as though it didn't have a worry in the world. I ran my hands round the steering wheel, fixed the rear view mirror, settled my posterior more firmly onto the squeaky leather and exhaled.

'You might want to think about turning on the lights before we get out onto the highway,' said Fleur, and I could hear an affectionate smirk in her voice. 'Perhaps the man had more sense than I thought.'

I laughed. 'The man had it in for me! How did I ever get mixed up with the lot of you anyway? You're all insane! You need a scorecard to know who's speaking to who on any given day.'

'Whom,' she said, and laughed back.

'I was thinking,' she continued, changing the subject, 'that since we're on the road, we could pass in at Neville's on the way home. We would kill two birds with one stone.'

I nearly ran the car into the ditch.

'You are crazy!' I replied. 'Let me see. You want me to drive you to Vistabella to console Sonabai's family. That's the Sonabai who drove into the middle of a cane field with a boyfriend young enough to be her grandchild, where they proceeded to do themselves in by plugging up the exhaust pipe of their car and breathing in all that lovely carbon monoxide. Just let me know if I've got that right. And then you want me to take you to Gasparillo so that you can pay a condolence visit with the boyfriend's family.'

'We wouldn't tell them where we've been. And, anyway, I have to go sometime. Neville is my cousin.'

'I thought you were related to Sonabai,' I said.

'No, no,' she replied, exasperated. 'Sasha is. Sonabai was Didi's brother-in-law's wife's niece.'

'Oh,' I nodded, sarcastic. 'Quite close then! How is Neville your cousin?'

'Neville is Indrani's boy.'

I knew the name from somewhere. 'Indrani?'

'Ma's sister-in-law's brother's second wife was Indrani.'

'Her brother's son? Which one?' I was confused.

'No, no.' Speaking to the village idiot. 'Ma's sister-in-law's brother was Calvin. He died. He had a sister, Indrani. Her son is Neville.'

Could it be more simple?

'But there's no blood, then!' I was bouncing up and down on the burnished leather. 'You're not related to him at all.'

Fleur was offended. 'We all grew up together. Indrani used to bring her children by us every year and we used to go with them to Mayaro for holidays.'

She had a brainwave. 'And Neville's sister married Pearlie's brother. Their son is Deso. You know Deso.' I did know Deso. He was studying in Toronto and we saw him at all of Fleur's parties. 'He won the Island Schol.'

'I thought Deso was somebody's outside child.'

I knew this wasn't true but liked to ride her about her relations.

Ruffled. 'No, you're thinking of Pearlie's other brother. He had two children with Laila Mohammed before she married Charran.'

Which brought everything full circle. Charran had helped carry the casket.

It is my belief that if you look closely enough, every Indian is related to every other Indian in Trinidad.

***

I had been to Sonabai's son's house once before and it hurt my heart to know that I was to drive the Benz into Vistabella, a suburb of San Fernando known to be the home to a proliferation of potholes and other vehicular nightmares. I dipped off Pointe a Pierre Road onto a narrow thoroughfare, its gutters practically gulleys, that leads to the swayback street that used to be called Jackass Alley, but which now goes by a much grander name that I always have difficulty remembering. The road was so steep downhill that only blackness was visible in front of me. I parked, yanked at the handbrake so that it practically stood straight up and turned the front wheels out towards to the road. There was no curb and I considered myself lucky not to have gone into a ditch I knew to be deep enough to swallow a smaller German car whole. I said a short prayer before climbing out, but I still managed to step down into a swampy culvert, sludgy liquid oozing over my shoes. The incline back up to the house was so steep that after I managed to close a car door that swung wide open again from the force of gravity, I had to push Fleur ahead of me with both hands. We reached the iron railings of the gate and held on.

The house appeared to be in darkness, but the yard was littered with cars.

'Perhaps they're out,' I essayed, hopefully.

'If your mother committed suicide with her toy boy, would you have all the lights blazing?' replied Fleur, scornfully. She shook the gate.

I looked down the road, past the Benz to the other side of the small valley. Lights twinkled in the distance and I could hear laughter not too far away. It was a perfect evening. For Sonabai's family to have felt the need to shut themselves off so completely from it, made me sad.

Fleur called out, 'Good night.'

'Hello? Who dere?'

'It's Fleur Sookbirsingh. Could I speak to Mr. Ramkhalawansingh, please?'

'Miss Fleur! Wait a minute an ah'll let yuh in. Boy, open dih gate fuh Miss Sookbirsingh.'

Fleur nodded to herself. 'Take your time,' she said, 'It is just me and my nephew.' I was in her good books.

There were about a dozen people in the dimly lit living-room: Christian martyrs all, hiding in the catacombs. Sonabai's son and his sobbing wife rose to meet us. Fleur, the oldest person there, was immediately accorded the respect she expected. She was escorted to an armchair, the previous occupant having scurried away. I recognized no one in the room and very little attention was paid to me. Did they think, I wondered, that I belonged to Fleur in some unsavoury but parallel way, a reflection of Sonabai's young man ?

Fleur squelched any such thought, 'This is Sasha Badri's husband.' Heads nodded. 'Aaaahh!'

I stood behind Fleur's chair, one of Calpurnia's attendants waiting for the orgy to begin.

'So what happened?' asked Fleur.

That's right, Fleur, lead into the tragedy gently!

'Oh Auntie, he kill she,' sobbed Sonabai's daughter-in-law. 'Mammy know he since he in short pants and she just tryin tuh help he get he business goin. He go tuh Presentation wit meh boy Lachlan here.'

Lachlan Ramkhalawansingh, the Scottish Hindu.

She pointed to a haunted-looking young man with two enormous orange ears.

'He always here wit Lachlan an we take he tuh dih house in Mayaro, an he play mass with dih family, an he like another grandson tuh she. She help he get a work in tong when he leave school. An he help she out arong dih house.' Stream of consciousness unadorned. 'An den he want tuh start he own business. He come tuh she and she give he cash tuh buy he inventory.'

Sonabai's husband nodded vehemently, and took over the telling.

'But den he come back and back looking fuh more. An she say, No, make do wit what yuh have, an get dih business off dih grong first before yuh expand.'

Now young Lachlan began to nod as well, his ears flapping slightly at the same time. His whole face seemed to ripple.

'An he ent listen,' he said. 'He come here an he stand by dih gate and bawl out tuh speak tuh she. Lawd, Lawd! She tell meh he harass she an he won't leave she alone.' Lachlan shook his head. I could feel the draught. 'Ah tell she tuh go tuh dih police, but she too sorf.'

His mother interjected, 'She sorf, fuh true.'

All three were nodding in unison.

'Den las' Thursday self, he take she in he car. He say he find a shop goin outta business an he can get tings cheap, an, Oh Lawd, she say, "Okay, I go go wit he an see fuh dih las". An den ah never see meh Mammy again. She musta told he, "Ah ent got no more money" an he get blasted vex an say he might as well be dead but he musta say he ent goin by heself so he carry she orf and he kill she.' Finally, she breathed. 'An den heself! An all she want tuh do is help he get on he feet.'

The whole room was nodding now, looking carefully at Fleur to see how she was accepting the story.

It didn't seem very likely to me. In the first place, Sonabai was one of the most self-centred people I had ever met and I had heard a lot of gossip about her in the last couple of days. How she was so cheap she once gave a pair of used panties as a Christmas present. How, at her own wedding, Fleur, her maid of honour, found her making out in the vestry with the best man — after the ceremony.

Fleur, however, slowly began to nod.

'Poor Sonabai,' she sighed. 'She was always too kind. And helpful.'

I was mesmerized by the nodding heads and found that mine was dipping in sympathy.

Fleur began, 'I remember when Sonabai and I were girls at La Pique…'

She held court. She told stories about Sonabai that made her appear a cross between one of the vestal virgins and Mother Teresa — although gradually the emphasis of the stories changed so that Fleur became their centre while Sonabai merely swam in her wake. The grieving family insisted we eat something before we left and a plate of chicken puffs, angel food cake and date loaf appeared. The puffs and the loaf looked exactly like the ones Clara had tried to get me to eat at teatime before they went bad. Wake food I knew, but the angel food cake was new and very good. I said as much.

'Mammy like she angel food cake, Mista Ee-an-uh. She ah angel she self. So ah make some fuh she,' explained her daughter-in-law, weepily.

Too much, I thought, just a little too much to make Sonabai, the septuagenarian siren, believable, but the charade was in full flight and we continued to nod sagely at one another.

'Well, we must be going,' said Fleur, eventually. 'We better get back. We have had our own loss, you know.'

Recrimination played at the edge of her voice.

'Oh my, yes! Is true! I forget. Ah so much on meh mind, Auntie. How dih funeral go? We go visit soon.'

We stood while Fleur gave chapter and verse about the wakes, the funeral and the burial, with herself as chief mourner. Then she pulled herself to her full height, shook her head and said, 'The family will miss him! The country will miss him! He was a great man!'

'Is true! Is true! Mammy did like Badri too bad.'

And the whole company nodded.

Back in the car, Fleur sighed.

'Well,' she said, 'they were so happy to see me. I'm so glad that I came.' She paused. 'Sonabai was always good for sheself.' A little lapse into Trini while she considered the matter. 'I always said she would come to no good in the end.'

I let down the hand brake and the car fled down the hill. We were half way up the other side before I got the key turned in the ignition.

'Lights, lights!' Fleur bawled. 'No wonder Badri never let you drive the car, you don't know what you're doing.'

I was too busy to reply.

'Gasparillo next,' she ordered.

***

I was surprised at how many people were there. I had forgotten that the boy's funeral — he was to be buried under Hindu rites — had been delayed until the family could contact an uncle who had been on a pilgrimage to India to visit Sai Baba. Also, as Fleur reminded me, the boy's brother was studying somewhere in the States and they were having difficulty finding him.

'Probably in prison,' she sniffed.

It was a low house, hardly raised above the ground, the wood unpainted. These must be the poor relations, I thought, as I walked behind Fleur up the dirt walkway to the front steps. A man in a white undervest stood in the doorway. He held a bottle of beer in his hand and waved it in the air.

'Dih wake arong dih back, Tantie,' he said, slipping down the three steps. 'Ooops!'

I could hear loud laughter behind the house and steered Fleur towards it. Our arrival was announced by three chickens scrambling ahead of us. Something approaching a party was in progress. Rented tables and chairs had been set up and a game of All Fours was being played, ferociously, to one side, the cards slamming down with gleeful alacrity.

'Take dat! And dat!' shouted one of the players.

'As Man! Watch meh good!' responded another, throwing down his hand.

'Ah ketchin meh nennen in dis ting,' moaned a third.

'Steups, boy,' sighed the fourth, shaking his head. 'Gopaul luck eh Seepaul own.'

Fleur walked towards the winner.

'Well, Neville, how are you? I missed you at Morton's funeral.'

Neville lurched to his feet and collided with the table. It scraped sideways to get out of his way.

'Tantie, tantie,' he called out, staggering over towards her.

I couldn't recall ever having seen him before, but several of the other people looked familiar and there were one or two I could have named had I thought about it.

'Ah ent know what ah go do! Meh boy! He gone!'

He took Fleur by the elbow and led her crablike towards the house, calling out as he went.

'Sulki. Sulki, come. Yuh see who here? Is meh Auntie from Canada. Come quick.'

A severe looking woman emerged from the house.

'What yuh bawling about now? Yuh son dead and you drunk. You is a disgrace!'

She opened her eyes wide when she saw Fleur.

'Sista Fleur,' she said, almost falling into Fleur's arms. 'He dead, meh boy dead, self!' She shrieked and collapsed at Fleur's feet holding on to her knees. 'What we go do?'

Fleur patted her reassuringly on the head.

'Come, sit down where we can talk,' she said, leading Sulki back through the door into a crowded sitting room. Neville wove his way behind them. I followed along in their wake.

The room was full of women. Their clothes matched their expressions --- sombre, subdued and carefully put together. They sat, ankles and wrists crossed, agile eyes looking about them, carrying on low buzzing conversations with their neighbours. We ran the gauntlet of those watchful eyes. Fleur, who does this kind of thing far better than I ever will, looked neither to the right nor the left, only scanning the room when she was seated and could face it full on. I nodded at a couple of faces that I thought I knew until my skittish glance landed on Mira sitting next to her sister Shammi.

'Hi, there,' I said, eyebrows raised high in mock astonishment. 'What are you doing here?'

Mira stifled a guffaw and slapped me on the arm. Mira and Shammi turned up at wakes like some people go the supermarket. It is a family joke that if either of them sees a likely candidate in the obituaries, she is on the telephone to the other and they arrange their schedule around a visitation to the house of mourning. Partap drops them off and picks them up later, during which time, they express their condolences to the grieving family, assess both the quality and the quantity of the comestibles, and take note of the fashion, its suitability, currency and cost. They do not have to know the deceased or its relatives well, although, of course, it adds an extra frisson to the event if the sympathy that they express going in is in any way, shape or form, heartfelt. To be fair, both Mira and Shammi see the joke as well as everyone else, and they defend themselves with steupses by explaining that, in addition to giving them a nice evening out, they provide comfort to the bereft and add to the body count. A wake would be a dismal failure if no one turned up to mourn.

Into Mira's ear I whispered, 'Are you sure you came to the right house?'

One notorious evening, Partap had dropped his wife and sister-in-law off at the wrong address. They didn't realize it at the time. Going up the front steps into the house, they found a wake going forward as advertised. They expressed their goodnights, said how sorry they were to hear of the widow's loss and shed a few tears with her. It seemed a bit strange, Mira admitted afterwards, because she had been under the impression that the deceased was a woman. Also, it had been a little surprising that they didn't know a soul there, but they sat, ankles locked together in the approved manner, ate some very tasty cake, drank a couple of cups of tea, spoke sympathetically to the other ladies present, and filed mental notes about an outfit cut on the bias made out of a very pretty voile.

At a prearranged time, they rose, made their goodbyes to the widow, who, they reported afterwards, looked at them a little doubtfully, and went back down the front steps. Partap was nowhere in sight. After five minutes of standing about in the dark street, Mira was beginning to be annoyed when they were drenched by the high-beams of a car parked further up the road. The car rolled towards them and Partap stuck his head out of the window.

'What all yuh doin dong here?' he asked. 'Dih wake back dere.'

It took quite a few minutes to sort everything out. Partap had dropped them, as directed, at Number 92 but the proper address, as he found out when he came back, was Number 29.

'No wonder ah ent recognize too many people!' declared Mira. 'But dih lady nice, Partap. It so sad she husband pass away so young.' She shook her head. 'An tree baby tuh raise. It go be hard fuh she. Oh my! Ah go axe yuh tuh carry she some mango tomorrow.'

'But yuh ent know who the France she is!' laughed her husband. 'Ah ent takin no mango tuh she. How she go know who ah am, an who send dem. Ask meh dat!'

'Fuh true, ah suppose,' Mira sighed. 'But still, is a good ting tuh do fuh a nice lady an ah ent want thanks anyway. So hush yuh mout!'

She moved on to another subject.

'Now back back dih car dong dih road an we'll just go into dih other wake fuh a few minute.'

Fleur had settled herself and was already being handed a cup of tea and some sahina puffs by the time I took my place at her side. Neville was hovering over her, and his wife, holding on to Fleur's hand, was seated beside her. She waved me away.

'Dih men outside,' she declared.

'Dis fella Alexandra husband!' Neville's words were slurred and he threw his arm around my shoulder. He was swaying slightly. I began to sway with him. 'He need tuh hear about dem kind ah nasty women.'

'So what happened?' asked Fleur.

Her usual subtle approach.

'Oh Auntie, she kill he,' sobbed Sulki. 'She know he since he in short pants and she have she eye on he. She lead he on, she tek he tuh Mayaro an all about wit dem nasty Ramkhalawansingh people. An yuh know how innocent meh boy, Anand, does be.' Ah, I thought, his name at last! 'He so sweet, an nice. A sweet, sweet boy!'

Neville took up the story. We were listing significantly to starboard.

'An she insist she find he a work when he leave school. An buyin him shirt an shoe an ting. She take he tuh Y. de Lima's in tong an buy he a gold watch. Look dih watch,' he said, nearly smothering me as he tightened his arm around my neck while he thrust the watch in Fleur's face. He was wearing it.

I had had enough of watches for one day, I thought, trying to free myself. I was in danger of suffocating in his underarms.

'She ent leave he alone. She come here an she stand by dih gate and bawl out tuh speak tuh he.'

I was beginning to wonder where I was. Hadn't I heard all of this before? In reverse.

'Ah tell he tuh go tuh dih police, but he too nice. When he start he business, he cyar get any time tuh open dih shop, she always after he!'

I rolled out from under Neville's torso. My ducking motion upset the swaying pattern we had previously established and threw his body off kilter. He hung suspended half upright for a moment before falling sideways onto the floor, glass flying out of his hand. One lose sandal made a lazy circle through the air before it landed with a crack at the far end of the room.

Sulki was oblivious.

'An den, las Thursday, he tell me he goin out after breakfast. "Ah goin out, Ma," he say, an he kiss meh an ting an he gone. Oh, Lawd!' She put her head on Fleur's chest and bawled. 'Ah ent see he again in life. Meh sweet likkle Nandy, he gone!'

Neville was rolling around the floor in a vain attempt to right himself, but he began to crawl towards Fleur when she hove into view.

'There, now! There, there!' muttered Fleur to Sulki, trying to peel her away from the front of her dress. 'What can I tell you! What can I say?'

For Fleur to be speechless was something new. I suspect it was the combination of a watery Sulki and the somersaulting host that did it, though I do realize words can sometimes fail in a situation like this. Mine certainly do.

Fleur pried herself out of the chair, half dragging Sulki up with her. She gave me a sharp look.

'Well, I think Ian wants to be going now. We've got to get back, you know.'

'No, Fleur, it's quite all right. We can stay for a few more minutes, if you would like,' I replied, airily. 'It's still early.'

'No, we better go.' She narrowed her eyes at me as Neville finally scurried to his feet. 'Now! And you've got a big day ahead of you, tomorrow.'

'But Ee-an-uh, boy,' said Neville, 'come an fire one wit me first.'

'No thanks, Neville,' I replied, 'I'd love to but I think Fleur really needs to get going. It's kind of late for her to be out.'

Sometimes I deserve a dig of my own.

Fleur was already through the door, having kissed Mira and Shammi on her way out. I waved a winking goodnight to them in passing. They would be there a while yet, taking everything in, along with the tea and the cake.

As we were on out way out, I noticed Paulie Goberdan in the yard. He must have stayed down south after the reading of the Will and, of course, he knew the family. He was seated with four men I had never seen before behind a litter of Carib bottles. Fleur didn't see him at all. He stared at me, nodded and went back to his conversation as we passed by. Paulie was doing the talking and the men looked properly out of patience. And yet they also seemed to be hanging on his every word. Oh Sasha, I thought, Badri's Will will be all over the South before the night is out.

Quiet Thoughts & Misappropriated Mangoes

By the time Fleur and I arrived home, the last visitors had departed, and, although lights were still on in several of the bedrooms, everything was quiet. Tomorrow would be my last day and, not being at all sleepy, I decided to do some packing. I never like to pack when I am leaving Trinidad. I delay it as long as I can, looking at the open suitcase on the side of the bed, knowing that I have to get on with it but not wanting to begin. I was made for the heat, and am willing to bake, grill, even singe in it. I would pack it with alacrity if I could capture it, close the lid on it and carry it with me. What I pack instead are clothes with that slightly musty, not quite mildewed tinge of the tropics.

Sasha was to remain for another week so that she could go through her father's belongings with Nessa, sorting out his clothes to give them to relatives or to charity. To do anything, she said, so that they would not have to hang in his wardrobe or lie pressed and wilting in his cupboard drawers until we came back. She had asked me whether any of his shirts would fit me. Many were still in cellophane wrappings, the best quality from Harry Rosen and Peter Jones, but they were not my size. They certainly would never fit James either, and Ag had pounced on them for Roh until she realized that most of them had French cuffs. Ag did not approve of French cuffs, though she wouldn't explain why. Perhaps it was a Calvinist thing: with Ag one never quite knew.

Sasha brought in a couple of her father's ties, silk and striped, to see whether I would take them. I knew it would please her if I did. She reminded me that I had said that I would lock the front gates before going to bed. It was a job I liked to do and it would get me out under the stars one more time, even though walking through the yard, down to the road in the dark, could be scary. The yard dog wagged his tail as I went down the back steps. He ambled contentedly ahead of me. Eleven o'clock. Everything was still, but the sounds of the night were loud and throbbing. I heard the croak of the huge, toad-like frogs that sometimes sit, plop, in the dog's bowl — how he hated them — and peered down at my feet in case I should tread on one, fretting that, in an absolutely perfect world, I would be staring up at the stars instead. I stood still, made sure my feet were safe from attack, and impressed the night on my memory, drawing its warmth into my lungs. The dog stopped too, sat on his haunches to scratch himself and waited for me to catch up.

I swung the two big gates closed, drawing them together with a metallic clang, looping the chain so they would not give access to the whole world of darkness right there on the other side of the wall, perhaps even now peeping in ready to maim or murder. The dog was sniffing at the edge of the culvert and I called to him as the gates closed. He lifted his leg against a bush before trotting back into the yard.

A cloud passed over the half moon.

I felt the lock with my fingers as I hooked it through two links of the chain, snapped it shut and tugged at it to make sure we were safe. Walking back towards the house, I could see that most of the lights were out now, people were sleeping, but Sasha was visible in her cotton nightdress combing her hair near the window. The night looked in on her, sneaking round the curtains, approaching her with its velvet touch, waiting for her to turn off the lights so that it could enter and envelop her at last.

I shouted 'Oy!' and she turned, although she could not see me in the darkness. She moved to the window and put her hand against the burglar bars.

'We don't need any today, thank you. Try again later in the week,' she laughed. 'Do you want a cup of coffee before we go to bed?'

'Too hot,' I replied, 'How about a coke?'

'A coke?'

'No, is there any soursop left?,' I changed my mind. 'For the last.'

'I'll check. What about a piece of cake?'

'No thanks, I've eaten so much cake this last week, I'm all caked out. Let me in, will you?'

You lock yourself out when you go out to close the gates.

We sat facing each other across a table already set for breakfast, swatting at the occasional mosquito, and waving away a random moth drawn by the single light above us. Sasha had made herself some tea and was attacking a ham sandwich. She had found a slice of paw paw in the back of a crammed fridge. I was spooning that, rolling the fruit around my mouth, fixing the taste in my memory before sliding it down my throat.

We had a lot to talk about: all the things I had to do when I reached home; what she wanted me to tell Nicolas; what chores she needed him to do for her before she returned. We lowered our voices — sounds carry even further in the still of the night — to talk about the events of the day; about what was likely to happen next; whether Anca would make the right decision; what that decision would do to the family.

'Poor Nurse,' she sighed. 'I'll call her tomorrow or the next day. Perhaps Soames will change his mind and let her come back.'

This was Sasha, through and through.

'Why would you want to do that? And, in any case, don't bet on it. Soames will think he's well rid of her. He'll be more worried about June and Anca than Nurse. And why do you need her back anyway?' And I added gently, 'Your Dad is dead, Sash.'

She smiled, 'I know, but somehow as long as she is here…'

'But you don't need her anymore.'

She didn't respond and I decided to change the subject.

'What about Ag? Think yourself lucky she's coming with me!'

'Ag will be fine when she gets home, out of Nessa's way. She is never comfortable here and, without Roh, there's no one to take her side. You lived here. Ag really just came as a visitor; she doesn't know what we're all about. She doesn't understand how we live.' She shrugged. 'She never wanted to learn.'

The tick tock of the clock in Soames' bedroom told us that the minutes were passing.

'A lot has happened this week,' I sighed.

One of the icons of the older generation had passed away and relationships among the rest of us would change. Adjustments would have to be made. Soames would be all alone in the big house when everyone left. Badri was gone and June would be staying away, at least for a while. Jolyon would drop in a couple of times a month but he had his own life. Didi and Rookmin were too old to come often. Fleur would fly in for Christmas and for three weeks in the summer, and Nessa and James would be here occasionally, though neither one of them liked the heat. If Roh hadn't come now, would he ever come back? In any case, he would bow to Ag: anything for a quiet life.

'Times change, Sash,' I said, softly. 'People change.'

She sighed. 'Two things never change.' She grinned at me over the table as she spoke. We had had this talk before. 'Manners. And family.'

I smiled back at her, reaching out to hold her hand.

'Yeah, yeah,' I said.

I knew that she would never change. Loving, unwilling to see the bad in people, Sasha goes about doing the best she can, opening her heart to everyone, sloughing off the hurts that are sometimes inflicted. I am only glad that she lets me be part of her life. Whatever happened on Sookbirsingh Hill, I would be her protector, her lover and her friend.

'Just remember to duck when you need to duck,' I said, 'and remember as well that, when the fighting starts about your Dad's estate, I'm the executor. Refer them to me. After all, I got the Benz to do the job.'

***

We were about to go in to bed when Fleur appeared in the doorway, her head wrapped in curlers, face bereft of makeup.

'I can't sleep. It's too hot. Could you stay here while I go up to Badri's quarters and find a book?' Badri had the best books. 'I won't be a minute.'

We unlocked the doors and Fleur went down the back steps towards the flat. She switched on the light before she went inside. We sat on the divan on the back gallery, looking out. Most of the yard was lost in a matte darkness. I settled down to wait, once again enjoying the witchiness of a tropical night.

Then, Fleur screamed.

I raced down the steps, across the yard and into the flat. Fleur was in the living room, staring through the wrought iron bars of the windows into the branches of a mango tree just feet away.

'What's the matter?' I asked.

'There's a man,' she cried. 'I see a man.'

'Where?'

'In the tree. Look.'

At first I couldn't see anything. It was dark, leaves were everywhere and he was almost hidden, but sure enough, there he was, sitting in the tree, legs thrown over a branch as though he were riding a horse. He was picking the ripe julie mangoes, and putting them into a satchel slung over his shoulder.

Fleur began to shout. It took a moment for me to understand what she was saying. The cool, sophisticated lady I had known for so many years had evaporated. In her place was a creature uninfluenced by the lotions and potions of decorum, a coolie woman in a fury.

'Tief! Tief!' she bawled. 'Get out meh tree. Is meh mango yuh tiefing! Put dem back. Get dong now!'

'Take it easy nuh, tantie,' replied the man in the tree, lazily examining the mangoes for blemishes, throwing them to the ground if he found too many. 'Ah only takin ah few mango self.' He reached for another.

Fleur spluttered and exploded. 'Get yuh blasted arse out meh tree or ah go call dih police.'

It was difficult to decide who fascinated me more: Fleur or the thief.

She had another thought. 'Ah go shoot yuh meself!'

'Ah nearly finish, tantie,' said the thief, amiably. 'Yuh want meh tuh pick a few fuh all yuh?'

Fleur was fibrillating with rage, holding on to the burglar bars, shaking them with both hands.

'Crapaud smoke yuh pipe! You're in big trouble if yuh don get outta dat tree dis instance, boy.' And in a shriek of desolation, 'Leave meh bleddy mango alone!'

By this time everyone in the house was standing behind her, peering out of the window at the man in the tree. He continued at his task.

'All yuh need a new dog. Dat does be one friendly dog.' His satchel was bulging with fruit. He laughed. 'No mango sweet like a mango from anoder fella yard.' He looked into the window at Fleur, 'Good night. An tantie, remember dis, dey is God mango, he only lend dem tuh all yuh. And ah sorry fuh allyuh loss. Ah gone!'

He shinnied down the tree and was swallowed up by the night.

The Executor Executes

We met in Badri's quarters the following afternoon so that those persons named in his Will could choose something by which to remember him. Soames suggested that, after the official business was over, everyone would go to the main house for supper and we could all have a glass of wine together, as Badri had requested. I wasn't so sure that everyone would want to do that, thinking also that Soames himself might feel less than comfortable having some of the individuals there, but he shook his head, saying that it should be done before I left, and that since Ag and Anca were leaving on the same flight, this was the only time.

Nessa and Sasha had spent most of the morning setting out items that they thought had real or sentimental value and which might appeal to those who were invited. It was doubly sad for them because Badri had hidden away some of their mother's personal belongings — clothing, toiletries — that they not seen for a long time. As Nessa said, suddenly there were two dead people in the flat. I spent part of the morning with Mr. Khan who gave me words of encouragement and advice, too many of them, about how to handle myself if, as he said, 'the sadness of the, umm, occasion imposes itself too much on the, ahh, situation' or, as I thought of it, if anyone ran amok in the flat.

I had suggested to Sasha and Nessa that I would like to ask Fleur and Soames to join the others and let each of them take a keepsake too. They had agreed readily. Soames, however, shook his head saying that he had been given too much already, and Fleur insisted that, since Badri had not included her in his Will, she did not wish to impose herself against his wishes. She would, however, be happy, she said, to drink his wine later. I called June and told her the time we would be meeting and to bring her boys, but I was far from certain that they would come. As for Nurse, Sasha, ever the mender of fences, telephoned her after breakfast to say that she hoped she would be there and that she would be welcome, but Nurse had screamed so loudly at her that it didn't seem likely. Soames, already on the front gallery devouring his morning newspaper, missed the call or he might have banned her.

I found it interesting that Nurse had fixated on Sasha as the origin of her woes. Nessa and she had never got on but, the dreaded finger incident aside, Nurse and Sasha had had a reasonable relationship over the years. When Sasha came to visit her father, they worked well together. Sasha made sure that Nurse was included at the dinner table and she was always invited to parties, not as a paid companion but as a guest. For a long time, if you had asked any member of the household what they thought of Nurse, I think the most negative comment would have come from Clara. Twice, in the safety of her kitchen, Clara had warned me to watch out for 'dat bleddy coolie woman, she bad too bad,' but she would never say more.

I went over to Badri's quarters at about three-thirty. It was one of those intensely still days, the air hot enough to burn the back of your throat if you breathed in too quickly. I opened the windows and the wide double doors and walked around to look at what Sasha and Nessa had accomplished. The dining table was covered a display of things that had belonged to their father — binoculars, his Mont Blanc fountain pen, silk shirts still in their wrappers, his initialled soft leather briefcase and much more. I had not seen some of the items for years. They took me back to a different time. I traced my fingers over the smooth head of a magnificent brass Buddha and hefted a Faberge paperweight in my hand.

Ann's china and crystal was neatly set out in the glass cupboards against one wall, and between the windows were framed pictures and paintings collected on Badri's travels. The Acropolis vied for attention with an ivory inlay of the Taj Mahal. Delicately embroidered Japanese flowers — fading now with age and the direct sunlight — faced row on row of coloured enamel plates brought back from Iran when it had still been Persia.

How do you dismantle a life, I wondered.

I saw that no one had turned the pages of the calendar, it was three months out of date, and I placed it face down on a bookshelf. I looked at Badri's books, rows of them, many beginning to yellow and fade as they do so quickly in the tropics, and I knew that he had read them all. If I opened one, even a novel, I would likely find pencilled notes in the margin; words of agreement, commentary or questioning. It was a catholic range of volumes and I wondered whether I had tried hard enough to know the man to whom they belonged. Had I wasted too much time convinced of his small-mindedness, when, in reality, I should have been thinking of my own, not paying enough attention to the breadth of his intellect or his interests?

Sasha came up behind me and put her arms around my waist. We sat down on the couch, her father all around us. I held her hand and we did not need to speak.

Almost at four on the dot, Jolyon, James and Nessa came to the door. Nessa looked around wanly. Anca came in from the garden, hot and nervous. She saw that her mother wasn't there and sat on the arm of the couch next to me. We heard a car pulling into the yard, and then another one, followed by the slamming of doors. Royston and Clarence came to the double doors frowning, June behind them. I rose to greet them and, like palace guards on duty, they moved aside to let me kiss their mother and escort her to a chair. She sat stiffly as everyone in the room, Nessa included, went over to kiss her on her cheek, a matter of duty. Only Anca did not move. She studied her sandals.

Suddenly, Nurse was in the room. She had entered through the kitchen. She threw himself onto a chair next to the dining table, not saying a word to anyone and not looking at them either. I went up to her and put my hand out to shake hers. She thrust an envelope at me instead and, still not looking up, said, 'Give dis tuh you wife when ah gone.'

Then, as I turned back towards the open door, the shade of Ag appeared.

'Hi Ag,' I said, heartily, 'come on in.' She took a seat next to June.

***

'Well, we're all here,' I said, tentatively. 'Ainsley's not up to it and won't be coming. He sent a message.'

My tongue felt thick, and I had to squeeze it against the roof of my mouth to make it behave.

'As you know, in his Will, Sasha and Nessa's Dad said that he would like each of you to have something, umm, something you would like to, umm, remember him by.'

I was turning into Mr. Khan.

'He didn't, you know, say that anything specific, umm, was to go to any individual, so we thought you might like to pick for yourselves what you would like, what perhaps you think is appropriate, what you would like to remember him by.'

I was really rambling now: how to stop was the problem.

'For yourselves. You know. Perhaps you would want to spend a few minutes having a look round first, seeing what there is, before we begin.'

I had hoped that everyone would jump up, move around the room, see the things that had been put on display, connect them to Badri, perhaps even examine them. And then choose. All properly civilized.

No one moved.

I cleared my throat. My voice rose half an octave.

'And when we have finished, Soames has invited us downstairs for supper and to toast the Doc's memory with a glass or two of his best burgundy.'

No one bloody well budged.

Sasha, rather nervously I thought, said, 'Ag, have you any idea what you might like?'

While Ag was in the process of opening her mouth to reply, Nessa invaded the moment.

'I'm taking the dinner china and Sasha is taking Daddy's crystal.'

Ag shut her mouth in a firm line of discontent. In point of fact, however, everyone knew about the china and the crystal. Ann had arranged their disposition with her daughters years before.

'What about the tea service, Ag?' Sasha asked, with a sideways glance at her sister. 'It's Limoges.'

Ag turned to me. 'Are you going to pay to send it home?'

I hadn't the vaguest idea.

'Well, no, I don't think so,' I replied.

'Then, it wouldn't be worth the bother, would it?'

There was a silence while we digested this.

Never having been one to outwit a silence, I thought of the one item in the room I would really have liked for myself.

'Perhaps Roh would his brother's Mont Blanc pen?' And nailing her with irrefutable logic, I added, 'You can carry it in your handbag.'

'A fountain pen, what would Roh want with a fountain pen?'

Said Nessa, sweetly, 'I thought the pen might be nice for Ainsley!'

Nurse piggybacked on her words.

'Dih pen fuh me. Yuh fader say I could have it when he kick off!'

'"When he kick...?" Well, you're not having it. It's for Ainsley.'

Nessa and Sasha had agreed that the pen should go to Ainsley, but Sasha wanted to conciliate Nurse. She crossed towards where Nurse was standing and said quietly, 'Perhaps, you could take something nice instead.'

Wagging a finger in Sasha face, Nurse shouted, 'You keep away from me! Don't you come by me or ah go cuff yuh dong!'

Everyone jumped.

'Now, wait a minute, there's no need for that,' I said, hastily.

Jolyon stood between them. 'Watch yuh mout, girl!', he warned.

Sasha clearly did not know what to do and it was Nessa who rescued her. 'Perhaps you would like his briefcase. It's pigskin. To carry your professional stuff in.' Butter wouldn't have melted in her mouth.

'No!' interjected Ag. 'Roh will like the briefcase.'

Jesus, I thought, this isn't pretty.

Nurse let out a high-pitched bleat, 'What ah go do wit a blasted briefcase? Ah want dih pen. Yuh fader promise!'

'But he didn't write it down and he didn't tell anyone, so you're out of luck,' I pointed this out with a certain relish and through clenched teeth. 'Auntie June, what about you? Is there anything that you would you like to have?'

I was trying balefully to move on.

'Ah ent know,' June replied tentatively, shrugging. 'Clarence, what yuh tink?'

'Uncle have some nice picture. What about dat nice picture of dih Taj Mahal, Ma?'

'Yes,' Nessa again, 'It would look good in your dining room.'

I looked over at James. He was smiling to himself. He must have read Nessa the riot act as far as June was concerned.

'Ah want dem tree, little, Persian carpet,' interrupted Nurse.

'Okay,' I said, trying to take some charge of where the conversation was going and to sound as though I could make a decision. 'You can take the matching carpets then. That will be good.'

Sasha and I had talked about how well they would look in our sitting room, but I was certain that she would not object.

'I thought Sasha liked the carpets,' said Nessa, taking umbrage on her sister's behalf.

'No, no, that's fine,' I replied, quickly. 'They are for Nurse.'

At this, Nurse rose, walked over to the nearest carpet, three by five it was, and rolled it up. She carried it to the side of the couch where the second one lay, removed a chair from one end of it and rolled that one up too. With one under each arm, she moved to the third one, half hidden behind June's chair. Clarence was standing on it.

'Move!' she barked, yanking it out from under him.

June flinched.

Nurse held the three carpets in front of her like ancient scrolls and, with everyone staring at her, manoeuvred them silently through the door. She was gone.

No one said a word until she was out of earshot and then Jolyon began to laugh.

'She vex fuh so! Oh Gawd, she a crazy woman! Good riddance!'

Shock turned to relief. Even Ag joined in the laughter and Nessa said, in a joking way, to June, 'Well, Auntie June, I guess you can't have the carpets!'

June laughed back, 'Ah never see more in meh life!'

After that, the afternoon proceeded smoothly and a little lightness crept into the room. June took the Limoges tea service, and one of her boys a matching coffee pot. Anca had wanted a painting of a peacock that was almost as tall as she was and she received it with simple, honest pleasure. We were surprised when Jolyon chose to take a number of old books. I don't think any of us had ever seen him open a book, but he said he rather liked the leather bindings and that books, more than anything else, reminded him of Badri. Ag said she would like Badri's Faberge paperweight, for her boys she said, and I raised no objection, saying yes before Nessa had a chance to open her mouth. James, bizarrely, asked if he might have the good steak knives from the kitchen. Nessa roared with laughter when Clarence told her she better watch out or she might end up in small pieces. I accepted the briefcase, just to be able to say that I had received something. I already had three at home. Perhaps Nicolas could use it. We sent a Waterford sherry decanter for Ram and Sasha asked me to pick out one of Badri's Bibles for Miss Marjorie. I quietly handed Badri's Swiss army knife to Anca and told her to give it to Sonnilal.

It was hot work and we were all thirsty by the time we were finished. Nessa led the way over to the house where an early supper was waiting. For a while it looked as though peace might even be established between Anca and her mother, but first Royston and then Clarence made remarks about Sonnilal. Anca let the remarks pass, but they didn't encourage reconciliation, and mother and daughter stayed at the opposite ends of the table while we ate.

Raising Our Glasses

The air was beginning to cool by the time the sun was setting, and I walked out onto the back gallery to look around the yard for the last time. We had left the doors to Badri's flat wide open and I went up the stairs to close them. As I was pulling them in, I felt Nurse's letter in my pocket. What, I wondered, was this about? I turned the envelope over in my hand and saw that it wasn't sealed. From the house, I could hear the murmur of conversation, the sound of crockery being cleared away, and occasional laughter. I sat down on the couch and considered what to do. Whatever was in the envelope would not be pleasant. Perhaps I should not let Sasha see it. Perhaps it was a case of least said, soonest mended, but I was sure that this was a relationship past mending and I had had enough of Sasha being hurt in the last few days.

I pulled the flap of the envelope open and took out the single sheet of paper. The note was hand-written, two paragraphs long. I scanned the words and my eyes filled with tears at the hurt they would cause. There is no need to quote it here. The letter was unkind, vindictive and self-serving.

I turned over the page. Nothing was written there and I turned it back again to read the words once more. Where, I wondered, did this come from? What would the family think? What would they say to Nurse if they knew? It would not do for anyone to see the letter: what good could come of it? I would simply tell Sash and Nessa that Nurse had resigned, and hope that the woman would disappear from our lives quietly, although I suspected that her version of what had occurred would be retailed at every job interview she might have and, worse, in every sitting-room she entered. I also knew that if I kept the letter, it would fuel my own fury. Sasha always says to forgive and forget, and, as I have said, Nessa never seems to carry a grudge, but there is something in me that needs to protect those I love, to ensure that they won't be battered and bruised twice over. And I never forget. I sat still for a moment, then walked slowly into the bathroom and lifted the toilet lid.

I tore the paper into small pieces. They fluttered out of my hands into the toilet, and I flushed them away.

Clara came to the door of the apartment to say goodbye. She was already late in leaving and I would be gone by the time she came to work in the morning.

'Look after Miss Sasha for me,' I said, 'and take care of yourself. We'll probably be back for Christmas. I want to drive my Benz.'

She laughed. 'I go polish it up fuh yuh, Mr. Ee-an-uh. An Miss Sasha be fine. Dey all be fine, but is good yuh takin Miss Agatha with yuh or ah go box she ears myself.'

I gave her a big kiss on the cheek

'Mind yourself and say goodbye to Miss Marjorie for me too,' I said.

'I go do dat, an ah'll tell she tuh be sure she does have plenty sugar fuh when yuh come.'

We walked out into the yard. Sonnilal was going to drive her down to the junction. It was almost dark now and it might be dangerous to take a taxi. Anca was sitting in the front seat of the car.

'Ah goin fuh a drive with Sonny,' she said. For a second it sounded as though she was asking permission to go, or my opinion of her going, but then she added, 'Meh suitcase pack up already. Don wait up fuh meh. Ah be here in dih morning.'

'You're sure?' I asked. I looked from one to the other. The question was directed at both of them.

'We sure, Ee-an-uh,' said Sonnilal, climbing into the car. 'We sure, not so, Anca?'

'We sure like you and Sasha sure,' she smiled and kissed me. 'Go look after yuh wife!'

As they were pulling out of the yard, Partap pulled in. Soames had invited him and Mira to come for the toasting. Shammi and Rookmin were in the car as well. It was a surprise that Rookmin had ventured out. She did not leave her house after dark, complaining that the night air, particularly in the country, brought on her rheumatism, but here she was.

'Dey need tuh fix dat road. It have so many pothole meh back achin. Chile, how yuh do? Come kiss meh.'

'I'm good,' I said. 'Come inside and I'll find a nice comfy chair for you.'

Another car pulled in. Bim and Perlie had brought Didi. The two old ladies, the matriarchs of their respective families, so different in every way, ambled slowly towards each other in the last moments of the twilight. Didi, grey in her orhni, slapping in her sandals, lined face shining; Rookmin, hair still black, lipsticked and powdered, high-heeled and fully bedecked. Old India and West India met in a comfortable embrace.

'How yuh do, girl?' asked Rookmin.

'Ah dere,' replied Didi. 'Ah dere!

'Ah bring angel food cake,' said Rookmin, 'Partap, where dih cake, boy? Take it out carefully. Mira, mek sure he ent drop it.'

'Yes, Ma,' said Mira, by rote.

'Ah bring gulloopjarmun,' said Didi. 'Pearlie have it.'

'Oooh, ah love gulloopjarmun,' said Rookmin and they helped each other up the steps, readying themselves to be greeted by everyone when they reached the top.

'Where Sasha?' asked Didi. 'Ah cyar see she!'

'I'm here, Didi, look at me here.'

'Come girl, let meh see yuh,' ordered the old lady. She peered up at Sasha and smiled. 'Yuh all right?' she asked. 'Yuh not too tired?' She smoothed her hand across Sasha's brow. 'Yuh sure?'

'I'm fine, Auntie.'

'What about me, Didi?' asked Nessa, 'You're not going to ask about me?'

'Pooh, Nessa, yuh as strong as a ox, girl.'

And she embraced Nessa too.

Ainsley arrived a little while later, but he refused to be coaxed out of his car. One by one, we went outside to encourage him to come in but he wouldn't move.

'Uncle gone!' he sobbed, when I went out.

He folded his arms over the steering wheel and rested his head on it. I left him alone in the warm night and went back to the party.

Didi didn't drink, and Rookmin professed not to do it too often, but when we began to pour the ruby red burgundy into the tall Waterford glasses, the mood of the evening began to change. We moved into the long living room and Soames made sure that everyone was served. Didi settled for Peardrax but everyone else, even the scotch drinkers, agreed to, at least, start with the wine. Soames, not a man to speak in public, raised his glass when we were all settled and said, simply 'To Morton.' There was much that each person there could have added but no one knew quite how to begin until Jolyon raised his glass again and added, 'Wherever he is!'

'Well, he's gone to a place you're not likely go to, Uncle Jo,' replied Nessa, on behalf of her father, laughing.

'Where I go, they'll have stables not libraries.'

'He's probably organizing a parliament or setting up a committee to discuss procedure or something already.'

'Do you remember that book he used to talk about, the one about how Christ died in Kashmir? He's probably trying to find out if it was true.'

'He'll be looking tuh find yuh mother, more like,' said June, looking down at her lap.

'Well, I'm sure, right now, he's looking down at us,' said Sasha. She raised her glass, 'To Daddy.'

Fleur said, 'Or looking up.'

'Watch it, Aunt,' replied Nessa, 'or he'll come and pull your toe!'

'I'd like to see him try.' Laughing.

'Do you remember that time…?' someone asked, and we began to reminisce.

***

'Ah remember how he lazy too bad tuh get up an get he own drink ah water,' said Pearlie. 'He wait till someone go near dih fridge an den he say, "As yuh on yuh feet". Steups.'

'An how he always looking at cartoon on TV. Ah always found it strange dat a man like he, ah man with a big brain, watch so much ah cartoon. Road Runner. Donald Duck. Mista Magoo.'

'Yuh remember how he like he dog?' said Partap. 'He dih onliest man ah know have dog in he bedroom at night.'

'It's true, and when Sarge died,' Sarge was the last Alsatian he owned, 'I think a little of Daddy died too,' agree Sasha, sadly.

'Do yuh remember when Sarge get hole ah dih cat and he take it by dih neck and shake it, an yuh Daddy chase he through dih house with dih broom!'

'An Sarge bury dih cat in Ann flowerbed and she get vex.'

'Lawd, she take off after Sarge and Morton take off after she!'

'Do yuh remember how he cry when Auntie Ann get sick?' asked Mira, pulling us out of our laughter.

'I remember how he use tuh get up in dih middle of dih night fuh cricket and listen on dih short wave.'

'An he never support dih West Indies. Always dih other team.'

'Not so! Only when dey vistin!'

'Ah remember when he young,' said Didi and we quietened to listen to what she had to say. 'He take Roh an he sista dong dih road every morning tuh school. An he barefoot, so clean an nice. He eye bright fuh so. He hair comb. He always want tuh get tuh school first, before dih other children, and Roh, he not want tuh go at all.'

'But Morton not always good in school, yuh know,' said Soames. 'He like tuh play marble too bad. An one time, he get in trouble when he tell dih teacher she wrong. Dih teacher get vex, but Morton still tell she she wrong.'

'Yuh remember he weddin, Didi?' asked Rookmin. 'Ann late getting tuh dih church an he standin dere goin from one foot to he next foot, waitin. Ah never see a man smile like he smile when he see she come down dih aisle.'

'He pushed Pa out the way to stand next to her,' said Fleur, 'And stood on my toe in the process.'

'Yuh remember when Nessa born, how proud he was. It ent matter yuh was a girl, Nessa.' June looked at her niece, with a hesitant smile. 'Everyone who came tuh dih house, he show yuh off. An den a little while later, dey tell he anoder one comin an he so excited.'

Everyone knew the story.

Rookmin took up the tale.

'Ah remember how he an your Grandfader sit on dih porch waiting fuh dih nex baby tuh be born, an when dih nurse come out an say it another girl, yuh grandfader pick heself up an leave, an even yuh Pa shake he head. Sasha, girl, he did so want a boy!'

'Don' make joke, he love he daughter,' said Jolyon.

'He certainly made sure we didn't go out with boys!' declared Nessa, laughing. 'If I even spoke to a boy he gave me a lecture about school and priorities and the importance of education.'

'He wanted to keep you on the straight and narrow,' said Soames.

'She fell off it anyway,' said James. Everyone laughed.

'Do yuh remember when he buy he first Benz? He drive dong from tong and turn in tuh dih yard,' said Soames. 'He so excited! Papa yo! He keep telling Ann, "Don't touch. Don't touch anything." An she say, "Where I go sit if ah cyar touch anyting!"

Joylon took over the telling.

'An Ann tell meh how when he driving down dih highway a huge over-loader drop gravel on dih road in front ah dih car and Morton swear bad, bad. An he stop dih car tuh see if it did leave mark on he bonnet! He so blasted vex, Soames had tuh calm he dong and give he a good doze ah Johnnie.'

'An den he take meh tuh look at dih Benz again,' said Soames. 'An, Lord, he have Desmond polish it up just so. An he drive back tuh tong slow, slow.'

And Soames refilled our glasses.

We smiled at the stories and thought our thoughts.

Then we began again.

The End Of The Story

My eyes were closed and I slept, still sweating slightly in the stale cabin air, as the plane flew northwards. I dreamt of the house on the Hill, the people there, the family and all that had happened in it, past and present. I imagined the future. The movie played, the engines droned, and the miles slowly evaporated. Gradually, Trinidad receded. Its warmth began to leach away. The rhythms of the place — its joy, its fun, its cheeky effervescence — ebbed like a lazy tide on a distant shore. I could try to capture it all, keep everything, remember each word, but some things would slip away and be forgotten until the next time I stepped out onto the ramp, breathed in the sweet, moist breeze, listening again to the nuance of its silly symphonies.

The bulkhead seats were occupied by a tribe of screaming infants on the return flight but there was plenty of space otherwise. Anca and I sat together. Ag, claiming the beginning of a migraine, moved towards the back of the plane to have a row of seats all to herself. She had hardly said a word on the drive to the airport. I, quite the opposite, had taken my rightful place behind the steering wheel, exulting that I was out on the open road and sad only that I would have to hand the Benz over to Sonnilal when we reached Piarco. It would be months before I saw it again.

I spent most of the drive telling him how to manage the car and how I wanted him to maintain it, until Sasha suggested that Sonnilal probably knew more about Benzes than I would ever know. If she wasn't precisely fair, she was at least accurate, but it didn't stop me in the slightest. They bore my talkative worrying with good humour and not a little sarcasm, until I nearly back-ended a maxi-taxi that came to a sudden stop in front of us at the Curepe roundabout. Then, even

Sonnilal suggested that I shut up and watch the road. Sasha began laughing when he drove the Benz off to the carpark after we had unloaded the luggage. I peered after it anxiously until it turned the corner out of sight.

'For God's sake,' she exclaimed, 'you look like a real poor-me-one. You've never cared about our car like that in your life.'

Our car was a Ford Tempo.

'Never mind that,' I replied. 'When you get back to the Hill, make sure Sonny washes it down and parks it in the shade. And don't you drive it!'

'Me? I don't want to drive your Benz. I wouldn't dare. I might hurt it. Can Soames drive it?'

She was pulling my leg, but I considered. 'Only in an emergency. He has his own blasted Benz.'

'Sasha mus be home by now,' said Anca, interrupting my vehicular thought processes. She said it so forlornly that I knew she was thinking of Sonnilal.

'Already? Not yet, it's only been forty-five minutes since we took off.'

'Umm, but Son said he go take dih highway an go quick quick so he can give dih engine a likkle outing.'

So I was right!

'I'll give him a little outing if he wrecks my Benz,' I declared.

'You keep yuh hand off my Sonny.'

She punched me on the arm.

'Are you sure, Anca?' I asked, 'That he's the one, I mean? I don't think Ram, or your Ma, are going to give in and change their minds. Not soon anyway.'

She shrugged. 'Pa and me don't pull and Ma, ah know Sonny not good enough for she. He got no class, but I ent looking fuh class. All ah want is he.' She was puzzling over the future. 'If ah get pregnant, it go get worse, but when ah have a baby, maybe dere is ah chance. Yuh know how Ma like baby. So we'll see. In dih meantime, ah hope Pa don' try someting.'

'Such as what?'

She turned in her seat to look at me. 'Come on, Ee-an-uh. Yuh hear all dih stories about meh Pa, like I do. It cyar all be nancy story. He a bad man an I know, from long, he don' like tuh be crossed.'

'Don't worry. Soames is on your side. And Jolyon. More important, Jolyon, in fact. He'll charm Ram round his little finger, see if he doesn't.' I said it, but I wasn't sure that even Jolyon could pull that off.

'All this talk about sides,' sighed Anca. 'Even Sasha have tuh take sides an Sasha talk tuh everybody. Dis one not talking tuh that one. I talking tuh you but not tuh he. You talking tuh he but not tuh me. Remember, it take two hands tuh clap.'

I thought about what she had said.

'Well, we — you and I — we should make a pact.'

'A pact?'

'An agreement. That whatever happens, whenever the commesse begins, we won't stop talking to each other. How about that?'

I put my hand out and we shook on it.

'What about that one six rows back?" I asked. 'She could cause trouble, too.'

'Ag's problem is she know she white! She tink she better than all ah we!' Anca laughed out loud. 'You know yuh not!'

'Yes, but it'll be sad if she comes between Roh and the girls. They say a lot about him, but he's their Uncle and they love him. It would break Sasha's heart to fall out with Roh.'

'Petticoat government, dat he!' she sighed.

I shrugged and shook my head. 'Anyway, it's me that's going to come into conflict with Ag.'

I told her about the trust funds for her boys.

'Yuh makin' joke! Uncle leave dat fuh you tuh look after? Boy, by dih time dem boys graduate, he go be owe yuh ten Benz.'

In my heart though, I think I knew that everything would work out eventually. Our manners had gone a little askew occasionally, even mine I would have to admit, but the family would bind its wounds and keep together. Blood will out and the family would show a united front against the world, whatever Paulie or Nurse said about what had happened. Ainsley would survive too, although one or two of his customers might not. June was too much a Sookbirsingh not to want to be part of her family and Nessa's tart tongue would be forgiven after a while. The more I thought about it, the more I became certain that if Anca had a baby, her mother would be there, on the doorstep, waiting to take it into her arms. Babies trump everything: and they have the blood!

I would even find a way, tranquillizers probably, to cope with Ag. Sasha and Nessa would comfort each other in their grief, and, in a little while, Sasha would come home. Eventually, Badri's estate would be settled and we would move on — me at the wheel of the Benz — to new things. The ties that bound us together were too strong to be torn apart permanently, and if they were in danger of snapping, well, we would have to make new knots that would strengthen them again.

On the ground at Pearson, back in a different world, it was as though we had never left. Nicolas met us at the gate and took over the luggage. I hugged him and he asked about how his mother was, how she was coping. He knows the family. He has the blood. We would drop Anca off on the way home, he said. Ag, held up at Canada Customs, came out at last and stood a little way off by herself. Nicolas walked over to her. He must have guessed something was amiss and I knew he would ask me about it later. A typical Trini, he loves gossip, but I also knew that he, the next generation, wouldn't become directly involved, unless someone attacked his mother.

'Hi, Aunt Agatha, how are you doing?' he asked her, bestowing the ritual kiss.

She sighed. 'Okay, I guess, sweetie. Tired. Have you seen Uncle Roh?'

'No. Is he coming? Traffic was bad on the 401.'

We searched the faces of the crowd. It was time to go. We were almost home. I looked at Ag, and said that we would help her find a taxi if she wanted.

She shrugged.

'I suppose so,' she said, and sighed.

'Wait a minute,' said Anca, pointing down the concourse, 'Look by dih escalator. See. He comin! Uncle Roh! He come!'

Genealogical Notes

Not for the faint-hearted, I enclose a few genealogical notes to clarify the relationships within the Badri and Sookbirsingh families. It took me years to figure them all out. Read on at your peril.

The Badris

Sasha's grandfather, Rajeev Badri, came to Trinidad from India during the time of indenture. He had siblings but, with the exception of Didi, his sister, they do not appear in this book. Rajeev sent back to India for her. After several years living with him, Didi married and bore several children, only one of whom appears here by name, Brimley (Bim). Brimley, in turn, married and he and his wife, Pearlie, had seven children. Though they were all most present at the events described in my book, the two who are specifically mentioned by name are their son, Stanley (who lisped), and Stanley's son, Percy. Percy, then, was Didi's great-grandson.

Rajeev himself had three children: Morton, Rebecca and Rohan.

Morton, named after the first Presbyterian minister to Trinidad, and whose funeral is the focal point of the story, married Ann Sookbirsingh. They had twin daughters. Vanessa (Nessa), the barely elder, married twice: to Krishna, whom she later divorced, and to James Wong Howe, 'the Chinaman'. Neither marriage produced children. The marginally younger daughter, Alexandra – known to everyone as 'Sasha' — is my wife. For the sake of completeness, I must add that we have one child, Nicolas, who appears only on the periphery of this particular story although he would be at the centre of many more.

Rebecca, Rajeev's daughter, died giving birth to her son, Ainsley.

Rajeev's younger son, Rohan, who unfortunately is absent from this story, married a Canadian, Agatha (Ag). She bore two children: boys, Daniel and Malachi.

The Sookbirsinghs

Sasha's mother's family is far more complex and, for the first several years of my marriage, the finer points of it completely defeated my limited, Anglo-Saxon understanding. For Sasha, however, the ties of blood are all important and I had to learn.

Ann Sookbirsingh Badri was one of ten children born to Soomar Sookbirsingh and his wife Shrimatie Teeluckdharry. Those who were alive at the time of Morton Badri's funeral were Irene, Soames, Joylon, Fleur and June. Irene, the black sheep of the family — to coin a cliché — had many children herself, but I do not know any of their names. Jolyon's five daughters were living abroad at the time and so remain unnamed. June married the shoe-magnate, Ram Ramdass. Their three children were Bianca (Anca), Clarence and Royston. Neither Soames nor Fleur married and Soames did not have any children, at least none that I am aware of.

Ann's paternal grandfather, Bhowanipersaud, fathered several children. Of concern to this story, in addition to his son Soomar, was a daughter named Shanti who married Bimboo. They themselves had several children, at least one of whom, Ooma, also had several children. One of Ooma's boys – a cousin of Sasha – appears here as one of Badri's pallbearers. At this point, it all begins to become too complicated, at least for someone who grew up with a finite number of aunts, uncles and cousins, and rarely saw any of them.

Soomar and Shanti Sookbirsingh, as we have seen, were brother and sister, married to Shrimatie and Bimboo respectively. These two, however, were also sister and brother. Their father, known to one and all as 'Old Mister Teeluckdharry', had what Sasha once described to me as 'a whole string band of children'. By far the most important of these, from the point of view of closeness to Sasha and myself, was Rookmin, long a widow.

Two of Rookmin's daughters, Shammi and Mira, whose husband is my good friend Partap, are especially close to the family. Another daughter, Sarojini, lived in England most of her adult life, but you may remember the story about the funeral of her husband, Mahadeo.

One of Rookmin's sisters was named Neeta. Neeta, 'the mad aunt', had a daughter who gloried in the wonderfully exotic Hindu name, Shakuntala. Shakuntala was one of the few persons in the family not known by a diminutive of her name. Alas, she emigrated to the United States and never came back. I met her only once in Denver.

Finally, there is Sonabai Ramkhalawansingh. Technically, Sonabai – buried the same day as my father-in-law – belongs to the Badri family. She was Didi's brother-in-law's wife's niece, as you will undoubtedly recall. However, it seems more appropriate to list her among the Sookbirsinghs since her young lover, Anand, was, as was explained (clearly, I hope), related by marriage to Sasha's grandmother. His mother, Sulki, was Shrimatie's sister-in-law's brother's second wife, Indrani. And the Badri family wanted nothing to do with Sonabai anyway.

And now, I hope, all the relationships will be perfectly clear!

Some Trinidad Words & Expressions

Achaa: Good, Everything's all right
Ah eh able: Give me patience; I can't do this
Ask meh dat, nuh!:   Of all the nerve
As man!:   An emphatic expression
Bad john: Bully
Basodie: Crazy
Behind God back: Very far away
Betaa: Son, boy
Beti: Daughter, girl
Bhaji: Spinach
Bubbalups: Fat, obese
Cat in bag: An unknown quality
Charge up: Drunk
Come with yuh hand shakin: Arrive without a gift
Commesse: Confusion
Crapeau smoke yuh pipe!:   You're in trouble!
Creole: Native to Trinidad
Cut cloth at Salvatori's: Work at an unskilled poorly paying job
Cut eye doh' kill!:   A threatening look can't harm you
Dead out: Tired
Doh think saltfish of yuhself: Having a high opinion of oneself
Dougla: A half Indian, half black person
Dulaha: Bridegroom
Every chalk have he cheese: There's someone for everybody
Fire one: Have a drink
Fuh dat!   How about that!
Fuh so: Very much

Give me breeze!: For heaven's sake!
Gopaul luck ent Seepaul own: Everybody is different
Gulloobjarmin: A fried, Indian sweet
Higher monkey climb, dih more he show he ass:
   the more he shows how foolish he is
Is so yuh stop!: So that's how you are!
Kick off: Die
Kiss meh arse chupid: Really stupid
Lime: Socialize with friends, gossip
Get licks like peas: Be beaten up in a fight
Look at meh crosses! See what I have to live with!
Make skylark: Exaggerate
Makko: Spy on
Mauby: Drink made from the bark of a tree
Meh fader lifted!: For heaven's sake!
Monkey know which tree tug climb:
   A clever person knows what he can get away with
More guts than a calabash: Foolishly brave
Morish: Wanting a second helping
Nancy story: Fairy-tale
Never see, come see: Impressionable
Ole talk: Gossip
Papa yo!: An exclamation of surprise
Pappyshow : Make fun of someone
Papsie: Weak
Pawpaw: Papaya
Petticoat government: Being ruled b women
Picknee: A baby
Picong: Banter among friends
Play mass: Dance and celebrate at Carnival
Please yuh mind!: Do what you want!
Po-me-one: A pathetic person
Pushing fire: Starting trouble
Saga boy: A swaggering male

She eh sof at all: She's determined
Shroud eh have pockets: The dead can't take anything with them
Sou souing around: Sneaking about
Steups: Sound of exasperation made by sucking one's teeth
Sweet eye: Flirting with one's eyes
Tantie: Aunt
Tie tongue: Speaking with a lisp
To besides: Also, as well
Touchous: Thin-skinned
Toutoulebay: Completely in love
Turning up the broom:
    If you do this, an unwelcome guest will leave
Watchicongs: Sneakers
Wet paper doh cut meh: Whatever I do fails
What is to is must is, it can't are:
    Whatever will be, will be
When cock get teat: It won't ever happen
Where molasses is, fly mus be: Some things are unavoidable
Yu head eh made fuh hat alone: Think!
Zug up: Spoil

Feci quod potui, faciant meliora potente

CPSIA information can be obtained
at www.ICGtesting.com
Printed in the USA
LVHW041045030523
745822LV00001B/19